Ivy and Abe

Ivy and Abe

ELIZABETH ENFIELD

MICHAEL JOSEPH
an imprint of
PENGUIN BOOKS

MICHAEL JOSEPH

UK | USA | Canada | Ireland | Australia
India | New Zealand | South Africa

Michael Joseph is part of the Penguin Random House group of companies
whose addresses can be found at global.penguinrandomhouse.com.

First published by Michael Joseph 2017

001

Copyright © Elizabeth Enfield, 2017

The moral right of the author has been asserted

Set in 13.5/16 pt Garamond MT Std
Typeset by Jouve (UK), Milton Keynes
Printed in Great Britain by Clays Ltd, St Ives plc

A CIP catalogue record for this book is available from the British Library

HARDBACK ISBN: 978–0–718–18500–8
TRADE PAPERBACK ISBN: 978–0–718–18502–2

www.greenpenguin.co.uk

According to 'M' theory, ours is not the only universe. Instead, 'M' theory predicts that a great many universes were created out of nothing.

Stephen Hawking, *The Grand Design*

Strange, isn't it? Each man's life touches
so many other lives. When he isn't around
he leaves an awful hole, doesn't he?

Frank Capra, *It's A Wonderful Life*

London, 2026

I'm aware of him looking at me.

Whatever intuitive faculty it is that informs of things we should not be aware of has kicked in.

I begin to feel flustered.

If I look up, will I catch his eye? If I do, will I simply smile in acknowledgement or will I be forced to look away, embarrassed?

I think I know him from somewhere but it's hard to tell. His face is partly obscured by the hat he's wearing, the kind Max used to wear when he was a student.

A Greek fisherman's hat, I had called it, but Richard had said, no, it was a Mao hat. 'I imagine our son is trying to capture the revolutionary-worker look rather than the Mediterranean fisherman,' he'd mused. 'Combined with a touch of Dylan and a dash of Guthrie for good measure.'

Max had been laughably image-conscious at the time but, then, most boys that age are.

Connor, who is just four, is the opposite: totally unaware, even when he comes out with me dressed as a tiger. 'Oh, look at you. Are you a tiger?' well-meaning strangers ask, and my grandson shakes his head or sometimes explains that he's 'just wearing a tiger costume'.

Today he is a regular little boy in blue shorts and stripy sweater, and I am the one who appears to be an object of curiosity, which is rare in your seventies.

I carry on scanning my items at the till. The self-consciousness of knowing I'm being observed lends an awkward deliberation to the routine act of shopping, moving the bread, croissants and chocolate buttons – to bribe Connor with on the walk back to my flat – from one side of the self-checkout to the other.

Hannah will say, 'I hope Grandma hasn't been feeding you too much junk,' when she comes to collect him after work. But she won't really be cross with me. Or maybe she will, in private. But if I'm the mother-in-law who meddles, she never lets on.

Eventually, I allow myself a quick sidelong glance. He definitely reminds me of someone, or perhaps it's just the hat.

I go back to my shopping, scan it all, pay and pick up the bag, meeting his eye now, smiling briefly.

And that would have been it, except he's finished and paid too.

'Excuse me.' He draws alongside.

'Yes?'

'It's Ivy, isn't it?'

'Yes.' Where do I know him from?

'Ivy Trent,' he says, not questioning now.

'Yes.' He's very familiar but from where? Is he a past colleague, someone connected to Lottie and Max's childhood? Or one of Richard's friends? He doesn't seem to fit any of those categories.

'This is my grandson, Connor.' I stall for time, hoping for some further clue. 'I don't think you've met him.'

'It must be at least sixty years,' he says, and then, seeing my confusion, he's about to introduce himself. 'It's –'

I get there first. 'Abe?' I ask, recognition slowly flooding through me. 'Abe? Abe McFadden?'

He nods.

I experience a sudden rush of emotion. There he is. My oldest childhood friend. My closest childhood friend. 'I can't believe it.'

An insufficient summary of everything I feel. I'd often thought of him over the years, wondered how he was and hoped life had been kind to him. Kinder than it had been when we were growing up.

Time seems to rewind and then jump.

It's leapt to a place where Abe and I are five years old, standing shyly in the playground on our first day at primary school. I had seen him and wanted him to be my friend. And then he is, and we're the kind of friends who are in and out of each other's houses, part of each other's families, the kind of friends people refer to in one breath, 'Ivy'n'Abe'.

I look at him again now. He's aged but the young Abe is still there, shifting on the spot, unsure what to say. His hair is grey but still thick and slightly unruly, the kind of hair that needs a close cut to tame it, the kind of cut he's too shy to have because it would expose his face with its peculiarly inviting set.

He smiles now, and I see it in the way the wrinkles appear, in grooves that have deepened over the years: an expression that suggests kindness, coupled with gentle humour and a trace of sadness.

Then my mind leaps to when it happened – the tragedy that would herald the end of our friendship.

And I'm brought back to the present by Connor, who is tugging at my coat. 'Grandma, I want to feed the ducks.'

'In a minute,' I say, stroking his head, still amazed at how happy the silkiness of his hair makes me feel. Being able to look after Connor has injected some real joy back into my life. Children make sense of all the pain and loss.

I wonder if I'd not had children how much harder their father's death might have been, and if Hannah had not just given birth to Connor, would I have been able to bear it when my brother Jon died almost a year to the day later? In Lottie and Max there are so many traces of my husband that they give me hope, even in my darkest moments. They are physical reminders that life goes on, that the particles of the universe keep on being reconfigured, the sun keeps rising and the world keeps turning on its axis and around the sun, towards new dawns and new seasons.

When the first shoots of spring begin to appear, I smile inside in a way that I don't think I used to. No matter how harsh the winter, spring always comes in the end.

'I just want to speak to this man.' I look at Abe again and Connor begins rooting around in the shopping bag I've asked him to carry.

'Can the ducks have croissants as well as bread?'

'No, they're for me!'

'Can't they have one? You don't need four.'

'I don't think they like them, Connor.'

Isn't there a sign somewhere in the park, asking people not to feed croissants to the ducks? Or is that something I made up? I'm getting increasingly forgetful, these days, as to what actually happened and what might have been a joke or a story, mine or someone else's.

'They should try them,' Connor persists. 'How do they know if they like something or not, if they haven't tried it?'

I laugh at him. He's so like Max, who sounded like me when he was little. Abe smiles. Is he a grandparent too?

'Can we go now?'

'Just a minute, darling. This man is someone I used to know a very long time ago, when I was about the same age as you.'

Connor looks up, interested in the solipsistic way that toddlers are when people relate to them in a way they have not previously realized. 'But you've always been old,' he says, with conviction.

Abe chuckles. 'You've always been young in my mind,' he says. 'It's such a surprise to see you again.'

'Can we go?'

'I'm sorry,' I say to Abe. 'We're going to the park to feed the ducks. Can you walk with us a little way?'

'Yes.'

The way he says it, it's more than a simple affirmation. It's as if he's been waiting for me to ask him and has already decided to drop whatever plans he already had.

'A redhead, just like you used to be,' Abe says, smiling at Connor as he throws bread at the ducks. 'Does your son have red hair too?'

'No, nor my daughter. It skipped a generation.'

My own hair, which had lightened rather than greyed, had finally turned to a silvery white.

'And my father's baldness skipped one too,' he says, nodding slightly as if to prove to himself that his hair was still there. 'My son is thinning, though, which seems unfair. But genes have a nasty way of remembering family traits.'

He is musing but of course the sentiment stirred up memories. He doesn't know. How could he? But he realizes he's said something.

'I'm sorry.' He looks at me. 'There's so much to catch up on. I don't even know where to begin.'

We didn't get a chance, not then.

'I'm hungry.'

'Connor, why don't you see if you can spot any frogs?'

'But I'm hungry.'

'Would you like a pig?' Abe fishes in his shopping bag, takes out a clementine and begins peeling it.

Connor looks suspicious but takes the segment.

I smile. 'You remembered?'

Abe nods. 'As if it were yesterday.'

It was so good to see him again but Connor is not entirely captivated. It is his day with me. Grandparents are supposed to be the adults who are not constantly distracted by other things.

'That man's not coming with us, is he?' he asks, when I suggest we go to the café for lunch.

'That's not very polite —'

But Abe interrupt: 'No, I have to be getting home.'

'Oh.'

I'd established he lived nearby, that he'd worked as a consultant for a firm of landscape architects, had children and grandchildren, but I hadn't worked out if there was anyone at home waiting for him. And I wanted to know. After all these years, I wanted to know. Was it the sadness I thought I could still see etched in the lines of his face? Was it because of my own loneliness, bearable now but ever present, that I needed to know if it was mirrored in the lives of others, just as I'd wanted to know when I first had children if other people had them too? Or was it simply because I'd carried something of Abe with me throughout my life and sometimes wondered if our friendship might have grown or morphed, if the circumstances had been different?

I read these things, occasionally, stories of people who'd used social media to dig up people from their past, wondering how they might fit into their present, often with disastrous results. Old lovers were allowed to rip through marriages, old friends unearthed in the hope of recreating times that were gone. When I read them, I thought of Abe and wondered, idly, what had become of him, what sort of man he had grown into, and about the people who were part of his life now.

Did I flush when I asked, 'Is someone waiting for you? Have I held you up?' I was aware of my hand moving towards my hair, smoothing a stray strand back behind my ear, suddenly conscious of the way I might appear.

'No. But I'm in your way now, Ivy. Perhaps we could meet up another time.'

'I'd like that.'

We swapped numbers and he gave me a hug. Then he touched my hair briefly. 'Ivy Trent,' he said. 'Ivy Trent.'

'What?'

'Just you.'

The way he said it made me smile, inside and out, and all the way through.

'But you've only just met him.' Lottie is incredulous.

I'm sitting in her kitchen, watching her make tea and, although I had planned to wait until it was ready and we'd carried it through to the living room, I've already told her about Abe and me.

'I mean, you haven't known him very long.' She scoops loose leaves into a yellow enamel teapot, with the same quiet sense of purpose she brings to everything, as her father used to.

'That's not true,' I remind her. 'I met him when I was four.'

'But you didn't see him for sixty-odd years.' She pauses before filling the pot with water and looks at me. 'You can't know him very well now. Not properly.'

7

She's not displeased or angry, she just doesn't understand, and I'm not sure if I can explain. I feel as if I've always known Abe. I don't need to spend months or years finding out about him, filling in the gaps. I know him instinctively, just as I did as a child.

There was a game we used to play in the living room at his house. There were two armchairs facing each other in front of the fireplace, a rug folded over the arm of one. I can't remember which of us thought of the game but it became a favourite. We'd take a chair each and opposite ends of the rug, sitting quietly at first before the catching of an eye signalled the start of a playful tug of war. One of us would pull at the rug and the chair of the other would move forwards slightly before the other responded. As the tugs became stronger so the chairs would slip and slide on their castors across the parquet floor in an increasingly energetic dance.

Sometimes we'd put one of Abe's dad's records on the gramophone and tug to the strains of Little Richard or Woody Guthrie. But always the game was accompanied by the peals and trills of our laughter. There was something about the way we communicated, wordlessly, through looks, and through the weft of the rug between us and the gentle competition for sole possession of it, that made us helpless with laughter.

At some point, one would wrest the rug from the other, sending both chairs spinning back a few inches across the floor and declaring themselves the winner. Somebody always won but it didn't matter who.

'Again,' we'd say, when the game was over, and we'd begin once more with the implicit understanding that it would go the other way this time, that whoever had 'won' on the previous occasion would allow the other to triumph now – not immediately, but when some unspoken signal indicated that one of us should tug a little harder.

Sometimes we'd carry on for hours.

'Daft apeths,' Jackie or Alan, Abe's older brothers, used to say when they saw us, and we'd laugh even more at the idea of a 'daft apeth'. I'd never heard the term before.

I find myself saying it sometimes now, when Connor is clowning or inventing strange games of his own.

'You haven't changed,' Abe said, the first time we met for coffee, just the two of us in a café on the high street in Richmond. He'd suggested the place but had never been there before, and as he sat down, we realized music was blaring from a speaker, loud enough to make conversation difficult for people our age.

I hadn't said anything. I'd simply looked at Abe, raised an eyebrow and inclined my head slightly. He'd nodded and we'd got up, a little too quickly, anxious to be out before anyone engaged us with offers of help or menus.

I laughed when we were outside. 'I feel like we've done a runner!'

And that was when he told me that I had not changed.

He said it on another occasion, in a café that was quieter and had a slightly older clientele. We were sitting in the window, visible to anyone who happened to glance in as they passed and Abe had put his hand across the table, taken mine and looked at me intently as he said it.

'I've aged a lot.' I squeezed his, not caring who saw us, happy at a time of life when I thought I'd had my fill of happiness.

'We both have, but you're the same person, the same warmth and the same spirit.'

'Thank you,' I said. 'This is . . .' I paused, unable to find the right words, looking at the rows of teapots on a shelf that ran around the room.

'What?'

9

'Just so nice.'

'The café?' he asked, as the waitress, a young girl with an air of bored wariness, approached us.

'No.' I shook my head. He knew full well what I meant.

'Are you ready to order?'

We asked for a cream tea for two and were given a basket containing several miniature pots of jam, hotel-breakfast-sized, which Abe removed from the basket and placed absentmindedly on the table between us. 'I've been think-ing,' he said.

'Yes?'

'A few years ago – actually, it was probably twenty years ago, maybe more – I pitched for a contract in Copenhagen.'

'For a fountain?'

I loved that Abe, whom I'd always thought would be an architect, had become a fountain designer. Until he told me, I'd never considered such a job existed. The knowledge made me start to look at things differently. Of course everything was conceived by someone: the star pattern of the paper nap-kin folded neatly under bone-handled knives, the knives themselves, the basket the jams had been in, even the lock on the sash window just above our eye level. We are sur-rounded by the products of people's working lives but hardly ever stop to wonder who'd decided that a scattering of tiny white stars on a yellow background was perfect for wiping away the crumbs generated by a cream tea, or that the brass of a window fitting should be bevelled.

'Yes, but I didn't get the job,' Abe continued. 'I think my design was too ambitious. I was trying to base it on an aspect of quantum physics I didn't fully understand.'

'Isn't that the thing about quantum physics?'

'What?'

'That if you think you understand it you don't?'

Abe laughed. 'Probably.'

'So what was this fountain like?'

'It was based on a clock.' He picked up one of the jam jars and began rearranging them in a circle on the table. 'If you can imagine the jams are jets of water . . .' He took a salt cellar from the table next to ours and placed it at the centre of the ring of jars. 'And this too.' There was an animation to his movements that suggested he must have loved his job. 'So, the salt jet represents the day and the jam jets the hours.'

I smiled.

'Obviously there were twelve but there's not quite enough jam! And then . . .' He looked about for further props and, in their absence, simply moved his fingers around the table. 'Then around those jets, there was another ring.'

I imagined them, where the warmth of his fingertips had left slight marks on the sheen of the wooden table.

'And around them a further ring of smaller jets, which represented the minutes.'

I watched his hands roaming deftly around the table, recreating the sequence as far as he could, trying to convey something of his work to me. They were like the hands of pianist: mesmerizing in their movements. Strong, but with a delicate dexterity.

He stopped the virtual illustration and moved the jars aside as the waitress returned with the tea, which sat untouched for a while, as we carried on talking.

'Do you still have your design?' I asked, curious.

'Possibly somewhere. But it never went beyond the planning stage. I'm only bringing it up because I remember thinking of you at the time.'

'Really?' I was pleased. 'Why?'

'Because the research I did introduced me to the notion of quantum entanglement. Have you ever come across it?'

'Perhaps somewhere. But I've no idea what it is.'

'As I understand it, and I'm still not sure that I do either, not fully – I'm told by a reliable source that if you think you understand quantum physics then you probably don't . . .'

I laughed. 'Then I'll try to appear clever and not understand quantum entanglement!'

'It's to do with the behaviour of particles, tiny ones, like electrons, that have interacted in the past then moved apart.'

'And how do they behave?'

'Well, the curious thing is, they say that even if they end up millions of miles or galaxies apart, they still continue to be affected by each other. Tickle one and the other dances, to use the correct scientific terminology.'

'It sounds uncanny.'

'Great minds,' he said. 'That's what Einstein thought. "Spooky action at a distance" was what he called it. Or *spukhafte Fernwirkung* in German.'

I laughed at his exaggerated pronunciation.

'Funny how these things stick in your mind,' Abe said, picking up the teapot and pouring for me. 'I can barely remember the names of everyday objects, these days, but *spukhafte Fernwirkung* is still there, stuck in the bit of the brain marked "useless information". Milk?' He pushed the jug towards me.

'And why, apart from the fact that Einstein and I obviously work along similar lines, did it make you think of me?'

'I know it sounds strange and probably a bit muddled. And it wasn't as if I thought of you all the time, but occasionally I'd get this very strong sense of you.'

'In what way?'

'I can't really explain. A bit like *déjà vu* but more that I'd forgotten you were someone from the past, not the present.'

I took a sip of my tea. 'I'm not sure I understand.'

'There were occasional incidents when I'd find myself thinking that I had to tell you something – you know, the way you do when someone has died recently and you haven't forgotten but it's still a habit.'

'I still do that with Richard, even though it's ten years since he died.'

It happened less often now but I still caught myself wondering if Richard would like to see a particular film or might want fish for dinner. And then I remembered, although of course I'd known all along, that he wasn't with me any more. Except he was, of course, in spirit.

'Sometimes the sense of you was so strong, it unnerved me. It was almost like seeing a ghost but without having seen one.'

'Go on.'

'There was one particular occasion, years ago, but I still remember it because, well, it was significant. Do you remember there was a bomb in Docklands?'

'Vaguely.' That's another thing about getting old: you forget events that unsettled you when they occurred.

'I was in the area at the time. I wasn't hurt or anything but close enough to see it happen and be shocked by it.'

'I'm sorry.'

'I was married, but immediately afterwards I remember thinking that I must let you know I was okay.'

'Me?'

'Yes. I suppose it was the shock. But that was my first thought. I must let Ivy know I've not been hurt. Ivy, not Lynn. And I thought that was weird. I hadn't really thought about you for years and suddenly I had to let you know I was okay.'

'Well, I'm glad you were.'

The waitress appeared and saw that the scones were still untouched. 'Is everything all right?'

'Yes, thank you,' I said, picking up the bone-handled

knife, cutting my scone in half and dismissing her with furious buttering.

'It happened again when I was pitching for that fountain in Copenhagen. I went out for a few days and Lynn came with me.'

Abe was still too intent on telling his story to make a start on his tea.

'I remember that because I called her Ivy over dinner one evening and she was furious. We were going through a difficult time and she thought I was having an affair. It took me a while to convince her that you were a childhood friend I hadn't seen or spoken to for years.'

'Did you know any other Ivys?'

'No. It wasn't as if I'd just called her Liz instead of Lynn. It was very specific.'

'Yes.' I bit into my scone, trying to imagine.

'But I told myself I sometimes got this strong sense of you, and it was only very occasionally, because a part of you was still with me.'

'I see.' I felt slightly unnerved by the conversation. I had thought of Abe from time to time but not in the way he was describing.

'I suppose what I'm trying to say is that I realized our early friendship wasn't just something that happened, it was something that had laid the foundations for all kinds of future relationships. Good foundations.'

'That's a lovely thing to say.' I smiled.

'In that sense, I suppose, when I skimmed the surface of quantum entanglement, I found myself using our friendship as a metaphor for it.'

There was something about the way he said it, the quiet, focused delivery of the words, that contrasted with his earlier animation, when he'd been talking about his fountain, and made me want to open up to him. There was nothing in particular I wanted to say, not then, but I could feel myself beginning to trust him, beginning to feel that he was a person in whom I could confide, exposing myself without fear of what he might think.

Is that what the beginning of love feels like?

'I'm not making much sense, I know.' Abe stretched his hands as if to signal he was winding up that line of thought. 'I'm just trying to say that a part of you stayed with me and I'm so glad to have met you again. I keep wondering what would have happened if I'd not been to the supermarket that day, if you'd not been taking your grandson to the park.'

He took my hand and squeezed it again, then looked at me, and I knew then, with a certainty that surprised me, in exactly which direction I wanted things to move.

But how can I explain this to my daughter, who has spent the past five years treading carefully as she tried to make up her mind as to whether her lovely, kind, steady, supportive boyfriend is the person she wants to spend the rest of her life with?

She'd finally decided and they're getting married in September. I worry she thinks I'm stealing her thunder. That's not my intention, but now that I've found Abe again I'm not going to let him go.

'I know it's a surprise to you,' I tell her, 'and I know it must seem odd, as if I haven't thought about it. But I don't need to. It's the right thing.'

'Have you always loved him?' Lottie asks, curious, and I wish we were not in her flat and that Richard was not looking at me from the framed photograph. It's right in the middle of mantelpiece that surrounds a boarded-up fireplace. Lottie was about six at the time. We're on a beach and I think it's probably Greatstone. We went there a lot when she and

Max were young, and you can just make out the shape of the dunes in the background. Lottie's wearing a swimsuit, sitting on Richard's shoulders, clutching his hair for support, and smiling. Richard's smiling, too, but his eyes seem slightly pained, perhaps because they're screwed up against the sun or because Lottie's pulling his hair.

'No. I haven't seen him for years,' I say, looking away from Richard's gaze and the clutch of objects that link Lottie to a past that was centred on our family unit.

There's a lump of the Berlin Wall, which Richard brought back from a business trip – he'd happened to be there when the Wall came down – and a tiny canvas painting of a bookshop on the banks of the Seine, which Max had bought her on a French exchange trip. Propped up on the floor next to the redundant fireplace is the strip of painted wood from the side of the under-stairs cupboard of our old family home. It's marked with the heights of the children at various dates. I'd thought perhaps I should paint over the markings before I sold the house but Lottie had wanted to prise it off and keep it.

'We were only children when we knew each other,' I say. 'And we didn't keep in touch after he moved away. But I do love him now.'

'But how do you know?' Lottie is so cautious and always has been.

I glance at the photo of her and Richard again. She couldn't quite give herself entirely to the thrill of being raised high on her father's shoulders, or to trust that he wouldn't let her fall: she'd had to cling to him. Max, always more physical, would have waved his hands around in the air, relished being so far from the ground and reached up higher. 'I just know.'

'Did you feel like that about Dad?'

'It was different.'

'How?'

'I loved your dad very much. He was a big man. He took on a lot, when he married me, and when we had you and Max, knowing the risks. It required a very special man to do that.'

I follow Lottie's gaze back to the photograph. I can imagine some of what she must be thinking. 'Lottie love,' I say, wanting her to look at me, 'I will always love your dad. He was and always will be a huge part of my life. Others would have run a mile from me and everything that went with me, but Richard was always ready to face the world and deal with whatever it threw up. He always supported my decisions, even when they were not the ones he would have taken. I loved him for all of that and so many other things. This is different.'

'Why?'

'I can't really explain. But sometimes you love someone because of the way they are, the things they do, the actions they take, and sometimes you just love someone for who they are.'

'So you loved Dad because of the things he did?'

'No,' I say, too quickly. 'Yes, I mean, but that doesn't make what we had any less. It made it more. Marriage is so much bigger than just falling in love with someone. Falling in love is not enough for it to work. There has to be more.'

'What?'

'Love, and a willingness to commit. It's easy to fall in love, easy to find your soul-mate, but maybe a soul-mate is not the person you should marry, not when you have your whole life ahead of you.'

'You seem so happy together, you and Abe,' Lottie says. 'There's something about the way you potter about that makes it all look so easy.'

'What?' I ask, laughing at the image of Abe and myself as elderly potterers. Of course, we're both in our seventies but I feel younger, so much younger, since I met him again or perhaps just more at ease, with myself and with the world.

The world, I have learned the hard way, can inflict a lot of loss on you but sometimes, when you least expect it, it tries to make amends for that in the most wonderful ways.

'There's a lightness to you now,' Lottie says, looking at me so directly that I squirm. 'You seem happier now than when Dad was alive, as if you're finally with the right person.'

'Perhaps it's just the right time,' I say.

I don't want to tarnish Richard's memory in any way. He was a wonderful man, but life for us wasn't always easy. Who knows if it would have been easier with anyone else?

'Abe and I,' I say, 'there's nothing for us to worry about now, apart from getting older. I loved your dad, but sometimes we got too caught up with the day-to-day to appreciate each other. And our day-to-day was not always easy.'

'I know, Mum,' Lottie says. 'I know that. It's just . . .'

I watch her topping up our cups from the teapot, which sits on the living-room floor, in the absence of a coffee-table, pouring it thoughtfully, considering what she will say next.

She looks at the picture of her and Richard again, as if she needs his approval. 'Do you think I'm marrying the wrong man?' she asks, finally.

'No, darling. Of course not. I think you're marrying a wonderful man who loves you and is willing to commit to you. The two of you are perfect for each other.'

I worry that I'm doing the wrong thing – that my planned marriage will affect my own children in ways I never imagined. 'It's different when you're young,' I say. 'Maybe you look too hard for things that aren't ever going to be there and you don't always see what is. At my age, you realize that all you were ever really looking for was someone to hold your hand through life, especially at the end. Maybe I knew that when I was young, too, but I don't think I was conscious of it.'

'Don't say that, Mum.'

'I didn't mean it to sound gloomy.'

'But what if Tim isn't the right man?'

'He is. You know he is.'

'I'm not as sure as you seem to be.'

'Lottie, there are probably lots of right men out there. You can't marry all of them. You won't even meet all of them. But you've met Tim now and you want to get married. That's the right thing to do.'

'It scares me sometimes,' she says quietly.

'You're not having second thoughts, are you?' I ask.

'Not really. I love Tim and I want to marry him, and I know it sounds ridiculous but . . .'

'What?'

'I feel a bit jealous of you. Because you're so sure of Abe.'

'I am now. Maybe if I'd met him when I was your age I'd have been less so. Time's not on my side.'

'There you go again!'

'Okay. Maybe it is. Maybe it's on both our sides.'

'What do you mean?'

'We've both got the time we've always had. You have to do what's right for you now.'

'I don't have much time, if I want to have children. What if Tim's not the right man, just the one who's here now, at the right time?'

'Then that makes him the right man,' I tell her, but she still looks unsure. 'Lottie, love, if my getting married is going to upset you, I won't do it. It doesn't really matter if we marry or not, although we'd like to. But I'm still going to be with Abe. Does it make such a difference?'

'No, Mum.' Her eyes well. 'I'm really happy for you. Really I am. It's just a bit of a surprise and it all seems to have happened so quickly.'

'I know,' I say. 'But I'm not getting any younger. None of us is. I've lost so many other people in my life, and now that I've met Abe again, I don't want to throw away a chance to be happy.'

'Oh, Mum,' Lottie says, and there's something in her tone that makes me move closer to her.

'What is it, love?' I put my arm around her. 'What's the matter? What is it that's worrying you?'

'Nothing,' she says. She turns and hugs me. 'Really, nothing.'

We hold each other for a moment.

'I think I'm just happy for you,' Lottie says, and her voice quivers, as if she's trying not to cry.

And I feel it too.

Happiness does that to you sometimes. It's so much closer to sadness than you imagine.

Max is less emotional when I tell him. He may have been as surprised as his sister but his questions are more practical.

'Where will you live?' He has poured us both a glass of wine, as if the conversation we're about to have requires a drink.

'I'm going to move into Abe's house with him and I'll put the flat in your names. That way you shouldn't have to pay inheritance tax.'

I thought he'd be impressed by my practicality but he's concerned. 'It's a good idea to hang on to it, just in case . . .' He stops and sips his drink.

'In case it doesn't work out?'

'You never know, Mum,' he said. 'It might not be right for you.'

'I do know.' I find myself repeating what I said to Lottie earlier in the day.

'How can you be so sure?'

'Because I'm going to make it work.'

'And what about his children? Are they happy?'

'I think so.'

Abe had lunch with Sam and Ruby today. I haven't seen him since but he called and reported that they were 'delighted'.

'Even though his wife died less than a year ago?' Max asks. 'They don't think it's too soon?'

'I know it might appear that way. But Lynn had been ill for a long time, not that that makes it any easier but I suppose he'd lost her, in many ways, before she died and he knew it was coming.'

'I'm not trying to be difficult, Mum,' Max says. 'I'm just concerned for you.'

'I know.' I touch his hand across the table.

He surprises me by taking mine and holding it.

'This is what I want, Max.' I look at him. 'It's what we both want.'

'Then I'll drink to it,' he says, and raises his glass. 'To you and Abe McFadden.'

Who knew? I certainly never expected to rediscover the joys of love and sex in my seventies when I'd thought that side of my life was well and truly over. At my age, I'd thought I'd be more concerned with death than sex. It's different, of course. The body isn't as willing, it doesn't yield as easily, but if the spirit is willing, the flesh can be made to catch up.

The first time I wasn't as nervous as I might have supposed. Abe and I had had the requisite number of coffees, lunches, dinners, trips to the theatre and visits to art galleries. We'd filled in enough of the gaps since we were children. We knew the bigger picture and a lot of the minutiae too.

*

'Alan became a stand-up comedian?' I laughed when he'd run through his older brother's career trajectory.

'For a while, in the early eighties, he tried to make a living out of it. Then he trained as an accountant.'

'And Tessa?'

'She started off as a teacher, then became something big in some educational think tank.'

'And they're still well? Your siblings?'

'Yes.' He touched the side of my face. 'I'm so sorry about Jon. It must have been very hard for you.'

'You know what it's like to lose a sibling.'

He nodded. 'It was a long time ago but it stays with you, something like that. Mum never really got over it.'

'How could you ever get over losing a child? Dad found it hard when Jon died. I think that was what really killed him, not the pneumonia.'

We had accumulated a lot of deaths of loved ones between us in the intervening years. Parents, siblings, partners. His wife Lynn had died more recently than Richard.

He described their marriage as 'very happy'. I wondered, initially, if I felt jealous in a *Rebecca*-esque way but I found I didn't. His happy marriage seemed to pave the way for us to have a future. A bad one might have made him more hesitant.

'Listen to us getting morose.' Abe shook his head. 'Do you still swim?'

'I do. I go to the local pool several times a week and the lido in summer.'

He laughed and put his arm around me, pulling me to him.

We'd come full circle. We were back where we'd been when we'd first met as children, drawn to each other in a way you cannot put into words. We still fitted, at least our personalities did, after all the years. Whether our bodies would was an unknown, but we would find out sooner or later.

'I'm not a brilliant cook,' Abe said, as we walked though the park one morning after we'd met for coffee, kicking up the autumn leaves like children, 'but I'd like to make you dinner one evening soon. At my place.'

'I'm not a great foodie,' I replied, 'so whatever you cook, I'm sure it will be lovely. And I'd love to come.'

'Tomorrow?' he asked. 'Or today even?'

'I'm picking Connor up after school so I'd need to go home first. But I could come round after Max collects him on his way home.'

'If you won't be too tired?'

'No. If I get the bus I could be at your house by about eight. Is that okay?'

'Perfect.' Abe was still looking at me. 'And I wondered . . .'

'Yes?'

'I wouldn't like you to take public transport home late. I could get you a taxi home. Or . . .'

'I'd love to,' I said, feeling myself flush as I spoke. We were standing near the entrance to the park, where a group of teenagers were skateboarding on a bit of tarmac.

'Good.' Abe put his arms around me. 'There's no pressure or anything. But it would be so lovely if you could stay.'

'Thank you.' I appreciated the reassurance, while enjoying the prospect of being with him.

He kissed me then, a moment of foreplay for the evening ahead of us. He kissed me until the teenagers on their boards stopped wheeling around and shouted, 'Get a room, Granddad!'

'There he is!' I spotted Sam seconds before Abe did: he was holding up a sign with 'Mr and Mrs McFadden' printed on it, surrounded by felt-tipped hearts and flowers.

'The kids made it.' He shrugged and dropped it to his side,

kissing his father twice and pulling him close at the same time, the way he always did. They were so easily affectionate together.

'Ivy, did you have a good time?' Sam let go of his father and planted a dry, warm kiss on my cheek.

'Wonderful. Really wonderful. And it's so kind of you to come and meet us.'

We'd both stressed that he didn't have to. He had enough on, with his job and two young children, but he'd insisted.

'Dad spent enough time driving me and Ruby around. And it was your honeymoon. You don't want to spoil it by sitting on the Tube for hours when you get back.'

He'd arranged the honeymoon too, with Abe's knowledge but without mine. It was a gift to us from all four of our children. They'd let Abe in on the details before they'd booked it, but told him to keep it a secret from me. 'We'll be by the sea and the weather should be warm but not too hot,' was all Abe would say when I asked him what I should pack.

'Is it northern Europe?' I wondered if he was going to show me his fountain on the waterfront in Hamburg. 'Or Spain?' Had he shown a little too much interest when I'd mentioned a work trip to Almería and said I'd like to go back? 'Or North Africa?' I knew the flight was short but perhaps we were going somewhere in Morocco.

He'd been several times with Lynn, Sam and Ruby. 'Such a beautiful country. The light, the colours and the hospitality of the people make it very special.'

I wasn't sure how I felt about honeymooning in a place where he'd spent so much time with his wife and young family, but wherever we were going, it was too late for me to do anything about it.

'Stop asking so many questions!' Abe said, as I probed.

'Have I read a novel set there?'

'Will I need walking shoes?'

'Should I bring mosquito repellent?'

'Honestly, you're like a child who needs to know what their Christmas present is before Christmas.'

'I just want to be prepared.'

'I've told you what to bring and I'll make sure we have everything else we need.'

'But what should I read? I like books I'm reading to resonate with the place I'm in when I'm away.'

'It's a surprise, Ivy,' Abe said firmly. 'Please, just indulge me and let it remain one.'

The real surprise was that Abe hadn't planned it. The children had got together in a way that meant far more to me than the trip itself. They'd all been so accepting, so happy for us and so unified in their desire to demonstrate it.

We had been in an Italian restaurant not far from the register office when Lottie handed me the card. 'This is from all of us,' she'd said over the clatter and chatter and Sam's iPod, which he'd hooked up to the restaurant's system so that, after his speech, he could play us a song he said had always been one of his dad's favourites.

'And now I know why!'

It was the Mamas and the Papas' 'For The Love Of Ivy', which I often sang to myself, as you do when a song has your name in it.

We were a noisy sprawling party, even though we'd tried to keep it to family and a few close friends. We had more of both than we'd known, and there had been thirty-five of us in a private function room that opened out on to a terracotta-walled courtyard filled with potted olive and bay trees. We could almost have been in Italy: the weather was warm, the food sun-drenched and aromatic, the waiters indulgent of the occasion and us.

'*Bellissima!*' the waiter said several times, as he topped up my glass with Prosecco, behaving as if I was a seventeen-year-old bride, rather than a woman of seventy-one.

But it was also the sense of family that fitted the Italian setting: Ruby and Lottie sat with their heads together on a bench in the sun, chatting conspiratorially as if they'd known each other all their lives. Ilona, Sam's Polish wife, was show-ing Connor and Tomasz how to fashion a swan from a table napkin while Sam and Max checked the cricket scores on each other's mobile phones and pretended they were not when Hannah asked what they were doing. They were miss-ing a Test match to witness their old parents getting married but they weren't going to miss it entirely.

'Open it,' Lottie said, as I looked at the envelope she'd just handed me.

The card was an Eric Slater painting, which showed a landscape that was English and picturesque but not instantly recognizable, unless you'd grown up in Sussex, which of course we had.

'The coastguard's cottages. That was one of my favourite places,' I said as I opened it. They were perched precariously on the edge of the cliffs where the meanders of the Cuck-mere river emptied out into the sea, and on the other side the distinctive white cliffs of the Seven Sisters.

'I know,' Ruby said. 'One of Dad's too.'

They'd all written inside the card: our children, their part-ners and the grandchildren had inscribed various versions of 'Mum and Abe', 'Dad and Ivy', and the heart-warming 'Grandma and Grandpa Abe', and 'Granddad and Nana Ivy'. They all congratulated us and wished us many years of happiness, and at the centre, a line in Sam's handwrit-ing: 'Hope you enjoy the honeymoon – from all of us, with love.'

I'd looked up at their expectant faces, touched beyond words.

There was a certain bitter sweetness, as Abe and I rekindled the relationship in a new and adult form, to my realization that I'd never before felt fully completed by another person. In all the adult relationships I'd had, every one good and loving in its own way, I'd always felt I was one half of it, not part of a whole.

With Abe I felt different. Perhaps it was just our age and that we'd met at a time of life when we could spend a lot of time together: life, work, careers and families were not distracting us from each other. I told myself so because I felt sad about the other men I'd loved and lost. I thought the separateness that had defined other relationships was natural, part of being an individual, to do with my not wanting to be subsumed by someone else and their needs. Now I wanted to be Ivy and Abe.

On the day it happened, I'd been out shopping in the morning. One of our neighbours had invited us to a party to celebrate their ruby wedding anniversary. It would be the first gathering Abe and I would attend together since we'd been married, the first invitation to go on the mantelpiece with 'Ivy and Abe' handwritten above the printed copperplate that detailed the time and date of the party. We'd been together again eighteen months and it was a little more than six months since we'd married and I'd moved into Abe's house.

We'd been to dinner parties together and family gatherings, both mine and his, but this was more of an occasion – enough to merit looking for a new dress.

'Will you be back for lunch or have something in town?' Abe asked.

'I'm not sure. I don't want to be too long but don't count on my being back.'

'I'll probably get myself a sandwich, but let me know if you're going to be back.' He'd looked at his watch as he said this, as if he was calculating the hours he'd have the house to himself.

'I'll find something out, I think,' I said. Perhaps he needed a bit of space.

'Okay either way,' he said, and kissed me.

It was early afternoon when I got back and Abe jumped to open the door.

'Is everything okay?' I asked, a little put out by his welcome. He was usually sensitive to the fact I liked a little time to myself, just to take my coat off and sort my bags out when I came in.

'Would you like a coffee?' he asked. 'I was going to make one for myself.'

'Okay. I need to put my bags down and go to the loo.'

'Of course.' He headed for the kitchen. 'I'll bring the coffee into the sitting room.'

I went upstairs and put my shopping bag, with the new dress, on our bed. The view from the bedroom window was barer than it had been when I moved in. The garden was small and low maintenance but the one it backed on to was larger and had had a magnificent sycamore tree, which we could see from our bed when the curtains were open. Now it was gone, cut down by a tree surgeon on account of disease. Abe had gone out to ask him when we heard the chainsaw and saw the branches falling.

'I miss the tree,' I'd said to Abe, more than once. 'And there don't seem to be so many birds now – I haven't heard our blackbirds recently.' We often woke to the sound of blackbirds singing, and a couple alighted regularly on the patch of lawn outside the sitting room.

'Our blackbirds', Abe had taken to calling them, and when he did I wondered anew at the beauty of nature. Having someone to observe it with seemed to intensify it.

The world seemed so much brighter with Abe at my side but the absence of the tree saddened me when I looked out of the bedroom window. Without it the garden seemed devoid of life, as if winter had come early. I tried to shrug off the slight melancholy I was feeling and went downstairs.

Abe was reading the paper in the sitting room. 'I've made you coffee,' he said, nodding towards a cup on the table by the window.

I paused before I sat down, irrationally miffed because Abe was on the side of the sofa I normally occupied, and in placing the coffee where he had, he was forcing me to sit somewhere else. I knew he wouldn't have meant anything by it but I liked the fact that we'd settled into a routine, which included having places where we 'normally' sat. It gave a sense of longevity to our relationship, which it did not have.

'Thank you.' I sat down, glanced out of the window and immediately understood why he was on my side of the sofa, his eagerness to see me off that morning, and the way he had jumped up on my return.

In the corner of the lawn where 'our' blackbirds could often be seen pecking at the ground, there was a patch of disturbed earth and, rising gracefully in its midst, a sapling. I burst into tears when I saw it.

'It's an apple tree,' he said, getting up and coming over. 'A semi-dwarf so it won't overshadow the garden but it should grow high enough to see from our bedroom window and bring in a few birds too.'

I was too moved to speak and I think Abe was perplexed by my reaction. He carried on talking. 'We'll probably get a few bluetits nesting in the spring, fly-catchers and warblers when the blossom is out, and in the autumn and winter, when the fruit is on the ground, thrushes, redwings and all sorts.' He was babbling as he sat down and put his arm round me. 'I thought you'd like it.'

'I love it,' I said, nestling into him.

'So why the tears? Here, have a tissue.'

I blew my nose and tried to put into words what I felt. 'Because I'm so happy,' I said, wiping my eyes. 'I've spent so much of my life not quite daring to look forward to anything, afraid of what the future might bring, but now . . .'

'That's a lot of emotion for the prospect of a few apples,' Abe said, putting his other hand on my knee.

We both knew it wasn't the tree I was talking about – not just the tree, anyway – but everything it symbolized: life and our new life together.

'Have you ever wondered,' Abe asked, taking my hand as we lay in bed that night, 'what might have happened if we'd met at a different time of our lives?'

'We did.'

'I mean later, not when we were children. If we'd met at the right time.'

'I had this conversation with Lottie not so long ago.'

'About us?'

'It was about her, really. Is there a right person or just a right time?'

'And what did you conclude?'

'I think there's a right person at the right time and a wrong person at the right time – and a right person at the wrong time. Who knows what would have happened if we'd met at another time? We might have been wrong for each other then, and you can't turn the clock back.'

'Unless you're North Korean.' Abe looked at the glow of

the LED display on the radio alarm by his bed. 'They put their clocks back as a symbolic gesture to show that they'd shrugged off the years of Japanese imperialism.'

'That didn't change the past, though,' I said. 'Who knows what another past might have brought?'

'We're so very lucky,' he said, turning towards me and putting his arm around me, 'to have met again when we did.'

I didn't say anything. I moved towards him and kissed him instead. It was a long kiss, and while it lasted, I struggled for the second time that day to find the right words to tell him what I wanted to tell him.

I wanted to tell him I felt complete, in a way I never had before. I wanted him to know how happy he made me, but he winced as we kissed and I stopped, wondering if he was uncomfortable. 'Are you okay?' I asked, snuggling close to him, enjoying the warmth of his body and his chest hair against my breasts.

'Yes,' he replied. 'I'm getting old, though.'

I laughed. 'We're both getting old.'

Abe let out a long, noisy breath. He sounded strained but I didn't want to ask again.

'I don't seem to be able to find quite the right words,' I said.

'You always say the right thing.'

Again he sounded pained but I went on, 'I've always been glad that we met when we did, when we were kids. We were lucky to have had that friendship. It was like a touchstone, something I could refer to at other times in my life, times when I felt unloved and undervalued. Our friendship was like a solid foundation to my life.'

I shifted around in bed to look at Abe. I wanted to make sure he was listening. 'Are you okay?' I asked again.

He seemed uncomfortable. 'Ivy,' he said screwing up his

face as he spoke. 'That's one of the nicest things anyone's ever said to me but my chest feels really tight.' He took another jagged breath. 'I think I might be having a heart attack.'

I switched the light on. His face was contorted with pain. I knew I had to call an ambulance.

'I think my husband is having a heart attack,' I said, standing naked in the light by the bed, then listened to them telling me to keep him still, to try to make him relax and rest while the ambulance came to us.

I felt bad getting dressed as he lay there, unsure if he would care that he was found naked and in bed by the paramedics, or if the pain had blocked out any of the thoughts I was still having.

But they'd clearly seen it all before, the young man and woman to whom I opened the door. They were professional and sympathetic.

Everyone was. The hospital staff, when we finally got there, the doctors, the nurses, were all kind and caring. Each and every one of them did everything they could. But it wasn't enough. He went into cardiac arrest not long after we arrived at the hospital. They tried to revive him but it was too late.

'I'm so sorry,' the doctor said.

'You can have a few moments with him.' The nurse held my hand briefly, before leaving me to sit with Abe, as the warmth and colour drained from his body.

I lay on the bed next to him. I couldn't think of him as a corpse. Not yet.

I held him, even though his heart no longer pumped and he no longer breathed, and I kissed him, even as his lips began to stiffen and turn blue.

And then I couldn't bear it any more. I don't think I've

ever felt so alone in the world, not after Richard died, or Mum, not even after Jon and Dad died. I'd opened myself up entirely to Abe. I'd let him in as I'd never let anyone in before, and now that he was gone there was a hole inside me that was too big to be filled by anything or anyone.

There was a gentle knock on the door and the nurse opened it tentatively. Did she smile when she saw me lying beside Abe on the bed? 'Do you need more time?' she asked, unshocked.

'No,' I said, although it was one of the hardest things I'd ever done, getting off the bed and walking towards the door.

'Hello.' The nurse is waiting for me outside. 'I'll get you a cup of tea and we'll call someone for you.'

She guides me to a chair. 'You're in shock,' she says, handing me a mug.

But I'm not.

I look at her, trying to gauge her age. I guess she's about twenty-seven. I wonder if her profession makes her more aware of the fleeting nature of life than I was at that age. Death then would have shocked me but it doesn't now. It is inevitable: the thing I always knew was coming had come earlier than I'd hoped for but, nevertheless, as I had expected.

Life is a series of moments. All of them fleeting. Yes, it goes on, but not in a smooth and seamless way. It jumps from moment to moment and eventually it ends. I wonder, not for the first time, how my life might have panned out if I'd met Abe at another point in it. I wonder how things might have turned out between us. But the only thing I know for sure is that eventually we'd have reached the end.

'Can I ask you something?' the nurse says, as I sip my tea. I nod.

'How long had you been married?'

I find that I'm not sure how to answer. 'Only a few months.' I register her surprise. 'But I first met him when I was a child.'

She smiles as if this makes sense. 'You seemed very close,' she said.

'We were.'

In string theory, the multiverse is a theory in which
our universe is not the only one: many universes
exist parallel to each other. These distinct universes
within the multiverse theory are called parallel
universes. A variety of different theories lend
themselves to a multiverse viewpoint.
In some theories, there are copies of you
sitting right here right now reading this in other
universes, and other copies of you are doing
other things in other universes.

Andrew Zimmerman Jones,
String Theory for Dummies

London, 2015

'You're turning into one of the diehards,' Tony said, as I
stood on the edge of the pool, adjusting my goggles.

It was late September and the water temperature was drop-
ping daily but I wanted to keep swimming outside for as long
possible. Someone had chalked '13C/56F' on the board at the
end of the covered walkway that bridged the indoor and outdoor pools and, underneath, one of the lifeguards had scrawled,
'Still warmer than the sea off Aberdeen in summer!'

'I don't know about that,' I said, to my newish acquaintance.

Tony was probably in his mid-thirties. I could never be
sure what age people were any more. He swam outside most
days in the large rectangular pool, which was flanked by a

row of coloured changing huts and overhung by trees in the park outside. I'd met him when I'd pointed out a greenfinch to him a few weeks ago, diving down to drink from the pool, and he'd said it looked like a canary.

'Canaries are more strikingly yellow. And you'd be unlikely to see one here.'

Tony was Australian. I supposed that accounted for his lack of knowledge about British birds.

'I saw a parakeet in Richmond Park,' he'd told me.

'I've seen a few about. I heard they escaped from an aviary during the hurricane in 1987.'

'I heard that Jimi Hendrix released a pair in Carnaby Street in the sixties,' he'd replied, grinning and pulling on a swimming cap. 'I'm Tony, by the way.'

'Ivy,' I replied.

'Good to meet you, Ivy. Enjoy your swim.'

We'd had a few exchanges since then, usually to do with the water temperature, the length of our swims or the quietness of the pool. Gone were the foreign students, who sunned themselves in tiny bikinis and tight swimming trunks but hardly ever got further than dipping their toes in, making a big deal of how cold it was.

Occasionally, Tony would ask if I'd seen any more exotic birds and I'd feed him the name of something that was really quite common to see how he reacted.

'A redwing? Really? Guess you don't see them very often?' I couldn't tell if he knew I was teasing him and that redwings were as ordinary as song thrushes – he probably saw them every day without knowing.

'What's the water like?' I said to him now. He was already in the pool, but paused between laps when he saw me.

'It's probably colder out there today,' he replied, and resumed his swim.

I liked the cooler temperatures. It meant the pool was fairly empty, where it had been crowded at the height of summer, and swimming more exhilarating. It made me feel fully alive in a way I had not since Richard had died and then Jon, almost exactly a year later.

A part of me felt guilty for having escaped the disease that had claimed too many family members, and the random way in which others' lives seemed to be cut short. But I knew that both Richard and Jon would want me to carry on living my life as fully as possible. I felt I owed it to them and to my mother: to appreciate the life I still had, especially now that I was over the worst of the grief. Time did heal, slowly.

Of course, there were still bad days but they were less frequent. On the whole, life was good. Swimming outside and feeling the rush of autumn's chill when I got out of the pool made me appreciate my life and living it.

'Are you training for something?' Tony asked, as I wrapped my towel around myself and we walked together towards the changing rooms.

I wasn't, but Tony was too much of a stranger for me to explain that coming here was part of a routine that was important to me. For so long my life had been held together by the framework of family. Now that the children had grown up and Richard was no longer alive, I needed something else to provide that structure so I clung to and created daily rituals: a cup of tea in bed when my alarm went off in the morning, breakfast with the radio on in the background, a short walk before a couple of hours' work, then lunch and my swim. It wasn't always the same: there was time, too, for friends and family, film and theatre. Sometimes work dominated my days but, even without it, they no longer felt long and empty, and my routines made sure they did not.

But I wouldn't tell Tony so. Instead I voiced a thought that had occurred to me a few weeks earlier. 'I was thinking of doing this trip where you swim between Greek islands.' I'd read an article, years back, and it had sounded wonderful. A boat transported your luggage and kept pace with a group of swimmers, offering somewhere to rest and recover if the swim was too arduous. It was not something Richard would have wanted to do. He hadn't been much of a swimmer, and while he was alive, I wouldn't have considered going off and doing it without him.

Now, if I wanted, it was a possibility, and while I wondered if I was too old, I could still swim reasonable distances.

'Wow, that sounds amazing,' Tony said, heading off towards the men's showers. 'Good for you, Ivy. You've got some balls.'

It was ridiculous to think of it as 'my' spot but I had begun to. The proximity of the café made the bench unnecessary. People sat at the tables and chairs outside, if the weather was good enough. I was the only person who carried their tea the extra few yards so I could drink it by the path that ran alongside the river. It was quieter there: the sound of the breeze in the cluster of ash and alder trees dulled the chatter from the café, and squirrels moved noiselessly through the branches of a horse chestnut. There was a narrow dirt path that ran between the bench and the river, worn away by joggers and cyclists, although most now preferred the tarmac track the council had laid down on the other side of the trees.

Today someone had occupied my bench and I hovered, wondering whether to sit there as usual or walk on and find somewhere to be alone with my thoughts. Sensing my presence, the man looked up and moved his drink, which he'd placed beside him, a little closer, making space for me. I gave him a half-smile, as I sat down, then removed the lid from my tea and emptied into it the sachet of milk. But I was too aware of his being there to lose myself entirely.

The first time I'd come here, I was exploring new surroundings. I'd moved just under a year ago to be closer to the children, who were now both working in London. I hadn't wanted to be in the family home any more. There were too many ghosts, too many memories. The rooms were no longer rooms but archives of the time we'd spent there. The narrow shelves in the alcove in Lottie's bedroom, which had been home to her collection of Sylvanian families, the rail across the passage that ran alongside the house, from which we'd hung a trapeze for Max's seventh birthday, the mismatched spindle on the staircase, which had replaced the one Max had broken climbing up the outside, and the narrow desk that ran alongside the back wall of the kitchen, so the children could do their homework there as teenagers: these were the markers of our life there.

But that life was over. There was too much space for one person. I spent most of my time in the kitchen, preferring to sit on the small sofa by the window than in the sitting room and to work at the kitchen table, rather than in the office extension Richard had created when my business began to take off.

I rattled around in it, which intensified my loneliness.

I felt cocooned in the flat I had now, which was smaller but, once I'd had it decorated and moved my things in, surprisingly familiar.

'It feels like being in a parallel universe where everything has shrunk,' Max said, when he'd finished helping me move furniture and put up pictures. 'You've still got the same painting over the fireplace and the same chair by the window.'

It was true, though I hadn't been aware just how much

mirroring of the old house I'd been doing when I'd chosen paint and put things away.

'Even the stuff on the shelf in the kitchen is exactly where it was before,' Lottie said, laughing.

That was also true. My mother's copy of *Mrs Beeton's Book of Household Management*, which I liked having but never used, was closest to the wall and next to it a row of other cookery books, bordered by a pile of three Polish pottery cereal bowls that Max had given me one Christmas.

'Have you been to Poland?' He was travelling a lot at the time.

'John Lewis.' He'd shrugged.

The rest of the shelf was lined with ceramics picked up abroad. There was a teal and azure flower-patterned plate from a holiday in Greece, another that depicted the running of the bulls in Pamplona, and a jug decorated with olive branches that we'd bought in Italy. Next to that was a yellow pottery lion, which Lottie had made in primary school, and the wonky penholder that Max had produced at the same stage.

'What, no ashtrays?' Richard used to say, year after year, when the offerings from DT classes were carried home in schoolbags. 'That's what we used to make when we were at school.'

I'd arranged the photographs above the mantelpiece in the living room much as before too, with the picture of my mother before she became ill next to the one of Richard and me on our wedding day, Richard looking smarter than I'd ever seen him in a new suit – the overall effect was a little spoiled by the folded sheaf of A4 that bulged from his breast pocket. 'My speech,' I remember him saying, patting it, whenever anyone commented.

I couldn't imagine meeting anyone else. Not now. I'd got

too used to Richard. The idea of someone new becoming as familiar as he had been scared me. Although he'd been dead for more than two years, I still felt his presence, or perhaps it was his absence. I still half expected him to appear: to climb into bed beside me, to call out when I put my key in the front door or to sit down, now, on the bench between me and the stranger. I could practically summon him up: see him rubbing his hands together as if it were cold, even though it wasn't really, and commenting on the breeze, taking a tissue out of his pocket and blowing his nose, out of habit, not because it was necessary.

All the little things that used to annoy me were now the things I missed.

And Richard was missing a life that was a little easier without the children at home or the pressure of full-time work. It didn't seem fair, after all the uncertainty surrounding my own health. Only a couple of years after I'd had the all-clear, Richard's had begun to fail.

I'd thought it was work that was bothering him. I knew something was causing his distraction. When I asked if anything was wrong he said no, but in a way that suggested otherwise.

There were the times when I'd called him at the office and been told he was out at a meeting he'd not mentioned. Later he was evasive if I asked about it. On occasion he'd close his laptop hurriedly, if I came into the room. And the physical side of our relationship, which had always been good, had waned suddenly, to a point at which it was almost non-existent. That had always kept us close, even when life made things difficult. We'd never stopped loving each other, never stopped making time for that side of our relationship. I'd begun to appreciate its importance in a way I'd not thought about when I was younger. It was not the only aspect of our marriage: we were friends and we had the children, we took an interest in each other's work and had a shared interest in the world, but all of that was condensed into the moment when we fell asleep, two people holding each other after making love.

Was it another woman? Was that why Richard now turned away from me in bed, claiming tiredness and leaving me to lie awake, trying to dismiss the suspicions that were starting to bother me?

I waited for a sign, some evidence that I was not simply being paranoid. So, 'Ivy, we need to talk', did not come out of the blue.

I'd been waiting for it, dreading it, but expecting it.

'Now?'

He'd just come in from work.

I was washing up. My hands were deep under the suds, scouring a frying pan. He hadn't even taken his coat off or put down his briefcase. It occurred to me he was going to leave there and then. Or maybe he thought I'd throw him out.

The children had already left home and I was getting used to the empty quiet again after twenty-two years of rumbustiousness. It seemed that the two of us, quieter and slower in our late fifties, would never be able to fill it again. Marriages often faltered when the nest was empty. I knew that, although I had not expected ours to. Richard had always seemed too solid. I couldn't begin to imagine a life without him.

'Yes, now.' He pulled a chair out from the kitchen table and slumped into it. 'Come and sit down.'

'I'll just finish this pan.' I wanted to delay what I thought was going to be a confession.

'Leave it. Just come and sit down.'

I dried my hands on a tea-towel. 'Do you want a drink?'

'Not really. But you have one if you like.'

His tone was too kind. He was going to do this gently.

I went to the fridge and took out a bottle of white wine, grabbing a couple of glasses from the shelf beside it. We might both need one.

'What is it?' I tried to sound neutral.

'There's something I've been wanting to tell you,' he began, 'but I've been too scared. I didn't know how to.'

'Go on.' I clutched the stem of my wine glass so tightly I wondered if it might snap.

'I've got cancer,' he said.

'Cancer?'

It's odd feeling relief when you've just been told something terrible. But there was a moment, before the implications of what he'd said dawned on me, when that was all I felt: relief that he hadn't said what I'd thought he was going to say.

'Bowel cancer,' he continued. 'I know I should have said something before but I was scared and I hoped it might be nothing. I've had a bit of pain in my stomach for a while now.'

'Bowel cancer?' I knew it was serious but I never imagined Richard would be dead eighteen months later. 'How long have you known?'

'I've been having the pains for a while,' he said. 'I thought it was just indigestion at first or that maybe I'd strained a muscle at the gym. But I went for an endoscopy a couple of weeks ago and I had the result today.'

'Why didn't you tell me? I would have come with you.'

'I didn't want to worry you if it was nothing.'

'But it's not. It's cancer.'

'There's a tumour that needs to be removed and part of the bowel with it. I'll be having chemo too.'

'But you'll be okay, won't you?' I hated myself for seeking reassurance, which he couldn't possibly give me, for wanting him to, when I was the person who should have been there for him.

'I hope so, Ivy,' he said. 'But I'm scared.'

I was scared too, but I didn't say so, not then, not out loud.

I said it when we made love later that evening with an urgency and sentiment that were new, even after twenty-five years of marriage, even after all the question marks that had hung over my own health; a clinging to life when it was in danger of being taken away.

That was the last time I felt really close to Richard. He began slipping away, retreating, even before he discovered the cancer had spread. It was as if he knew it would happen and he needed to dull the pain of death before it came.

There was something about the flow of the river, fast at that particular bend, that absorbed me. It seemed to reflect the fleeting nature of life, as it carried flotsam towards the sea. It mirrored my own heightened consciousness that we're all flowing in an inevitable direction. The closer we get to the open sea, the faster the current seems to be.

Maybe that was why I'd chosen that spot: to remind me that Richard hadn't been singled out for an early death but that it would come to us all, sooner or later.

And then I saw him. At least, I saw someone of about the same height and build, somewhere between bald and balding, walking towards the bench, in rapid pursuit of a toddler on a bike – one of those bikes with no pedals. He walked fast to keep pace but without breaking into a run. Then the child looked round. 'Granddad can we –' He fell off, landing in a heap at my feet.

I was part of a triumvirate, involved in solicitations towards a crying child.

'Oh dear,' the man beside me said.

'Are you okay?' I asked.

'Jump up, little man.' The man who had reminded me of

Richard picked the bike up with one hand, extending the other to his grandson.

The child stopped crying, reassured and a little embarrassed. 'I fell off because I was trying to talk to my granddad at the same time,' he said, lest the two of us on the bench were in any doubt about his cycling prowess.

'It's hard to go straight when you're looking behind you,' the man beside me said.

I didn't say anything because there was a lump in my throat.

'Off we go.' The grandfather set the bike down, nodding briefly to us.

I was still getting used to the way grief raises its head at bizarre and inappropriate moments. What had triggered it this time? The similarity in stature had made me do a double-take when I first saw them, and that he was with a grandchild had got me going.

Richard had not lived long enough to help any grandchildren learn to ride a bike. I wasn't aware that I was crying until the man beside me asked if I was all right.

'Oh, yes, no. I'm sorry,' I felt foolish but unable to stop now that I'd started. 'It was just that man. He reminded me of someone.'

'Here, have a tissue.'

'Thank you.' I smiled, and wondered if he had already taken one from his pocket and blown his nose when he sat down, out of habit.

'I don't want to intrude,' he said, as I handed back the packet, 'but it can help to talk.'

'That's kind of you but I'll be okay. Thank you.' I looked at him properly for the first time. He was about my age, with a thick head of hair, not yet grey, salt-and-pepper, with dark eyes. 'I was just thinking about my late husband.'

'It's a good spot to think. That's why I come here.'

His voice was soft and gentle and there was kindness in the way he spoke that made me tearful again.

'I'm sorry,' he said. 'I didn't mean to upset you further.'

'You haven't. It's not you. But thank you.'

'What for?'

'For being nice.'

He laughed, shifted slightly, and we lapsed into an awkward silence, broken when a small bird landed where the boy on the bike had been and began pecking at the ground. 'You could almost be in the country here,' he observed.

'It's peaceful,' I agreed, just as an aeroplane roared low overhead.

'Well, some of the time.'

'It still doesn't feel like London,' I said, as the plane descended in the direction of Heathrow.

'Have you always lived in London?' he asked, and although I'd wanted to be alone I found I didn't mind his questions.

'For most of my adult life,' I told him. 'But I lived in south-east London, until recently. I moved here after my husband died.' I swallowed.

'I'm sorry.' He'd noticed my reaction. 'I've stirred up difficult memories again.'

'No, it's not you. It's just the way I'm feeling today.'

'Would it help,' he said, 'if I bought you another cup of tea? Yours must be cold by now.'

I looked at the cup on the ground by my feet, forgotten, and found myself saying, 'Thank you. That would be nice.'

'Shall I bring it here or would you like go to the café?'

'Let's go to the café.' Moving would stop me dwelling.

'Do you want to get that table in the corner,' he asked, 'while I go to buy the tea? Would you like anything to eat?'

'No, thank you. Here, let me give you some money.'

'I'll get it. You grab the table.'

'Thank you,' I said, again, when he returned, carrying a tray.

'I've ordered a couple of scones too. Just in case you're hungry.' He sat down. 'I won't be offended if you're not . . . hungry, that is.'

'I am, actually.' I'd not had anything after swimming and it always made me hungry, even though I'd thought I could wait until I got home to eat something.

'I'm Abe, by the way.' He put out his hand.

'Ivy.' I took his outstretched palm and we shook before he opened the lid of the teapot and stirred, with measured deliberation, as if trying to achieve just the right strength of tea.

His dress was careful, not showy but presentable. He was wearing a pale grey shirt, a taupe cardigan, and his shoes, I'd noticed, were freshly polished, as if, for him, it was worth making the effort, even for a stroll in the park. Polished shoes always remind me of my own father, lining his up on a sheet of newspaper on a Sunday evening, a box of brushes to hand, then polishing several pairs so that he could have a change during the week, asking my mother, when he'd finished, if hers needed cleaning or any of ours.

I watched Abe as he focused on the tea. He had a nice face. I imagined he was handsome when he was younger, perhaps intimidatingly so, but his face was softened by age and the lines etched around his eyes indicated kindness and a predisposition to smile.

'I'm sorry.' He looked up, aware that I'd been studying him. 'I didn't ask how you like it.'

'Strong! Carry on.'

'It used to drive my wife mad.' He smiled at me now. 'I always used to forget that she drank her tea so weak it resembled dishwater.'

'You're widowed too?' I asked, as he poured tea into one of the cups and pushed it towards me.

'No. Separated.'

'I'm sorry.'

'It's been seven years now, so I'm used to it.'

'Nevertheless.' There was something about him – the solicitude he had shown towards me and the care with which he appeared to operate – that made me feel sad he was on his own.

'It was my fault,' he said, as if reading my thoughts. 'I messed things up. I caused my wife a lot of pain. I think Lynn's happier now and we're still friends, good friends.'

'Perhaps I'll see you again,' was how we left it, after our first encounter. No asking for numbers or anything. And there was no reason we should. He was just someone who had shown me kindness and consideration when we'd found ourselves in the same spot at the same time. And yet I had warmed to him in a way that made me want to see him again.

'Where are you, Mum? It sounds windy.' Lottie had called when I'd gone back a couple of days later at the same time.

'I'm having a cup of tea by the river.' I felt as if she had caught me out, somehow, yet I wasn't doing anything I didn't normally do. As I said, I felt it was 'my' bench and I often went to sit there. Except this time I had gone hoping that Abe might be there too. I had lingered a little longer, bought a second cup of tea and taken it to the bench, even though I was beginning to feel cold. And I had been disappointed out of all proportion when I didn't have to share my bench with anyone.

'Are you okay, love?' I asked Lottie.

'I'm on my way to visit a client in the area and wondered if I could pop in on my way back to the office. It's my last call of the day so I don't need to rush away.'

'That would be lovely.' Lottie was a social worker, which

didn't altogether surprise me. She'd always been caring and unfazed by extreme circumstances. Perhaps the extremes of my own family's illness, which she'd experienced at first hand with my mother and Jon, helped her take things in her stride.

I hadn't been enthusiastic about her decision when she'd told me, not because I didn't think she'd make a good social worker but because I wanted her to be free of having to care. Max worked as a sports psychologist, which married his intellect with his own sporting prowess and put two fingers up to the way his life might have gone, if he'd carried the gene that had destroyed my mother's and brother's physical abilities, rendering them incapable of doing anything without help.

Max's work was a world away from that. Lottie's felt somehow closer and I wondered if she would be happier to be free of it too. But she was adamant. She could see herself doing it. She worked with families now, families who found it hard to cope with whatever life had thrown at them – children with physical or psychiatric conditions, refugee or homeless families. She saw and heard a lot of distressing things, but her capacity to give of herself never seemed to diminish.

Sometimes I felt guilty for having moved to London, hoping my children didn't feel obliged to fit me into their lives.

'But if you want to get back to the office and finish off for the day, don't feel you need to call in just because you're near,' I said to Lottie now.

'I don't,' she said, and I could almost hear her smiling. 'I want to see you, as long as you're not busy?'

'No. It'll be lovely.'

I stood up and glanced around, still willing Abe to materialize, as I'd half expected to see Richard the last time I was there. Honestly, Ivy, you're behaving like some lovestruck teenager, I reprimanded myself, and began to stride along the path beside the river towards home. I tried to remember the name of the boy whose house I had circled on my bicycle when I was a teenager. There was a route of a few blocks that took me past it and I used to ride by again and again, hoping each time that he might emerge from the front garden and I could pretend it was a chance encounter, that I just so happened to be passing his house as he came out.

Sometimes Fate throws someone in your path; at others you have to tempt it.

I looked back as the path forked to the left, giving the bench one last glance, and saw someone sitting there. Was it Abe? It might have been, and I was tempted to turn and walk back. And do what? I asked myself. Act as if you've just turned up, when you've been sitting there for the best part of an hour? Why? What are you hoping to get from him?

I had no answer to that, and if I did go back and he was there, I'd miss Lottie.

I went there a few more times, during the week, and each time was less disappointed by Abe's absence, so that when, the following week, I sat down with my tea and my thoughts, and a voice asked, 'Do you mind if I join you?' it took me by surprise. After that we swapped emails and arranged to meet, rather than bumping into each other accidentally on purpose.

When I got home I began behaving like a teenager again, checking my emails more often than I otherwise might have done.

Although I was slowly winding down the travel PR company I'd set up when the children were in their teens, I still worked for existing clients. I hadn't taken on any new ones for several years and wouldn't. Eventually there were a couple of work-related emails in my inbox but nothing from Abe. I opened one of the work ones and was flicking idly through suggestions for a spring media campaign I was working on when his name popped up in the corner of my screen, attached to a message with the subject: *Meeting up*.

I delayed opening it. I went to do some washing up and pottered in the kitchen, savouring the anticipation of the moment when I would read and reread the few brief lines.

Dear Ivy,

I'm glad to have bumped into you again today and enjoyed our chats on both occasions. Like you, I'm a regular visitor to the park and, while I don't want to intrude in any way on your time, if you ever want company on your walks or someone to talk to over a cuppa then it would be good to talk some more.

The deer were gathering as I left. I'm always moved by the sight of them.

Hope to see you again.

Abe x

It was considered and considerate. I wondered how long he'd spent trying to get the words right and if he'd consciously tried to strike a balance between appearing keen to see me again but not wishing to force his company on me.

I moved about the flat distractedly, drawing the curtains in my bedroom and the blinds in the bathroom, putting today's newspaper in the recycling box and formulating my reply as I did so.

Eventually I returned to my computer.

Dear Abe,

It was lovely to see you again too and I really appreciated your kindness towards me when we first met.

Lucky you to have seen the deer. My route does not take me through that part of the park but, yes, perhaps we could walk there together some time.

Ivy x

I went to make dinner, lingering over the sautéing of mush-rooms, the grilling of a chicken fillet and the boiling of rice. I sat at the table to eat, my copy of *Thérèse Raquin* open on the table beside me. My plan to get rid of some of the books, which were too numerous for the shelf space in the flat and towered in piles on the living-room floor, had failed. Instead I was re-reading them.

But today the shenanigans of Thérèse and Laurent were not absorbing me. I was thinking about Abe McFadden, wondering if he would reply to my email and when I would see him again.

I woke up my computer after dinner and saw another message in my inbox.

I am free on Friday and the weather forecast is good, if you'd like to meet for a walk then. Ax

I'd love to!

We arranged to meet just near the park gate at eleven o'clock.

'Ivy!'

Abe was waiting. He waved when he saw me and kissed me, warmly, on the cheek when I drew level.

'What a beautiful day,' I said. 'I think this is my favourite time of year.'

The weather was as forecast and the low autumnal sun slanted through the leaves of the beeches, dappling the air beneath them.

'You look beautifully autumnal yourself,' Abe said, step-ping back to take me in.

I was wearing a mustard-coloured scarf, which Lottie had given me for my birthday, and an olive green tweed coat I'd bought in Dublin years ago. I suppose the combination and the slight rust of my lipstick reflected the burnished colours of the season.

'Shall we go?' Abe touched my arm lightly and we headed off along a path through the bracken to the woods and a clearing beyond, where about thirty red deer stood grazing in the grass. 'Aren't they beautiful?' he said softly, and we watched them for several minutes, then moved off along the path that bordered their spot. 'It reminds me of Scotland,' he said. 'I spent part of my childhood there.'

'Really? You don't have an accent.'

'I know. I'm a Sassenach, really,' he said, adopting a gentle brogue. 'I was up there for a few years in my early teens but the family moved about a lot.'

'So you don't consider yourself from anywhere?'

'Not really,' he said. 'How about you?'

'I grew up in Sussex but it's not really a place people identify with. I didn't anyway.'

We carried on walking and talking. He told me a bit about his work, as a fountain designer, his children, Sam and Ruby, and Lynn, the wife from whom he was separated. The more we walked and talked, the more at ease I felt with him. Ease, tinged with a frisson of . . . what?

Our walks became regular. Sometimes we'd go to the park, at others we'd wander by the river. From time to time we sat on the bench in companionable silence. There was something about him that I was drawn to and I suppose, if I was honest, I found him enormously attractive. I wasn't sure how to deal with that – if I wanted more than someone new to talk to.

*

'How might you feel about lunch?' Abe asked, as we walked by the river a few meetings later.

'I'm generally in favour,' I replied.

'Next week?'

'As long as you can spare the time.'

'I can make time for you. Will *you* have time?'

'I work for myself. I can make time too.'

I don't need to work now – my living expenses are moderate and Richard's life insurance policy gives me a regular income – but I need something to keep me going.

'Good. We need to spend a bit more time together.'

His manner was assured, as if he'd already decided that we were, or would be, more than just two people who met to walk and talk. He wasn't pushy and it felt natural. But it still unnerved me. It had been so long since there'd been anyone other than Richard, and Abe was still married.

His phone had rung earlier, when we were walking. He'd taken it out of his pocket and looked at the caller ID. 'It's Lynn,' he'd said to me. 'I'm sorry. I need to take this.' He'd hung back a little as I idled by the river, trying not to listen or to read too much into the way his face seemed to soften as he chatted, as if he was talking to someone he could relax with completely.

'Okay, I'll pop round. Yes . . . See you later then, love.' He wound up the call. 'Sorry,' he said to me. 'There seems to be a bit of an issue with the lock on the front door. The Chubb's not working and Lynn doesn't like leaving it unlocked. The house was broken into a couple of years ago.'

'Oh dear. I hope nothing too important was taken.'

'No,' Abe replied. 'Mostly electronic items. All replaceable. But Lynn's a bit more nervous when she's by herself now, which is understandable.'

I tried to weigh up the significance of 'when'. Did he still stay there sometimes? Did she have a new man in her life?

He'd told me they'd been separated for a long time but they weren't divorced. I wanted to know more about why they'd split up but the right opportunity to ask never seemed to come up.

'Look. I know this must be odd for you.' Abe appeared to read my mind. 'It is for me too. I know you've only recently lost your husband and I know I'm technically still married. I don't want to do or say anything that makes you feel awkward or uncomfortable.'

'But?'

'I'm glad I met you. I'd like to see more of you. But if you're not ready –'

'I'd like to see more of you too,' I interrupted. 'But . . .'

'But?'

'I don't want to rush into anything.'

'I'm not asking you to. I'd just like to have lunch with you. Will you have lunch with me?'

'I already said I'd like to, didn't I?'

'Yes, you did. But I worried I might be scaring you.'

'No,' I said. 'You're not.'

A couple of lunches later, I was a little nervous that I'd invited him to my flat. I almost wished I'd invited him to breakfast rather than lunch. I wasn't coping with the waiting. There's only so much preparation you can do when you've decided to make chicken casserole with rice, not much tidying needed for a small flat that you live in on your own, only so many times you can look in the mirror and realize there's nothing you can do about your appearance because that is what you look like.

But I couldn't settle, couldn't concentrate on anything, even though I had work to do.

I returned to the kitchen and glanced around for something to keep me busy. I went to the shelves above a cupboard, on which various plates and bowls were stacked and behind which the faces of friends and family, no longer with us, stared out, smiling and happy. That was where I propped up the funeral service cards, which seemed to be accumulating at an alarming rate. Was it morbid to leave them there? Would it be off-putting for Abe to sit in the kitchen with my late husband, my brother, a work colleague and a friend looking down at us from beyond the grave?

I stood on a stool, gathered them up and put them in a pile beneath my diary, feeling a little guilty about Richard's. I traced the outline of his face. 'I've not forgotten you, my love.' I kept to myself the joyful thought that I was beginning to feel a sense of possibility again but I added, 'You don't mind, do you? My asking Abe for lunch?'

I knew that he wouldn't. He'd said, not long before he died, 'I hope you find someone else, Ivy. You deserve to be happy.'

Richard had deserved it too and I hope I made him happy, that what we'd had had been enough to sustain him in his final moments.

Why had I invited Abe to my flat? Partly because I wanted to bring someone there – hardly anyone ever came, and I wanted it to feel more like home. Partly because I wanted Abe to see where I lived, and partly because I thought it would be easier. There were things I wanted to ask him, which I thought it might be more natural for us to talk about in private, things I'd not felt able to ask him in a crowded restaurant.

I began to relax when he arrived.

'These are for you.' He handed me flowers, an arrangement in a jam-jar tied up with a bit of twine. 'They're from my garden.'

'They're lovely. Thank you. Shall I take your coat? And

hat?' He had in his hand a navy woollen cap, the kind I imagined Greek fishermen wore.

'It was my dad's,' he said, as if the hat needed explaining. 'There's quite a chill today. Very autumnal.'

I caught him looking at a photograph on the wall, as I hung the hat and coat on the pegs behind the door. 'That was in Cornwall, years ago.'

'You look happy.' Abe studied the picture of us all picnicking at the foot of sand dunes. Lottie couldn't have been more than about eight and Max was still tiny.

'We were.' I allowed him to look for a moment longer, then said, 'We're in the kitchen.' I walked down the hallway and let him follow me.

'Something smells good.' He looked around. 'I've brought some wine. I didn't know if you preferred white or red so I got a bottle of each.' He fished in a bag and placed them on the kitchen table.

'That's very kind. And you shouldn't have. Not as well as the flowers.'

'You've made the lunch,' he said. 'Which would you prefer?'

'I don't mind.'

'Red?' he asked. 'Shall I put the other in the fridge and you can have it another time?' Abe came a step closer and put his hand on my arm. It was a gentle, reassuring gesture but I still felt anxious.

'Red's good,' I said, laughing nervously. 'I think I need a drink.'

'Me too,' he said. 'I know there are probably a lot of things you want to ask me. Do you have a corkscrew?'

I took one from a drawer and handed it to him. 'I'm not going to interrogate you,' I said, as he took it and began removing the cork from the bottle.

'But you want to know more about me.' He pulled the

cork and poured the wine. 'I want to know more about you too. Here.' He handed me a glass.

'Thank you. Cheers.'

We took a sip.

'Lunch will be about ten minutes.'

We sat at the kitchen table.

Some small talk. And then: 'I don't want to pry.' I did. 'But . . .' How to phrase this without seeming presumptuous? '. . . I'd like to know more about your wife. Why you separated and . . .'

'It's not prying. You're entitled to know. We separated for a number of reasons.' He sipped his wine. 'And I think we both have different point of views about what went wrong.'

'What's yours?'

'It was partly the children growing up. They'd been so much the focus of our life together that when they no longer were we were a bit adrift.'

'We felt a little of that.'

'I'm sorry, Ivy. I know it must sound ungrateful, selfish even, ending a relationship I could have stayed in when you had no choice about yours.'

'Maybe Richard and I would have found life more difficult, post children, if he'd lived longer. His cancer gave us another focus.'

'That's why it seems selfish, but after Ruby and Sam had left home, there just didn't seem to be anything left of us.'

'A lot of people feel like that.'

'Lynn got pregnant quite soon after we met,' he said. 'We were thrown into family life almost before we really knew each other.'

'Oh?'

'It all happened very fast. Meeting each other, finding out we were going to be parents. We got married a few months before Ruby was born and a couple of years later we had Sam. And we were happy, really happy. The kids were fantastic. They're wonderful children. We were a happy family, but you know what it's like with young children.'

'Yes.'

'There's very little time for you, as a couple. Lynn worked in television, long hours often, and I was absorbed in my job. The kids took the rest of our time, and when they grew up, we didn't really know each other any more or how to be with each other.'

'I'm just going to look at the rice.' I stood up and moved to the cooker while Abe carried on talking.

'I suppose that was when we should have begun making more time for each other, but I didn't make the effort and I wish I had.'

'So you just drifted apart?' I was stirring the rice, my back to him.

'I had an affair. I know you'll think less of me now but I did and, unsurprisingly, created more distance between us.'

'What happened?' I turned the gas low and sat down again. 'I mean how long did it last and how did Lynn find out?'

'A couple of years.' He drank some more wine and looked at me, then quickly away. Embarrassed? 'I met the woman through work. I was very drawn to her. I can't say it meant nothing because it did and she did. I loved her. I still loved Lynn and I was terrified of hurting her but at the same time the other woman seemed to offer something else. Another life.'

'You wanted to leave your wife?'

'I thought about it and agonized about what to do, but in the end it wasn't my decision.'

'What happened?'

'She finished it. The other woman. I'd talked about leaving Lynn. I don't know if I actually would have done, if it had come to it, but I think it scared her.'

'So she ended it before it went any further?'

'Yes. I was devastated but relieved too. I didn't have to worry about how much I'd hurt Lynn if I left her, and I was grateful to be spared that, but . . .'

'She found out anyway?'

'The irony is that I almost got away with it, although I know that sounds awful. But I also wonder if the circumstances that led to her finding out happened for a reason. Maybe we needed to end the marriage because by now neither of us was really happy in it.'

'Go on.'

'The other woman lived outside London. She travelled up for work and we met here most of the time but, on that occasion, she'd asked if I could meet her midway. She said she needed to talk, and she had to be at home that day. She had younger children. I went to meet her at a country pub about fifteen miles from where she lived. She suggested it. It was anonymous and not on her patch.'

'And she told you it was over?'

'Yes. I won't go into details. We both knew really that it couldn't go on for ever, not as it was, and she didn't want to break up her family. I understood that, even though, if she'd felt differently, maybe I would have left Lynn.'

'So you accepted her decision?'

'I did. I was upset, of course. She was too, but she'd made up her mind. She said she had to stop seeing me.'

'So what happened?'

'On my way back there was an accident. A lorry carrying hay bales jack-knifed in the middle of the road and shed its load. I was a couple of cars behind. The ones in front of me braked, swerved, and there was a collision.'

'Was anyone hurt?'

'Miraculously, no. The road wasn't busy or it might have

been worse. But the police were called and there was some issue with the lorry, with the way the hay had been secured. I was a witness to an accident. They needed my details.'

'Of course.'

'A week later, Lynn took a call from the police. The officer explained that I'd witnessed an accident and they wanted to take a statement. Of course I hadn't told her – I should have been at my office that afternoon.'

'So it all came out?'

'Yes. In the worst possible way. Lynn was devastated. I was too. But I had no right to feel sorry for myself. It was a terrible time.'

'I can imagine.'

'We had counselling. We tried to make a go of our marriage. For a time, I thought we might pull through. But there were too many cracks to paper over.'

'So you decided to separate?'

'We were arguing, bickering, all the time. We couldn't be nice to each other. Eventually I suggested I moved out, just to give us a break.'

'And that was the beginning of the end?'

'In a way, or maybe it was just the beginning of a different relationship between us. We got on better when we were living apart. We still see each other. We go to the theatre and meet for lunch. We've built a close friendship now that we've put the marriage aside.'

'That's good,' I said, but I felt unnerved by it nevertheless.

'Of course I regret that we couldn't mend our marriage. I thought, given time, Lynn would be able to forgive me, to trust me again, but I don't think she ever will.'

'Do you still love her?'

'Yes,' he said simply, which was half what I wanted to hear and half what I didn't. What sort of man would he be if he didn't love someone he'd been married to for so long, the mother of his children?

But where exactly did that leave me?

'She'll always be the woman I was married to. She'll always be the mother of my children, and she'll always be my friend.'

'Thank you,' I said, and got to my feet to dish up the lunch. 'What for?'

'For telling me,' I said, removing a pan from the hob and putting it on a trivet on the work-surface.

I couldn't pretend I was happy about the situation, or that I might not have found it easier if he and his wife had fallen out so badly that they never spoke. Of course it was better that they were still friends, and I wasn't surprised. It said more about him than if they'd split up acrimoniously. And I hadn't known him long, had no idea how he thought of me or where our friendship was leading. But I knew that I really liked him, and that if it was leading anywhere, I'd find it more difficult than I might have if his wife was completely out of the picture.

'Would you like some coffee?' I asked, when we'd finished eating.

'Yes, please, if you're making it.'

I walked over to the side and put the kettle on. 'Shall we go into the living room? I'll bring the coffee through.'

'Can I help you with the dishes first?' Abe got up and brought our plates to the sink.

'I'll do it later.'

'Okay.' He hovered close behind me, as I busied myself with mugs.

'Ivy?'

I turned, and almost bumped into him. 'What?'

'What I told you about Lynn. I know it's not straightforward

62

and I might be asking too much of you, especially as it's not that long since you lost Richard but . . .'

'Yes?'

'I still see Lynn. We're friends, and I know that might not be easy for you, but since I met you . . .'

'Go on.'

'You're all I can think about!' He laughed. 'I know that sounds daft but it's true and, well, I'd really like it if we could just see how things go.'

'What do you mean?' I knew, really. I knew he wanted to kiss me. I took a step closer.

When you don't have sex for a long period there comes a time when you don't miss it any more. It becomes a distant memory, rather than something you need or crave. It had been two years since Richard had died and I'd pretty much forgotten what it was to feel aroused by someone's touch. But it didn't take much to bring it all flooding back, for my body to respond instinctively to Abe's kiss.

'Are you all right?' he asked, after a while.

'Yes.' I tried to formulate my thoughts. I was scared of being with someone new, after so long. I was scared that I wasn't ready. I was scared by how much I wanted him in my life. I was scared that if I gave in to those feelings, admitted them even, I'd get hurt, and I was only just beginning to stop hurting. 'I'm not sure I can do this,' I said to Abe, unsure of what I actually meant.

'It's only kissing,' he said, stroking my hair.

'I suppose it is.'

I looked around Abe's living room, trying to absorb a little more of him through the accumulated items of his life. It was lined with bookcases, which were filled with classics, travel books, contemporary novels and coffee-table tomes on architecture.

A week had passed and he'd invited me for lunch at his flat, the one he'd been renting on his own since moving out of the family home but which was still full of enough of the trappings of family life not to feel like a bachelor pad: photographs of young children, a garishly painted clay pencil pot on his desk, not unlike the one I have, a corkboard in the hallway tacked with drawings and notes that must go back years.

'Daddy, my tooth fell out today,' read the childish handwriting on a yellowed scrap of paper. 'Dad, Lewis Hamilton won the Grand Prix!!!' said another, written in a slightly older hand. 'I recorded it for you.'

'All the things I missed, working late,' Abe said, catching me looking at it.

'It's nice that you kept them.'

'Actually, it was Lynn. She never throws anything away. She put them all on the board when I moved out.'

He said it casually, as if this was the way it went when you separated after the children had grown up, but I knew couples who had simply walked away from each other and that period of their lives, as if it had never happened. It said a lot about Abe that the relationships he had with Lynn and his children were still good and ongoing but it was hard to know where I might fit in a life that was already crowded.

On a unit in the corner I spotted a record player and beneath it a stack of LPs. I flicked through them, as I waited for Abe to bring the coffee. There were a few newer albums, Arctic Monkeys, Laura Marling and Rufus Wainwright, but most of them dated way back: Bob Dylan, Little Richard, Hank Williams, Woody Guthrie and the Mamas and the Papas. I pulled out the latter.

'You want to put it on?' Abe asked.

I shook my head. 'Just seeing if my song is on it.'

'"For The Love Of Ivy"?'

'You know it.'

'I used to love it when I was younger,' he said, and I experienced a slight sense of *déjà vu*.

Next to the record player, a shorter bookcase was covered with family photographs. 'Are these your children?' I asked, peering at one, as Abe returned with a tray. It showed a young boy, who looked much as I imagined Abe had when he was young, sitting on steps next to an older girl, his sister.

'Yes. Ruby and Sam.'

'Sam's like you.' I studied the photograph more closely and noticed something on the step between the two children. 'Is that a tortoise?'

'Yes.'

'I didn't think you were allowed tortoises as pets any more.'

'Fred was mine when I was a child,' he said. 'He's still alive but Sam has him now. He became his when they were growing up.'

'That's lovely,' I said. 'To have a pet that stays with you all that time. And is this Lynn?'

'Yes.' Abe stood next to me. 'It was taken years ago on a holiday.'

She must have been in her mid-fifties but was still strikingly beautiful. She had shoulder-length ash-blonde hair, piercing blue eyes and the sort of bone structure that enabled women to retain their looks well into old age. I felt plain in comparison, or if not plain, because I knew I hadn't aged too badly, unable to compete. 'She's very beautiful.'

'And so are you,' Abe said. He kissed me for what seemed like a long time before he stopped and asked, 'Shall we move somewhere?'

Was he suggesting we move from our standing position in

front of the mantelpiece and sit on the sofa? Or was he suggesting we go to his bedroom? I'd glanced at it earlier on my way to the bathroom and taken in the neatly made double bed with the stack of books piled on the table beside it. A large abstract painting hung in the space above the headboard and there was an open-plan unit along the wall in which a row of shirts hung above drawers, which, I presumed, contained other clothes.

I'd looked at the bed, with its grey checked cover and woollen blanket folded across it. Did Abe sleep on one side or stretch out across it? Did he sit there and read late into the night, or wake up early and reach for a book? And could I imagine myself there with him? And, I wondered, wishing I had not, had Lynn ever slept there? Did she still, sometimes?

I had had friends who, in the throes of the bitterest divorce, still had sex. In a long marriage sex becomes as much of an addiction as it is a habit, and the fact that you can no longer stand the thought of sitting opposite someone at the dinner table, night in, night out, doesn't mean you're ready to forgo the intimacy of the bedroom.

'Let's sit down,' I said, in response to Abe's question, moving towards the sofa.

'Are you all right?' he asked, putting his arm around me and drawing me closer to him.

'Yes.' I relaxed as he kissed me and as I felt the warmth of his body moving closer to mine, but I tensed again when he began fumbling with my blouse, pulling it free from the hem of my trousers. 'Not yet,' I said.

'Sorry.' He smoothed the fabric back into place. 'I'm sorry. I don't mean to . . . It's just . . .'

'What?' I knew, really, what he wasn't saying.

'You're so lovely, Ivy.'

66

'I'm sorry,' I echoed his words, feeling guilty for not being able to respond to his desire, for not being able to give in to the desire I felt too. 'I'm just not ready.'

'Really, Ivy, please don't be sorry,' he said, sitting up straighter. 'But can I ask you something?' He took my hand, when he said this, and stroked it.

'What?'

'Will you tell me about your mother?'

I'd explained about her illness and its effect on the rest of the family but I hadn't gone into any great detail.

'How old were you when you first found out that something was wrong?'

'She started to show symptoms when I was in my early teens but I didn't find out what it was and how it might affect me until I was twenty.'

'So you lived with the knowledge for most of your adult life,' he said, stroking my fingers.

'Yes,' I said, enjoying the feeling that I could sit there and talk to this man who, a few months ago, I had not known existed.

I told him a lot about her illness, about the risk to me and my siblings, how living with the risk had affected each of us in different ways, and about how a lot of the decisions I had made in my life had not been entirely my own but swayed by the knowledge of the faulty gene that ran right through my mother's side of the family.

I don't know how long we sat there, holding hands and talking or if he felt, as I did afterwards, that the words we'd exchanged were more revealing of ourselves than anything else could have been, that what I had told him and his responses were as intimate and unguarded as any lovemaking.

*

'I'm so glad I found you, Ivy,' Abe said, a few weeks later, after an afternoon in town.

We'd been to the National Gallery to see Maggi Hambling's *Walls of Water*: huge paintings of giant waves splashed over vast canvases. Abe had appeared utterly absorbed in them, and I took the opportunity to gaze at him, to take in every aspect of him, as he stood transfixed by them.

His face was strong, determined almost, but softened by the kindness of his eyes and the gentleness of his manner. Even though he was wrapped in the paintings, something in him sensed the presence of another and he moved aside a little, ceding his position directly in front of a canvas without taking his eyes off it. I found it hard to imagine Abe ever upsetting anyone, not intentionally, and even though I now knew more about his marriage and how much he had hurt his wife, I found it hard to hold it against him. After all, his crime had been to love another. It seems wrong that that simple fact can cause so much pain and suffering.

'Okay?' He caught me watching him and smiled. 'They're quite spectacular, aren't they?'

'Yes,' I agreed.

We shared an attraction to water, although it manifested itself in different ways. Abe, who had worked as a fountain designer, liked to direct and manipulate it; I like to immerse myself in it. But one way or another, we never seemed to be far from water, and when we emerged from the gallery, it was into a sea of people rallying in support of the journalists killed at the *Charlie Hebdo* magazine in Paris. Placards saying *'Je Suis Charlie'* bobbed up and down above their heads, as we made our way around the periphery of the crowd and up St Martin's Lane. I thought of Nathan, a man I had known briefly, for the first time in years, and something he'd said to me about how I'd never know what it felt like to be hated because of what you are.

I shivered, the way you do when a memory from a long-ago past resurfaces and Abe, noticing, took my hand and led me towards the fountain. 'Here,' he said, fumbling in his pocket and taking out a fifty-pence piece. 'Make a wish.'

I looked at the coin. 'It's a swimming one, from the London Olympics.'

'Then your wish has your name on it!' He took another coin from his pocket and threw it into the fountain.

'What did you wish?' I asked him.

'I didn't,' he said. 'It was a thank-you throw.'

'Who did you thank? And what for?'

'Fate,' he said, taking my hand again. 'For throwing us into each other's path. I'm so glad to have found you, Ivy.'

I squeezed his hand in return and tossed the swimmer on the face of the coin into the water at the foot of the bronze lion. I wish I could hold on to this feeling, I said silently to myself. I was happy, really happy, for the first time since Richard died, but a couple of things still unsettled me.

One was the existence of Abe's wife.

I tried not to feel jealous when he said, 'I'm going to the cinema with Lynn tomorrow evening,' or 'I'm going to be over at the house on Saturday. There's a bit of DIY to do.'

'Does she know about me?' I'd asked him once, and had been surprised by his reply.

'Yes. I told her I'd met someone special.'

'And does she mind?'

'I don't think so.' There was hesitancy in the way he said it, as if he suspected that she did.

I didn't tell him I thought I might, if I was in her shoes. I wasn't sure I would be generous enough to be entirely happy for him. If she'd not been able to forgive him for an affair that was now almost a decade old, would she forgive him for seeing someone else now? It might be irrational but people are irrational beings.

I was in town a week or so later. I had a meeting with a client who ran small-group historic-interest holidays aimed at the over-fifties. They were adding the area around Ancient Stagira in northern Greece, Aristotle's stamping ground, to their portfolio and I would be handling the PR.

The meeting was at the Greek Tourist Office near Oxford Circus, and as I was a little early, I popped into a computer shop, thinking I might get a new keyboard as some of the keys on mine had begun to stick.

That was when I saw them: Abe, with a woman I knew, from the photographs I had seen, was Lynn. She was sitting in front of a desktop and Abe was leaning over her shoulder, while a shop assistant hovered beside them. 'So can we get a FireWire, so I can transfer everything from her current computer to this one?' Abe was asking.

They seemed so cosy, so like a couple who had been married for years, looking for a new computer together. I was about to turn around and walk out but the assistant had seen me. 'Yes, we sell that too,' he was saying to Abe but looking at me, causing them to turn.

'Ivy!' Abe sounded surprised. 'What are you doing here?'

'I'm on my way to a meeting,' I said, flustered. 'I was a little early and I need a new keyboard.'

'Ivy?' Lynn said. 'Ivy your friend?'

'Yes, sorry.' Abe shook his head and beckoned me over as Lynn stood up. 'Ivy this is Lynn. Lynn, Ivy.'

'It's lovely to meet you,' she said, extending a slim, manicured hand.

'You too,' I said, unsure.

'I've heard a lot about you.' Her demeanour was warm and friendly. 'Abe said you work in travel?'

'I do PR for a few travel companies,' I said. 'Not a lot of work, these days, but a few clients still use me.'

'It sounds like a wonderful job,' she said. 'We're just trying to get something for Ruby's birthday. It's her thirtieth so we thought we'd splash out a bit.'

Had Richard and I ever shopped for any of the children's birthday presents together? I didn't think so. We discussed them but I usually bought them, unless it was something sporty for Max or techie for either of them, when Richard bought them by himself.

'When is it?' I asked.

'Next Tuesday,' she replied, and I glanced briefly at Abe, who looked a little awkward. 'But she'll be at work so we're taking her out for a meal on Sunday to celebrate and we need to get the present sorted by then.'

'Of course,' I said.

Abe hadn't mentioned that when I'd asked if he'd like to go to the cinema on Sunday evening. There was a film I wanted to see at the local picture house. 'Well, I should leave you to get on with it,' I said, glancing at my watch. 'I ought to be at my meeting.'

'But your keyboard,' Abe said.

'I'll have a look afterwards. I was really just killing time,' I said. 'Anyway, it was lovely to meet you, Lynn.'

'You too,' she said. 'I don't often get to meet Abe's new friends.'

'I'll see you,' I mumbled, to Abe, unsure what to say and put out by 'new friends'. Were there a lot of them or was she stressing that that was all I was, all that was possible?

Seeing them together, caught up in the purchase of a computer, made me feel excluded. And I wasn't sure if I was prepared to open myself further to someone who still had a life from which I would always be excluded.

Perhaps Abe guessed what I was thinking because a few days later he made an announcement and a suggestion. He said he thought it was time to tell his children about me and asked if I would meet them.

I hadn't told mine, not yet. I wanted to be sure the relationship was going to last before I broached it with them. But if Abe wanted me to meet his, he must think there was a place for me in his life, even if I was finding it hard to envisage.

'And what did your husband do?'

There appeared to be a subtext to the question, to almost everything Sam had said to me. He exuded hostility.

'Richard specialized in designing building refits.'

'He was a builder?'

'An architect,' I corrected him.

'Richard's firm designed the interiors for some of the suites in the Shard.' Abe helped me out. 'And Ivy has her own travel PR business.' We were in a restaurant just off the Fulham Road, the Thai Brasserie.

'A contradiction in terms,' Abe had joked earlier, as we set out.

'Ruby's fairly level-headed,' he'd told me. 'But I never know quite what to expect from Sam. He was quite a volatile child. I'm never sure how he's going to react to anything.'

'You mean to me?' I was nervous enough as it was.

'To the idea of you,' he said. 'I'm sure, once he's met you, he'll like you. How could he not?'

Easily, it seemed.

'And you met Dad on a park bench?' Again, Sam's tone was hostile.

72

'Yes, by the river,' I said. 'It's a spot we both like.'

I could understand why Sam was hostile, but it might have been easier, for all of us, if he'd tried to disguise it.

'Dad said he went there after visiting Mum,' Ruby said.

I hadn't known Abe had seen his wife just before we met. Why would I? Why should he have told me? No reason at all. I mustn't let it bother me.

'There's something about watching water that helps you accept the transience of life.' I dared them to challenge me. 'Whether it's a river, or the tide coming in and out.'

'That's very poetic,' Ruby said.

'I'm not sure I've explained myself very well.'

She looked away.

'I go there, to the place where I met your dad, because it helps me put my husband's death into some sort of context.'

'Ivy's had a lot of difficulties in her life.' Abe played the sympathy card, although I didn't want to go into the details of my family history. They'd find out in time, if we had time. They didn't need to know everything immediately.

'Mum's life hasn't exactly been easy,' Sam interjected.

'I know that.' I hoped acknowledging the situation might help.

'Not since Dad left her. And before that.'

'I know.'

'And she's had health problems since.'

'I didn't know that.' I looked at Abe.

'She had a stroke a few years ago,' Abe said. 'It was a very minor one. She wasn't even sure she'd had it and it hasn't affected her.'

'But it scared her,' Sam said.

'To be fair, Dad was there for her,' Ruby said.

'He took her to hospital when she had all the tests. I

remember because I'd have gone but I was stuck in Spain, after the volcanic-ash thing.'

'Ivy's aware of the situation between me and your mother,' Abe said. 'And I won't ever not be there for her, or either of you.'

'And that makes it better, does it?'

'What?' Abe tensed.

'You two carrying on at your age.'

'Sam.' Abe banged his hand on the table, causing everyone to look at him, including diners at neighbouring tables.

'What?'

'That's enough.'

'It's okay.' I tried to play peacemaker.

'It's not,' Abe said. 'If he's angry with me, that's fine, but he has no right to be angry with you.'

'I'm sorry,' Sam said petulantly.

'Would anyone like dessert?' Ruby changed the subject.

'Not for me,' I said.

'Are you sure, Ivy?' She appeared to be trying to atone for her little brother's behaviour. 'You've not eaten a great deal.'

'I might just have some coffee.'

Everyone passed on the pudding and ordered coffee.

We drank it, when it arrived, in an awkward silence.

'I'll hail a taxi and head home,' I said to Abe, as we left the restaurant.

We were walking a little ahead of Sam and Ruby, who both planned to take buses in separate directions.

'Are you sure you won't come back with me?' Abe asked.

'I think it might be better . . .' I lowered my voice and glanced over my shoulder '. . . if I go straight home.'

'Not even for . . . a coffee? I'll call you a cab afterwards?'

'I just think it may be easier if I leave now and you

74

three have time to talk.' That wasn't all of it. If I was finding it hard to see where I fitted in, given Abe's continuing closeness to his wife, it was even harder now with his children's attitude.

'No. I'm not going to let them win.' Abe said.

'It's not a question of winning –' I stopped as Ruby drew level with us.

'That was a lovely dinner, Dad,' she said. 'Sam and I thought we might have a drink before we go home.' She nodded towards the pub at the end of the road, the Cock Inn. We'd passed it before and Abe had told me that it would once have been a venue for cock fighting and the colourful image of a comb-headed bird advertised this to illiterate locals.

'So perhaps we should say goodbye now,' Ruby was saying. 'Unless you want to join us?'

'No, we should be getting home.' Abe had stressed 'we'.

'Okay. It was lovely to meet you, Ivy.' She put out her hand and I shook it before she turned to kiss her father.

'Good to put a face to the name,' was the best Sam could muster. 'Dad,' was all he offered his father, with a brisk nod.

'I'll call you, Sam.' Abe watched them walk away.

'I'm sorry,' I said to him.

'What for?' He started towards the Tube.

I caught up with him. 'Won't you wait while I find a cab?'

'Are you sure you won't come home with me?'

'I can't,' I said. 'Not now, not after that.'

We faced each other in the middle of the pavement.

'They're not normally like that,' he said. 'They're normally so bright and friendly and engaging.'

'I'm sure they are. It's difficult for them.'

'They'll get used to it,' Abe said. 'It doesn't have to change things between us.'

'It's a difficult situation. For everyone,' I said.

He was silent for a while.

'What do you want to do?' I said, apropos his children.

'I want you to come home with me,' he said. 'I know the evening didn't turn out well and I'm sorry if it upset you. I'm upset too and I want you to come back with me. I want to try and make everything all right.' He reached out and took my hand, pulling me a step closer to him.

I was so tempted. He was right that we were both upset. We could have looked after each other. Maybe it would have made things better. Maybe everything would have been all right, but something stopped me.

'I'm sorry.' I seemed to be saying that a lot. 'I don't think I can, not now, not tonight. I'm still too wound up.'

'Ivy,' Abe said, turning to face me, putting one arm round my shoulders and stroking my hair with his free hand.

'Maybe another time.'

'What is it that's bothering you?'

'I can't explain.' I couldn't tell him that I could still see Sam, eyeing me suspiciously over the dinner table, and hear him saying, 'So you and Dad met on a park bench?'

And I could see Ruby, as blonde and pretty as her mother looked in the holiday photograph on Abe's mantelpiece, trying her best to be nice to me as the evening wore on, but having to try nevertheless.

'I love you,' he said, gazing at me in a way that told me he meant it. 'I really do, and I want to be with you, and if you need more time, I'll wait, and if you want me to back off a little, then I will, but you have to talk to me. Please tell me what it is that you're afraid of.'

'I can't,' I said. 'Not now. Please, help me hail a cab.'

'If that's what you want.'

'I'm sorry,' I said yet again, as a cab slowed and stopped at the edge of the pavement. 'I'll speak to you tomorrow.'

He kissed me, a peck on the cheek, and I climbed into the cab, utterly bereft.

When I finally got into bed that night, I missed Richard more than I had since I'd met Abe. I missed the familiarity of our night-time routines, the warmth of his body and the patterns of his breathing as he slept.

I missed the sensation of knowing another person so well that their presence is like an extension of yourself, rather than new territory, which has to be negotiated.

I wished I could have asked him what I should do. I wished that he was still alive and I wasn't in the position I was in now, and I wished I wasn't so scared of embracing a future without him.

Abe didn't call the next day. Or the one after. Or the one after that. And that was unusual. But neither did I.

I was missing him but I didn't know what to do. I wasn't sure what to say. I wasn't sure how I felt so I kept myself busy, arranged to see a few friends, gave my full attention to the bits of work I had to do, looked up the Greek island swimming trip and thought about booking myself on to it the following summer. I swam endless lengths of the pool and tried to sort out my thoughts while I did so.

I'd just come out into the foyer one afternoon when I heard a distinct antipodean twang. 'Hey, Ivy!'

'Hello, Tony.'

'I saw you in the pool,' he said. 'Looked like you're training to swim the Channel.'

'I've been looking into that Greek island swim I mentioned.'

'Good on yer,' he said, keeping pace with me as I made for the exit. 'Which way are you going?' he asked. I nodded in the direction I was headed. 'Mind if I walk with you?'

'No. Where are you off to?'

'My dad's over on a work trip with his new wife,' he said.

I looked at him, wanting to see if there was anything in his expression that gave away his feelings towards her. 'Oh? Have you not met her?'

'Yes, I have. Last year when I went back home. Dad's been seeing her for a while but . . .'.

'But?'

'I don't think we made it easy for him. Me and my siblings. I've got three sisters. He and Mum divorced years ago, but you never think your parents have the right to stop being your parents.'

'I suppose not,' I said. My mother had had no choice in the matter.

'Anyway, I'm going this way,' he said, as we reached a T-junction. 'See you, Ivy.'

'Goodbye,' I called after him, as he quickened his pace and walked off to meet his father and the new wife.

After a few more days, I broke the stalemate. I called Abe and was reassured by how normal he sounded: relaxed and apologetic. 'I'm sorry I haven't called,' he said. 'I wasn't sure what to say.'

'I know.'

'I suppose I was a little naïve not to expect Ruby and Sam to react with some . . . well, to find it hard. I was so caught up in you that I didn't really stop to wonder how they might feel.'

'It's normal that they're wary of me.'

'I know. I should have anticipated their reaction and thought a little more about how that might make you feel.'

'Perhaps we should have talked it over more beforehand.'

'Can we talk now, Ivy?' Abe asked. 'Or at least soon? I'd like to see you if you're not still angry with me.'

'I was never angry with you.' I'd felt sad, frustrated, excluded but not angry.

'Are you free at all later this week?'

'I haven't got a lot on tomorrow. Would you like to come round?'

'I'm visiting Lynn in the morning,' he said. 'The roof of the house needs a bit of work. She's got a builder coming round to do a quote and I said I'd be there.'

'Right.' I reacted with a petulance born of jealousy each time he mentioned Lynn's name. I didn't like it and knew it had to be addressed. I couldn't go on letting Abe think I'd just fit into his world. I had to let him know how hard I was finding it.

'I could come to you afterwards but I don't want to impose,' he said. Already there was a distance that had not been there before.

'You won't be. I'll make lunch.'

'I could take you out if it's too much trouble.'

'Why would it be?' I wanted him to answer that. I wanted him to tell me why he'd started dancing around me. But he didn't.

'Okay. I'll text you when I'm leaving the house.'

'This looks lovely, thank you.'

I'd just dished up a Spanish stew.

I was eating better since I'd met Abe, cooking for him, being cooked for and taken out. I hadn't bothered much when it was just me. I'd liked the way having met someone was turning meals and other ordinary things into small occasions.

'Cheers,' Abe said, albeit a little half-heartedly, raising his glass.

79

I took a sip of wine. It felt more like fortification than celebration. 'Have you spoken to Ruby and Sam since the weekend?'

'I met up with them on Monday evening.' He toyed with his food.

'Oh?'

'We went out for a meal.'

'A nicer one than the one we had?' I didn't manage to disguise the pique that had crept into my voice. I didn't like myself for it but the image of him sitting around the table with his children, enjoying a meal, when ours had been so strained, was hard not to resent.

If Abe noticed, he ignored it. 'Yes. As I said, I probably should have had more of a dialogue with them before I introduced them to you. I rushed them into something they weren't ready for. I should have realized they wouldn't be happy straight away. But I was too caught up in you to think straight.'

He'd used those words before, but where once they'd made me smile, now they seemed awkward and inappropriate. 'And you think it will take some getting used to?' I asked.

'I think they'll get used to it,' he said. He reached across the table and took my hand.

'And Lynn?'

'What about her?'

'How does she feel about me?'

'She accepts the situation.'

'But she's not over the moon about it.'

'That's not what I said. She's fine with it. Why wouldn't she be?'

'Because she might find it difficult. Because your children find it difficult. And . . .'

'And what?'

'I find it difficult, Abe. I love seeing you, but your life is hard to fit into. It feels too crowded.'

'Things are as they are, Ivy. Lynn and I are separate but we're still friends. I'm not going to stop looking after the house and . . . things.'

'I'm sorry,' I said. 'I don't want to appear selfish and I don't want you to stop seeing Lynn or doing all the things you do for her. I admire you for the way you've managed to maintain your relationship, that it's still good, despite everything.'

'We were married for a long time, and we'll always have the children. Nothing changes that. Imagine if you'd been in this position with Richard. You'd have wanted him still to care for you and the children, wouldn't you?'

'Of course. And, as I said, I'm not asking you to stop. It's just . . . it makes me anxious. I feel as if maybe . . .' I didn't know how to put this without appearing rude, without making Abe seem callous and calculating. I sometimes wondered if he understood what he was asking of me.

'Go on.'

'I wonder if I'm just a way of you working out how you really feel about Lynn. I don't mean you're doing it consciously or deliberately but in the scheme of things. I worry that seeing me might make you remember what you had with Lynn. I worry that Lynn might too. People often don't move on entirely after splitting up until one of them meets someone else. It makes it seem more real. The fact that I'm on the scene might make Lynn reconsider what she wants from you.'

'I know this isn't the easiest situation, Ivy,' he said, 'but my marriage is over. I know we're not divorced but it's still over.'

'Do you ever think about getting divorced?'

'Not really. It seems unnecessary, involving solicitors, getting into all of that. The arrangement we have suits us and I suppose it just seemed too . . .'

'Final?'

'No. Well, yes, I suppose. I don't know. Why do you say that?'

'Because it's difficult for me, always feeling like the other woman.'

'But you're not that. I really do care for you, Ivy. I want you to be a part of my life – a big part – but Lynn and the children are already a huge part. I can't change that.'

'I know.'

'If there's anything I can do to make it easier for you, then tell me. Meeting you when I did, it felt like a gift. I don't want to lose you. I really don't.'

'I don't know that there is anything you can do,' I say.

'You're amazing, Ivy, and when I met you, everything about the way we were felt so right. It still does. And I'm sorry if you feel I'm rushing you into things that you're not ready for. I don't mean to. I don't want to do anything that might drive you away. I want you to take as much time as you need to get used to the situation, but let's not allow other people to spoil what we have.'

'But they are,' I said. 'If it were just you and me it would be so much easier, but it's not and it never will be. I just don't know if . . .'

'If?' He put up his hand and touched the side of my cheek.

'I don't know if I can do this any more.' I hadn't intended to say it, not now, but I'd been thinking it. I didn't want to lose Abe, any more than he said he didn't want to lose me, but I didn't like feeling as I did either. Too much was getting in the way of what could have been a lovely relationship, too much that was making me unhappy.

'What do you mean?' He was clearly anxious.

'It's not you.' Such a cliché. 'It's everything else. There's so much to deal with and I'm not sure I'm strong enough for that. Not now. Not yet.'

'It's not just Lynn and the children, is it?' Abe asked.

I realized that everything I had said had not been entirely fair to him. He was right. It wasn't just Lynn, it was Richard too. 'No,' I admitted. 'It's me and it's Richard too. I don't really understand myself, Abe. I thought I was over the worst of it. I felt I'd moved on.'

'I don't know what to say. I wish you didn't feel like that. But I can't do anything about Lynn and the children. I can't make them disappear and I can't replace your husband either.'

'I'm not asking you to do any of that.'

'So what are you saying?' He sat back in his chair and looked at me expectantly.

'I don't know quite how to put it,' I said.

'Try.'

'When I met you, well, like you said, everything seemed so easy. I felt so at home in your company. My only reservations were that it seemed too soon after Richard dying. I wasn't sure I had the right to be happy, not with someone else anyway. I was beginning to feel that I could be happy on my own, where previously that had seemed impossible. But then I met you, and I was happy when I was with you.'

'I felt the same way. I feel the same way.'

'But it's changed. It's difficult hearing about Lynn or "the house" and the children. Like I said, the relationship feels too crowded and it's too soon.'

'Too soon to be with someone else?'

'Partly but not just that.'

'What do you mean?'

'It feels too soon to be unhappy again. I don't think I'm strong enough yet to deal with all the other emotions I'm having to deal with. I'm sorry but I think I need to be on my own again.'

'Oh, Ivy.' He took my hand again. 'I never wanted to make you unhappy.'

'I was all right when I met you. I felt strong again. I was over the worst of the grief, after Richard died. I was okay again, but now I'm not and I can't cope with the way that makes me feel. I'm so sorry.'

'So you want to stop seeing me?'

'I don't *want* to.' I couldn't say any more. There was a lump in my throat.

'Do I get a hug?' I asked, as he put on his coat and stood ready to leave.

'Ivy.' He stepped forward and took me in his arms. I put my arms around his neck and drew him to me in a long, lingering kiss that I wanted never to end.

'We could be so good together,' Abe said, when it did, pressing his face into the side of my neck.

'I know,' I said. 'I'm so sorry.'

'Don't keep saying that. I'm sorry too.'

'It's not your fault. You haven't done anything wrong. It's just the way things are.'

'And neither have you.'

'I love you, Abe,' I said, putting all my effort into not crying.

'I love you too, Ivy,' he said, and wiped a tear from his eye. 'I really do. I feel as if I've been waiting all of my life to meet you and now that I have . . .'

'. . . it's not the right time,' I finished his sentence for him.

'I'm so sorry I've made you unhappy,' he said, stroking my cheek in a way that was almost unbearable. 'But I'm still glad I met you. In another life . . .'

He trailed off and I nodded because the tears I had been trying to suppress had started to flow.

84

He held me again and we stood in the hallway clinging to each other, sobbing for what seemed like an eternity.

Perhaps my younger self would have held on to him for longer still, unable to contemplate being alone in the world again, without Abe at my side. But I knew from experience that time did heal and that I was not alone. I had my children and the knowledge that, throughout my life, I had been loved.

If a coin comes down heads, that means that the
possibility of its coming down tails has collapsed.
Until that moment the two possibilities were equal.
But on another world, it does come down tails. And
when that happens, the two worlds split apart.

Philip Pullman, *The Golden Compass*

London, April 2010

I was trying to keep myself busy and not worry so I'd decided
to wash the downstairs windows, which were covered with a
thick, yellowish grime. 'I wonder what's made them so disgusting,' I said, as I filled a bucket with water and took a
cloth from under the sink.

Max was sitting at the kitchen table, having breakfast and
flicking through his phone. I didn't expect an answer. They
were generally in short supply before midday. 'It's been sci-
entifically proven,' he had told me earlier in the week, 'that
teenagers are not suited to early starts.'

'Seriously?'

'Yes. It's much easier for old people like you.'

'I'm only in my fifties!'

'Exactly. It's much easier for you to start work at the crack
of dawn than it is for me.'

'Thank goodness for your timetable, then.'

He was in his final year at college and most of his lectures
seemed to be scheduled later in the day. Today he had a class

at midday and was slowly coming to life with the aid of a pot of coffee and several peanut-butter-laden pieces of toast. 'It's ash,' he said, looking up. 'On the windows. From the volcano.'

'Really?' Lately I had been preoccupied so the minutiae of the news had passed me by. The headlines had been dominated by a plane crash in Russia, which had killed the Polish president and dozens of political and military leaders. For a few days Smolensk had been a place name on everybody's lips. Now newsreaders were trying to get to grips with 'Eyjafjallajökull', after the Icelandic volcano, whose name it was, had erupted, creating a giant ash cloud over northern Europe. 'It can't be the same ash,' I said. 'Can it?'

'Yes, I read it.'

'Already?' The eruption had only just happened and its effects were not yet being felt beyond Iceland.

'Apparently it had been spewing stuff for a while before it erupted big-time,' Max said, refilling his cup from the cafetière. 'That's why the cars are all gunky.'

'I thought it was because we haven't had any rain for a while.'

'Nope. Volcanic ash,' Max said, before returning to whatever it was on his phone that held such interest for him.

I took the bucket outside, and ran my finger down the window pane, rubbing the accumulated dirt between finger and thumb. Could particles from another part of the world really settle here so quickly? I stood on a stool and began to wipe the glass with a soapy cloth.

A few days later, when the volcano's eruptions had caused chaos, dirty windows were the least of my worries.

Richard was in Latvia. His company was building a new hotel in Riga. He was supposed to be away for just a couple of days but that had changed. 'They've grounded all the flights,' he told me from the airport. 'Nothing's taking off today at all.'

'Oh dear. What will you do?' I was in the changing room at the local swimming pool, about to get into my swimsuit, still trying to fill the days so I could not dwell on the news I was about to receive.

'I'll go back to the hotel for another night and try again tomorrow,' he said.

A week later Richard was still in Riga and I was making my way, alone, to University College Hospital for the result of a blood test.

'Can't you ask them to reschedule the appointment?' Richard had asked, the previous evening.

I was reading in bed. The space beside me had now been empty for ten days. Richard was more or less confined to his hotel room.

'They're going to have to get air traffic moving sooner or later. Could you see if they can delay the appointment for a few days? I want to be there with you.'

'I know you do but I can't bear the waiting any longer.' It was nearly two weeks since I'd gone in to give a blood sample. 'I just want to get it out of the way. I'll call you as soon as I have the result.'

'I really don't think you should go on your own.'

I could heard concern in his voice, mingled with frustration. I imagined him sitting on the bed in his hotel, the TV on with the sound turned down, a tumbler with a finger of whisky beside the bed.

'Can you ask a friend to go with you?'

'Maybe,' I'd said. 'But I think I'd rather go alone. I'll make sure there's someone I can go and talk to on the way home, if I need to.'

I snuggled down in our bed.

'Promise you'll do that?' Richard was insistent. 'You shouldn't be on your own afterwards. Promise me you'll arrange to talk to someone afterwards. Whatever the result. And I'll call you.'

'I'll let Helen know. She's the only person I've told I'm having the test.'

'I still wish you'd wait until I get back. I feel so useless being stuck here.'

'There's nothing you can do about it.'

We chatted for a few moments longer, then said goodbye. I switched off the bedside lamp and rolled, out of habit, towards the empty space where Richard should have been.

So, there was no one with me as I sat in the waiting room at the hospital, flicking through a magazine, unable to find an article to stop me thinking about the moment that lay ahead – a moment that would be life-changing, whichever way things went.

It was Max who had provoked my change of heart. Whatever I thought about the odds, I had begun to feel they were diminishing with time. I was in my mid-fifties, and if I was going to succumb to the same ugly disease that had killed my mother, it should have presented itself already. So the possibility that I had it felt easier to ignore.

But as Max approached his eighteenth birthday he was looking for certainty. He would be an adult. He didn't need my permission to have the test: he could make the decision on his own. He was planning to go to university to read sports science. Max played tennis. He was good enough that his coach thought there was a chance he might be selected to play for the country in the Commonwealth Games in four years' time.

It seemed impossible that such a physical child could

possibly have inherited the faulty gene that had been responsible for so much pain and suffering on my side of the family.
My children had never met my mother. She had been robbed
of the chance to meet any of her grandchildren, though
spared the indignity of them witnessing her body slowly losing control of its every function and being taken over by
alarming spasms.

They had witnessed my brother Jon's steep decline, and
the thought of my own son having to go through what Jon
had was too much for me to contemplate. I felt that his phys-
icality would protect him, although I knew full well that it
could not. If I had the gene and had passed it on to Max,
nothing he did and no amount of innate physical strength
would protect him against the disease.

He was stacking the dishwasher one evening after dinner
when he brought the subject up. It was just the two of us,
tidying the kitchen in a quietly companionable way.

'Mum?' Max tried to squeeze a saucepan on top of some
plates.

'Yes?' I expected him to ask for money or if he could stay
out late.

'I've been thinking.' He was still struggling with the saucepan, adjusting it to fit into the machine better and to avoid
looking at me directly.

'What's that, then?'

'When I'm eighteen I want to have the test,' he said, standing still.

'What's prompted that?'

'I've just been thinking about it.'

'Is it after seeing Jon?' My elder brother was deteriorat-
ing fast.

'No. Yes. Well, sort of, I suppose, but not just that.'

We'd visited Jon and Anne last week. Jon was in a

wheelchair and could hardly communicate any more. I could tell that Max was appalled by his uncle's condition: he had to be helped with everything, even on to the toilet.

Lottie had taken it more in her stride. She'd sit opposite Jon and feed him, chattering away as she wiped his chin and paused to clear his mouth with her fingers if he started to choke. It didn't appear to faze or scare her.

But it alarmed Max, more than he let on. Of course it did. How would he deal with the possibility that he might end up in the same position?

'I've been thinking about uni. I still want to read sports science and I could maybe become a sports psychologist but it seems pointless going down that route if . . .'

'You'll still have time,' I said. 'Even if . . . Before . . .'

Neither of us wanted to put the possibility into words.

'But I have choices now and I want to make the right one. If I'm going to end up like Uncle Jon, I want to know now.'

I took a dishwasher tablet from the cupboard under the sink and didn't reply immediately. I pictured myself at that age, coming home from a year abroad, sitting in my own parents' kitchen and being told that the strange symptoms my mother had been showing for several years now had a name. That there was a reason for her mood swings and muscle spasms, that there was no cure but, worse, it was genetic, it ran in the family, and the likelihood that Jon, Cathy and I carried the same gene was fifty–fifty. I was on the cusp of adulthood. The world should have been opening up to me; instead it seemed to be shrinking.

I remembered sitting with Jon in the kitchen, after my father had helped Mum up to bed, and trying to get my head around it all. I hadn't had the choice that Max had now. There was then no test to confirm or not the presence of the markers that would tell me if I would suffer the same fate as my mother.

The only option open to me was to learn to live with the uncertainty, and that had informed my character. I had become someone who was perhaps more able than others to go with the flow, but Max, from an early age, had liked to know, as far as possible, how things were likely to pan out.

'Will the tide be in or out when we get there?' He would pester us with questions in advance of an outing. 'Will we put our rugs by the dunes? Will we swim before lunch? What sandwiches did you make?'

He didn't like surprises – diversions on the roads, museums that were closed when we got there or restaurants that had changed their menus and scrapped the dish he'd decided to have as soon as we booked a table.

I was not surprised that Max wanted to take advantage of the test, which had been developed when he was young, even if I would rather he did not. It was my decision, mine and Richard's, not the children's, to make when the test was first developed and I had decided I didn't want to know, that I'd rather carry on in the hope that everything would be okay than be told, for certain, if it would or would not.

But as they grew older I began to worry whether the decision I still thought had been right for me was actually right for them.

From a fairly young age, Lottie and Max had watched Jon's health slowly deteriorate, knowing exactly what was causing it. When they were in their early teens we had explained there was a chance it might affect them too. I had been ignorant of that possibility for longer and had watched my mother believing, until I reached adulthood, that it was nothing, that she would get better, never thinking it might also affect me.

'I'm sorry, Mum,' Max said. 'I didn't mean to talk out of turn about Jon.'

'I know that, love.' I looked at him: such a beautiful boy.

He was as tall as Richard now and solid but with deftness to his movements that belied his strength. He looked well too, tanned from the time he spent outdoors. And the blond highlights in his hair, which were less noticeable in winter, had begun to show again in the early spring sunshine. It seemed impossible that he would not always be so full of vitality.

'It may not be necessary for you to have the test,' I told Max. 'You know the symptoms usually begin before people reach their mid-fifties and I haven't shown any signs yet.'

'But they could start after?'

'They could, but it's unlikely.'

'I just want to know,' Max said. 'I've thought about it a lot. I'd rather know before I decide whether or not to go to university.'

'But even if I have the gene, even if you do, that shouldn't affect your plans,' I said. 'You can still go to university. It shouldn't stop you doing what you want to do now.'

That was the mantra by which I'd lived my adult life but it wasn't the one my son wanted to live his by.

'Yes. But I still want to know. I need to know.'

'Okay.' If that was how he felt I couldn't argue with him.

It was how Jon had felt too. I'd never wanted to know. Even now when I believed the test result was likely to come back clear, I'd still rather not.

'I've done loads of reading on the internet, Mum,' Max said. 'And I've talked to other kids online who've had the test. They all say it was the right thing to do.'

'Let's talk about it more when Dad's back.' I stalled him.

'I'm not going to change my mind.' Max shrugged and picked up his iPod.

'Are you off up to your room?'

'Yeah. I know this isn't easy for you, Mum, but it's what I want.'

'Okay, love.' Although I didn't tell him just then, I knew that meant I'd have to have the test myself. If I had it and was clear then Max and Lottie would know that they were too. I didn't want Max to have to go through all the genetic counselling sessions and the test if I could spare him by having them myself first.

And if I was positive? Then the children would have to decide what they wanted to do.

So today I'm in the waiting room at University College Hospital, having already been there for three counselling sessions.

'Why have you decided to have the test now?' the counsellor had asked on my first visit. I had explained that my son needed to know and I'd take the test so that if I was clear he wouldn't have to.

'That's quite common,' she said, and outlined implications I'd already been through in my mind more times than she could possibly imagine. 'How do you think you'll feel if you're clear?' she asked.

'I don't know.'

You'd think I'd be overjoyed but I didn't know how I'd feel. I'd lived with the uncertainty for so long. It was part of me. To have it taken away from me, to know that I'd escaped something that was blighting my brother's life, something that had killed my mother, felt wrong. I might feel lost without it, guilty for having survived.

But I'm about to find out. One way or another.

'Ivy?' The counsellor is approaching me. 'How are you?' She smiles and I try not to meet her eye.

She must already know. I don't want her to give anything away. 'Nervous.' I follow her into the consulting room.

94

'Is your husband not with you today?'

I sit down and explain that he's stuck in Riga.

'And you're sure you don't need someone to be here with you?' she asks.

'Does that mean it's bad news?'

'I'm not going to discuss that yet. I want to make sure you're all right with being here on your own. We could reschedule the appointment.'

'I've arranged to meet a friend afterwards. She lives nearby. I said I'd call in on her. She'll come home with me if I need her to.'

'Okay, if you're absolutely sure?'

'I am. Now that I've started the process, I just want to get it over and done with. I can't bear to wait any longer.'

'All right,' she says, and reaches for a folder on the desk with my name: 'TRENT, I.'.

It reminds me of the nametapes I used to have on my clothes at school.

She opens it and tells me the result of the blood test.

I walk out of the consulting room and down the stairs of the hospital on autopilot. I go out into the atrium, where there is a Costa coffee shop. I join the queue and order a double espresso. I take it to a table in the corner and sit down opposite a man I don't even begin to register.

I may say, 'Do you mind if I sit here?' but I don't remember.

It's a blur. Maybe I drink my coffee. Maybe I don't touch it. I have no idea.

The next thing I know the man opposite is asking if I'm all right.

It's only when I try to answer that I realize I'm crying. I'm not even crying quietly. I'm crying huge, undignified, uncontrollable sobs that can't possibly leave anyone in any doubt as to whether I'm all right or not.

'Here,' the man says. 'Have this.' He's handing me a tissue and he's coming round to my side of the table and he puts his hand gently on my shoulder. 'You've clearly had some sort of difficult news,' he says. 'Is someone with you?'

I shake my head.

'Is there someone I can call for you?'

'No. It's okay.' I take a deep breath and try to pull myself together. 'I've just – I just –' I can't begin to explain. 'I should be getting home.'

'Where do you live?' he asks.

'Highgate. Not far from the Underground. I'll catch the Tube.' The practical details of the journey divert me enough from the emotion, which is overwhelming me. I focus on them. 'I'll take the Tube from Warren Street. It's easy.'

'I don't think you should go on the Underground,' he says. 'You're not in a fit state.'

And the next thing I know I'm standing on the pavement outside the hospital and the man, this kind stranger, is hailing me a cab. 'Highgate,' he says to the driver, as he opens the door for me to get in, and I see him hand over a couple of notes. 'That'll cover it, won't it?' he asks the cabbie.

I'm fumbling with my bag, trying to unzip the pocket that contains my purse but my hands are shaking. I can't seem to open it.

'Don't worry. You just make sure you get home safely.' He leans though the door and does up my seatbelt, as if I was a child.

'But I can't –' I begin.

'You've had a shock,' he says. 'You've clearly had some upsetting news. I know what that's like. I just want to make sure you get home safely.'

Only then do I look at him properly for the first time. He's tall and around my age with a kindly face and a thick head of unruly salt-and-pepper hair. 'But I have my purse,' I say, still unable to locate it.

'Please don't worry,' he says, takes a card out of his pocket and hands it to me. 'If you feel you need to pay me back then this has my address and number. But it's really not necessary.'

'Thank you.' I put it into my pocket. I give the cab driver Helen's address, and when we get there, he hands me change, a lot. The stranger must have given him far too much money.

'Oh, Ivy,' Helen says, her eyes welling when she opens the door and sees the state I'm in. 'Come in. Come and sit down.' She leads me to a chair in the kitchen. 'It's bad news?'

'No.' The floodgates open once more. 'I'm clear. I don't have it. The kids don't have it.'

'Oh, thank God,' Helen says. 'When I saw you, I thought the worst. I'm so happy for you all.'

But she cries too, and I think she understands why I can't stop. It's as if everything I've been bottling up all my life is coming out now.

'Have you called Richard?' Helen says.

'No. I've been in too much of a state.'

'You must let him know. I'll put the kettle on, or do you want a drink?'

'A cup of tea would be lovely.'

'I'll make it while you to talk to Richard.'

He's delighted, of course, and frustrated he can't be with me.

'I should go now,' I say, when we've talked for a while. 'I need to get home and tell the children.'

After Helen's made the tea, she asks me to try to explain to her the mix of emotions I'm grappling with.

'It's really hard,' I say, 'but I feel a strange sense of loss. I know how ridiculous that sounds. I've just been given a new lease of life. But I've got so used to living the way I've been living that I'm grieving for an affliction I'd learned to live with.'

'I think I understand,' she says kindly. 'It's a bit like kidnap victims missing their kidnappers when they're released.'

'I suppose so. And of course it's the best possible news. I don't know what I'd have done if they'd said I was positive. But I feel bad for Jon. It doesn't seem fair. I don't know how I'm going to tell him and Anne.'

'Give it time,' Helen says. 'You don't have to tell them just yet. Are you going to see the counsellor at the hospital again or is that it now?'

'There are follow-up sessions. I didn't think they'd be necessary, if I was clear, but I guess the state I'm in means they are.'

'She can probably help you decide when's the best time to tell your siblings and how.'

'You're right,' I say. 'And I'm sorry. I know I've just pitched up and cried all over your kitchen but I really need to get home.'

'Shall I come with you?'

'It's really kind of you but I'll be okay. Thank you.'

Helen gives me a big hug and kisses me. 'I'm so relieved for you,' she says. 'Let me know how you get on with the kids.'

They're thrilled – relieved and thrilled. Lottie cries and Max puts his arm around me and says we should celebrate.

'We should.'

I put a bottle of champagne that someone gave us at Christmas into the fridge. 'Let's have a takeaway too. I'm too tired to cook. Would you mind going out and getting one?'

'What do you want? Chinese? Indian? Fish and chips?' Lottie asks.

'I don't mind. You decide. I'll give you some money.' And this time, when I pick up my bag, I have no trouble finding my purse. I take out two twenty-pound notes and hand them to my daughter. 'Are you going with her, Max?' I ask.

'No,' he says. 'I should stay here with you.'

'Oh, it's really not . . .' I begin, but actually I want him there. 'Thank you.'

'Can I wear your coat, Mum?' Lottie's already halfway into it.

'Go on.'

She leaves, and when she comes back she piles boxes of chicken curry, pilau rice and vegetable korma on the table, then takes poppadums and naan bread out of carrier bags. Last, she reaches into the pockets of my coat and hands over the change. 'Do you want the receipt? '

'No.' I sit on the sofa that runs along the side of our kitchen, too tired now to do anything other than watch my two teenage children fussing over me.

'And this?' Lottie holds up a card.

'What is it?'

'It says "Abe McFadden, Landscape Architect". Do you need it?'

'No,' I say, not even sure how the card got there. 'It must be one of those cards people put through the letterbox.'

She throws it into the bin with the receipt and later, when I've eaten, she ladles the leftovers into the bin on top of it.

It's only a few days later, when Richard is back, when he's asking me to go through the details that I've already been through with him on the phone several times, that I remember the stranger, the good Samaritan, who witnessed my upset and helped me get home.

The bin liner has been transferred to the bin outside and the refuse collectors have taken it away.

I would have paid him back. I would have got in touch to say thank you.

Instead, by the time I remember that the name Lottie had read out to me belonged to him, his card is lying somewhere at the bottom of a landfill site.

'Things aren't like this,' he kept repeating.
'It shouldn't be this way.' As if he had access
to some other plane of existence, some parallel
'right' universe, and had sensed that our time
had somehow been put out of joint.

Salman Rushdie, *The Ground Beneath Her Feet*

London, March 2000

I can't believe I'm doing this. This isn't me. I'm not that sort of person. Is that what everyone thinks? That they're not that sort of person, whatever that sort of person is? And do they suddenly find that they are?

Is Richard that sort of person? Is Abe? Is everyone, when it comes to meeting someone whom they feel instinctively drawn to, when the choice is walking away or becoming that sort of person? The sort of person who is willing to deceive their partner and risk their children's happiness because they've met some bloke and they can't let him go?

Am I just a cliché? A woman in her mid-forties who's a little bored with life and seeking excitement elsewhere?

I'm not sure I can go through with it. If Abe was a little less persuasive, a little less sure, then perhaps I wouldn't be sitting on the train, travelling into central London when I should be at home with the children.

'It's a totally separate thing,' he's said, every time I say, 'I can't,' or 'I really don't think I can go any further.'

'I don't want to do anything that will disrupt your life. This is just extra.'

'But it could,' I protest. 'It could destroy everything.'

'Not if we don't let it,' he says. 'We're both married and we both need to stay married. What we have is aside from that.'

I almost believe him, but the way he talks about his wife makes me wonder: has he used the unhappiness he implied to elicit my sympathy and push me in the direction he wants me to go?

It seems unlikely, but he is the one pushing and I am the one who seems to have all the qualms.

I'm imagining that the other occupants of the train can tell where I'm off to from looking at me but I can still hear their projected thoughts in my head, as if they were saying them out loud.

'Have you thought about the consequences?' the woman opposite is saying, as she catches my eye while reapplying her makeup.

'Are you thinking about his wife and child?' a tired-looking woman asks, as our reflections stare at each other in the semi-darkness just outside the window.

'You do realize you're being completely and utterly selfish and thinking only of yourself?' says the elderly man opposite, smart in a three-piece suit and tie.

Perhaps he's been there himself.

I look at him more closely. He's probably in his early seventies. His face is still handsome, and there's an openness in his smile when he catches me looking at him that is attractive.

I smile back and take a deep breath.

Abe's booked the hotel room. I've said I'll meet him in the pub around the corner – the Marquis of Granby. We've met in a different Marquis of Granby before.

'There are lots,' he had told me on another occasion. Thank goodness for the Marquis. I was going to need a drink first. I was going to need a drink anyway.

'There's no pressure. You can change your mind at any time,' he'd said to me on the phone earlier.

I could barely speak and managed only 'I'll see you later.'

Perhaps we'll just have a drink, change our minds and go home again. But the thought of the room round the corner is tempting, if only to have some privacy from the world. And Abe has booked it.

What if someone sees us going into the hotel?

The train is nearing Waterloo now and my phone beeps. A text alert. I look, thinking it will be Abe asking if I'm on my way.

It's from Richard: *Can't find Lottie's monkey* . . .

Lottie can't sleep without her monkey. I sat it on the head-board that morning, as I always do when I make her bed. Has she moved it? It's only a toy but it signifies enough to make me want to turn straight round and go home again. I could tell Richard my client meeting was cancelled and I'm coming home. I could tuck the children up and kiss them goodnight. I could buy a bottle of wine and a takeaway and make the most of Richard being back early.

I call Richard. I'm all ready to tell him I'll be home after all. 'Hello, it's me.'

'What's up?' His tone is brusque, the way it is if I call him at work and he doesn't wish to be distracted.

'You left a message, saying you can't find Lottie's monkey.'

'Oh, I sent that text ten minutes ago. We've got it now.'

'Oh. Okay. That's good.'

'She's asleep.'

'Great. Is everything else okay?'

'Fine.' Richard sounds irritated. 'I can manage, you know.'

'I only called because you texted.' And because I wanted to talk to you. I wanted you to want to talk to me. I wanted you to say something that would make a difference.

'Okay. Well, have a good evening.'

It's as if he can hardly wait to get me off the phone.

'Thanks,' I say, and pause, hoping he'll say something other than 'Bye, then.'

But that is all he says.

I stand up to put my coat on as the train pulls into the station.

'Excuse me,' the old man opposite says. 'Is that your umbrella up on the rack?'

'No. I think I've got everything.'

'Excellent.' He smiles.

Do I imagine that he adds, 'It's easy to forget what's important,' or did he really say it to me?

I look at him rising, with effort, from his seat, using a stick for support, preoccupied with the task.

I don't concern him.

Abe has already checked into the hotel, been to the room and claimed it, before he left again to meet me. That was enough to make him appear familiar with both the hotel and the room when we go there together.

He nods briefly to the receptionist, while I try to avoid eye contact with anyone. Only when we're alone in the lift do I look at Abe.

'Are you okay?'

'I'm not sure.'

He says nothing but puts out his hand and touches my cheek.

It's enough.

Enough for me to walk out of the lift and follow him

along the hotel corridor, scanning it anxiously for people I know. I imagine the hotel to be full of people I work with, parents from school, colleagues of Richard's and old friends from college days.

'After you.' Abe opens the door.

I walk past him, only a few paces. Any more will take me right up to the bed.

The room is small and claustrophobic. Abe is standing behind me. He puts his arms around me and holds me. No kisses. Just the warmth of his body and the reassuring feel of him.

It's the right thing to do. I relax.

I turn and put my arms around his neck. We kiss and I know there's no turning back now.

'I'd better take my coat off!' I pull away, remove it and hang it over the back of a chair. Then I sit on the chair, away from the bed, still unsure.

Abe sits on the end of the bed, less than two feet away. 'Come here.' He pats the space beside him. I join him. 'I've wanted to be alone with you for so long.' He puts an arm around me and draws me to him. My body tenses. 'Are you okay?' he asks again.

'I think so.' I'm so nervous.

Abe pushes a strand of hair away from my face, a solicitous gesture, and runs his fingers down my cheek. 'God, you're beautiful,' he says.

We kiss again, and when we stop, I bend down and unzip the boots I'm wearing. 'I'll just go to the bathroom,' I say, and head for the tiny en-suite.

I don't need the loo and I don't want him to hear me pee. How ridiculous is that? I'm about to get undressed and get into bed with this man. Why worry about him hearing me pee? But I do.

In the bathroom, I simply look at myself in the mirror, not out of vanity. I'm trying to take in my face. I wonder if it will look different afterwards, if it will give anything away.

I hitch up my dress and remove my tights. I do this out of vanity. At some point, Abe will remove my dress or I'll do it myself. I don't want to have tights on when that happens. I know that's a funny thing to worry about, but it deflects the anxiety about getting undressed in front of someone new when you haven't done it for years.

When I go back, Abe has taken off his shoes and socks and he's sitting on the bed, propped against the pillows. I sit next to him and all the worries, all the voices, all the thoughts, the images of Lottie unable to sleep without her monkey, Max clutching his stomach and saying he feels sick again, recede so far into the distance as to be practically forgotten.

All I can think about is Abe: his touch, the surprising softness of his skin, the sprinkling of hair on his chest, the stubble grazing mine as he kisses my breasts and the strength of his tongue as it works its way down my body. All the anxieties I'd thought I'd have, about being in this position with someone new, have disappeared and long-forgotten sensations are creeping back: the anticipation as we undress, the way my body comes alive to his touch, standing naked next to someone who has never seen me naked before, it all feels natural, as well as new and exciting, the way it only ever is at first, before things settle into something more secure but routine.

I'd almost forgotten what it's like to have a man's head between my legs and the moment of pure pleasure it produces. I abandon all other thoughts. I can think only of the tension between my not wanting it to stop and longing to have him inside me, and the look in his eyes when he eventually comes, so quietly I'm not sure that he has.

And afterwards, when we lie spooned around each other and some of the thoughts begin to creep back and a part of my mind is asking, What have I done? he kisses the back of my neck as I clasp his hand tight across my breast and hold my breath, so I can hear him, because he says it so quietly.

'I'm so glad I found you.'

I feel as if I'm floating as we dress afterwards, as if I belong to another world, and later I realize that I do: a world in which people risk their marriages for the thrill of the unfamiliar. The reality begins to sink in as I walk back to the station, checking my phone, in case Richard has called.

He hasn't but someone does, as soon as I put my phone back into my bag.

I forget about Richard as soon as I see the caller display. 'I wanted to hear your voice again,' Abe says. 'Are you on the train?'

'Not yet. I'm just heading towards the station.'

'Thank you for coming,' he says. 'I know it's not easy for you, having to leave your children and come all this way.'

'I wanted to see you.'

I look around as I approach the station concourse, wondering if any of the people in the throng around me will be remotely interested in my conversation. But why should they? I've reached the age when I'm invisible to most people. Teenagers and young men in the street don't even register my presence, too engrossed in their thoughts or conversations to move aside when I approach. Even people my own age don't see me. They see a middle-aged woman, rushing between work and her family. They know the type.

It used to feel depressing to know that I'd become someone whose presence doesn't register, but now it has, with one man, at least.

'And you don't . . . you don't regret it, Ivy? Do you?'

'No,' I say. 'I don't.'

It hadn't occurred to me until now that the encounter may have been a one-off. Now that it has, I worry about the implications. Was that all he wanted? To get me into bed? Will he stop talking to me now, stop making time and disappear back to his wife?

'Good,' he says. 'Me neither.'

That doesn't tell me anything, doesn't assuage the fear that what I've just done was meaningless, that what I've been telling myself about the connection between us was simply justification for doing what I did to satisfy my own lust.

'I'm just going through the ticket barrier now,' I say. 'I don't like talking on trains.'

'Okay,' he says, and I think that will be that, but then he gives me the reassurance I need. 'I will see you again, won't I?'

'Of course.' Relief floods through me.

'When?'

'I don't know. Next week?'

'That seems ages away.'

'I know, but . . .' What else can I say?

'I'll speak to you before then. Can I call you tomorrow?' he asks, and I tell him I'll be at home, working on my own, for most of the morning. 'Goodnight, Ivy,' he says. 'And thank you.'

Monday mornings are always a little tense and the following one was unusually so.

'I want peanut butter in my sandwich,' Lottie was insistent.

'But you can't take nuts into school any more. There's a new boy and they make him very sick.'

She had brought the note back in her bag last Friday, announcing the arrival of a child with a severe nut and avocado allergy. 'Who'd have thought anyone was allergic to avocado?' I'd commented.

'Who'd have thought children would take avocados to school?' Richard had said. 'What's wrong with an apple or a tangerine?'

'You don't know the half of it. Parents compete over lunch-boxes. Lottie asked me the other day if she could have some of the "new carob" chocolate bars. Apparently one of her friends brought some in for lunch and impressed the rest of them.'

'Jesus, we haven't gone down the old carob route yet, have we?' Richard looked at me as if he suspected I might have become a secret food faddist without his knowing.

'You know me,' I replied.

I was intolerant of food intolerances and fads. Everyone these days seemed so concerned with their health when, for most of them, it was something they could take for granted, not something they needed to worry about.

'I do.' Richard had grinned and kissed me.

His confident assertion that he knew me made me feel instantly guilty.

But this morning the atmosphere was different.

'The new boy isn't going to eat my sandwiches,' Lottie complained. 'He can have his own.'

'Well, I'm making you cheese.'

'I don't want that cheese,' Lottie said, picking up the packet of Cheddar. 'It's mouldy. Why do we always have to have mouldy food?'

'I'll cut the mould off. It's perfectly fine,' I reassured her. 'It's what penicillin is made from and that makes you better when you're sick.'

'That's stretching a point,' Richard said, opening the bread bin. 'And the bread's mouldy too. Is there any more any-where?'

'Why? And where would there be?' I resented the implication that the lack of fresh bread was my fault.

'Seriously, Ivy, this loaf is completely past it.' He was tetchy now.

'There are some rolls. I'll do one for Lottie.'

'I wanted some toast for breakfast,' he said, and begun muttering, more to himself than to me. 'I've got an important meeting this morning. Is having something to eat before I go to work too much to ask?'

'Look, I'll run to the corner shop and buy some bread, if it's such an issue.'

'Don't bother. I haven't got time,' Richard said.

'Can I have a peanut-butter roll then?' Lottie asked. 'That's not a sandwich.'

'It's not the sandwich that's the problem, love,' I said, as my phone, which was on the kitchen table, beeped with a message alert.

'You've got a text,' Richard said, picking it up and handing it to me.

I looked at the display. It was from Abe. 'Just work,' I said, panicky. 'It can wait.'

I slipped the phone into my pocket and did not reply until an hour or so later, after I'd taken the children to school and was back at my desk, ready to write some promotional material for one of my clients.

Eventually Abe called me. He had a meeting that morning, near Blackfriars, and didn't have to go back to the office until later. Was there any chance I could meet him? He knew it was short notice but he really wanted to see me.

The children had after-school clubs on Monday. I didn't have to pick them up until later. I could ask a friend to be on call, tell them I had to go into town for a meeting, in case anything happened.

We discussed a few other things, made the necessary arrangements, and a couple of hours later, I found myself looking for Abe in the bar of a Premier Inn, then following him towards the lift, stepping out, walking down a corridor, watching him as he took the key card out of his pocket and opened the door to the room.

There was none of the hesitancy of our previous encounter. As soon as the door was closed, I was in Abe's arms and he was kissing and beginning to undress me. We were in bed within seconds, making love with an urgency that was at odds with our having seen each other a few days earlier. Had I ever felt such intense overwhelming desire for anyone before? Did the illicitness of the encounter make it seem so? I couldn't be sure. All I knew was that I wanted Abe more than anything else in the world at that moment. And then it was over, too quickly, all our energies spent, and Abe was looking at his watch in a way that made me feel awful.

'Do you have to get back to the office?' I hoped I didn't sound as peevish as I felt.

'Not just yet,' he said, and we lay for a while, my head on his chest, talking about life, about how random it is, about the possibility that we might never have met but we had.

'Do you want a bath?' Abe asked, and I suppose that was as nice a way of signalling that he had to make a move as any. 'We could have one together.'

He went to run it, calling me from the bathroom and allowing me to get in first before stepping in behind me, opening his legs so that I could lean back against him in the water. It was almost unbearable, the thought of having to get dressed and leave, as he ran his hands all over my body, smoothing the bubbles of the bath gel over my skin.

He got out first, wrapped a towel around himself, then held one out for me, wrapping it round me and rubbing me gently until I was dry. He looked at his watch again and I took my cue.

'We should get dressed.'

'Do you have to go now?' he asked.

'I thought you did.'

'I've still got time, if you have.'

I nodded.

'Let's go back to bed,' Abe said, and when I lay down, on top of the covers, he walked to the foot of the bed, bent down and kissed the inside of my ankles, slowly, gently, before working his way up the inside of my thigh and kissing every part of my body, except where I was longing to feel him kiss me the most.

He was kissing my stomach, moving up and over my breasts, and then his mouth was on mine and I wanted to him to head back down to the area he'd skirted, but instead he put his hand there and began stroking me. I reached out to touch him too but he moved my hand away.

'Not yet,' he said, looking at me. 'I want to see you. I want to look at you, while I touch you.'

The Ivy who had been married to someone for several years would have been under the covers with her eyes closed, but the part of me that had been brought to life by someone new, and the unfamiliarity of the way he explored my body, lay on the bed, watching, as the man who was not her husband moved his hand expertly, and allowing herself to look into his eyes as she moved against it.

'Ivy,' Abe said, and I wondered if the intensity of the feeling that flooded through me registered in my eyes.

He held me afterwards, not allowing me to reciprocate. 'Next time,' he said quietly, taking my hand as if it to signal that this was going somewhere. I didn't allow myself to wonder where, that was too scary, just luxuriated in being with someone who made me feel things I'd not felt for so long: as if I was alive, not just living but really, truly alive.

If you asked me to pinpoint the moment when I started to drift away from Richard I'd say it was after Jon and Anne's party, after hearing Cathy's news. Quite why my sister's revelation should have thrown us off course is hard to say. Perhaps we had been storing up different resentments, and that was the point at which they began to emerge . . .

'Why don't you go on your own and I'll stay at home and look after the children?' Richard asks. He phrases it as if he's doing everyone a favour but I know he was never keen to come in the first place. So it's not a favour, it's an excuse.

'No. I'll sort something out,' I say tetchily. 'Lottie can always go with Max, if necessary, or she can come with us.'

'But wouldn't it be easier if –'

'No! I want you to be there. I don't want to go on my own.'

We have this argument, or a version of it, too often at the moment.

At the last minute, Richard will say he's too tired to do something we've planned to do together. 'You go on your own,' he'll say, as if it doesn't matter to me whether he comes or not.

'But I'd rather you were with me.' It will spiral from there.

Richard works hard. I know he's under pressure and the children don't make home the most relaxing of places but I'm tired too. I work for myself, so theoretically I can fit in with the children but in practice this often means I have to finish off projects late at night, after they've gone to bed.

My preference is often for an early night rather than going out. But if we never make time to do anything together, if we don't make sure there is still an us, not just Mum and Dad, Max and Lottie, I worry it might happen again.

Richard's an architect. It's not a career that attracts a huge number of women. When one appeared in his office while I was knee deep in nappies and not paying him much attention, the attraction proved too great to resist. That is, of course, a gross simplification of what happened.

I remember the physical shock when I read the text message. We were on holiday in Corfu. We'd rented a villa with a pool on the north-east coast with views across the narrow strait to Albania. Richard had brought binoculars and would use them to focus on the opposite shores picking out high-rise buildings and declaring them 'brutalist Communist monstrosities'.

'We should go,' I'd suggested. There was a day trip to Tirana from Corfu Town. 'I could practically swim there!' In the past, people had tried to cross the two-mile strip of water to escape the oppression and deprivation of the regime there. Some had made it. More had drowned or been shot by Albanian soldiers, who patrolled the waters in military vessels.

We never went. Max and Lottie were more than happy to spend their days by the pool and on the beach, punctuated by ice creams and meals in waterfront tavernas or chatting to the elderly Greek woman who came to clean and change the sheets every other day.

'Lottie,' she would call out in a happy sing-song voice, pronouncing the *ie* with two syllables: 'Lott-y-a'.

'Lottie, is this your friend?' She'd pick up a toy from the floor and tuck it carefully into the freshly made bed.

'Maximilian!' she would call to Max. Clearly both names were too short for her to relish. 'I've found a work of art,' she said, indicating one of Max's inexpertly crayoned drawings.

They would follow her around the house, enthralled and happy. We all were for a few days.

'No phones,' we had agreed before we left home, but of course we had brought them.

I hadn't switched mine on but Richard would check his daily, commenting on the number of messages he'd had from the phone network, welcoming him to Albania. The narrow passage of water formed a geographical border between Greece and Albania but mobile-phone signals had no respect for such.

'I dread to think what the bill will be like, when we get home,' he'd say. 'I don't think Albania is covered in my contract.'

But the phone bill was the least of his worries.

The children were napping one afternoon and I'd gone to read on our bed, where it was cooler, when Richard's phone had vibrated loudly from the drawer in the unit on his side of the bed.

I hadn't been looking to catch him out. In hindsight, when I thought about it, I'd been deliberately ignoring the signs that were there, subconsciously thinking that if I did not look then I could not be upset.

When I stretched across the bed and opened the drawer, I was thinking only that I might take the phone to him but it was the initials that intrigued me. There was a message from 'CPG'. Why no name? Maybe it was just another mobile phone company, I told myself, as something spurred me to click on the message and open it. *I'm sorry. I know we said we wouldn't get in touch while you were with your family.* I could hardly bear to go on, to scroll down further but I was compelled to do so. *But I miss you so much. Call me if you get a moment. I just want to hear your voice Cxx*

I deleted the message and put the phone back. I decided there and then that I would say nothing until we were home again. I tried to pretend that nothing had changed but Richard could tell something wasn't right. I was short with the kids and tetchy with him.

'What the hell's the matter?' he snapped angrily one evening, as we both got ready for bed.

'You tell me,' I said, glaring at him accusingly, and he began to crumble, his anger towards me replaced by fear.

'How?' he said, sitting on the bed and putting his head in his hands. 'How did you know?'

Somehow we got through the next few days, and talked – I screamed at him – when we got home. He ended it and we struggled on for a few months, for the rest of the year, but I was surprised by how quickly his affair became a thing of the past and how well the wounds healed.

We could talk about it now, prompted by news of friends caught in the aftermath of infidelity or a storyline in a TV drama. 'I suppose I felt like that when you had your fling,' I could say with equanimity, finding that time and the fact that we were still close had erased the hurt.

'It wasn't because I didn't love you,' Richard had said back then. 'It just happened.'

His words weren't particularly comforting, yet they were probably true. Richard was ambitious at work, he had grand plans for projects and envisaged a bright future for himself, but in his private life he seemed never to think far beyond what was happening at the moment.

That had been part of the attraction when I'd met him, a year after Mum died, a year after a brief but promising dalliance had ended in a way that made me wonder if I'd ever have a relationship that lasted. It was hard to blame that particular boyfriend for running away. He'd found himself thrust into a family in the midst of grief and reckoning. I'd have done the same if I'd been him.

I met Richard by chance, and when that happens it's easy to convince yourself that Fate brought you together.

We'd been to the theatre, Dad, Jon, Anne and I. It was a treat for Dad's birthday, Michael Frayn's new play, *Copenhagen*. Dad had let us buy the tickets but he insisted on pre-ordering and paying for the interval drinks. I was still pondering the first act when we made our way to the bar. Two physicists meet in the Danish capital and years later, after their deaths, their spirits discuss the various ramifications of that initial meeting. 'What if the atomic bomb had never been built?' they ask. 'Would the future that is now the past have been inevitable or uncertain?'

'I'm not sure I quite understood it all,' I said to Dad.

'I'm not sure you're supposed to,' he replied. 'Now. Can you find our drinks? They're under my name.'

It was crowded in the bar so Dad let me swim through the sea of theatregoers to locate our order. I've forgotten what everyone asked for, only that I'd wanted white wine and Dad a glass of red. I found an order, which included both, under the name 'Richard'. There were two gin and tonics alongside the wine. That must have been what Jon and Anne ordered. I took a sip of my wine, then picked up the tray with the two G and Ts and Dad's red, to carry them through the crowd to the periphery where my family was waiting.

'Excuse me.' I heard a voice at my shoulder, turned round and looked up at my future husband. Of course I didn't know that yet, any more than Niels Bohr and Werner Heisenberg knew what the consequences of their work on the atom would be when they first met in Denmark in 1941.

'I think those are my drinks,' the man said.

'No,' I contradicted him. 'They're ours.'

'Richard Smith?' He pointed to the name on the sheet.

I hadn't looked properly and the 'Smith' had been obscured by a glass. 'Oh, God, sorry. You're right. I'm looking for Trent, Richard Trent.'

'Just along there. Almost took your drinks myself,' he said, smiling.

'But I've already had a sip of the white.' I was flustered. 'I'll get the one that's ours and bring it back to you.'

'It's okay,' he said. 'The white's mine. I don't mind you having a sip of it, unless you're carrying some deadly disease?'

'No.'

He'd meant it as a joke but the play, the what-if scenarios, being with Dad on his own, and Jon and Anne, knowing what they knew, I didn't laugh and some of my thoughts must have been reflected in my face.

'It was a joke,' Richard Smith said.

'Yes. I'm sorry for the mix-up.'

'Easily done,' he said.

I thought, That's it, I'll never see him again, but afterwards I was waiting in the foyer for Dad and Jon, who had gone to the Gents, and Anne, who was in a longer queue for the Ladies.

'So, did you enjoy the play?' Richard Smith had appeared from nowhere.

'Yes. It was interesting. Did you? And your friends?' I looked around to see whom he was with but he seemed to be on his own now.

'Work colleagues,' he said. 'One left his briefcase in the auditorium. They've all gone back to look for it.'

'Oh. I hope they find it.'

'I'm Richard, by the way,' he said, and put out his hand. 'Richard Smith.'

'I know that!' I laughed. There was something about him and his directness that I liked. 'Ivy,' I said. 'Ivy Trent.'

'And are you here with friends?' he asked.

'Family. My dad, my brother and his wife.'

'Ah.'

'So what are you and your colleagues?' I asked.

'What do you mean?'

'You said you were with colleagues. What do you all do?'

'Oh, I see,' he said, as I caught sight of Dad and Jon coming down the stairs to join me. 'I'm an architect.' He fished in his pocket and handed me a card.

I took it and nodded towards Dad. 'I ought to go now.'

'Well, if you ever want to discuss a physicists' work outing to Copenhagen in more detail,' he said, 'you've got my number.'

I did. I put the card with Richard Smith's name and work number in my purse and the following Monday, when I was at work, I called. It felt bold, and I was relieved when his PA answered and I was able to ask her to tell him that Ivy Trent had rung and to leave my number.

Minutes later he called back.

Perhaps Richard told his friends 'it just happened' with me, as the affair with his colleague 'just happened'. He tended to let things happen and didn't worry about the consequences.

I told him about Mum early on, and outlined the implications but they didn't seem to scare him. He'd lost his mother too. Perhaps that was another factor in us being drawn to each other. He rarely speaks of her now, finding it easier not to. She died in a car accident when he was ten. But, occasionally, one of the children will ask him something.

'You're luckier than Mum because you've got a mum but Mum doesn't,' a confused Max said to him.

'But I don't have a mother either.' Richard was perplexed. 'That's why you've only got granddads, no grans.'

'But Mum is your mum,' Max said.

'No, Max.' Richard had laughed. 'Mum's my wife not my mum.'

'Then why do you call her "Mum"?' he'd asked earnestly.

Richard and I had looked at each other and laughed, but it saddened me too. It was only when Lottie was born that he'd started to call me 'Mum'. After Max, I'd still been Ivy.

119

It was as if he'd made a conscious decision to think of me as someone else, a mother, no longer his wife. Lottie's birth had been difficult where Max's was surprisingly easy. She had turned at the last minute, come out feet first and nearly strangled herself with the umbilical cord. Richard had had to watch while they pushed her back in and whisked me off for an emergency Caesarean. I know it affected him but he doesn't like to talk about it, any more than he likes to talk about his mother and the spectre that looms over my family.

That suits me. Another man might have wanted to keep torturing me with what-ifs but Richard is happy to live in hope that the worst may never happen. Another woman, another version of myself even, might have thought longer and harder before opting to make a life with Richard. I might have wondered if Richard was right for me, if he was my soul-mate or if there was someone better suited to me. Perhaps Richard pondered the advisability of marrying and having children with someone who might be destined to die young and pass on that fate to his children.

'We'll deal with it when and if we have to,' is all he will say on the subject.

We chose not to think too much, to accept what was good and make a go of us.

'Dad's mother died before you were born, Max,' I'd told him, 'so she never got to meet you.'

'She'd have loved you, though,' Richard added.

Max was now eight and Lottie six. They should have been having sleepovers with friends while Richard and I went to Jon and Anne's party. But Lottie's friend is sick and her mother's not sure about having her. Richard wants to use the excuse to stay at home. 'What's the party in aid of this time anyway?' he asks.

'Anne's got a new job.' I ignore the jibe. 'And Cathy's home for a bit too, so it's a chance for us to see her.'

Cathy has been working on a health outreach project in Kenya. Something to do with Aids. I sound as vague as Dad when he talks about her work but I'm not sure what it involves. She's only ever home for a few weeks' leave and I know she'll come up to London and see us but her visit will be rushed, as they always are.

And I want to see Jon and Anne and celebrate Anne's new job. I admire the way they make the most of the small things and don't let the bigger issues cloud the rest of their lives.

Jon tested positive four years ago. When he found out he was a carrier, that his genes are marked in exactly the same way that our mother's were, he and Anne decided not to have children. He didn't want them to go through what we went through with Mum. He didn't want a child of his to have to face what he knows he will have to face himself.

I wonder if I might have done the same, if the test had been available earlier, before I had my own two. I'm thankful it wasn't, that I didn't have to make a decision then that might have meant I'd never have a family of my own. I love them more than I thought it was possible to love anyone, and I love Richard for making it all possible and for understanding why I don't want to know, why I'd rather live with the uncertainty than have my future mapped out for me by doctors and therapists.

Jon still shows no symptoms of the disease but he knows, as he approaches his fifties, that it won't be long before they start to appear. Until then he's decided to work hard, play hard, and celebrate whatever he thinks is worth celebrating.

Now that we're here, now that Max's friend's mother has agreed that Lottie can spend the night at her house too, Richard's relaxing a little, as he helps Jon fill a dustbin with ice and booze. Perhaps it helps that he has a beer in his hand.

'By the way I've asked William Ross,' Jon says casually, as they faff about with the drinks. 'Do you remember him?'

'Billy?' He was one of my best friends through infant school.

'Yes, but he calls himself William, these days.'

'I'd almost forgotten he existed.'

The kids find it odd that I cannot name all the people I went to school with when I was their age; I have largely forgotten that time of my life.

'Who is he?' Richard asks.

'Ivy's first boyfriend.'

'He wasn't my boyfriend!' I protest. 'We were children.'

'He was a bit soft on you, though,' Jon says.

'We were friends,' I say to Richard, who is looking at me with a raised eyebrow. 'His mum was a good friend of Mum's.'

'He wrote to me after Mum died,' Jon tells Richard. 'He still lives locally. I think he's an estate agent or something.'

I try to picture Billy as a child but I can't remember what he looked like or anything much about him, other than that I'd liked him and we'd spent a lot of time with each other and each other's families.

I'm curious to see what he's like now and keep an eye open for him when the guests begin to arrive.

'Hello, stranger.' Cathy's one of the first. She's come from Dad's house but will stay at Jon's tonight with us.

'Hey! How are you?' She looks well, tanned and slim. My big sister.

'I'm . . . fine.' She hugs me.

The pause before she said 'fine'.

'Are you?'

Her eyes dart around the room, as if she's looking for someone other than me.

'Oh, you know . . .' She speaks with the curious lilt she's developed since working in Africa. She drags her words out and uses an upward inflection at the end of her sentences, forming questioning statements.

'She's such a bloody hippie,' was Jon's verdict. 'That or she's stoned half the time.'

'How long have you been home?'

'Oh, me, I have been here since . . . Wed-nes-day.'

'And have you been staying with Dad?'

'I . . .' She looks around again and never resumes whatever she started to say.

'Is everything okay?'

'Yes,' she says. 'I'd better find Jon. And I need a smoke.'

Maybe she was a little stoned already. 'He's with Richard on drinks duty in the conservatory,' I tell her, and she briefly touches my arm.

'See you in a bit.'

I'm talking to one of Anne's colleagues when Billy Ross appears in my peripheral vision.

'Ivy,' he says, kissing my cheek.

'Billy?' If Jon hadn't told me he was coming I wouldn't have had a clue who he is.

'Am I so tired and grey that you don't recognize me?'

'No, not at all,' I say hastily, but in truth, the middle-aged, thickset, balding man bears no resemblance to the image of Billy Ross I'd tried to dredge up from my memory.

'Are you still Ivy Trent?' he asks. 'You're married now, aren't you?'

'Yes.' I glance around to see if Richard is nearby – he's pouring wine on the other side of the room. 'But I'm still Trent.'

That was the thing. We'd sat next to each other when we started school because our names followed each other in the register. There were no children with surnames that began with S.

'I was sorry to hear about your mother,' he says. 'And your family. Jon told me his news. It can't be easy for any of you.'

'No,' I reply, appreciating the fact he'd acknowledged it. Many people preferred to skirt round it. 'It's good of you to say. We're all used to living with it now but it's never easy.'

He seems nice as an adult, but I feel a little awkward, as if the years since I'd last seen him had left me with nothing to say to him. 'Is your mum still around?' I ask.

'Yes. But she's got Alzheimer's. She's in a home now and doesn't really know what's going on a lot of the time.'

'I'm sorry. That must be difficult too. But how are you? Jon said you still live locally.'

'Yes, with my wife, Sarah. I'm afraid she couldn't make it. We've got a fairly new baby.'

'Congratulations. Is it your first?' Perhaps that accounts for the tiredness.

'No, we've got an older boy, Matthew. He's nearly two.'

'How lovely. And what do you do?'

'I'm a surveyor. I work for a local firm.'

'I thought you wanted to be an astronaut.' Have I remembered that correctly?

'Didn't everyone at the time?'

'Ivy!' Jon's old school friend Simon gives me a huge bear hug. 'How the hell are you?'

'Good.'

I'm about to introduce Billy but Simon goes on, 'Sorry to barge in on your chat but I have to drag this woman away. Grub's up and I absolutely have to sit with you, Ivy, while I eat mine.'

'Simon Hopper is intensely overbearing,' I said to Cathy, the following morning, as she and I cleared away debris from the night before.

She might not have been stoned when she arrived at the party but she was the next time I saw her, standing in the garden, smoking, making no attempt to disguise it from one of the partners at Jon's firm.

'I suppose.' She seemed down now.

'Did you speak to him?'

'Briefly. I wasn't really in the mood.'

'Oh?'

'Like you say, he's a bit much.'

'I was talking to Billy Ross. I haven't seen him for years but Simon butted in.'

'Hmm.'

'Billy's a surveyor now.'

'That fits.'

'Does it?'

'He's your type.' Cathy gave a heavy sigh, as if she wasn't interested but I pursued it.

'What do you mean?'

'Well, you know.'

'No!'

'Architects, surveyors.'

The way she said it, it was a criticism, and unlike Cathy. 'But he's nothing like Richard.'

She picked up a plate from the floor and put it on the coffee-table, saying nothing.

'Do you think Richard's like him?' Richard wouldn't be pleased.

'Who is Richard like?' Richard appeared in the doorway.

'No one,' I said, adding another plate to Cathy's.

'We probably shouldn't leave it too long,' he said, 'before we get going. We need to pick up the kids.'

'I'd like to pop in on Dad on the way home.'

'As long as we don't stay too long. I've got work I need to get done before the morning.'

That was Richard's way of saying he'd had enough of my

family. He liked everyone well enough but less so if he was exposed to them for more than twenty-four hours. 'I know,' I said, inclining my head to convey that I understood and that I was grateful to him for having come. He had been tired after a difficult week at work and I understood that he wanted to spend a bit of time at home, just being there, without the pressure of having to socialize.

'Half an hour or so?' he asked, and I nodded. He headed off to the kitchen.

'He's got a lot on at work,' I said to Cathy, feeling the need to apologize on his behalf.

'But you will call in on Dad before you go back?'

'Yes, of course.' She didn't need to ask me. I saw Dad as often as I could, which was more often than she could.

'When are you going back?'

'I'm not sure. There's something I need to talk to Jon about. You too. It's hard to find the right moment.' She gestured to the empty room, as if it were still full and all the people in it were getting in the way of her talking to us.

'Cathy?' My stomach turned. 'It's not? Is it?'

'I had the test,' she said, sitting down. 'That's one of the reasons I came back.'

'Oh, God. Oh, no.' I sat down too. 'Is it? Are you?'

'No,' she said, reaching out and taking my hand. 'It's not. The test results were negative.'

'Oh, God, Cathy.' I was crying now. I think we both were. 'When did you have it? What made you?'

'I've met someone,' she said. 'There's a guy in Kenya. We're not getting married or anything. It's just, working there, with so many people dying of Aids, I wanted to know either way.'

'Oh, Cathy.'

We stood and I hugged her but I couldn't stop crying. 'I'm sorry. It's just all so . . . I don't know.' More tears.

'No. I'm sorry,' she said. 'It's been so difficult, finding the time and . . .' she looked towards the kitchen '. . . I haven't told Jon. I don't know how to tell him. It seems so . . .'

'What's going on?' Richard reappeared.

We discussed it in the car on the way home but I don't think Richard understood my reaction. I didn't really understand it myself. Of course I was relieved that Cathy had been spared the horrible slow death that our mother had suffered. Not just relieved, delighted. But Jon . . .

'It must be difficult for Jon,' Richard said.

'Yes. It seems so unfair.'

'He was very good about it.'

He had cried too, which wasn't like him, but I think it was because he was pleased for Cathy, not because he was feeling sorry for himself.

'Are you okay?' Richard rested a hand on my thigh as we headed up the motorway back to London.

'I think so,' I said.

'Is it making you wonder again about having the test yourself?'

'Not really.'

'Are you sure? Because the chance now . . .' he paused '. . . now that you know Cathy's clear . . .'

'You think the chance of my not being positive is higher?' I spat, angry with him for voicing what I was thinking. It was irrational, I knew it was, but I was allowed to be irrational because I was me. Richard had no such right. I know. That's irrational too. 'It's still the same,' I snapped. Although that wasn't what I was feeling. Cathy being clear had made me think the chance of my being positive was diminished. 'It's still the same,' I repeated.

Richard knew that.

Richard's good at maths. His career is founded on being good at maths. He knows that if there's a fifty–fifty chance of something being behind a closed door it remains a fifty–fifty chance, even if one of your siblings has opened the door and found something there and the other has opened it and found nothing.

Just because you toss a coin up ten times and it comes down heads each time, the chance of it coming down tails on the eleventh is no more likely than it was before. It's still fifty–fifty. But human psychology and statistics aren't on the same syllabus.

If Cathy had tested positive, I think I might have felt that my chance of having the disease was reduced, even though it would still be the same. Still fifty–fifty.

'I just thought you might feel differently now. About the test,' Richard said.

'No.' I said to him what I had been thinking.

'Are you sure?'

'Absolutely.'

'Okay,' he said, apologetic, and laid his hand on one of mine.

I let it rest there although I resented its presence. How dared he ask if I wanted the test? Why could he still not understand what we'd been over a million times before? I could live with the risk that I might have the gene that my brother knew he had but I didn't know if I could live with the certainty.

And there was something else, a reaction to Cathy's news that I hadn't expected. I was delighted for Cathy, delighted that she was clear, delighted that she was so relieved and happy to know for certain. But I wasn't sure I would feel the same if I was in her position. It was as if the risk of having the disease was so much a part of my identity that I didn't want to lose it. For me, the test offered two outcomes, neither of which I was ready to face. I might find out that I carried the gene and my life would begin to shrink and disappear. Or I might discover that I didn't, that the risk I had lived with all of my adult life was no longer there. And I wasn't sure I was ready for that either.

'It's your decision,' Richard put his hand back on the steering wheel, 'but if you want to talk about it, I'm always ready to listen.'

'I don't,' I said angrily. I wouldn't let him pressure me into doing something I didn't want to do.

'Okay,' he said gently.

I didn't respond.

Why, when I felt suddenly vulnerable, did I push away the person who was there for me to lean on?

Again, human psychology and logic are not on the same syllabus.

Richard and I fell into an uneasy silence and he switched on the radio.

A traffic report warned us of delays further up the M23. 'A lorry carrying hay bales has shed its load and a section of the motorway is closed while the road is cleared,' said the announcer.

'I don't know why they can't secure them a bit better,' Richard said. I didn't think he required a response so I didn't give one.

I felt as if we'd had that conversation before, which scared me because that used to happen to Mum.

A week or so later I was feeling conspicuous as a lone woman sitting in the hotel bar. But drinking alone in my room felt lonely. I was familiar with Copenhagen and could have found another bar, somewhere close to Tivoli Gardens, but

I was tired after travelling and had a long day ahead of me. And the hotel had a courtesy lounge. Drinks and food were thrown in with the room. It seemed a waste not to take advantage of it. And when I looked around almost everyone else appeared to be on their own too.

There were several configurations of armchairs set around small tables. But each configuration had a lone occupant, unless you counted mobile phones and the odd laptop as people. Most of them were sitting, drink in hand, plate of food on the table, and deeply engaged with either a computerized device or a sheaf of documents. Businessmen, taking little pleasure from a night in a hotel on expenses.

'Do you mind if I sit here?'

'Go ahead.' I wished the man who was hovering would sit anywhere else.

'There are no free tables.' He knew what I was thinking. 'But if I'm disturbing you . . .'

'No, no, no.' In my mind, a triple negative exuded a positive. 'It's fine.'

'It's fine' was something Max had begun saying when things were anything but, when I knew something was bothering him but he wouldn't tell me what it was.

'It's fine' really meant 'I'll put up with whatever it is but I'm not really happy about it.'

My fellow hotel guest put a plate of cold meat and bread on the table. 'I'm going to get some wine.' He gestured towards my nearly empty glass. 'Would you like a top-up?'

'No, thanks,' I said, although I wanted another drink.

'Are you sure?'

'Oh, well, okay then, if you don't mind. I was having the Sauvignon Blanc.' I allowed him to take my glass and watched him as he approached the bar.

'Sauvignon Blanc,' he said, when he returned.

'Thank you,' I acknowledged the small kindness and returned to my book.

He, the interloper, arranged a sheaf of documents on the table, alongside his plate of charcuterie. They were covered with drawings. He was making slight alterations and notes alongside and he caught me looking and smiled, before going back to his work, clearly not wanting engage in conversation.

But my interest had been piqued and I peered over the top of my book. A series of what looked like water jets was splashed across the paper.

Their creator caught me looking. 'Are you here on business?' he asked, removing his glasses.

'Yes.' I shrugged, acknowledging my intrusion.

He looked at me expectantly.

'I do PR for travel companies. One of my clients operates in north Zeeland. I'm here to see it for myself.'

'I haven't been outside the city but I've heard it's a lovely part of the country.'

'The home of Karen Blixen.'

'*Out of Africa* Karen Blixen?'

'Yes, but also Øresund coast Karen Blixen, where she returned to live and write.'

'*Babette's Feast* country?' he asked, and I had to admit that I'd neither seen the film nor read the book. 'You should,' he said. 'It might help with your PR and it's a wonderful story.'

'I'll try to get hold of a copy,' I said. 'What about you?'

'What about me?' He was half smiling at me, teasing.

'Are you here on business?'

'Yes.' He gave a warm, open, engaging smile. 'I am.'

'Any clues?'

'To what exactly?'

'What it is you do!'

'I design fountains.'

'Really? Is that a job?' I asked.

'Yes.' He raised an eyebrow. 'It is. At least, it's what I do for a living.'

'Sorry, I didn't mean to sound rude.'

'You didn't.'

'I don't think I've ever met a fountain designer before.'

'There are only a couple of companies in the UK and they employ just a handful of people so not many people have met one.'

'I have now.'

'Not properly.' He leaned forward and stretched his hand across the table. 'Abe,' he said, taking mine and shaking it long enough for me to note the smoothness of his touch and the clack of his wedding ring. Long enough for me to note that I was noting all of those things.

'Ivy.'

An awkward pause.

'So, I guess you've seen the Tivoli fountain?'

'It's kind of compulsory, isn't it?'

'And the bubble fountain?'

'I liked that. It's mesmerizing.' I'd sat and watched the water-filled tubes dotted around a circular pond, bubbling away on a previous trip. 'It's not one of yours, is it?' The Tivoli fountain clearly predated him but the bubble fountain looked contemporary.

'No.' He shook his head. 'It was designed by Niels Bohr in the sixties. I'm not that old!'

'I wasn't suggesting you were. I'm not very good at dating fountains.'

'Early sixties, and although I was born in 1955, I didn't work as a child.'

'Me too!'

'You weren't a child labourer?'

'No, but I meant I was born in 1955.'

'You look younger.'

'Only because you've taken your glasses off.'

He put them on again. 'No. You definitely look younger than forty-five.'

'Thank you,' I said, embarrassed now. 'The bubble fountain. Who did you say designed it?'

'Niels Bohr, a quantum physicist who worked at the university here. You've probably heard of him.'

'I saw a play about him a while ago.'

'*Copenhagen*?'

'Yes. Have you seen it?'

'No. But I've heard it's good.'

'I can't remember much about it, except that I met my husband that night.'

'Ah. So it made an impression.' A slight pause. 'You've been married long?'

'Ten years,' I say.

'Children?'

'Two, a girl and a boy, eight and six. You?'

'Just the one.'

He looked down at the table, not to be drawn, so I switched the subject back. 'I caught half a documentary about Bohr recently. Something to do with a row he had with Einstein?'

'They famously differed over the nature of reality.'

'In what way?'

'I don't fully understand it myself but Bohr claimed that what cannot be observed does not exist.'

'That doesn't seem likely.'

'That's what Einstein thought. He cited the moon as existing even when you can't see it. But Bohr believed that for very small particles it was true. They only came into being when you measured them. He challenged the nature of reality.'

I didn't fully understand so I asked him more about his work. 'What's the design you're working on now? Does it exist?'

'Not yet.' He laughed. 'But I've been measuring the dimensions, at least on paper.'

'Something to rival the Tivoli?'

'Nothing quite so grand. It's basically a clock.' He pushed his drawings in my direction. 'The middle ring represents the hours,' he indicated a circle of jets, 'and the outer ring the minutes. It will only tell the time every five minutes. Otherwise the jets will be random displays of water.'

'And what do they represent?'

'I'm trying to convey something of the randomness of life between the precise measurements of time.'

'That's interesting. I'll look out for it.'

'It's not even commissioned yet. But there's a new urban park being built on the outskirts of the city. They want to include a fountain. My company is pitching for it.'

'I hope you get it.'

'Thank you.' He pulled the papers back towards him. 'It's been lovely talking to you . . .' He looked at his watch, for a precise measurement of time.

'You too.' I smiled.

'I wondered . . .'

'Yes?'

'I mean, you probably have plans and you don't know me and, well, I don't want to make you feel uncomfortable, so I won't be offended if you say no.' He stopped.

'Say no to what?'

'I just wondered if you might want to join me for dinner, either here or maybe somewhere in town.'

'Um . . .' I hesitated. I wanted to but wasn't sure that I should.

'Unless you already have other plans or would rather not?'

'No,' I said. 'I was just going to get something to eat here.' I've never liked dining on my own, although it's a necessary part of the job, but I wasn't sure if it was wise to take up Abe's offer, although I was tempted.

'There's a place just around the corner,' he said. 'Less than a five-minute walk. They do great fish and you can always make your excuses if I bore you!'

'I'm sure you won't,' I replied.

'But I'll understand if you'd rather just stay here. You've probably got a busy day tomorrow.'

'I'd love to go to the place round the corner,' I said, reassured by the effort he was making to give me a get-out.

'I don't,' he said, as we got up to go, 'make a habit of asking strange women out for dinner every time I'm away for work.'

'Am I strange?'

'No.' He laughed again. 'The opposite, really.'

'Normal?' I was teasing him now.

'Strangely familiar. Does that sound odd?'

'No.' I'd never met him before, our paths had never crossed, yet he did seem familiar, so familiar that accepting his invitation to join him for dinner did not even begin to unnerve me. I shook my head, the way Mum used to when she experienced *déjà vu*.

'I'm sorry I'm late,' I say, scanning the restaurant for anyone I know before I allow myself to kiss Abe.

'It's so good to see you,' he says, as I take off my coat and hang it on the back of my chair, still anxious that perhaps this restaurant is a little too close to home, a little too likely to be somewhere a friend may come or someone I know from the children's school.

'Are you okay?'

'Yes. It's just been a difficult day. I had some work to finish for a client but I had to pick Max up from school early and then Richard was a little late home from work and it all felt a bit . . .'

'What?'

'You know.'

Stressful, deceitful, wrong, unnecessary were all words I could have used to describe how I'd felt when Richard came home, fed up after a day at work and having forgotten that I needed him to look after the children.

'Where are you going again?' he'd asked.

'A client meeting,' I'd lied. 'Dinner with the manager of that chain of restaurants.'

I was banking on him not being interested enough to ask too many questions.

'Oh. Okay.'

He clearly wasn't. If he had been, I might have felt worse. 'There's a bit of chicken and bacon pie in the oven for you and some potatoes. The children ate earlier and they're both ready for bed.' I couldn't be accused of neglecting anyone. 'I had to pick Max up from school early today because he said he felt sick but he seems to be fine.'

'You're too soft on that boy,' Richard said.

'What else could I do? The school called and said he was unwell. I had to stop working on the report I was writing so I'll have to finish it tomorrow now. And I may have more work for this client if the meeting goes well.'

'Okay. Enjoy your dinner.'

'I'm sorry, Ivy,' Abe says now.

'What for?'

'For making things difficult,' he says, as the waiter approaches our table and asks what we'd like to drink.

'A bottle of the Merlot.' We've already agreed on that. 'And some sparkling mineral water.'

He has the same wine preference as my husband and took a similar route into his job. Abe worked as an architectural model-maker before he moved into fountain design. Richard is an architect although these days he describes his job as 'endless office refits'.

He's bored, and am I simply bored with him? Am I a total cliché? A middle-aged woman having a mid-life crisis involving a man who is really just another version of what she already has?

'You didn't,' I say, when the waiter has gone. 'Make things difficult. It's just Richard's not exactly stressed with work but by the boredom of it. It doesn't excite him any more and he can't seem to see a way out of the rut he's in.'

'And that affects you?'

'I suppose. Kind of. I feel disloyal for saying so.'

'It's not disloyal to talk to someone,' he says, as the waiter returns and pours a little of the wine into his glass. 'That's fine.' He's quiet as our glasses are filled. 'I'd like to feel you can talk to me about anything, Ivy,' he says. 'It won't go any further. My wife always says it helps her to moan. It gets things off her chest and stops her feeling resentful.'

There was something about the way he spoke of his wife, with an easy affection but with the hint of a suggestion that they had their ups and downs.

'Sometimes I feel as if I've trapped Richard, by being married to him and having the kids, in a job that he doesn't really enjoy any more.'

'What do you think he'd rather be doing?' Abe asks.

'I don't know. When he started out he had big plans. He wanted to be the next Richard Rogers. He wanted to design ground-breaking buildings, but most of the work he does is remodelling or extending existing ones.'

'And how did meeting you lead him on to that path?'

'It didn't, really,' I say. 'I suppose the pressure of having a mortgage to pay and mouths to feed pushed him towards a steady job.'

'He wouldn't have wanted that anyway?'

'Well, yes.'

'It doesn't sound as if you need to beat yourself up over his frustrations. Everyone gets bored with their jobs now and then.'

'Do you?'

'Occasionally.'

'And do you moan about it?'

'Yes, but I'm not going to now. I've been very lucky. I landed a job I love pretty much by accident.'

He's told me this before. How he went to art school, wasn't sure what to do when he left, got the job as an architectural model-maker with a firm of architects and was thinking about training to be one himself. Then one of the partners left to set up a fountain-design business and asked Abe to go with him.

'Sometimes that's the way things happen,' I say, thinking that our meeting had been entirely serendipitous and all the more wonderful for it. 'But if I'm going to unburden myself about things at home, you're allowed to moan about your job, or whatever, too.'

My comment was intended to be light-hearted, and maybe I was trying to define parameters too. This is what it is, I was telling myself. We are two people who met by chance and got on well, and because our worlds are separate, we can talk about them more openly than we otherwise might. And in some ways this much is true but I know something else is driving our desire to meet, something far more dangerous.

'But I don't want to, Ivy,' Abe says, looking directly at me.

'I don't want to dump any of my frustrations on you. I want my company to be a source of pleasure to you.'

There is no physical exchange, only words and a look, but my body reacts as if he had leaned across the table and kissed me. My face is hot and I try to quell the restlessness I feel by reaching for my wine glass and sipping too quickly, then mumbling a heartfelt but slightly awkward 'That's nice.'

'Oh, and before I forget,' Abe is reaching for his jacket, which is hanging over the back of his chair, 'I've got something for you.' He takes out a paper bag, the kind that could double as wrapping paper if necessary, yellow with a scattering of white stars. He passes it across the table to me.

'Thank you,' I say.

It feels like a book. I open the bag and take out the slim volume inside. '*Babette's Feast*!'

'You haven't already bought a copy?'

'No. But I did mean to. This is lovely.' I look at the blurb on the back, then at Abe. 'Thank you.'

Our eyes meet and linger for a moment too long before I look away.

'So, is your son okay?' Abe asks, topping up my wine glass and letting his hand settle briefly on mine as he puts it down.

It was a deliberate gesture and from then on our conversation is accompanied by moments of physical contact.

'Yes. He seemed fine as soon as I got him home. He sometimes gets a bit panicky and I think he genuinely felt sick but it seemed to pass,' I say, letting my hand lie on the table where it had been when he touched it.

'That's good.' Abe covers it with his own for longer this time.

'I hope so. I've got a lot on at the moment and if he gets sick he'd inevitably pass it on to Lottie and I'd have one or other of them off school for weeks.'

'That's an advantage of having just one,' Abe says. 'A natural isolation unit.' He shifts in his seat so that his knee rests against mine.

We are having one conversation with words and another with our bodies.

'Did you never want to have another?' It was something I'd wanted to ask since meeting him, but the moment never seemed to arise naturally.

'To be honest, Ivy, I never really wanted children in the first place.' He removes his hand from mine and picks up his glass.

'Oh?' I'm surprised and a little disappointed.

He is so gently charming, so interesting and easy to talk to, and I find him so physically attractive that I'm already wondering what might have happened if I'd met him at another time. I'd always wanted children despite all the risks that entailed.

I move back in my chair, away from him.

'Don't get me wrong. Ruby's the best thing that ever happened and I wouldn't be without her for anything, but Lynn's pregnancy wasn't planned.'

'Ah,' I say, not wanting to overstep some boundary or pry too much into his home life.

'We hadn't been together very long and when she got pregnant I wasn't really prepared.'

I take a sip of my wine.

'But Lynn wanted to keep the baby and I was beginning to think, well, it was time for me settle down. Plenty of my friends had children. It was something I always seemed to shy away from. There was another woman I'd been seeing before I met Lynn. She wanted to settle down and have a family but it ended because I didn't feel ready to commit to that.'

'I think a lot of people feel the same. A lot of men. Women too.' Although in my experience women are often ready to think about children at an earlier age than men, I'm not ready to tell him that, for me, the decision whether or not to have children was more loaded than it is for others.

'I did love that other woman but it all seemed to move too fast for me. I seemed to be heading towards marriage and children, I got scared.'

'What happened?'

'I blew it. I told her I didn't feel ready and that effectively ended the relationship.'

'Do you still see her?'

'No.' He shakes his head. 'I'd have liked to stay friends with her. I just didn't feel ready to get married. I know I really hurt her. So I had to let her go.'

'The one who got away?'

'I suppose so. When I met Lynn and she got pregnant, I felt maybe it was what I needed. The baby, although I was terrified at the prospect, felt like something concrete, something that would stop me running away.'

Not for the first time, I feel grateful for Richard's lack of hesitancy about having kids, for the way he never let what might have been an issue become one, for giving me two wonderful children and a wonderful life, for allowing me to turn into the person I have turned into, the person sitting here in a restaurant now, the person who is attracting the man I'm sitting opposite.

I would not be that person without Richard. I'd be a shyer, less confident version of myself.

I shouldn't be here now with Abe, I think. It's not fair on Richard. But at the same time I can't help myself. I want more, even if that means hurting the people I love most in the world.

'And the other woman. The one you ran away from. Do you know what happened to her?'

'She married someone else. I hope she's happy. She's lovely. She deserves to be. You remind me a little of her.'

'Really?' I say, flattered.

'More than a little, in fact,' he says, stretching his hand across the table and putting it over mine again.

'But it all worked out in the end,' I say, turning mine so that I'm holding his hand.

'There's no point in thinking about what might have happened if she hadn't got pregnant and we hadn't stayed together,' he replies. 'Because she did and we did.' He removed his hand when the waiter returned with the starters.

'That's my philosophy for life,' I say.

'What do you mean?'

'It's probably going to sound a bit heavy but it's kind of important.' I say.

'Go on. I'm listening.'

I tell him my story, in all its complicated details. I try to finish where I started. Or where he left off. 'That's why I decided not to have the test,' I tell him. 'Because I can't change anything. What will happen will happen or, if it's not to be, it won't.'

'You're a brave woman, Ivy,' he says, as he takes my hand again and looks at me.

I return his gaze, wondering if what I've told him will put him off but I can see from the way he looks at me that it makes no difference. 'I don't know if it's brave,' I say. 'But I seem to find it easier living with the risk than to contemplate the prospect of living without it.'

I know now that unless I do something decisive – stop agreeing to meet him for lunch, or drinks or dinner, stop texting and emailing him – that what we've begun will become more dangerous, will threaten to destroy everything I hold dear and hurt the people I love.

But I lack the willpower to stop, not yet, not now that I've met him.

'Here's a funny thing,' Richard says one evening. He's sorting out his 'office'. In reality it's a corner of the sitting room where he has a desk and numerous piles of papers and boxes. He's been talking about sorting it out since the kids were born.

The sitting room has become a repository for everything pertaining to everyone, except me. I am less of a hoarder but Richard doesn't like to throw things away. Add a doll's house, various boxes of Lego, computer games and consoles, cricket sets, toy farmyards to the boxes that belong to Richard and you have a room in which sitting is only possible when you've picked your way through or over the ever-increasing mass of stuff.

'What's that?' I ask, as I try to match stray Lego pieces to models.

Max and Lottie are, for the moment, quiet in front of the television, giving us the chance to tidy up, a prerequisite for a building project Richard has proposed for our own home: an office, somewhere to close the door on the kids.

I'm happy working at a desk in an alcove in the kitchen – the huge purpose-built kitchen Richard masterminded before thinking about anything else. I don't particularly want an extension of the sitting room into the yard outside. But Richard needs to do it. He needs a project. For now, it's just sheets and sheets of paper, covered with calculations, drawings and boxes of things that need to cleared away, if a builder is ever going to be able to turn his plans into reality.

'Have a look at this,' Richard says, holding up a photo-graph.

One of the boxes is full of them. Richard has no albums but several boxes of photos, accumulated throughout his life. Most of them were taken by others. He's never been keen on taking photographs himself. 'You miss the moment,' he says. 'You only see what you see through the lens. You can't see the bigger picture.'

But he's held on to the moments other people have doled out: early Polaroids that his mother and father took of him and his siblings on family holidays, official photographers' records of key moments, like his graduation, and glossy duplicates that friends must have had made when they took their rolls of snaps to be developed.

'What is it?' I pick my way through piles of discarded images to take a look at the one in his hand.

'It's from a party,' he says. 'It must have been in the early eighties. I vaguely remember it.'

There's a group of people standing in a garden at dusk, cans of beer and joints in their hands. One of them is a youthful Richard. 'Nice hair,' I comment. It's overly spiky. 'Whose party was it?'

'I don't know. I'm not sure I even knew then,' he says. 'Someone on my course was invited and I went with him. But I do remember the place. It was at this house which backed on to the British Museum.' He pauses, as if expecting me to pick up on the significance of this, then adds, 'But look.'

Richard stands up so he's looking at the photo over my shoulder, from the same angle. I think his general excite-ment for whatever it is I'm missing must have to do with the building itself. Should I be able to see a bit of the British

Museum, one of his favourite places, over the shoulders of the group he's standing with? 'I know it's blurry,' he says, pointing, 'but look at the background.'

And then I see, behind the group, standing by the wall, a young woman on her own, a few feet away from a couple of young men, deep in conversation, unaware of the camera. She's looking up, as if she knows a photo is being taken, although she's not central to it. She has shoulder-length red hair.

'It's you, isn't it?' Richard says. 'We must have been at the same party.'

'Yes,' I say, studying the image more closely. 'It does look like me.'

'You don't remember the house?' Richard asks.

'It doesn't ring any bells. I must have been invited by someone during my temping years.'

'It's weird, isn't it?' Richard says. 'We might have met before we did. I wonder what would have happened if we had.'

'Yes.' I'm still staring at the photograph, not really listening to Richard, who is saying something about history. 'What's that?'

'"Our world, like a charnel-house, lies strewn with the detritus of dead epochs,"' Richard repeats. 'It's a Le Corbusier quote.'

'Meaning?' I look at him, although I'm still transfixed by something in the photograph.

'Well, in architecture it means that you shouldn't let the past stifle future projects,' he said. 'But I sometimes think it just encapsulates the way bits of the past keep cropping up. You know?'

'It's weird, isn't it?' I repeat his words, and Richard thinks I'm as struck as he is by the chance, by the coincidence. And

I do think it's strange. But I'm struck by something even stranger, something even less likely to happen. The two young men to the right of the redhead in the photo. Of course I didn't know him when he was younger but I'm still sure it's him. One of the men, deep in conversation, is Abe McFadden.

Not only did I almost meet my future husband several years before I actually did but I almost met the man I'm considering . . . I can't think it. The only words I could use make it sound too tawdry. The fact that he's in the photo and that I met him again, at another time in another country, make what's about to happen feel like fate.

I keep reading articles in magazines I would not normally read, looking for vicarious advice. 'You think you can keep it separate from the rest of your life,' an agony aunt writes to a reader on the brink of a putative affair.

'Do you think I can get away with it?' sums up the woman's letter.

'No,' is the short version of the long reply. The longer version includes: 'People often think they can contain an affair. Very often it starts out as sex. Both of you being married might make it appear safer.'

And then, of course, there are the buts. And the general gist of those is that 'One or other of you will inevitably start to have feelings, which will get in the way. It will no longer be just sex, or separate. But something intrusive and dangerous.'

'Don't do it,' is the advice.

It's always the advice.

Who knew we are such a moral nation? I sometimes wonder if French agony aunts, in a country we think of as having learned to accommodate extramarital activity, dish out the same advice.

'But what if it wasn't just sex in the first place?' I'm always on the lookout for the letter that asks this. 'What if you were drawn together by an overwhelming feeling that this person was the one you'd been looking for without even knowing it? And now you've found him.' I want someone to ask on my behalf. What if, in your moments of guilt and personal recrimination, that person holds you tight to him, kisses the back of your neck and whispers, 'We should be together,' with such conviction that your guilt evaporates?

What if you get used to seeing someone who gives you something extra, something that makes you so happy that you find it's worth the risk?

What if the risk begins to recede, because your other half does not appear to suspect anything?

What if the change in you, which you think is so obvious that everyone must notice it, goes completely unremarked, even by your nearest and dearest?

What if you have told yourself it's just an escape from the reality of life and it begins to feel real?

What if you've started to love him and you can't imagine not having that man in your life? You know the situation is, theoretically, impossible but it seems to be working out. No one is any the wiser, so no one is getting hurt.

Except you.

You miss him too much when you can't see him and those times seem longer and more difficult to handle. You suspect he's cooling towards you and you can't quite bear to broach the subject because you're afraid you'll fall apart if he ends the affair. You've begun to act resentfully towards him for being the person you always knew he was – someone else's husband.

'Are you around next week?' I'm toying with a plate of egg and chips in a greasy spoon around the corner from a seedy hotel where Abe and I have just spent a couple of hours.

The hotel and the café seem to reflect the change in us over the past couple of years. Yes, it's been nearly two years. At the start, we went to places that were nice. Now we opt for cheap. Cheap makes me feel cheaper but it was me who pushed to meet this afternoon so I can't complain.

Abe had suggested a drink one evening but I'd pushed to spend more time alone with him. My neediness won out. I almost wish it hadn't now. There was an atmosphere between us and we're booked into Room 101.

'Is that a sign of something?' I joked, as Abe put the key in the door.

He ignored me.

'Sometimes it feels like just sex,' he said later, as we lay in bed after an unsuccessful attempt at lovemaking. It had happened a couple of times recently, another sign that Abe's heart was no longer in it.

'Let's go and get something to eat.' He swung his legs over the side of the bed and scooped his clothes off the floor, then headed to the bathroom.

'I'm in Frankfurt next week,' Abe says now, in the café.

He'd already told me about plans for a new square in an old industrial area of the city. His firm is tendering for its centrepiece fountain. It's based on the Fibonacci sequence – the mathematical progression which shows that things that appear to be totally random in fact conform to a strict set of rules. The seed patterns of sunflowers and even the bumps of pineapples adhere to Fibonacci's rules. The jets of Abe's fountain will too. 'It starts with two single ones, then two together, three, five, eight until you reach the pools.'

'When are you back?'

'I'm going on Tuesday. I'm not back until Friday.'

'I've got a client in Frankfurt,' I say tentatively.

It's not true. I'm wondering how he will react if I hint that it may be possible for me to join him.

'Lynn's coming with me.' He looks past me with such purpose that I think he must actually be looking at something, rather than trying to avoid my eyes.

I turn my head, as far as I can, owl-like, and look at the shelf with rows of ketchup, mayonnaise, brown sauce and condiments. It gives me a moment in which to be disappointed without letting him see. 'Really?' I say. It sounds a little more accusatory than I intended.

'What do you mean?'

'Nothing.'

'Lynn's mother has offered to look after Ruby. She likes going there and it will give Lynn a bit of a break.'

'I know.' I can't keep the plaintiveness out of my voice. 'It's just . . .'

'What?'

'It seems to be getting more difficult for us to see each other.'

'We're seeing each other now,' he snaps. 'Don't spoil it.'

'I'm sorry.'

We sit in silence and I'm sure the waitress, who is squirting cleaning fluid on to the table next door so liberally it makes me sneeze, is listening to our conversation and knows exactly what's going on. She dabs it half-heartedly with a lurid green sponge and glances in our direction.

149

'I'm sorry,' I say again. 'Do you want a coffee?'

'Aren't you going to eat your meal?'

My food is mostly untouched. 'I'm not really hungry.'

'I'd better get back to work. I've got a conference call at five.'

'Okay.'

'I'll go and pay,' Abe says. He slides out of his seat and approaches the till.

Normally I'd offer to go Dutch but I let him pay because I'm angry with him.

'Which way are you going?' I ask, in the street outside.

'I'll walk to the Tube,' he says, knowing I'll head for the railway station.

'Bye then,' I say, more awkward in his company than I have ever felt before.

'Bye, Ivy,' he says, and kisses me so briefly that I want to cry.

You meet him for lunch a couple of weeks later. Just lunch. But every encounter is charged. You wish he didn't have to go back to work and you could slope off to a hotel for an hour or so. But Abe has stressed he doesn't have much time. The atmosphere is awkward. You ask how his trip was but he is unforthcoming.

Halfway through your meal, his phone rings. You've switched yours off. But he's expecting a work call.

'It's Lynn,' he mouths and gets up, moves away slightly.

You're sitting at the back of the restaurant, near the toilets. They offered you a better seat but you wanted to be hidden, out of the way.

'I'm with a client but go ahead,' you hear him lie.

And he turns away from you, hunches his shoulders, as if further to exclude you from the conversation.

You hear snatches.

'Are you okay? Is Ruby okay? Do you want me to come home?'

When he returns to the table he says he's sorry but he has to leave. Something's happened.

'What is it?' You're concerned.

'It's Lynn,' he says.

You already know this.

'Is she all right?'

'I really need to go.'

He's agitated. You let him leave. You get the bill. You wonder what's happened.

You hear nothing. Why should you? There's no reason you should. It worries you. Are you worried about him or yourself? You don't answer that. You don't want to scrutinize your feelings.

The next day, nothing. Finally he calls. 'I'm sorry about the other day,' he says. 'Lynn and Ruby were involved in an accident.'

'Oh, my God.' That seems an apposite response. 'Are they okay?'

'Yes.' Relief. 'What happened?' It sounds like something and nothing.

Lynn, or 'his wife', as you prefer to think of her, had been visiting her mother. She lives outside Guildford, an hour's drive from their London home. Ruby was with her, strapped into the child seat in the back, singing along to 'The Wheels on the Bus'.

'She said it all happened very suddenly,' he tells you. 'There was one of those lorries with hay bales and she could see it starting to sway, as if it wasn't quite secure.' He tells you the load began to topple. There was a flurry of bales.

Lynn couldn't see the road. She slowed right down but one of them struck the car and bounced on the bonnet, blocking the windscreen and causing her to swerve. She'd hit the brakes.

'Oh, my God.' Again. 'How scary. But she wasn't hurt?'

'No,' he says. 'But she was very shaken.'

'I can understand.' You try to understand.

'It was very close,' he says, and you resist the urge to say, 'But it didn't happen.'

It's not the moment to embark on your theory about the world of difference between 'almost' and 'actually'. As far as he's concerned, his wife had a brush with something much worse than a near miss.

You think it is this which has changed things.

I don't hear from him for a few days. There are no texts. No calls. I dwell on how distracted he seemed, when we last met, even before the phone call from Lynn.

I text him as nonchalant and cheery a message as I can muster: Hope everything's ok? I'm around today if you have time for a quick chat xx

He doesn't reply, nor the following day when I text him again.

Hope everything's ok at home and no repercussions? A bit worried, not having heard from you. Let me know how you are xx

I hope he'll text and ask if he can call me. I want to be reassured by the sound of his voice.

But he doesn't reply, not for a couple of hours anyway. Not until, I try again: Hi Sweetheart. I go for it this time. Guessing you're busy. Can I email you?

I always check before I do, just in case someone at work is sitting at his computer.

Eventually, he replies.

Sure x Curt and not giving anything away.

I agonize over the email I eventually send him. I'm supposed to be preparing a press release. One of my clients is about to launch a new package, cycling in Galicia. I should be putting together a list of journalists to send the press release to. I need to get that done and sent out before I pick up the kids from school, but instead I spend an hour composing and deleting, saving draft versions and hovering over the send button, then starting again.

In the end, it was short and sweetish.

Dearest Abe,

I hope everything's okay? You seemed a little distant the other day I know you've got a lot on and not so much time on your hands. I don't want to ask for anything you can't give. You know how much I like to see you, and I know it's not always possible, but if anything's up, or you're having second thoughts, then talk to me, won't you?

Hope you're not too snowed under at work and everything's ok at home.

Xxx

He replies.

Tied up in a meting. Taking the rest of the week off. Will try to get back to you before I leave the office today xA

Not what I was hoping for.

I leave work and pick up the kids.

'Mum, I have to dress up as someone for world sports

day,' Max chatters excitedly. 'But I don't know who to go as.'

'You could go as Celestine Babayaro,' I suggest. Max supports Chelsea and this is one of the names I have registered. I have no idea what he looks like. The name sounds French or Italian.

'I can't,' Max says. 'I'm allergic to facepaint!'

'Oh.' It dawns on me that the player is black. 'You don't have to take the dressing up too far, Max.'

'I could be John Terry,' he says.

'Good idea,' I reply, distracted by not having heard from Abe. I check my emails, too often, all evening.

'Is there a problem at work?' Richard asks.

'No,' I say, and begin to worry that my behaviour is making him suspicious.

I switch off my computer and don't switch it on again until the morning, when Richard's gone to work and the children are at school.

There is an email from Abe in my inbox. It was sent very late at night. He must have known I wouldn't open it until he was out of the office. There is no subject heading.

I read it, hoping for an explanation of the coolness, the way he has been behaving towards me, other than the one I fear. He doesn't even afford me the consideration of being unambiguous. He's clearly trying to end things but without actually saying so, as if he wants to make out the decision is mine, when it isn't. It's his. The email itself is a muddle of 'will always care for you', 'knew the first moment I saw you there was something special about you', 'I can never give you what you want so it is better for me to remove myself from the picture' and 'I need to spend more time at home.'

He is ending the relationship without having the guts to

say so clearly. And, as if to make himself feel better about it, he behaves as if the whole affair was something I instigated and found easy.

> I never should have allowed myself to be sucked into something that threatened to hurt the people closest to me. I have found it increasingly difficult to deal with the guilt and wonder that you find it all so easy . . .

I'm upset and furious in equal measure. How dare he brush me off in an email that doesn't even make sense, when he'd had a chance to say it all to my face? How dare he do it just before he takes time off, knowing I cannot contact him at home? How dare he make such smug assumptions about how I feel? In doing so he has revealed he has absolutely no idea how I've felt about any of it.

I break one of our cardinal rules: don't text me when I'm at home. *Sorry to disturb you but your email is ambiguous and unclear,* I tap into my phone. I press send.

I hear nothing for at least half an hour, in which I fret and pace and look at my watch, willing him to reply before I have to pick up the kids from school. Then I think about trying to pull myself together before I see them. I cannot be this agitated. I have to be normal. And I have to behave normally when Richard gets back from work.

My phone bleeps and I open the message from Abe: *I can't talk. I'm with Lynn x*

Then you should have talked to me when you were with me I reply, regardless.

I tried. He pings back.

Then, before I have time to reply, another: *I'm going to switch my phone off. If you want to reply to my email I'll check mine later.*

I don't know what to say because what can I say? I always

155

knew it would have to end one day. But not like this. Did he really care for me so little that he could end a relationship I thought was important like this?

I'd thought Abe was my soul-mate. I'd really thought there was something special between us. I'd risked my marriage to be with him because I'd believed him when he said he was glad he found me and that 'we should be together'.

I do email him but it's curt and to the point.

'I think, at the very least you owe me an explanation.'

I want this much. I feel I deserve this much, but when his reply arrives in my inbox, I feel cold with the shock of the reality of what we have been doing.

'Dear Ivy,' he replies.

I know I should have said this to your face but I found it too hard. I knew I was going to hurt you and I didn't want to hurt you. So I am taking the cowardly way out. We always knew things would have to end one day. Perhaps I allowed them to go on longer than they should but they cannot go on any longer now.

Lynn's pregnant. Not quite three months so we have not told anyone and she's been very sick so I'm taking time off to look after her and Ruby. When they were involved in that accident, I had a taste of what it might feel like if I lost them and I knew then that I couldn't keep doing something that made that a real possibility. My future is with Lynn, with my own, about to get bigger, family and that yours is with yours.

I'm sorry not to have dealt with this better.

But I must stop all contact with you now.

Love

Abe x

*

I am stunned, shocked, saddened, and sorry for myself but mostly brought up short by my own behavior, by how selfish Abe and I were being, by how close we came to destroying the lives of the people we care for.

I miss him. I miss him so much it hurts but I also begin to resent him for that and for causing the black moods to which I find myself increasingly susceptible. I've never felt depressed before. Desolate, yes. Grief-stricken, after my mother died, but not this feeling down all the time. He has done this to me.

Richard notices. He hadn't spotted anything before. 'You're probably having some sort of delayed reaction,' he says gently. 'It was bound to happen. A reaction to Jon's test result and then Cathy's. You've been so optimistic and brave but you're bound to have times when it's more difficult.'

'It's not that,' I say, because I feel so bad that he's being so nice to me. He should hate me.

'I knew you'd been finding things difficult,' Richard continues. 'I spoke to the doctor and he said it would probably hit you at some point. I didn't like to say anything because I know it's bad enough for you without having to worry about other people worrying about you.'

'Oh, God,' I say, because I can't believe his generosity of spirit.

'I'm not pressuring you to have the test,' he says.

'I didn't think you were.'

All this time I've been sloping off to another man, justifying my behaviour because I thought Richard hadn't noticed, he's been worrying about me. All this time, instead of urging me to talk, he's kept quiet, not because he didn't notice that anything was wrong but because he did and thought something else was bothering me.

What was it Abe said about Niels Bohr when we met? What cannot be observed does not exist? No doubt I'm completely misinterpreting this facet of quantum physics and applying it wrongly to my own life. But because Richard couldn't see that I was having an affair, for him it was never real. I pray that it stays that way. 'I'm so sorry, Richard,' I say.

I almost want to tell him, in the hope that he'll forgive me, but if I do, I'll only hurt him and I know what it's like to be hurt. This wasn't some casual fling with someone in the office. I had real feelings for the person involved.

'You've got nothing to be sorry for,' Richard says.

If only he knew. If he did, he wouldn't be as kind to me as he is.

'Whatever happens, I'll be here for you.' He's determined to do everything in his power to make me feel better. He does everything he can to show me that he loves me and I know he does, more than I ever did before, which makes me feel worse.

I can't let myself off that lightly.

I don't want to feel the way I do but I can't stop. I can't talk to anyone so I swim endless lengths of the local pool, hoping the repetitiveness of counting strokes and laps will take my mind off Abe. I can no longer enjoy it as I normally do. And I can't get away from the feeling that I was duped, that nothing Abe ever said was heartfelt or true.

I can't quite believe how naive I was to think that Destiny had brought us together. Now I see that all I was, all I ever was, was a bit on the side. It floors me, in a way that other blows in life never have.

Two years of my life. Two years of feelings for someone,

so intense that he was rarely out of my head, have been reduced to nothing.

I read somewhere two sentences that stay with me: 'One day it will seem as if it never happened. You will be surprised how much it never happened.'

According to Greek mythology, humans
were originally created with four arms, four legs
and a head with two faces. Fearing their power,
Zeus split them into two separate parts, condemning
them to spend their lives in search of their other
halves. And when one meets the other half, the
actual half of himself, whether he be a lover of
youth or a lover of another sort, the pair are lost in
an amazement of love and friendship and intimacy
and one will not be out of the other's sight,
as I may say, even for a moment . . .

Plato, *The Symposium*

London, 1996

It's just before eleven when I decide to phone Tessa. I know it will worry her, make her wonder who's calling at that time of night. But I hope she'll still be up, watching the news discussed on *Newsnight*, as I have been. Perhaps she's even thinking about calling us, just to make sure Abe is okay. If anyone is likely to be worried about him, it's his sister.

'Tessa, it's Ivy. I'm sorry to call so late.'

The phone rang for a long time before she answered. I was aware that I might be waking Harry and the children too.

'Is everything all right?'

'I don't know,' I say, and all the feelings I've been trying to suppress over the past months begin to crowd in on me.

The part of me that is still clinging to there being a rational explanation tries to hang on in there. The part of me that fears the worst is pushing to the forefront. But there's still another part that thinks it's not the worst, it may simply be something else, something bad, but not the worst.

'You've heard the news?' I ask.

'Not this evening,' Tessa sounds concerned now. 'Why? Has something happened?'

'Yes.'

I'd thought Tessa and Harry would have watched it or caught it on the radio. When Abe's at home in the evening, which has become increasingly infrequent, we sit and watch the news together before bed. I imagine others doing the same.

Perhaps, even if they had, it wouldn't have registered as a cause for concern. Perhaps they aren't aware that Abe's office is in Canary Wharf. I have no idea of the exact location of Jon's office, even though it's in the place I grew up. Why should Tessa be any more aware of where her brother's office is? Why should she and her husband have any idea that he takes the Docklands Light Railway from South Quay station at around seven o'clock every evening?

Perhaps they've heard about the bomb on the news but it hasn't crossed their minds to wonder if Abe is safe.

'There's been a bomb. It's the IRA.' I focus on the details rather than the thing I fear most. 'They've broken the cease-fire.' I start to gabble. 'Part of the South Quay Plaza has been destroyed and a lot of the station. There've been lots of injuries and —'

'Ivy,' Tessa interrupts. 'Is it in the Docklands?'

'Yes.' I look towards the television screen where more images of the rubble are flashing across it.

'Is Abe okay?'

'I don't know.' My words are practically inaudible.

'Ivy?' Tessa raises her voice, as if it's the line and not me.

'He's not home from work.'

'When did it happen? How long ago?'

'Just after seven. They say there was a warning beforehand and the area was evacuated but lots of people have been injured and that's usually about the time Abe gets the train home when . . .' I pause. Now is not the time to let my other concerns cloud what I am trying to tell Tessa.

'And he hasn't called?'

'No. I wasn't worried until I switched on the news. I wasn't sure if he was coming home late or not.'

'So he might be at a meeting?' Tessa is going through exactly the same thought process that I have already been through. 'Perhaps he's somewhere else and doesn't even know there's been a bomb.'

'It's possible.' I try not to acknowledge, even to myself, how distinct a possibility I fear that may be.

'Have you called his office or . . .' The alternative hangs in the air.

'There was no reply from the office but there never is, not at that time. I've tried the police and the hospitals. They say they have no record of Abe among the injured but it's still confused . . .'

'Well, that's good,' Tessa says, but I can tell she's as worried as I am.

'They're still in the midst of dealing with it all. People are still being brought in. He might not have been taken to one of the hospitals I tried . . . And perhaps he wasn't even caught up in it. Perhaps he had a meeting after work and he's oblivious to everything that's going on.'

'Wouldn't he have told you?' Tessa asks.

'He might have and I may not have taken it in.' I cover

for him, even though for the past few months Abe has been increasingly vague about his whereabouts and angry if I ask him.

I suspect the worst. Or, rather, what I have been suspecting was the worst, before this new spectre appeared.

'Are the kids okay?' Tessa asks.

'They're asleep.'

I had got Minnie off to sleep just before nine, when I sat down to watch the news.

'I wanted Daddy to read me a story,' she'd said, wide-awake and a little petulant, when I had finished reading her a second Alfie and Annie Rose story. 'Daddy does better voices.'

When he's at home, Abe throws himself into bedtime stories. He gives all the different characters in Minnie's favourite Shirley Hughes compendium different voices.

'Och, aye, let's have a look at this, then.' He gives Mr McNally a thick, guttural Scottish accent, the accent he says he had when he lived there but is much softer after the years he's spent in London.

'But I read you two stories,' I reasoned with Minnie, tired and desperate to go downstairs.

'But you sounded cross and no one in the stories is supposed to be cross.'

'I'm sorry, Mins,' I said, putting the book on the shelf.

I'm worried that Minnie is picking up on the atmosphere. She hasn't got the right words to articulate what she feels but clearly there's something. I don't think I sounded cross but I admit I was distracted when I was reading to her. I was too busy wondering where Abe was, even before I'd switched on the news, to give the story my full attention. I thought I'd read it fine. But kids are harsh critics and acute observers.

'Daddy can read to you tomorrow.' I tucked the duvet around her chin.

'Promise?'

'If he's home in time.'

'That's not a promise.'

'Well, you can't make promises that other people have to keep.' I switched off her bedside lamp. 'But I promise that I love you more than anything in the whole wide world. Now go to sleep, gorgeous.'

I hope neither of the kids wakes up. If they pick up on my anxiety they'll never go back to bed.

'Oh, Jesus! I just switched the news on,' I hear Tessa saying. 'It's a mess.'

'I know.' My voice catches.

'Shall I come up? I could drive up and be with you in an hour or so.'

Tessa lives in East Sussex, in a village not far from Hastings.

'I can't ask you do to that,' I say, although I'd like some company. 'As you said, he might be fine. He might walk through the door any minute.'

'But what will you do?' she asks.

'I'll keep calling,' I say, unable to think what else to do. 'And I'll wait up until he gets back.'

'Let me know when he does, won't you?' Tessa says, and I can hear that she's trying not to let me hear her yawning.

'Of course.'

'I was on my way to bed. But I'll wait up. Call me again, if you hear anything. Or just . . . anyway.'

'I will.'

There was a point earlier in my marriage when Abe's incessant watching of the news infuriated me. When the children were younger, and I hardly ever got to sit and watch anything myself, he still somehow managed to claim his divine right

164

to give it his undivided attention. You'd have thought he won the Gulf War single-handed, simply by sitting on the sofa, blotting out the noise made by tiny Minnie and infant Charlie and watching hours of wall-to-wall coverage.

This evening, though, the extended news is a godsend. It gives me something to do while I decide whether to phone the hospitals again or wait a little longer. I search for clues in the images of rubble and the snippets of information.

'Two people are feared dead,' the reporter is saying, and I go cold. 'They are believed to be the owners of a newsagent . . .' I relax again.

Not Abe, then, unless he was in the newsagent buying something. How is anyone to know who was where doing what minutes before that vast crater appeared in the newest part of London? But surely if he were among the dead or injured someone would have contacted me by now.

The phone rings and I have to steel myself to answer it. It's probably Tessa, I tell myself. After all, she'd said she would call. 'Hello,' I say.

'Hello.' The voice is a woman's but not Tessa's. I don't recognize it.

'Hello,' I repeat.

The onus is on whoever it is to say something.

'Is that Ivy McFadden?'

That's not a good thing to say. It's going to be bad news. I never changed my name when we married. I'd been thinking about it recently, because it feels odd not having the same name as the children but I haven't done anything about it. I'm still Ivy Trent. Only someone connected to Abe would call me that, presuming I have taken his name. Only someone who is looking after him in hospital or . . . Or worse, whichever form worse takes. I've been trying to stop myself worrying about the other, because right now it doesn't feel important. Correction. Shouldn't feel important but still does.

'Yes.' I wait for the caller to say more.

Please don't let it be bad news, I say to myself. Please don't let it be a call from a hospital. And please don't let it be another woman. Let it be someone from the hospital instead. Is that such a terrible thing to think?·

As I worry that my husband may have lost his life I still don't want mine, ours, to be disrupted by anything else.

'Who is it?' I say, because the caller has gone quiet.

'I just wondered if Abe was at home,' she says, and then I know.

I know.

All the late nights. All the avoiding of searching questions. All of the things I tried not to confront, in case it was true.

I know now.

'Who is it?' I ask again, even though I don't really want to know.

'I'm a friend of Abe's.'

I wonder if she's rehearsed what she's going to say because it all comes tumbling out.

'A colleague, really. I just saw the news and I know he works nearby and he was due to call me about a project this evening. I'm sorry to disturb you but I just wanted to check that he was okay. Is he?'

I say nothing. I can't quite believe the cheek of it. How dare she call here? How dare she validate her concern by calling me? She has no right to be worried about Abe. I'm worried about him and Tessa's worried about him. We're the people who should be worried about him. Not her.

I'm about to say some of this when I hear the keys turning in the door. 'Please don't call here ever again,' I say, surprised by the coldness in my voice.

'I'm sorry,' she begins, and I delight in her pleading tone. 'I just needed to know.'

And I shall not tell her, not now, not tonight. No doubt tomorrow Abe, who is now in the hallway, hanging up his coat, will let her know. But I'm going to have a sleepless night. She can bloody well have one too.

'I don't know who you are,' I say, lowering my voice because I don't want Abe to hear me. 'But I do know why you've called and you have no right. Goodbye.'

I hang up as Abe comes into the room, looking ashen. I'm too relieved to be angry, too upset to be relieved, too confused to know what to say. I take in this apparition of the man I used to think I knew instinctively. 'Who was that?' he asks.

'Tessa,' I lie. 'I was worried. What happened? Where have you been?'

'There was a bomb,' Abe says, and sits on the sofa at a right angle to me.

He looks stunned and a little dusty but he's not injured and he's not dead. I'm caught between relief and fury. 'I know. I've seen the news. I've been calling the police and hospitals for the past two hours. I didn't know where you were. I thought . . .' I can't say it. 'Why didn't you call me?'

'I don't know. I'm sorry.'

'Why didn't you come home?'

'I just . . . I was on my way to the train and . . .' He's clearly distressed.

'Where were you? What happened?'

'We were told to evacuate the building, but I thought it was just a hoax.'

'Go on.'

'I had a call I needed to make.'

'Who to?'

167

'It was just work,' he says, too quickly. 'And I couldn't get through but I tried a couple of times and then – I know you won't believe me but . . .'

'Try me.'

'I forgot about the warning. It was almost six and the office was quiet but it just felt as if everyone had gone home. It's often like that when I'm working late.'

'And you've been doing a lot of that recently,' I say, knowing now is not the time but unable to help myself.

'I'm sorry, Ivy.' He looks directly at me, for the first time since he came in. I can see fear in his eyes, real fear, and it scares me too.

'Tell me what happened,' I say.

'I didn't leave till just before seven. It was only when I did that I remembered the warning, because the place was deserted, and then it just suddenly . . .' Abe struggles to find the right words. 'It was like an earthquake. Everything shook and the ground opened and buildings began collapsing, and if I'd been a few moments earlier . . .' He puts his head into his hands and I move to sit next to him.

I put my arm around his shoulders and he starts to cry. 'It's okay,' I say. 'It's okay. You're okay. You were lucky.'

He sits there crying, saying nothing.

Eventually I break the silence. 'Why didn't you come home? I've been worried sick. Where have you been?'

'I told you I might be late tonight,' he says.

How can he? Not now. Not after what's happened. 'I don't want to talk about that now.' I bite back my anger. 'I want to talk about what happened this evening. I want to know where you've been and what on earth was going through your mind that you didn't think to call me and put me out of my misery. What was going on, Abe? Where did you go? What have you been doing for the past five hours?'

'Walking,' he says.

'Walking? Where?'

'I ran at first,' he says. 'When it happened, I ran. I had to get away.'

'Yes?'

'I'd been so close.' He looks at me again. 'I can't describe it, Ivy. It was like a warning. It was as if someone was trying to tell me, "You could lose it all". Life is so tenuous.'

Jesus, does he think I don't know that?

'I needed to get my head around it. I know it doesn't make sense but I just couldn't talk to you. Not just you. Not to anyone. A few people asked if I was okay. I don't know what I must have looked like. I just had to keep walking. I didn't even know where I was. I was just walking and thinking and then . . . I was here.'

'You walked all the way home?'

We live in Hither Green, a good eight miles from Canary Wharf. 'You walked all the way home?'

'Yes,' he says. 'It hurt. The realization that life is so . . . That it can be snatched away. It really hurt. I thought if I kept moving the pain would go. It was only when I turned into our street that I realized I was home.'

'And now that you're here?' I stare at him so that I'm sure he understands what I mean, even if I don't say it. 'Are you home? Are you back with me and the kids?'

He looks away. And I know that he knows that I know. He knows what I'm asking. 'I'm so sorry, Ivy,' he says. 'I just –'

'Don't,' I interrupt. 'Please don't say anything. I don't want to know, not now, maybe not ever, not after this. I just need to know that you're back. The rest we'll deal with later.'

'Yes,' he says. Tears are streaming down his face, streaking it through all the dust. 'Yes,' he repeats. 'I don't deserve you, Ivy, but I'm back.'

I start to fuss with practical details. 'You're cold and exhausted. You're probably still in shock. And you're covered with dust.'

He glances down at his clothes, as if noticing for the first time.

'I'm going to run you a bath.' I get up, go upstairs and turn the taps on. I leave them running and come down again. 'I must call Tessa,' I say. I'd forgotten.

'I thought . . .' Abe says, and stops, realizing. 'Yes.'

I make the call. It's quick. She's relieved, tearful, but she understands I cannot talk now. Neither can her little brother. 'I'll phone you again in the morning,' I say to her.

'Let's go up,' I say to Abe.

He climbs the stairs obediently, and stands, like a child, in the bathroom, while I test the temperature of the water. He undresses and climbs into the bath. I sit on the edge and soap his back. I look at the paleness of his skin and the scattering of hairs on his shoulders, at the mole, which I was worried about but has been checked. I run my soapy hands over all of these landmarks on his body, the body I know every inch of and love. I can't bear to think what I start to think as I look at him. And then my own tears start to flow silently. I'm not sure Abe notices them. He doesn't say anything but stops my hand, holds it to his shoulder.

'I'm going to bed,' I say, after a while. 'You won't be long, will you?'

'No,' he says, and even before I'm out of the door, I hear the water sloshing as he gets out of the bath.

I look in on Minnie and Charlie, sleeping, utterly oblivious to the world, and I know I'll do everything in my power to keep it that way.

Abe gets into bed next to me. He lies there still, not touching, and then he says quietly, but not so quiet I cannot hear, 'I'm so sorry. I never meant to put you through any of this.'

I don't react as I thought I might. I don't want to lie without touching. I don't want to turn my back on him or push him away. 'Hold me,' I say.

Abe turns and puts his arms around me, and the warmth of his body, the familiar smell of it, the softness of his breath against my face, I cannot lose that. Nothing is going to take that away from me. Not yet. Not now.

When we meet someone randomly, we want to believe that Fate intervened. We cannot allow that the randomness of the universe makes it quite possible that we might never have met the person we fall in love with. But does Fate intervene or are we simply destined to love someone? Anyone? No one in particular?

When I met Abe I was running away. I wanted to be on my own. Or, rather, I wanted to get accustomed to the idea that I might end up on my own. I was resistant to the idea of another relationship. My job description even forbade it.

I was getting bored of my job with Alex, even though the travel company he'd set up was flourishing, and I'd got used to the sword of Damocles that hung over my family. I felt restless and I wanted to get away. I'd been seeing someone for a couple of years. A guy called Chris. I'd met him through work. He'd designed the company's new logo. The relationship, too, had reached a point where it had plateaued and we either needed to move it up a gear or leave it. Chris was fun to be with but he didn't take anything particularly seriously, not even Mum's illness and its implications.

'It's a long way off,' he'd said, when I'd told him it could also affect me.

I suspected he wasn't planning on sticking around for that

long way off. So I applied for a job abroad, with another company, similar to the one Alex had set up. 'I could find you something somewhere else,' he'd said. 'You don't have to leave the company. Just hang on a bit and we'll find something at the start of the next season.'

'I'd love to carry on working for you, Alex, but I need a change and this job's come up.'

I told Chris and he knew that if I took it we would split up. He encouraged me. 'Even if you only do it for a year or two, you'll have a great time and you'll have something else to put on your CV. If you stay in your current job any longer you'll go mad.'

The job was as a tour guide in Morocco. If I wasn't destined to settle down and marry, and I didn't seem to be, I wanted to see some more of the world. Abe was in the fourth group I was to take into the Atlas Mountains that season. He arrived with a friend. They had just finished training as architects and were having a break before they began new jobs.

I don't know if I believe in love at first sight, but as soon as I saw him at the airport, I knew there was something more than just attraction. He felt at once both new and familiar.

'Are you Abe McFadden?' I asked, looking at the list of clients' names. I didn't need to hear his answer. I knew.

'Yes, and this is Tim Hollings.'

I ticked their names off on my list and motioned them towards the rest of the waiting group. 'We're just waiting for a couple of others to come through.'

'You didn't tell us your name,' Abe said, touching my arm.

'Ivy,' I said, distracted by the arrival of two more people. 'You must be Judith and Helen?'

I ushered them all out of the arrivals hall and into the minibus, aware that Abe McFadden was walking behind me, aware that even though he was saying something to one of the others, about this being the first time he'd travelled outside Europe, that he wasn't really giving them his full attention: it was on me.

So I wasn't surprised, after we'd loaded all of the bags into the back of the van and everyone began piling in, that Abe held back until almost all the seats had been filled and there were only two left.

'After you,' he said, before sliding into the seat next to me. 'How long have you been here, Ivy?'

It was the start of something.

We were accompanied on the trip by a small team of muleteers, who led animals laden with luggage and camping equipment. They moved ahead of the group, setting up camp for the night before we arrived there.

On the fourth night, I'd decided to wash. The camping was basic, no toilets or washing facilities. I found it easier than I might have supposed to spend a week without washing. It made the shower, when we returned to the *riad* in Marrakesh, all the more luxurious and the trip to the *hammam* to be scrubbed clean of ingrained dirt a real treat.

I enjoyed the freedom of not having to worry what I looked or smelt like. Brushing my teeth, putting on suncream and tying up my hair was all the attention I paid to myself. But Abe's presence had made me self-conscious, especially as he'd been making an effort, despite it all.

His shirts changed regularly, and when I fell into step with him, as I tried to with all of the clients over the course of the walking day, I'd never noticed anything other than a sweet, slightly musky smell that I presumed was his.

It was easier for men to take themselves away from the camp and find a bit of river in which they could strip down to the waist, but not all bothered. They tended to fall into two camps: those who, like me, embraced letting things go, and the others who, like Abe, still found a way to shave and keep up appearances. The latter group tended to be more polite, more sensitive to the locals we encountered, more keen to engage with our guides. Abe was all of those things. It did not surprise me that he found a place to wash each day. I found myself slightly embarrassed that I did not.

So I took myself off to where I knew from previous trips there was a bend in the river and a bank from which there was easy access to the shallows, far enough from the local village to avoid the embarrassment of anyone catching sight of a Western woman trying to wash. I had a towel, a cup and a small bottle of shampoo, borrowed from one of the other women. I took off my shirt and knelt on a rock by the side of the river, from which I could dunk my head and face in the freezing water to let it and the shampoo wash away some of the accumulated grime.

It's surprising, when you're not dressing up or wearing makeup, what a difference clean hair makes. By the time I'd finished, dressed and begun walking back to the camp in the late-afternoon sun, I felt as if I'd spent a day being pampered in a spa.

I encountered Abe near the fork in the river, sitting on a rock. 'Hi.'

'You look nice,' he said.

'Clean. It's amazing the difference it makes!' I wondered if he realized my wash was for his benefit.

'You never have your hair down usually.'

'It's usually too dirty.'

'Do you want to sit?' He shifted a little on his rock. 'I was watching the colour of the rocks change as the sun goes down. It's incredible.'

I perched next to him. 'I often do that. It's like one of those sound and light shows.'

'But without the sound,' Abe said. 'It's so peaceful out here. It makes me feel calm.'

'You are.' His calmness was one of the things I liked about him.

'Not always,' he said. 'I was pretty stressed before coming out. It's partly why I came. I needed to get away from . . . from things.'

'I suppose . . .' I didn't really know what to say.

'Just pressure of work and life. I've had quite a lot of decisions to make lately. It's great not having to make any here. You tell everyone what to do!'

'It's hard work. I'm really stressed having to decide what to do with you every day.'

Abe laughed. We both knew the timetable for each day was always the same and required very little decision-making. I had to worry about what should happen if someone became ill, or the group dynamics were strained, which they often were, or if someone couldn't manage all the walking. But this group was a good one. No one seemed to have brought any of their problems with them. Everyone got on with it.

'I'm sure it's not always easy,' Abe said.

'Every group throws up different things,' I said, looking at him.

'And what has this one thrown up?' he said, returning my gaze.

'I think we both know that,' I said, surprised by my directness.

'Yes,' he said, still holding my gaze as if by doing so he was making absolutely sure I understood what was being said. 'It's taken me a bit by surprise.'

'Me too,' I said. 'Like you, I came out here to get away from things.'

'And do you mind?' he asked. 'My being here?'

'No. The opposite.'

That was when he reached out and took my hand.

'You find things where you least expect to find them,' he said, before looking back at the rocks, which were now glowing purple in the dusk. 'The stars here are so bright.' He stroked my hand as he spoke. 'They make you feel so small and insignificant.'

'We are.'

'Tiny particles on a pale blue dot,' Abe said. 'Being tossed about at random.'

'Maybe not everything is totally random.' I looked at him and he kissed me.

I had a few more washes.

'You're very clean and shiny this week, Miss Ivy.' Abdul had noticed the change. 'And happy.'

'I'm always happy here.'

That was true. There was something about the landscape and the people, the locals we met, as well as Abdul and his team: they were always courteous, hard-working and smiling. Every evening, when they'd cooked and served our dinner, they would sit a little way from the fire. Initially, I encouraged them to join the rest of the party but Abdul insisted they worked for us and therefore could not. But he would himself from time to time. 'A different happy,' he said, a little too knowingly.

The terms of my contract stated that guides must not get involved with any of the clients. Group cohesion was important and a liaison would be likely to cause divisions. So I'd made absolutely sure I didn't speak to Abe more than any of the others during the day. If anything, I spoke to him less.

But on the final evening, the day before we would return to Marrakesh and the airport, I was a little less cautious. 'I can't believe we're going back tomorrow,' Abe said, as we walked during the day. He'd been with Tim but when I fell back to speak to them both, Tim marched ahead.

'This week has gone so quickly.'

'Too quickly.' Abe looked around, aware of the rest of the group.

'We'll have a bit of a feast tonight,' I told him. 'We always do on the final evening. Abdul gets a lamb from somewhere and they roast it over the fire. There's dancing afterwards.'

'Dancing? To what?'

Occasionally someone brought a radio with them but that was the only sound, apart from us, that ever punctured the peace of the surroundings. 'Pots and pans mostly.' I laughed. 'When the guys have done the washing-up they bring everything out and play it. It's surprisingly good.'

It was. The sounds they produced with whatever was to hand made instruments seem obsolete.

'I look forward to it,' he said. 'But . . .' He glanced around again, making sure the others were out of earshot. 'I guess it rules out the chance of spending even the tiniest bit of time with you.'

'The place we camp at tonight,' I told him, 'is in a kind of oasis on a riverbank. The tents tend to be more spread out. I'll pitch mine at the edge. Maybe after the party . . .'

'It's a party now?'

'It's the closest we get here.' I laughed. 'But, anyway, maybe after.'

'I could come to your tent and ask if you've got any Alka-Seltzer?'

'Not that sort of party!'

This was an Arab country: none of the guides drank and

most of the guests held back out of respect or because they didn't want to carry it with them. After the first night in Marrakesh there was nowhere to buy alcohol.

'Maybe you can just slip away when everyone else has gone to bed.'

'Wild horses.' He smiled. 'But I don't want to get you into any trouble.'

Without saying any more, I let Abe catch up with Tim and the first part of the group while I dropped back to join those at its rear.

After the lamb, the pots and pans came out and the muleteers performed a rousing rendition of a song that sounded like 'housy housy'. The group mirrored their actions as they danced on the spot around the fire. When it had died down everyone said a slightly emotional goodnight to everyone else. Even the crew stepped across their self-imposed divide, embracing the people they'd helped look after for the week, then made their way back to their tents. I crawled into my mine, left the flap open and waited.

It wasn't long before I heard footsteps, the sound of canvas being pulled aside, and Abe's face appeared, silhouetted against the dark. He crawled through the flap and sat next to me on my sleeping bag. 'Come here,' he whispered.

Afterwards, before he went back to his own tent, we whispered in the dark.

'This week,' Abe said. 'Meeting you, being here with you. I don't want to say anything to scare you.'

'Try me.'

'I know you're here and you will be for some time but I can't imagine not seeing you again. To be honest, I can't imagine . . .' He paused. 'I can't imagine not being with you.'

I didn't answer immediately because when I did I wanted to make sure I said the right thing. But I must have been silent a little too long.

'I'm freaking you out, aren't I?'

'No,' I said. 'You're not. It seems a bit ridiculous. I hardly know anything about you but you're familiar.'

'I feel the same.'

'So, can I write to you?'

'Of course.'

'And find a way to see you again?'

'I'd like that.'

'I don't want to presume.'

'You're not.'

'Because now that I've met you, I don't want to let you go.'

He kissed me again and I knew, without being able to say why, that things would be different with Abe, that if they went the way I wanted them to, I wouldn't be able to walk away from him as easily as I had from Chris.

We'd known each other less than a week but I was already affected by Abe in a way I'd not been affected by anyone before. I knew that if things didn't work out, I'd be deeply hurt, and I knew that if they did, the thing I lived with would cause him to suffer in ways I did not want him to. But he felt so absolutely right that I had to give it a go. I had to expose myself to being hurt and to the possibility that I would cause him pain too. If I didn't try I'd never know.

So we wrote. Every week.

He wrote to me and I wrote back. He told me what he was doing, about plans he was drawing up for a new office development in the East End, about how he was looking for a new housemate, as one of the girls he shared with was moving in with her boyfriend, about how he liked to put his bike on the train and head to the coast at weekends and cycle in

Kent and Sussex, about films he'd been to see and bands he'd heard play.

I told him about the new clients who arrived every couple of weeks, about how the route I'd walked with him through the High Atlas was now blocked by snow. Instead we were trekking in Jebel Siroua. I wrote of how Abdul's wife was about to have another baby, and each time we returned to Marrakesh he went home anxiously, wondering if there'd be news.

We kept up the correspondence for the next two months and then one day, when I returned to the hotel in Marrakesh after a ten-day trip in the mountains, there was a message for me. 'Your father called and you need to phone home,' the receptionist told me.

I knew him well, because we always came back to the same place. His name was Ibrahim and he was always warm, friendly and ready to share a joke. But he was serious.

'Is everything all right, Ibrahim?'

'You must phone home. You can use the telephone in the office.'

'Thanks.'

'And there's a letter for you,' he added, fishing out an air-mail envelope from a pigeonhole.

I recognized Abe's writing. I wanted to tear it open but first I had to make the call.

'Miss Ivy?' Ibrahim knocked on the door of the office and opened the door slowly.

I was sitting at the desk.

'Can I bring you some tea?'

I nodded. I was in shock. 'I have to book a flight home,' I said.

'Yes.' He seemed to know. Dad must have told him when he called.

'I will get you some tea and then we will phone the airline.'

'Thank you.'

It was all so sudden, yet the timing was good. It had happened on the day I could be reached by telephone. If it had happened ten days earlier, there'd have been no way of letting me know. That added to the guilt I felt now for not being there.

But it wasn't expected, not yet. It was too soon.

There was a flight that evening. I barely had time to get my things together or to worry about who would replace me. 'We'll sort it,' my employer said, when I phoned London to tell them.

But I had a few moments, when I'd put everything into my suitcase and while I was waiting for the taxi to the airport. I took out a postcard I'd bought from the souk a while ago. The picture was of the Koutoubia Mosque, which towered over the Jemaa el-Fnaa and the city. No other buildings in the area were permitted to be taller than palm trees. 'Allah is bigger than man,' Abdul had explained.

On the reverse I wrote,

Dear Abe, Sooner than I planned, I'm coming home. I know this is probably not the best way to tell you but I feel very alone just now. I have to tell someone. Mum died today. She'd been ill for a long time but we weren't expecting her to die. Not yet. I know this comes out of the blue but I needed to tell you. I'm flying home tonight. Ivy xxx

I didn't post it until a few days later when I was back home.

And when I saw him again it was in the midst of a period of turmoil and grief. I wasn't myself. Or perhaps I was. Perhaps grief strips away everything else, all the outward signs of control and knowing what you want, and reveals the person underneath, exposing you in a way that you don't want to be exposed, especially to someone you've only recently met.

I'd been home three days when the phone in the hall rang. I answered it because, although Jon had been fielding calls so that Dad did not have to speak to anyone, he wasn't around just then.

'Hello,' a voice that was both familiar and strange said. 'I'm really sorry to disturb you but I'm trying to get hold of Ivy Trent.'

'Abe?'

'Ivy, is that you? You sounded different. I thought maybe it was your sister.'

'No, it's me. How did you get the number?'

'I looked it up in the phone book.'

'Of course.' I wasn't thinking straight about anything.

'I'm so sorry about your mum, Ivy. I should probably have just written but I wanted to talk to you. Is this a good time?'

'As good as any.' I picked up the phone from the table and moved with it so I could sit on the bottom stair. It was no longer the cosy place it had once been to take a phone call. The stair lift was in the way and knowledge of the part the stairs had played in Mum's death. I shifted, wishing I could take the phone elsewhere. 'It's so nice to hear from you,' I said to Abe, sounding like Jon had sounded so often over the past few days.

'No, it's Jonathan,' we'd hear him saying to whoever had called after seeing the notice in the paper, assuming the mantle of eldest child, dealing with things Dad hadn't the strength to face. 'It's very good of you to call . . . We're expecting the funeral to be sometime next week . . . I'll let him know you're thinking of him.'

'It's really good to hear your voice,' Abe said. 'But I wish it was in other circumstances. Do you want to tell me what happened? You said your mum had been ill but you weren't expecting her to . . .'

'Not yet. She had a degenerative condition and we knew she wasn't going to get better. We thought she'd get a lot worse but she had a fall and hit her head. It was much sooner than any of us expected.'

'God, I'm so sorry.'

'In a way, I suppose it spared her from the worst of it. And Dad. It was going to get harder for him to look after her. At least she was still at home and . . .' It wasn't the right time to go into all the details, not on the phone. I hadn't told him anything about it yet. I'd been wanting to avoid the subject for as long as possible, until I had some idea of whether it might become an issue or not.

'Listen, Ivy,' he said. 'I know you've probably got a huge amount to do and you'll be tied up with your family and the funeral arrangements, but if you need anyone to talk to, you know I'm here. I'd like to think you could call me. Or I could come down to Sussex for an hour or so. I'd love to see you but I realize this isn't a great time.'

'I'd like to see you too. But I can't ask you to come down here and I can't leave Dad for long, not at the moment.'

'If I got the train to where you live, maybe we could go for a walk or something. Just for an hour or so. Think about it.'

I didn't need to. 'If you're sure you don't mind. When could you come?'

It was several days after the funeral when I made my first foray out of the village. Abe had been down two or three times in the intervening period. It was strange the way my family assumed he was my boyfriend and how at ease Abe seemed to be with them in the midst of all the madness. And I was grateful to him, for letting me cling to him.

On his first visit I told him all there was to know about Mum's condition and how it hung over the rest of us too. I told him it might affect me and that it seemed to scare people off.

'I'm here,' he kept saying, as if none of it mattered. But the fear was there, and I think it was probably just the sequence of events that led him to suppress it until much later, when it emerged in a way that would damage us both.

Three days after Mum's funeral I went up to London.

'Are you sure you don't mind my going?' I was worried about leaving Dad, even though Cathy was still staying and Jon lived nearby.

'It's only for a night or so, Ivy. You need to catch up with your young man.'

I was still raw with grief when I went back with Abe to his London flat and, desperate to feel someone's warm, living body next to mine, to make love as if my life depended on it. A part of me felt as if it had died with Mum. I needed someone to make me feel alive again.

Perhaps if Abe hadn't been around, I'd have found someone else to go to bed with, to ease the pain of loss and the fear of what my future might hold. But Abe was there. He didn't appear to have any qualms about entering a relationship in the midst of such intensity. I felt as if we were being fast-forwarded to a place that, had things been different, might have taken us months or years to get to.

And then we were catapulted to another place altogether.

The travel company I'd been with in Morocco had given me work in their head office and an old friend of Cathy's had offered me a room in her flat. I wasn't sure how long I wanted to stay in either but I was occupied.

One evening after work Abe took me out for dinner. He said it was six months since the day I'd gone to wash my hair by the river.

'So long? How can you remember?'

'I can't, really. But it must be about six months. I just wanted to do something nice. That felt like an excuse.'

'You don't have to find an excuse. I'm always up for doing something nice.'

'Can I say something, Ivy?' he asked, pouring us both a glass of red wine.

It always made me anxious when something about to be said needed flagging up.

'I just wanted to say you're amazing,' he said. 'I mean, I thought that anyway, when I met you, but the way you're coping now.'

'I'm just muddling through.'

'No,' he said. 'You've been really strong. You are really strong.'

'Thank you,' I said, but I was unnerved by the speech. Had he had enough? Had he been there for me when I needed him to be and now wanted to beat a retreat?

When we went back to his flat that night, I was scared of losing him for the first time since I'd been with him. I'm not sure what had alarmed me but there was something about the way he'd spoken earlier, something about the way he looked at me when he was undressing me, something about the way he stressed the 'do' when he said, 'I do love you,' as he made love to me, something about the intensity of the way we made love that night, and something about the way he seemed quieter the next day and over the next few weeks – more reserved, as if he was thinking hard, too hard.

I didn't want him to think. I wanted him to go with the

flow. But I had no idea until a few weeks later which way the flow was taking us.

'Are you all right, Ivy?' Louise, a work colleague, caught me holding on to the edge of the washbasin in the Ladies.

'Yes,' I said, looking at her reflection in the mirror. 'I suddenly felt a bit dizzy and queasy.'

'Do you want to go home?' she asked. 'You do look a bit pale.'

'No,' I said. 'I'll be fine. I just feel a bit weird. You haven't got any toothpaste, have you?'

'I've got some in my desk,' she said. 'Do you want me to get it?'

'If you don't mind.' I peered at myself in the mirror and saw someone who looked slightly different gazing back at me. 'I've had this weird metallic taste in my mouth, which I can't seem to get rid of.'

'You're not . . .' Louise hesitated.

'What?'

'You're not pregnant, are you?'

The most difficult part of my pregnancy was telling Abe about it. I believed that he loved me. I'd never been so sure that anyone did, but I knew he was afraid of that. I could see the fear written all over his face when I told him, and the way he had to steel himself to ask me what I wanted to do.

I understood the enormous range of emotions it must have triggered when I said I wanted to keep the baby. God knows what I'd have done if, at that point, he'd run away. He had every right. I could have forgiven him for that, as I would forgive him for things that hurt me later. I loved him enough not to want to screw up his life.

'I won't blame you if you don't want to be a part of it,' I

said, wondering how the hell I would find the strength to do it on my own. How could I possibly cope with a baby – or a child – especially if I started to show the symptoms my mother had shown when I was still a child?

But I also knew that asking anyone to stand by a newly pregnant newish girlfriend was a huge thing, especially when her mother had just died of a disease she might also be carrying and might pass on to their child.

I loved Abe so much for putting aside his fear, or trying to. And he really did try over the next nine months and after Minnie was born. When she was three months old, he asked me to marry him.

But Charlie, and the way he arrived, seemed to bring it all back to the fore, to magnify the risk of being part of a family with me.

Everything about Minnie was easy, from her conception and my pregnancy to her birth and early years. Abe couldn't help but be happy. She brought with her an air of possibility. She was a living, breathing embodiment of 'life goes on', arriving just over a year after Mum's death and bringing with her an unexpected legacy.

The night before she was born, Abe's father, Greg, telephoned. When I heard the phone I was expecting it to be his wife, Pam, and was all ready to tell her that, no, there was no sign of the baby yet, then mouth to Abe, 'It's your mum,' and smile, as he crept out of the room while I made excuses.

'He's just gone to buy milk'; 'He had to go into work for a couple of hours'. Anything other than 'He hasn't got anything to add to whatever he told you when you called this morning!'

When Greg rang, I'd just taken the ice tray out of the freezer and was about to fill a bowl with cubes ready to munch my way through. It was a peculiar craving, which Abe was doing his best to tolerate. 'The baby's going to be freezing when it comes out,' he'd say, but I knew he meant, 'The noise of you crunching is giving me the shivers.'

By this time Minnie was ten days overdue and Pam seemed unable to stop herself calling to ask if there was any news, although she tried to pretend otherwise. 'I'm not calling about the baby. I just wanted to ask if you've enough Baby-gros. They've got some on special offer up here,' she would say breezily, but I knew she was desperate for news so that she could book her flight down and help.

This was not her first grandchild. Alan, Abe's eldest brother, already had children but his wife's mother was nearby. Pam said she felt like the interfering mother-in-law when she offered to help. With no mother of my own, I would welcome her.

So, when I heard Greg's voice on the phone, I thought Pam had told him to call in her place: 'Oh, they must be sick of me calling. You phone them for a change.'

'Why would I ring them?'

I imagined some such exchange. 'I'm afraid we're still waiting. Not a twinge to report,' I said to him.

'I'm sorry,' Greg replied. 'You must have had enough of the waiting. And I'm sorry too, because that wasn't actually why I called.'

'Oh?'

'Just something I've been meaning to mention to Abe,' he said. 'Is he with you?'

'Yes. He's in the garden. I'll get him.'

'Your dad's on the phone,' I called to Abe, who was raking early autumn leaves. He'd taken time off work, in case the baby came, and had done just about everything he could think of around the house we'd rushed to buy.

'Is he as fed up with waiting as you are?' he asked, touching my arm briefly as he passed me to go into the house.

I didn't reply. I waited in the garden, my attention transfixed by an apple, which fell from the tree at the edge of our tiny patch of garden and rolled a short distance across the lawn. 'Not far from the tree,' I said to myself, and the thought made me smile.

I didn't know if I was having a boy or a girl. I hadn't wanted to be told. Whichever it was, it was a part of me and a part of Abe, a greater amalgamation of us than we could ever be. The baby kicked, as if aware of my thoughts, and I turned, registering Abe's presence in the doorway. 'Is all well?' I asked.

'Yes.' He smiled. 'Want a cup of tea?'

'I've got ice inside!'

Abe grimaced. 'Well, I'm going to have one. Come and talk to me while I make it.'

I went inside, curious now, and pulled a chair out from the kitchen table, wincing slightly with the effort of everything.

'You okay?' Abe asked, and I nodded, doing my best to ignore the twinge spreading across my stomach.

'What did your dad say?'

'You know my aunt Katrina?' he asked, and I nodded as I felt the baby squirm again, then another twinge, a bigger one this time.

I'd never met Katrina but Abe had talked about her a lot, his mother's older sister, who had lived near them in Scotland. She didn't have children of her own and had therefore been more involved with Abe's family than she might otherwise have been. She'd died several years ago, long before I met Abe, but he spoke of her with a fondness that made me wish I had met her.

He had his back to me now, as he put the kettle on.

'What about her?' I asked, as another twinge began to take hold.

'Apparently she left us some money.' He took a teacup off a hook and put it down next to the kettle.

'Really?' I was surprised he hadn't discovered this nearer the time of her death. Another twinge stopped me saying more.

'Yes.' Abe carried on talking, as he poured water into the cup. 'I didn't know this but apparently she left each of us ten thousand pounds, but we'd only get it after the birth of our first child.'

He turned to me now, and I shifted in my seat, trying to mask my discomfort.

'Wow, that's incredible. And you didn't know?'

'No.' He picked up the cup and sat opposite me. 'She left us all the same amount but she didn't want us to squander it when we were younger. Apparently she thought if we came into the money at the same time as a baby was born we'd use it wisely!'

He laughed, as if at the memory of her, and I smiled too, though partly to disguise a further tightening across my belly.

Abe and his siblings had always said Katrina was resolutely practical. There was a story they told about her killing a deer when she swerved while driving to avoid a hay bale in the road. The car had been badly damaged and she must have been shaken, but she'd pulled into the verge, opened the boot, somehow dragged the body of the deer into it and taken it to the local butcher: it would have been a waste just to leave it there, she'd told them.

'That's wonderful –' I abandoned my sentence to a sharp intake of breath.

'Has it started?' Abe asked, looking at me keenly.

'I think so,' I said, standing up as the contraction subsided. 'What can I do?'

'Nothing,' I said, turning and putting my hands on the table, pushing against it as hard as I could, allowing the wood to absorb some of the force that was taking over my body.

'Ivy.' Abe was at my side now, hovering, clearly unsure what to do.

I laughed in the brief lull before the next contraction.

'I can't believe it, Ivy,' Abe said. 'Our baby is on its way.'

Nine hours later Abe was sitting on a chair next to my hospital bed, holding Minnie in his arms, while the midwife checked me for tears.

'You're fine,' she said, familiar with the indignity and emotion of the occasion. 'You did really well.'

'Thank you,' I said, more grateful than I could articulate for her role in the delivery.

Abe had cried when she handed our baby to him. 'She's beautiful,' he said. 'She's perfect. She's so perfect I can't quite believe it.'

'I'll leave you together for a while now.' The midwife finished what she was doing. 'Do you want a cup of tea and some toast?'

'I suppose so.' I was oblivious to everything but the baby.

'I'll get you some.' She smiled at us and left the room.

Everything felt surreal. What I had just been through was already fading, as the presence of our daughter loomed large in the room. The pain and the effort were forgotten as soon as I saw her face.

'It's going to sound odd,' Abe said later, 'but when Minnie came out, there was a moment when the midwife picked her up, before the cord was cut, and she looked at me, and she seemed so knowing and so like Auntie Katrina, it was almost as if, just in that moment . . .'

I reached for his hand and squeezed it.

'Does that sound weird?' he asked.

'No,' I said. 'It makes sense. She looks like Mum too.'

'Of course she does,' he said, and smiled, but it didn't mask the shadow.

I shouldn't have said she looked like Mum, not then.

I could see fear on Abe's face as soon as I said it. I could see him recomposing his features, trying to be all optimism when he kissed the top of Minnie's head. 'Look at you,' he murmured to her. 'You've no idea how wonderful it is to have you here.'

Charlie's entry to the world couldn't have been more different.

He was conceived deliberately, after we'd spent months talking over whether we should have another child or not. I wanted one for myself and for Minnie, before the age gap was too wide for her to make the most of a younger sibling. Abe was hesitant, wondering if it was responsible to bring another child into the world, knowing the risk.

In the end, it was the risk that swayed him. 'I suppose it makes sense to have another, a kind of insurance policy.'

Put like that, it sounded a little grim, but Abe was happy when I got pregnant, excited in a way that I loved him for all the more – I knew how he felt, deep down.

Charlie burst upon us three weeks before he was due, shattering my belief that he, too, would be late. I'd just dropped Minnie off at nursery and Abe was due to fly to a meeting in Copenhagen later that day.

I was walking up the hill from the nursery when the first twinge came. By the time I reached the top there was another, but they were gentle and far apart. I suspected it was the start of a slow build, but when I got home, the contractions were coming more regularly, often enough for me to think that this wasn't a false alarm.

Abe was making coffee in the kitchen, his overnight bag sitting in the hall, ready for him to leave.

'I seem to be having quite regular contractions.' I paced around the kitchen, the desire to keep moving more distracting than the contractions themselves.

'Already?' He stopped what he was doing and came over to me.

'Don't touch me.' I didn't mean to snap but a huge restlessness had come over me. I had to keep pacing and didn't want to be touched.

'Sorry,' he said. 'What should I do?'

'I don't know.' I felt irritable. 'Maybe they'll stop. It's too early and they're not very strong but . . .'

'Was Minnie okay at nursery?'

'Fine.' I grabbed hold of the work surface edge, as a stronger contraction took hold. And I heard myself letting out a noise that was familiar to me, a deep primeval howl that shocked us both.

'Is it getting worse?'

I didn't reply because it happened again. The sudden intensity of what my body was doing was overwhelming. I howled again, scared.

I was unprepared. The pain was different from what I'd experienced with Minnie, more intense and less manageable. It happened again, too soon. There was no time for me to recover.

'Do you want to lean on me?' Abe asked.

I shook my head, bearing down on the work surface.

'Can you call Caroline?' I said, when it had receded. 'Let her know.'

One of my nursery-mum friends had agreed to have Minnie when I went into labour. She wouldn't be expecting a call just yet.

'Should I call the midwife?' Abe asked. 'Or is it too soon?'

'I don't know,' I gasped, in the brief lull between increasingly intense contractions.

Minnie's birth had been so easy, so textbook, that we'd planned to have this baby at home. But now that it had begun I wasn't sure I wanted to stay there.

I heard myself screaming. It was the sound of someone being tortured.

'I'm going to call her,' Abe said.

'No. I think we should go to hospital.'

'But I thought –'

'It doesn't feel right. It's too –' I had to stop again. This time my waters broke and already I felt the urge to push.

'Jesus,' Abe said, 'what do we do now?'

'Can you take my knickers off?' I was desperate to push although it worried me.

'Shoes first,' he said, bending down and trying to pick my foot up, as if I was a horse being shod.

I think I may have kicked him when the next contraction began. 'It's coming now,' I screamed.

'I need to call someone!' He was panicking when I needed him to be calm.

'An ambulance!' I was shocked by my own insistence.

This wasn't what we'd planned. This was not how I wanted it to be. The pain was like nothing I'd experienced before and I was terrified that there was a reason for it.

The ambulance operator must have heard my screams when Abe called. It arrived quickly and the paramedic confirmed my fears. The baby was breech and the wrong way round, its spine wedged against mine. 'That's why the pain is so intense.' The paramedic gave me gas and air, while his colleague examined me. 'Try not to push,' she said.

'It's coming.'

'The baby's in the wrong position,' she said. I heard the note of panic in her voice. 'I'm going to have to try to push it back inside you. You must try not to push.'

I tried but I couldn't. The urge was too strong to resist. But the pushing had no effect. This baby appeared to be going nowhere.

'The baby's stuck,' I heard the paramedic say. 'We're going to have to get them to hospital. '

'But I can't move.'

How could they possibly transfer me to hospital? They had to do something here. Now.

'You'll both be all right.'

If she was trying to sound reassuring she was failing.

'We're going to put you on a stretcher, get you into the ambulance and take you to hospital.'

Somehow they managed.

Afterwards was a blur. When I came round from the general anaesthetic, I felt sick, woozy and detached.

'Where's Abe?' I asked the doctor who was with me. 'What happened to the baby?'

'The baby's been taken to intensive care,' he told me. 'It's a boy.'

I knew I should have asked if he was all right but I was too shocked.

'Is Abe okay?'

'Yes, of course. He's with the baby. '

'Can I see him?'

'You can see the baby in a little bit,' the doctor said kindly. 'I just need to check you over.'

'Can I see Abe?' I started to cry.

I felt completely alone in the world. That I had a husband and two children didn't alleviate the feeling. I felt lonelier than I'd ever felt before. I'd brushed too close to something I wasn't ready to encounter.

When Abe came in, he looked different: exhausted and upset.

And distant. That was the worst of it.

'I thought I was going to lose you.' He sat next to my bed, blunt and to the point. 'I thought you and the baby were both going to die.'

'Is the baby okay?'

'Yes,' he said. 'But he's got a collapsed lung.'

'What?'

'It happens sometimes apparently.' He sounded utterly detached.

'It's not uncommon after a stressful birth,' the doctor reassured us. 'A needle has been inserted to let out some of the air. He should recover quickly.'

'But can he breathe?'

'Yes. We just need to monitor him. He needs to stay in intensive care.'

'When can I see him?'

'It won't be long now, I promise.'

Afterwards, in the early weeks, Abe did all the right things. He spent a lot of time with Minnie so that I could be with Charlie. He cooked and washed and nursed me, while the Caesarean scar healed. But he didn't bond with the baby.

And he seemed to be detaching himself slowly from me.

I didn't say anything. I thought it would pass.

I knew women often felt depressed after giving birth. Even if they didn't suffer full-blown postnatal depression, I knew they could have 'baby blues'. But I'd never heard of men being similarly afflicted.

A few months after Charlie's birth, it dawned on me that something was missing in the sitting room. It was my photograph of Mum holding me as a baby, framed, and usually on the mantelpiece. Dad had the same picture by his bed at home. He'd had it copied and given it to me after Minnie was born.

Abe must have moved it when he'd tidied the house.

'Have you put the picture of me and Mum somewhere?' I asked, expecting him to say, 'Oh, yes, it's on the bookcase. I'll put it back.'

But he didn't. 'I can't bear it, Ivy,' he said, turning round so fast that it startled Charlie, who was in a sling around my neck. The baby started to cry and I jiggled to try to soothe him.

'What?'

'All of this,' he said, gesturing towards me and the children. 'And the picture of your mother, looking at us all the time as if she was a part of it, which she's not. She's gone.'

'But we've got a picture of your auntie Katrina there too.' I was genuinely perplexed.

'It's not because your mother's not here. It's because of why she's not here,' he said. 'When you were in the hospital after having Charlie I really thought I might lose you both and I didn't know if I could bear it.'

'But you didn't.' I stepped towards him to try to say something reassuring.

'But I might. The chances are that I will. It's too hard sometimes.'

'But it won't just come from nowhere.' I wondered why he was saying all of this now. 'If I get ill, there'll be signs. We'll have time to get used to it. It won't be for years. There might even be a cure by then.'

We'd discussed all this before, of course, the risks and the possibilities, but it had clearly seemed more abstract for Abe than it was now.

'I wish there was a way of knowing for certain whether you carry the gene,' he said.

'Do you? Would it help?'

'Of course it would.'

'Why?'

'Because then we'd know for sure.'

'Well, there isn't,' I told him, and bent down to undo the straps of the sling Charlie was in, lifting him out and handing him to his father. I didn't tell him that, even if there was, I wasn't sure I'd want to know. I thought he wouldn't understand.

He didn't, a few years later, when Jon invited us to lunch with Dad and Cathy. Cathy was working for a health organization, helping people with Aids. She was thinking about doing VSO. There was talk of Malawi. Perhaps that was why Jon had brought us all together – soon Cathy might be out of the country.

It was a beautiful spring day and hot, too hot for the time of year. The kids were toddling around Jon's garden in T-shirts. Anne, his girlfriend, was cooking. 'Roast lamb,' she said. 'But it'll be a while yet. Do the children need anything to keep them going?'

'They're fine.'

I liked Anne. She was younger than Jon, younger than me too, so much younger that I'd been slightly suspicious of her at first, perhaps because she might not stick around for long with someone ten years her senior and with our family history. She was a legal secretary at the practice where Jon worked. 'Can I do anything?' I asked.

'You could shell the peas,' she said. 'They're in the bottom drawer of the fridge.'

I opened it and the first thing I saw was a bottle of champagne. Did they have an announcement to make? They'd been together a few years. It would make sense.

So, I was waiting, as we all sat around the table and tucked into the lamb, for someone to clear their throat and say something.

And, sure enough . . .

'It's great to have everyone here,' Jon said, as I cut some lamb into tiny pieces for Charlie. He was sitting next to me on a pile of cushions, strapped to the chair with a belt. He looked a bit precarious but seemed happy. 'And I've got something I want to tell you all,' Jon continued.

I caught Anne's eye, wanting to see her smile and colour, but she looked more worried than happy.

Jon appeared serious too. 'I went to the doctor a couple of weeks ago –'

'Oh, no.' It was Dad who interrupted him and, even though he spoke only two words, he sounded scared and upset. 'Oh, Jonathan.'

I think we all individually anticipated the worst. I could hear it in the way Dad said Jon's name, see it in the shock on Cathy's face. I went cold and something shrivelled inside me.

It had been only a matter of time before one of us began to display the symptoms that our mother had shown when I was in my early teens, to note the occasional involuntary jerk of a limb or muscle spasm and try to write it off as 'one of those things', to wonder if hormones were to blame for mood swings and uncharacteristic angry outbursts, or if it was something whose name we all knew and the terrible, unforgiving prognosis.

Had the doctor confirmed Jon's suspicions? Had he been

told that, yes, he had the disease and, no, there was still no cure, no relief even from the debilitating symptoms, nothing to look forward to but a steady decline in which he would lose control of his limbs, his bodily functions, and eventually this would kill him?

'No, Dad!' Jon's voice was urgent. 'It's not that. It was something else entirely. Nothing to worry about.'

'Oh, thank God,' Dad said.

I looked at Abe who was looking at me. He must have seen my reaction. I breathed out now, relieved, so relieved, for the time being.

'I'm sorry. I didn't meant to alarm you,' Jon continued. 'It is related. But not in a bad way. The doctor told me something and I thought you should all know. Maybe you've heard already.' He looked at Cathy and me.

I shook my head. 'I've no idea what you're talking about.'

'They've developed a test for . . . for Mum's condition,' Jon said, refusing to dignify it with its name. 'They isolated the gene last year and now they can test for it. We can have a blood test and find out one way or another if we carry it.'

There was a perceptible pause while we all took in what he had said. There was a test that would tell us if we carried the faulty gene, a test that had not been available to Mum or her father and had only very recently been developed and approved.

Nobody said anything until Dad asked, 'And will you?'

'We've been talking and I'm thinking about it,' Jon replied. 'You have to have counselling first. They won't let you have the test without understanding all the implications. But I've thought about it quite a lot and I want to know.'

Abe was looking at me expectantly, but I didn't know what to say. I busied myself helping Charlie spoon up potato and gravy.

'I'm sorry,' Jon said. 'I didn't mean to spring it on you. This probably wasn't the right way but there's something else.'

He looked at Anne and this time she smiled. 'The reason I'm thinking about it really,' he said, 'the reason I think I want to have the test is that I've asked Anne to marry me and she's said yes. Before we decide whether to have children or not, well, we think we want to know.'

'Oh, Jon, that's wonderful!' I jumped up from my seat, nudging Charlie, who ended up at a wonky angle in his makeshift high chair. 'Sorry, baby.' I propped him up again, while around me the others were moving to congratulate Jon and Anne.

'There's some champagne in the fridge,' Jon said.

We celebrated.

'That's great news, isn't it?' Abe said to me, as we were driving home.

Minnie and Charlie had both fallen asleep in the back.

'Wonderful,' I said. 'I really like Anne and she and Jon seem happy.'

'I meant about the test.' He glanced sideways at me.

'Oh. I suppose so.'

'Don't you think?'

'I'm not sure.'

'But you could find out if you've got it or not. You could know for certain, one way or the other.'

'I'm not sure I want to,' I told him.

I'd been thinking about it all day, ever since Jon had told us, and I knew that Abe would tell me I probably needed more time to think but I wasn't sure I did.

If I had the test and discovered I was free of the gene it would be wonderful, but what if I wasn't?

'Why not?' Abe asked.

'I don't know if I could live with the knowledge,' I said. 'I feel that I can live with not knowing. Maybe if I started to have symptoms I'd want to find out. But if they told me I had the gene, I don't know if I could carry on living as I do now.'

'I don't understand.'

I tried to explain that I could live with the possibility that I might carry the gene but not the certainty.

'But it would make life so much easier if we knew.'

'Or so much more difficult.'

Neither of us said anything new. We kept reiterating our different positions. We were never going to see eye to eye.

'It's different for Jon. He hasn't had children yet. He wants to know before they decide to have them.'

'And you already do and you could find out if their mother will still be around when they're older or not.'

'And what if I won't?'

'Then at least we'll know.'

'But I don't want to know,' I repeated. 'Not yet anyway.'

'It's your decision,' Abe said, although he clearly resented me making it.

'I'd never forgive my husband,' women say.

There's a multitude of things they claim they won't forgive them for: being violent towards them or their children, spending family money on drink or drugs – or themselves – losing their job and lying about it, having a sex change. Once you start imagining things you won't forgive your husband for, with a group of unforgiving women, the list is endless.

'I wouldn't forgive Tony if he spent that sort of money on a season ticket without telling me.'

'I wouldn't forgive Mark if he bought a season ticket at all.'

'I wouldn't forgive John if he didn't buy a season ticket

and get out of the house every Saturday afternoon so I can have some time to myself!'

This is the sort of conversation I have with my friends. Top of the list of unforgivable things is infidelity. I've always felt uncomfortable in that conversation. How they can be so sure? I've always hoped I'd be able to forgive Abe pretty much anything because the alternative would be losing him altogether and I've never wanted that.

Perhaps at the root of my friends' inability to forgive is a lack of love.

'Would you leave Abe if you had more money?' one asked casually, over coffee one morning. 'I mean, if you could afford to strike out on your own, would you?'

'No!'

'Don't you ever fantasize about it?' she pressed.

'No,' I said truthfully.

'God, you and Abe are so . . .' She drained her coffee, irritated.

'What?'

'I don't know. Happy.'

'Not always.' She had no idea. 'No one is happy all of the time.'

'Attached, then,' she said. 'You're so attached. You don't even fantasize about leaving him.'

'We've got a family. He'd have to do something pretty terrible.'

'Such as?' And we were back on familiar territory, but even there I couldn't agree with her.

'I'd definitely chuck Mark out if he was unfaithful.'

'Even if it meant losing everything? Your home? Your family? Your friends?'

'I'd be so furious. It would be a total breach of trust. Wouldn't you?'

'I don't know what I'd do,' I told her. 'You never really know what you'll do in a particular situation until you find yourself in it. You never know how hard you'll fight to keep hold of someone or something.'

'So you could forgive him?'

'You don't know how much you can forgive, how much pain you can put behind you until it happens to you. Nobody does.'

I can't talk to any of these women about the phone call on the evening of the bomb. I don't talk to anyone about what I now know to be true. I don't want anyone else's opinions weighing in on my marriage.

Nobody but us knows the full story, the circumstances under which we met, the things that Abe had to shoulder when he took me on. And nobody knows how much I love him or that I would rather bear almost anything than lose him.

So I don't speak to them.

I don't even want to talk to Abe about it, but after the initial shock, the numbness and relief I felt on the night of the bomb have turned to anger and upset. The overwhelming urge to lash out is not prompted by anything in particular.

We've circled each other for days without saying anything. He goes to work and comes home on time. We're both on our best behaviour. It's a scene of domestic bliss that suddenly offends me so much that I want to smash it.

It's breakfast time. I feel strangely detached, like an extra in a cereal commercial. Minnie and Charlie look more than usually fresh-faced. This is down to nits. Their heads were crawling: I forced them to shower before breakfast and made them wash their hair, then began an assault on the nits, making my way meticulously around Minnie's head and combing it so hard, it hurt. I was a little more careful with Charlie. Minnie's hair is now in two neat plaits. Charlie's is still wet, combed away from his face so that he looks Brylcreemed.

I wonder what the imaginary cereal company, paying for the imaginary ad, would think if they knew my children's wholesome look was down to an infestation of parasites.

'Do you think the owls will come into the classroom?' Minnie chats about the day ahead.

There is some sort of avian visit to their primary school. I signed the consent form, saying I had no objection to them spending time with owls. I wonder what grounds for objecting there could be.

'I want to hold one,' Minnie goes on.

I wonder what parasites live on owls and if they can spread to humans.

'I want to turn my head all the way round like owls can.' Charlie tries but can only twist his head far enough to see Abe preparing their packed lunches, just like the perfect dad you'd want in a breakfast commercial. 'Do I look like an owl, Dad?' he asks, widening his eyes.

'Did someone say something?' Abe grates cheese. 'I thought I heard a too-whit or a too-whoo.'

'Twit. Twoo.' Charlie laughs.

'Twit. Twoo,' Minnie echoes, smiling.

'Do you want tomatoes in your sandwiches, baby owls?' Abe asks.

And that is what makes me snap.

'For fuck's sake. They're not baby owls.'

Charlie's wide eyes widen further still. 'Mummy said the F-word!'

Minnie can't quite believe it.

'Right, kids, have you finished your cereal? Time to brush

your teeth!' Abe is all mock-jovial and starts chivvying them out of the room.

I start to tidy the table, to give myself something to do. I pick up a pint of milk and take it to the fridge. I'm feeling sick with the enormity of everything I've been trying to suppress these past few weeks.

I don't know how it happened – I'm not aware of it slipping or of my letting go but I've dropped the milk. The bottle smashes and the milk runs all over the floor.

'Mummy dropped the milk,' Charlie says, concerned, and then I lose it.

'Oh, for heaven's sake, Charlie! Why don't you just do as your father says and go and brush your teeth?'

Abe doesn't tell me I'm being unreasonable. 'Do as Mummy says. Go and brush your teeth.' Then: 'What's going on, Ivy?' he asks.

I can't even begin to find the words.

'What brought that on?' he asks, as the children trudge upstairs chatting animatedly.

'Mummy said the F-word!'

'We're not fucking baby owls!'

They laugh but I know my outburst has disturbed them.

'I couldn't stand the pretence any longer,' I tell Abe.

'I don't understand.'

'This.' I gesture at the room. 'Us playing perfect happy families. You and me dancing around each other, pretending that everything is fine when we both know it's not. We need to talk.'

'I know.' Abe comes over to where I'm standing and tries to put his arm around my shoulders. 'Are you okay?'

'Not now.' I shrug it off. 'I have to take the kids to school. You've got to go to work.'

'I'll take the day off.'

'Not here. I don't want the house tainted. I don't want to have the conversation we're about to have here, in our home.'

'Where, then?'

'Let's drive somewhere.'

Abe nods.

'Where shall we go?' He pulls out of the parking space.

'I just want to get away from here.'

Abe says nothing and takes a left turn at the end of the street. I stare out of the window, worn out from the pressure of trying to keep a lid on what I know. Still not really wanting to confront Abe.

The landscape of terraced houses opens out a bit. The buildings become detached, and before long we're in open countryside, driving down the A20. Abe presses down on the accelerator and manoeuvres into the fast lane. The road signs point us towards Dover. 'Shall we go to the sea?'

'Okay.' I continue to focus on the shifting landscape. He can decide where to go and what to do. That's the least he should do.

I feel exhausted – and must have fallen asleep because I wake as Abe is backing into a space carefully, even though the car park is empty.

'Greatstone,' he says, almost triumphantly, as if he created the beach himself.

'Really?' It's a favourite beach of ours. Only an hour's drive from London, with a huge sweep of golden sand backed by a long chain of dunes. The kids love it. We love it, Abe and I. In the summer after we met, when I was newly pregnant with Minnie, we used to drive there in the evenings after work, getting there just in time to swim before the sun went down. Then we'd find a pub, eat sandwiches and chips and go home drunk on fresh air, seawater – and each other.

Once, in late September, we got stuck in traffic and arrived after dark. The sea felt too cold to swim, but we paddled and spread a rug out in the dunes and made love. It was dark and late and we were hidden by the landscape.

And there's a picture of Minnie jumping from the top of a dune on to the sand below. The angle the photograph was taken from makes it look as if she's jumping from the most enormous height although it was only a few feet.

'We never came here last summer,' I say.

Abe was always too busy. The children would have loved to come and I could have driven them myself after school. But it was an outing for the family, not just the kids and me.

'We'll go this summer,' Abe says. 'I'll come back from work early and we'll go after school.'

Two months earlier, this suggestion would have been full of promise. But now . . .

Now that we're here I feel a quiet sense of dread. Abe is opening the door. 'Ivy,' he says. He's out of the car and has opened the passenger door. He's coaxing me out as if I'm an elderly lady. I allow myself to be helped. I allow Abe to take my hand and lead me across the car park on to the beach. It's late March and the cut of the sea air hits us as we walk. Despite myself, I move closer to Abe for body warmth, and he puts his arm around me.

'We must look like lovers,' I say, imagining how we would appear to others, although the beach is deserted.

'I do love you,' Abe says. 'I always have and I always will.'

'Then why?' I demand, shaking free of his arm as I turn to look at him. 'Why are you doing this to me?'

'I didn't mean to hurt you,' he says.

'Is she someone from work?' I ask, for the first time since I found out.

I know it sounds odd for a couple who live together to

spend six weeks dancing around a subject that others would fall upon the moment it's reared its head. But I needed time. I didn't want it to destroy us. I don't want it to destroy us now. I am the one who could let it. I know that. But we may have to deal with more important things than an affair. I know that, too. If we can't deal with this, will we be able to get through worse, if it happens? That's why I have to get through this.

'Sort of,' Abe says. 'I met her through work. She's associated with one of the clients but I don't work with her. I don't have to see her again. I haven't, not since . . . And I won't.'

'I can't bear to know the details,' I say, and all the cool detachment I have somehow managed to muster for the past weeks evaporates. I'm crying.

'Let's sit down somewhere.' Abe is trying to usher me towards the dunes but I don't want him to touch me.

I stride ahead, almost running, and when I reach the dunes I keep walking, winding along the path that leads through them, ahead of Abe but I can hear him behind me.

'Ivy,' he calls, and I stop. 'Let's sit down.'

A little way from the path, there is a sheltered bowl, created by the lie of the dunes; the spring sunshine is beating down on it. It looks inviting. I nod.

Abe waits as I turn, then walks in front of me, takes off his jacket and lays it on the ground. He sits and pats the space next to him. I sit.

'Will you promise me it's over?'

'Oh, God, Ivy, you know I will. It was over even before it started. I never loved –'

'Don't.' I'm scared he's going to say her name and I don't want to know it. I don't even want him to say 'her'. That's an acknowledgement too far.

'I don't know what to say. You want to talk but you won't let me say anything.'

'Why did you let it happen?' I ask him. 'That's all I want to know. I don't want to know who or where. But I need to know why. Was it because it was easy, because you could, because you thought I wouldn't find out? Or did you want me to?'

'No – God, no, never. If I could have the time back, if I could spare you any of this . . .'

'Were you thinking of leaving me?'

'Not for a moment. The complete opposite.'

'How can the complete opposite of leaving me be having an affair with another woman?' I'm shouting now there's no one to hear. 'A part of you left me,' I say, saddened by the veracity of my words. 'A part of you left me years ago.'

He says nothing.

'When did it begin?' I ask.

'Nine months ago. But I only saw her a few times. I mean, I saw her more but we only . . .'

'Don't.' I'm trying to protect myself from details.

'I'm sorry,' he says. 'But I have to try to explain, Ivy. It had nothing to do with you.'

'Thanks.'

'No. I mean, it had everything to do with you but not in a negative way, not in a way that reflects badly on you or the way you are. You're a wonderful woman and I love you more than I could ever love anyone. I couldn't even begin to be me if I hadn't met you. You mean everything to me.'

'Then why?'

'Because of that, really. Because of the way I am. Because I'm scared of losing you. I always have been. Practically from the moment when I met you at the airport, I was scared I was going to lose you. Even before I knew there would be an us, I was scared of losing you, and then, when there was an us, and I knew that I could lose you, I was even more scared.

Sometimes I'm so frightened of what the future might hold I can't bear it. I can't bear to feel what I feel for you. I was trying to run away from that feeling because it gets too much for me.'

Sometimes I think Abe's life has been too easy. It was all happy families, when he was growing up: four siblings, big houses with sprawling gardens, foreign holidays and camping trips. He had his mother's depression to cope with but he managed to reach his forties without losing anyone close to him – even his beloved tortoise, Fred, was still alive. His aunt Katrina was the first person he'd loved who'd died. He was scared of losing me because he didn't know that when you were robbed of the people you cared for, you could carry on.

'I'm scared too, Abe!' I'm still shouting at him, but my words are carried away by the wind so I don't sound as angry and upset as I feel. 'Think what it's like for me having to live with the knowing and the not knowing – knowing the children may have to live with it too. I was scared of loving you in case you couldn't take it. I was terrified of falling in love with you in case you couldn't carry on. But I let myself love you and I've continued to, even though these past few years you've been holding back from me. That hurt. I was already hurting before this. I'm hurting even more now.'

'I'm so sorry,' he repeats. 'And it feels disingenuous to make excuses but please listen to me.'

'Go on.'

'I know it's not an excuse, not a reason, but it's the only explanation I can really give for behaving in a way that is inexplicable, even to me. I keep asking myself the same questions you are asking me now. Why did you do something that meant you risked losing the one person you love more than anyone in the world? And I do love you, more than anyone, more than the kids even. I'd be devastated if anything happened to you. I suppose I was trying to protect myself against the possibility of that hurt.'

'But that's what loving someone is,' I say. 'That's what really loving someone means.'

'I don't understand.'

'You open yourself up. You make yourself vulnerable to knowing that they will cause you hurt and pain, and that the more you love them the worse it will be. Do you think I don't feel the same? Don't you think everyone does? Everyone's afraid of loving another person because they know that with the love comes loss, sorrow, pain, all of that – that's part of it. Can't you see it?'

'Maybe. I don't know. Perhaps other people are better at dealing with it than I am. It felt so right when I met you. You felt so familiar. I felt as if I was meant to be with you and I let myself go with it.'

'I was the same.'

'And for a while everything was perfect. You, me, the children, but at the same time, having it all, it just meant there was more to lose.'

'I know,' I say.

'I thought you were going to die when you were in labour with Charlie and I couldn't bear it. I really didn't know how I would cope if anything happened to you.'

'But it didn't.'

'But the fear is still there, all the time. The only way I could deal with it was to distance myself from you.'

'And that helped?'

'No.' He shook his head sadly. 'I was lonely. And that was when . . . I know you don't want to hear and I know what I did was inexcusable and if I could do anything to turn the clock back I would.'

'In another life,' I say.

'But there is no other life. All I can do now is tell you how sorry I am and make promises you may not believe.'

'If you were lonely,' I say, 'you could have come to me. I love you, Abe. I always have, even now, even though I don't really want to. I still do. Why would you want to throw that away?'

'I didn't. I don't. Jesus, Ivy, I may not be explaining myself very well but the last thing I wanted – the last thing I want is to lose you.'

'But you did something that made it a possibility,' I say.

'The possibility was already there,' he replies. Then he asks the question. 'Are you okay, Ivy? Not with this, obviously. I mean are you okay?'

'Yes,' I say. 'I'm fine. It's not that. It's not what you've been thinking, if that's what you've been thinking. If I'm going to get ill, it's still only a possibility, and if I'm going to die of it, that's a really distant possibility. But what you've done . . . that makes losing me a distinct and real possibility, much more than some far-off thing that may never happen.'

'Please don't say that.'

'I'm trying not to. I don't want to. But it hurts. It hurts so much.' I start to cry and Abe puts his arm around me. I let him.

'When the bomb went off. It was so close. It was like when you were having Charlie again but opposite. If I'd been a few minutes later, I could have lost you all. I knew then that it had to stop, that I couldn't risk it happening. By the time I got home that night, I knew I was going to put a stop to it. But you already knew. I could see it as soon as I walked in. I've been trying to kid myself that maybe that wasn't it, that maybe you were worried about your health, but deep down, I knew you knew.'

'Did you? How?'

'Because I know you. I always have,' he says. 'You're a part of me, and if I lose you I won't even be myself.'

There are a million more things to say and there is nothing more to say.

I put out my hand and lay it on his thigh. It's quiet here but the quiet is punctuated by the sound of gulls, a strange squawking.

I turn my head as far as I can, like Charlie did at breakfast, and I spot them, a pair of mating gulls on the dune above our heads. They stop squawking when I look in their direction, then the female stares straight at me and dips her beak before they carry on, a flurry of ruffled feathers and sounds of contentment.

I look back at Abe and he laughs. 'Can I kiss you?' he asks, and I realize that is what I want more than anything.

I nod and his lips meet mine, tentative at first, but then it becomes more urgent. Our tongues explore each other's mouth, tentatively, then with more confidence. We know how to do this. We know how to kiss, and we know how to touch each other, how to move our hands and explore each other's body. I can feel Abe's hand tugging the T-shirt that is tucked into the top of my jeans, so he can feel the skin underneath, and then it's moving to the waistband and under, and only momentarily do I think, We can't. Not here. Not on the beach.

But there's no one around. We've not even seen a solitary dog-walker, and if we do? They can walk on past. We need this, Abe and I.

I stop his hand and glance around as I undo my jeans and pull them down to my ankles. Abe does the same and I feel him inside me, where he belongs. We are one person: one person with four arms and four legs and two heads who will, when this is over, remain together for a little while before moving apart, becoming two again. Two individuals or two halves who must be together.

'Thank you,' Abe says, rolling away from me, pulling up my pants and covering himself. 'We should probably get back. Or the kids will be wondering where we are.'

I do up my jeans and we stand up.

Abe kisses me again. Then we walk back along the beach. I shiver.

'Are you cold?' he asks.

'Not really,' I tell him. 'I just had an enormous sense of *déjà vu*.'

For the next few weeks we carried on as if we were okay, as if we were going to be okay. Abe was trying. Really trying. He was solicitous towards me at home. He made sure he let me know if he was going to be late back from work and exactly where he would be. He told me if he had meetings scheduled, in case I tried to contact him during the day.

I tried too. I really tried. To trust him. To forget.

But I felt as if I was acting, playing a part in my own life. I went through the motions. I ate breakfast and dinner with Abe; I watched television with him in the evenings. We discussed the children and our days. And we made love. But it was always there, the knowledge, sharper now for my having acknowledged it. He'd let me down, broken the trust between us. I wasn't sure I'd ever be able to trust him fully again. And that was eating into me, however hard I tried not to let it.

In the end, it was a tiny thing, which, had everything been fine, would have gone unnoticed that triggered my reaction.

It was a Saturday morning, just over three weeks since we'd driven to the beach. Abe had come home early from work the preceding evening, had picked up a takeaway and a bottle of wine on the way 'so you won't have to think about cooking' and a couple of videos: *Toy Story* for the children to watch and *Apollo 13* for us.

We had a pleasant evening. Minnie was so proud of herself for liking 'spicy food' and, while Charlie ate mostly plain rice, he was appreciative of the occasion. 'It feels a bit like Christmas,' he said, running his fingers along the edge of the foil containers as Abe unpacked a carrier bag filled with rogan josh and chicken tikka.

Minnie was asleep by the time *Toy Story* had finished, and Abe had to carry her up to bed, while Charlie congratulated himself on still being awake and not needing help getting ready for bed. 'I don't have to let Mummy undress me. I can do it by myself.' But he, too, was asleep when I'd finished easing Minnie out of her skirt and tucking her into bed.

'Another drink?' Abe asked, patting the seat on the sofa next to him, when I went back downstairs.

Apollo 13 was ready to play. He'd brought the bottle in and set two glasses on the coffee table.

It was a good choice of film, for a couple still negotiating their way through the hurt caused by infidelity. It put the smallness of us and everything we do into perspective. What were our troubles compared to the possibility of being permanently stuck in space? And the alcohol took the edge off what I still felt so that I could curl up on the sofa with Abe and later, when we'd gone to bed, let his hands start the familiar exploration that signalled he wanted to make love, enough for me to respond to the prompts that were a part of our marriage and try not to allow thoughts of what he might have done with 'her' to obliterate the familiar sensations he knew how to arouse and produce.

I slept quickly afterwards, and slept in the next morning. It was nearly nine when I woke and Abe was already downstairs making the children breakfast.

'I was going to bring you a coffee,' he said, smiling at me when I went down to the kitchen.

I don't know what it was about the way he said it, or the accompanying smile or just the normality of the scene that greeted me and the near normality of the night before, but all I could think, when I looked Abe, was that I didn't know him. I didn't really know him at all. Here he was, acting the part of the perfect husband and father, carrying on as if nothing had happened and, yes, he was trying, but he had no idea how hard it was for me.

'I don't want a coffee,' I said, with an edge to my voice that made Minnie look up from her breakfast. 'And do you have to let the kids put so much milk on their cereal? We'll run out and they don't even finish it.'

'We'll get more,' Abe said, eyeing me warily.

'That's not the point,' I snapped.

'I know,' he replied, resigned to the fact that our reconciliation was not a full one: whatever he did, however hard he tried, he was going to have to do more, try harder.

And I knew that, while I wanted to forgive him, was trying to forgive him, I still wasn't sure if I ever would, not fully.

'Ivy,' he said, when the kids had finished and gone upstairs to get dressed, 'I'm trying as hard as I can.'

There was a plaintive note in his voice that infuriated me, as if he expected me to feel sorry for him, as if I was the one at fault for not being able to wipe my mind of the knowledge and the thoughts that went with it. 'Jesus Christ, you're so fucking . . .'

'What?' he asked.

'Selfish,' was the best I could come up with.

'And you're never going to let me forget it, are you?'

An old school friend invited us to his wedding. I'd been to primary school with Billy Ross and kept in touch, mostly because he still lived in the same village, and until she died my mother had kept up with his. He was marrying someone who'd also been in our class, someone I vaguely remember him being soft on when they were five or six. I hadn't known they still knew each other but Dad, who was still in touch with the Rosses, filled me in.

'Apparently Beth's family moved up north when she was nine or ten,' he told me. 'Then she turned up working for the same company as Billy. They're both surveyors.'

'It's rather sweet when you think about it.' I showed Abe the invitation.

'Do you want to go?' He read it. 'It says no children.'

'We could ask Kirsty to look after them?' I suggested, unsure about a wedding but at the same time wanting an excuse to revisit a period of my life that had been more secure and safe than it had become not long after.

'I'll call her later,' he said. 'I'm sure she will if she's not busy.'

Abe's sister Kirsty lived in London. She was usually happy to babysit. She said she loved spending time with her niece and nephew.

'And if it's a problem,' Abe added, 'you could always go on your own and I could look after the kids.'

'No,' I said. 'If I go, I want you to be there too.'

'Good,' Abe said, looking at me as if he understood this was important. 'I want that too.'

*

It was strange being in the church we'd gone to as children, Jon, Cathy and I, with more faces from my childhood than there had been at my own wedding.

'Ivy, you look well,' people said to me, as we arrived at the church. Some, lowering their voices, said, 'I'm so sorry about your mother.' Then, brighter again, 'Is this your husband?'

'Abe,' he kept saying, putting out his hand to people from my past.

I don't know that I'd have recognized Beth if I'd seen her anywhere other than there. I had a vague memory of a small, chubby girl with pigtails, but she was tall, slim and beautiful in an ivory wedding dress – and happy.

Billy's face lit up when he turned to watch her coming down the aisle and taking up her position at his side for the ceremony.

I couldn't help thinking back to our own wedding, seven years previously, as we stood up to sing a hymn, remembering how happy I had been then to have found Abe, to be marrying him, to be knowing that I would go through my life with this wonderful, kind, sympathetic man.

If I'd known then . . . I thought.

But instead of trying to push the thought away, as I did whenever the worst of them surfaced, I let it run its course. If I'd known then what I knew now, would I have married him? I found myself thinking and believing, really believing, for the first time since the night of the bomb, that, yes, I probably would, despite everything we'd been though, despite what we were still going through, I would still have married him.

I glanced sideways at Abe, at his profile, took in the look of concentration as he studied the order of service and the slight shadow on his cheek that always began to appear by early afternoon, even when he had shaved in the morning.

And I marvelled that looking at him still stirred me in a way that no one else had or did.

Billy and Beth were saying their vows now. 'To have and to hold,' they repeated in turn after the vicar, 'from this day forward . . .'

'For better, for worse,' said the vicar, as Abe took my hand and clasped it gently but firmly.

'For better, for worse,' Beth was saying, and I squeezed my husband's hand in return.

For small creatures such as we the vastness is
bearable only through love.

Carl Sagan, *Contact*

London, 1987

I tried the doorbell a few times but no one answered. So I sat on the hay bale that was placed incongruously against the wall of the house and took my book out of my bag, happy to read as I waited. I glanced every now and then towards the phone box on the corner, thinking, if no one turned up soon, I would try the number I'd called earlier.

The hay seemed to absorb the sun, and after a while I put my book down and undid my hair, which was knotted in a loose bun, and let it cover my neck, which I worried might start to burn.

'Comfy?' a man walking a dog on the other side of the street called. I shrugged and smiled.

The exchange was never going to be more than that, never long enough to explain what I was doing there or tell the dog-walker that I, too, had wondered at the presence of the bale, propped against the wall of a terraced house in east London. Walthamstow was at the end of the Tube line but not so far out that you expected elements of the countryside to encroach.

'I'm sorry. I'm so sorry.' A man on a bicycle was cycling towards me. He looked to be in his early thirties, around the same age as me.

'You must be Ivy,' he said, as he stopped alongside and dismounted. 'I'm sorry I'm late. I got tied up with work. Have you been here long?'

'Only about five minutes.' I stood up so he could prop his bicycle against my makeshift seat while he rooted about in a backpack, looking for keys.

'They're in here somewhere,' he said, pushing a tuft of thick, unruly hair off his forehead.

He was dressed in the kind of smart-casual way that was becoming more common: a pair of navy trousers and a grey cotton shirt, unbuttoned at the neck. I guessed he might be a teacher, or a journalist, or maybe a doctor.

'I should have been back an hour ago,' he said, putting his bag on the ground and bending down to release his trouser leg from a bicycle clip. He opened the bag a little further. 'Ah, here they are!'

'Where do you work?'

'Only about a mile away,' he said, unlocking the door and gesturing for me to go into the house.

He pushed the bike in after me, leaving it in the hallway and showing me through to the kitchen, which was small but had been designed to maximize the space. The kitchen units were arranged along one wall and French windows opened out into a small courtyard.

I noted the piled-up crockery and wine glasses on the open shelving, and on a higher shelf an arrangement of tiny model buildings that might have been made with Lego but in black and white bricks. 'Work.' He saw me looking as he opened the French windows.

'What do you do?'

'Architectural model-making,' he said, stepping out into the courtyard, which was bursting with fuchsias, geraniums and busy lizzies. 'For a local firm. Here's the bike.'

It was propped up against the only bit of free wall.

'You've picked up a bit of hay,' he said, as I went ahead of him to look at it.

'What?'

'On your top.' He nodded to the long, loose shirt I was wearing over cropped trousers, ready to cycle back if I liked the bike. It was printed with a red and grey geometric pattern.

'Oh,' I said, slightly put out that he'd noticed.

I brushed myself down as he moved the bike away from the wall and stood it for me in the middle of the courtyard.

'Have you had many other enquiries?'

'A couple, I think,' he said. 'It was Lucy, my girlfriend, you spoke to. It's her bike.'

I'd picked up a copy of *Loot* at lunchtime and called from my desk about the three that seemed suitable. I hated travelling to work by Underground and thought cycling would make me feel less deskbound, if I topped and tailed each day with a ride in the open air.

'I've given it the once-over and everything seems to work,' the man was saying. 'Do you want take it out and have a ride?'

'Yes, please.' I watched as he lifted it over the back step into the kitchen and wheeled it through to the hall.

'Can you hold it for a sec,' he said, 'while I move mine out of the way?'

He pushed his into the sitting room. It was a tiny house, two up, two down, not really big enough for one bike in the hallway, let alone two.

It would give them a bit more space if I bought it.

'Thanks.' He smiled, took it from me and carried Lucy's bike out into the street where he held it for me as I mounted, as if I was a child learning to ride. 'There's six gears,' he said, touching my hand, which was now resting on the handlebars, as he indicated the dial. The brief contact didn't seem to bother him, because a moment later he put his hand on my arm, as I was about to cycle off. 'I'll wait here,' he said.

There was nothing flirtatious or forward about the gesture, he just appeared to be tactile. And charming, I thought, as I pedalled around the block, changing gear and shifting ahead in my thoughts too. It's a shame he has a girlfriend.

When I got back to the house a heavily pregnant blonde woman was talking to him in the street. 'How did you get on?' she asked.

'Yes, I like it.'

'Ivy, this is Lucy.' The man introduced her.

'Abe's probably shown you everything there is to see,' she said, smiling and touching her stomach as she spoke, as if to reassure the baby that was pushing out the fabric of her dress. 'Do you want to ride it any further or do you want to come in?'

'I'm happy with it. I'll take it if you'll let me have it,' I said, delving in my bag for the money I'd already got from the cashpoint. 'Oh, that's great,' Lucy said. 'I wanted it to go to somebody nice. Would you like a cup of tea or anything while you're here?'

'I'd love a glass of water, if that's okay?'

'Of course, come on. Abe, will you put the bike inside while I get Ivy a drink?'

'It's not the roomiest of houses,' Lucy said, putting her bag on a chair in the kitchen and fetching me a glass from the shelf below the miniature houses. 'Getting rid of the bike will give us a bit more space. And I can't ride it now.' She patted her stomach, this time inviting me to comment.

'When's it due?'

'Six weeks,' she said. 'You'd think it was any day now, judging by the size of me, wouldn't you?'

'You're not that big,' Abe came into the kitchen and grinned at her, running his hand along her shoulders briefly as he stood next to her. 'My bike's going to have to go out the back now so we can get a pram in the hallway.'

'Honestly, Abe. I'm sure Ivy doesn't want to know all this.' Lucy gazed at him adoringly as she spoke, and I drained my glass, thinking I should be gone.

'What's with the hay bale?' I asked, as Lucy opened the front door and I wheeled my new bike past her.

'Oh, Abe saw it in the middle of the road when we were driving back from my parents' house. It must've fallen off one of those lorries. He was worried it might cause an accident if we left it. I did tell him he could have moved it to the side.'

'Well, it gives people somewhere to sit while they're waiting.' Abe followed the two of us out into the street. 'And read,' he added. 'You left your book.'

'Oh, how stupid of me.' I must have put it down when he arrived and forgotten about it.

'*Babette's Feast*,' he said, as he handed it to me. 'Any good?'

'I'm enjoying it.' I put it into my bag and thanked them both, as I got ready to ride off in the direction of Tottenham Hale.

'Good luck with the bike,' Lucy said.

'Good luck with the baby.'

They stood outside the door, waving to me, the way my parents used to wave off guests. Abe had his arm around Lucy and she was leaning back against him, allowing him to take some of her weight.

I thought about them as I cycled across London. There was something about them. I felt slightly jealous – not of either of them, just of the way they were together. They seemed so right for each other.

The multiverse, she said, was like an old library
whose shelves were packed with books arranged by a
cataloguing system that ranked them according to
similarity, each book containing within its covers a
story that varied only slightly from the stories of its
immediate neighbours, but by increasing degrees
from those of increasingly distant books.

Paul McAuley, *Evening's Empires*

London, 1983

'And where exactly is that?' I asked, when he called me at the
office and suggested a picnic after work.

It was June: the days were long and, for the past few days
anyway, seasonably warm.

'You know the Ready Money fountain,' Abe had replied,
as if I would, as if everybody did. I suspected that most
people had probably walked past as many times as I had
without realizing what it was called or why.

One of the things I loved about Abe was that his outlook
on the world was different from mine. He knew things and
absorbed details that seemed to pass me by. I loved living in
London but for me it was about forging my career and meeting people. The details of the city, which I would have read
about if they were in another country and stopped to photograph if I was there, I allowed to escape me. But Abe drew
my attention to them. 'Those bollards are made from

Napoleonic cannons,' he'd say, as we strolled along the South Bank. 'That raised kerbstone was Wellington's mounting block,' if we were wandering along Pall Mall, and 'This is where they used to watch cock fights,' as we climbed the steps in a small passageway near St James's Park. We would often meet after work and stroll around the city together, stopping off at a pub for a drink or a restaurant for a bite to eat.

Today Abe had suggested meeting in Regent's Park for a picnic 'by the Ready Money fountain'. He'd had to explain that this was the drinking fountain in the middle of the Broad Walk, and I circled it, as I waited for him, admiring its granite spire and marble columns and reading the plaque in one of the arches above the water spouts. It had been donated by Sir Cowasjee Jehangir, 'a wealthy Parsee industrialist from Bombay who donated it to The Regent's Park in 1869 as a thank you for the protection that he and fellow Parsees received from British rule in India'. No mention anywhere of Ready Money.

'You found it!' Abe came up from behind and kissed me.

'Who knew this was a gift from Sir Cowasjee Jehangir?' I said, putting my arm around his waist, beneath the bulk of the rucksack that I imagined was filled with food. 'And why is it called the Ready Money fountain?'

'It was Sir Cowasjee's nickname. I guess he always had it and was generous with it,' Abe said. 'Are you going to have a drink while we're here or shall we find somewhere else for this?' He held up a carrier bag and I could see the foil-covered top of a champagne bottle poking out of it.

'You got the job?' He'd been for an interview earlier in the week. 'I thought they weren't going to let you know until after the weekend.'

'Let's find somewhere to sit first,' he said, smiling in a way that told me he'd got the job but that I'd have to wait for the details.

We walked through the park to the boating lake and Abe laid out his jacket on the bank beneath an alder. The park was busy with people trying to capture a bit of the weather after work, and young families packing up after a day out. There were several pedalos and rowing-boats crisscrossing their way across the lake, disturbing the ducks and swans that lived there.

'It's not Cordon Bleu,' Abe said, unpacking bread, cheese, cold meat and tomatoes from his bag, along with a couple of plates and plastic cups. He took the bottle from the carrier bag.

'Go on, then.' I was all eager anticipation. 'Tell me the good news.'

'Well,' he said deliberately, 'I got the job.'

'I knew it!' I threw my arms around him and hugged him. 'I knew you'd get it. That's so brilliant. I'm so happy for you.'

He'd applied for a job as a model-maker with a good firm of architects.

'Thank you,' he said, allowing the smile he'd tried to contain earlier to spread across his face. 'I'm really pleased.' He popped the cork and filled the plastic cups.

'To you,' I said, attempting to chink but foiled by the plastic.

'It feels as if everything's falling into place,' Abe said, sipping his drink. 'No more temping, no more job applications for a while. It's nice to be able to feel a bit more settled.'

'It's wonderful,' I said.

Since graduating from art school, he'd had a series of temporary jobs, ranging from paint-mixing, van-driving and office admin to wrapping-paper and greeting-card design. At the same time he'd been looking for something more permanent, without being sure what he wanted to do.

When he'd seen this job advertised, it had appealed to him

but it wasn't until he'd applied for it that he decided he really wanted it. He'd liked the people he'd met on the day of his interview, the projects they'd shown him and the opportunities it offered someone like him, with an interest in buildings and an eye for design but no architecture degree.

'I'm so pleased for you.'

We sat, sipping our champagne and discussing the new job. After a while, Abe asked if I wanted to eat. 'I've got a knife,' he said, delving into his bag again. 'It's in my pencil box.' He carried with him a small wooden cigar box filled with charcoal pencils and in idle moments he would bring them out and sketch something he saw. He handed it to me. 'I'll unwrap the cheese,' he said, picking up a wedge of Brie and watching me strangely as I opened the cigar box.

The knife was not immediately apparent. In fact the box appeared to be entirely empty. But when I shook it something rattled.

'Open it further,' he said, and I slid the box away from its lid to reveal a gold ring, set with sapphires and diamonds, five stones in all.

I wasn't sure as I looked at it, frozen with a mixture of emotions, until Abe started gabbling: 'As I said, I feel settled now. Everything seems to be falling into place – being with you, getting the job, and I wondered . . .'

'Yes?'

'If you'd consider marrying me.'

'Yes.' I didn't need to consider it. 'Yes, I will.'

'Really?' He looked as if he didn't quite believe me.

'Really, absolutely. There's nothing I'd rather do.'

'The ring might not fit,' he said, gabbling again. 'It was my grandmother's and she left it to Auntie Katrina and she gave it me when I was twenty-one for just this purpose. But if you don't like it . . .'

'I love it,' I said, slipping it on my ring finger. 'And it fits perfectly.'

'Oh, Ivy,' he said, a little tearful, leaning forward to kiss me.

Three weeks after I'd met him, I woke up in the narrow single bed in Abe's room. It wasn't really conducive to sleeping but we weren't doing much of that. I opened my eyes and looked through the gap in the curtains. I could just make out the façade of the British Museum. Abe lived in a large shared house which backed on to the building, with a clutch of people doing jobs that all seemed interesting.

One of his housemates had invited me to a party there, Chris, who'd designed the logo for the fledgling travel company I worked for. After a couple of years' teaching English abroad, I'd wanted to come home. Mum's condition hadn't got any worse but I knew she wasn't going to be around for ever. I wanted to be in the country so that I could visit her and Dad, see more of Jon and Cathy, when Cathy was around, to acknowledge that maybe my restless period was over and I wanted something a bit more settled.

I signed up with a temping agency in London and had only spent a couple of weeks with them when I saw the job advertised: assistant to the managing director of Voyager Travel. I imagined a huge organization but it was just the two of us, Alex and me, in a tiny office in Hammersmith. Alex had been running guided tours in four different European countries from his bedroom for the past two years. The office, the assistant and the newly designed logo all amounted to expansion.

'We're having a party at the weekend,' Chris had said casually, as we signed off on an image of the earth unravelling, as if it were an orange that had been peeled. 'You two are welcome to come.'

I wondered if he thought we were a couple and hadn't realized Alex was gay.

Alex thought he was interested in me. 'You should go. You'll never meet anyone stuck here with me all day.'

'Maybe I'm not looking to meet anyone.'

'Ivy, everyone wants to meet someone. Do me a favour. Go to the party.'

If I hadn't gone, I'd never have met Abe.

'This is such a lovely place to live,' I said, pulling the curtains open a little more. My own shared flat in Stoke Newington paled in comparison.

'Well, you can stay here now.'

We'd known each other just a few weeks but it felt longer. There seemed to be a tacit acceptance that our relationship had the potential to go somewhere but I wasn't going to voice that for fear of spoiling things.

'Coffee?' Abe didn't need to get up but I had to go to work. He went downstairs, returning a few minutes later with two mugs. He put them on the bedside table. 'Shove up.'

In his absence, I'd allowed myself to take up most of the tiny bed. Now I squashed myself against the wall, watching Abe as he took off his dressing gown and climbed in beside me. 'Come here.'

I moved into his arms.

We lay there for a moment, knowing it wouldn't last or turn into anything else.

'I'd better have my coffee now.' I broke the quiet. 'Or I'll be late for work.'

Abe removed his arms and half sat, propping up the pillows and passing me a coffee. 'What are you up to today?' he asked.

'Flights to book, visas to sort, phone calls to make. I really should get up.'

He took my cup, put it on the table next to his, then held my face and kissed me. 'Go on. Get up!'

'Let me past then.' I nudged him.

He twisted round throwing his legs over the edge of the bed and ran his hand across my buttocks as I stood up.

'Can I wear your dressing gown to the bathroom?'

'You don't have to keep asking, Ivy,' he said, as I put it on.

'Thanks.' I glanced at my watch and headed for the door.

'Just a sec,' Abe said.

'What?'

'Come here.'

'Really, I have to get dressed.' I smiled.

'I just want to tell you something,' he said. 'It'll only take a few seconds.'

'So tell me.' I stood opposite him as he sat on the bed, and he slipped his hand under the dressing gown. 'That's not helpful.'

'I just wanted to say I'm so glad I met you.'

He pulled me a little closer and kissed my breast. 'Now go and get your sodding shower!'

The particular Marquis of Granby pub we'd arranged to meet in was just around the corner from the National Portrait Gallery.

'There are quite a few of them,' Abe had told me. 'He was an eighteenth-century general who gave his officers money to set up pubs when they retired. Lots named them after him.'

'How do you know that?' The bits of information Abe fed me were like gifts. I glanced at the picture of the marquis on the board outside. I'd never have suspected he was a military philanthropist.

'I'm so sorry I'm late,' I said. Abe was sitting at a table in the corner. 'I got held up at work. Have you been waiting long?'

'Only this long.' He held three fingers to the edge of his pint, indicating how much he had drunk.

'How long is that?' I tried to remember who used to measure cake in minutes.

'It doesn't matter because I was happy with my pint, knowing that at some point you would walk through the door.' He stood up and kissed me. 'What would you like to drink?'

'A glass of white wine, please.'

'I'll be back,' he said, touching my cheek before going to the bar.

'So, how was your day?' he asked, when he came back, bearing drinks.

'Very good.'

'Very?'

'It was, actually. Alex, my boss, has asked me to work on a new tour in India.'

'And what does that entail?'

'Lots of extra work. Lots of phone calls. Lots of meetings. Lots of trying to get through to people in places where it's hard to reach anyone. More responsibility for no extra money!' I grinned and took a sip of my drink.

'And the very good thing "actually"?' Abe asked.

'It's my tour. If I do all the planning and organizing from start to finish, it'll look good on my CV and it'll be interesting to research and plan and . . .' I paused for dramatic effect – and to tease Abe.

'Oh, is that the time?' He looked as his watch, mocking me. 'Go on, then. What is it?'

'I get to go there, probably in the autumn, to check out the transport links and hotels and all of that.'

'Wow!' he said. Was he a little put out? 'That does sound exciting. How long for?'

'Only a couple of weeks,' I said. 'But if it works well and

the tour attracts customers, there will be other trips.' Maybe you could come on one, I wanted to say, but didn't dare, not just yet.

'Which part of India?'

'Rajasthan,' I told him. 'Alex wants to set up a two-week tour, taking in Delhi and the Taj Mahal, then Jaipur and Jodhpur and Udaipur.'

'That's a lot of purs,' Abe said.

'They're amazing places,' I said. 'I've been looking them all up this afternoon. I'm really excited about it.'

'And a little nervous?' he asked.

'Not really. Why? Do you think I should be?'

'Travelling on your own to a country you don't know, with a job to do? I would be.'

'It's what I want to do,' I said, wondering if he was anxious for me or simply that I'd be away too much. 'It's the reason I took this job. I'm sure I'll start worrying nearer the time but at the moment I can't quite believe I'm being paid to do things I want to do anyway.'

'I love your spirit of adventure, Ivy,' he said, smiling at me.

'Well, you only live –' I changed tack: 'You're only young once.'

'I guess so,' he said. 'Well, that's great. I'm really pleased for you. It sounds as if Alex has a lot of faith in you.'

'He's a good boss,' I said. 'And it's a small company so I get opportunities I wouldn't if I worked for a bigger one.'

'And where does Chris fit into it?' he'd asked.

I'd introduced them briefly at the party where we'd met.

'He's freelance. He does design stuff.'

'And were you looking to meet a penniless art student when you came to that party with him, or did he think you'd go home with him afterwards?' he asked, turning the conversation into one that you keep having in the early days of a

234

new relationship, when you go over and over things, holding on to the initial meeting and wondering at it.

'I wasn't looking to meet anyone. I only went because my boss told me I ought to.'

'So you were keeping Chris sweet?'

'Something like that.'

I still couldn't quite believe this was happening and that it felt so right. 'Were you going to kick me out for gatecrashing when you asked who'd invited me?'

'No. I was hoping you'd gatecrashed and that Chris hadn't invited you because if he had I didn't think I stood a chance.'

'Really?' I wanted more. I had to know that he'd felt the same as I had when I first saw him.

'No, not really,' he said. 'I thought you'd just strayed in off the street and needed redirecting to the British Museum.'

I slapped his thigh lightly.

He caught my hand and held it there. 'You know why I came over and talked to you?'

'There must have been far more interesting people you wanted to talk to.'

'I saw you and thought you looked nice but maybe a little dull. Who knew? I took a gamble!'

I laughed. 'I'm not going to ask if it paid off.'

'Seriously, Ivy, I saw you and thought you looked like a lovely person, and as soon as we started chatting, I knew you were. But I thought it might be a bit less straightforward than it seems.'

'What do you mean?' Had he guessed that I was holding something back? Every conversation we'd had during the past few weeks had been one in which we'd got to know each other a little better. We'd talked about our backgrounds, our families and friends, and filled each other in on what we'd been doing all that time before we met. But I hadn't told him about Mum.

This was the first time, since I'd found out, that I'd been with someone whom it felt important to tell. But when was the right time? He needed to know only if the relationship was going somewhere. If I told him, would it scare him off? I didn't want to risk that, not yet. But I didn't want to hold back and be accused of deceiving him later either. It lay, awkwardly unrevealed, between us.

'To be honest, I thought you'd probably already be with someone. I wasn't sure how old you were. You could have been married with kids for all I knew,' Abe said now.

'I don't look that old, surely.' I was partly relieved that he'd been on entirely the wrong track, but at the same time wishing he'd been on the right one. Abe's only a few months older than I am.

'You can be married at sixteen in this country,' he said. 'You don't have to wait until you're in your fifties.'

'Well, I'm not.'

'Never have been?'

'No.' I grinned and took a sip of the not particularly nice wine I was drinking. 'Well, only briefly at sixteen, but it didn't last.'

'I knew it.' He put his arm round me and pulled me to him. 'I knew someone would have snapped you up as soon as possible. What went wrong?'

'Oh, you know. We were too young. It was never going to last. He was a psychopath. That kind of thing.'

'I've got psychopathic tendencies too. Is it a problem?'

'I've noticed. I'm still trying to decide if it's going to be an issue or not.'

We laughed.

'But I imagine there's been someone who was important to you. Was it the psychopath who made you a child bride before he tried to kill you?'

'No,' I said. 'There was someone before him.'

Abe spluttered into his beer and laughed but I was half serious and wanted him to be serious now too. 'Go on,' he said, and appeared to be concentrating on his beer, not looking at me.

I had the chance to give him one of the covert sidelong glances I liked giving him when he didn't know I was looking at him so that I could take in the contours of his face and the thickness of his hair, remind myself what he looked like and marvel that he was there, with me.

And I wondered, although I knew I was making a giant leap of faith by doing so, if, when we were in our fifties and Abe was driving somewhere and I was sitting in the passenger seat, I would still snatch sidelong glances and marvel that he was with me.

I hoped so. But I didn't dare hope too much.

Sometimes I didn't dare hope that I'd reach my fifties.

'Well, there was a boy at primary school I was very fond of.' I thought back to what seemed like another life.

'I had a girl like that. I was very shy and so was she.'

'I was shy at school too.'

'I can't imagine that. You seem so self-assured.'

'Do I? Thank you.'

I didn't feel self-assured except when I was with Abe, when I felt I could be the me I'd like to be.

'What happened to her? The sweet shy girl?'

'I've no idea. We moved away. What about Primary School Boy? What happened to him?'

'I don't know either.'

'And after him?'

Abe was probing and I was enjoying it. It's part of the dance you do when you first meet someone: the wanting to know about their previous relationships and the slight sense

237

of triumph that they went wrong, because you're hoping that the new one you're embarking on now will be the one in which everything turns out right.

'Oh, you know,' I said. 'There was someone in the sixth form and a guy I met when I was travelling whom I went out with for a while, but when the time came we went our separate ways happily enough.'

'Not your soul-mate?' Abe asked.

'No.'

'And since then?' He looked at me intently.

'A few people, nothing that's lasted very long.' I stopped because I almost said 'until'. 'It's all fairly unexciting,' I finished, although, of course, there were moments when it had seemed the opposite: having sex properly, for the first time with Nathan, a brief affair with a Greek waiter, a two-week tempestuous fling with a cycle courier when I first moved to London. There were moments of my love life that had been exciting, but in a different way from how I felt now.

I didn't know what it was about Abe but it already felt as if it might last. Perhaps you always think that at the start of a new relationship.

But, as I said, I didn't dare to hope.

'What about you?' I asked him.

'There was someone I was with in the sixth form I really liked.' He paused. 'But then, well, by the time I got to art school I was that much older than everyone else.'

He'd told me before that he'd intended to go to uni, had been planning to read architecture but had changed his mind and worked for a few years before deciding to go to art school. 'There was stuff going on at home,' he told me now. 'With my parents. It kind of stalled me.'

'Was that when they split up?' I knew his parents didn't live together. He'd told me before that they were both in

Oxfordshire but his mum had moved out of the family home. I hadn't probed further at the time. But I'd wondered how old he'd been when they'd separated and how it had affected him. I hadn't asked yet because I feared it would lead to him asking about my parents and I hadn't been ready for that.

Maybe now was the time.

'Yes. I suppose so. Kind of. They're not exactly . . .'

'What?'

'Well, they don't live together any more but they're not divorced or anything.'

'So they're separated?'

'It's not as simple as that. It's all a bit weird. It was really strange at the time and I still find it odd, especially telling other people.'

'You'd better tell me.' I picked up my glass and slugged my wine.

'Ivy,' he said, 'it's nothing bad. Well, it was. It was hard for all of us and it's difficult for Dad but it's not the sort of bad that will affect you and me.'

'Sorry.' I put the glass down again and held his hand.

'It's the sort of thing that if I was a different person I'd probably have told you at the party. It would be my party story. But it does upset me and I just wanted to get to know you better first. You'll probably think I'm just being daft but it's not the kind of thing I'd have told you if we were just going to be a flash in the pan.'

I said nothing but I held his hand a little tighter, thanking him silently for that.

'Do you want another drink?' He looked at my glass, which was nearly empty, while he had still drunk only five fingers.

I shook my head.

'When I was doing my A levels,' he began, 'we lived in

Oxford and Mum had an admin job just outside, at a hospital in Thame. More of a rehabilitation centre, really.'

'Go on.'

'She used to drive there every day. She only worked a few hours. It wasn't great money but she'd been at home with all of us for years. She liked the people and she enjoyed getting out.'

'Yes.'

'There was an accident one day, on the road, when she was coming home. There was this lorry carrying a load of hay bales. Mum always used to have a thing about them. She thought they never looked safe so she'd always slow down and keep her distance.'

'And something happened?' Had his mother been injured in an accident? Was she in a hospital or a home somewhere now?

'Yes, but not to Mum.'

'Oh, okay.'

'Not directly anyway.' He took a sip of beer. 'The thing is, the bales started to fall off the lorry and there was a girl riding her bike on the side of the road. The car behind the lorry, which was just in front of Mum, swerved to avoid the bale and it went straight into the girl on the bike.'

'Jesus.' I could imagine the scene.

'Mum stopped. Everyone stopped. The driver of the car in front was really shaken, obviously. He hadn't meant to hit the girl. He'd just swerved instinctively because there was a bale falling towards him. But the girl was pretty badly injured.'

'And your mum saw it all?'

'The girl had hit her head and she was barely conscious. Someone went to call an ambulance. The driver of the car that hit her was in shock, the lorry driver too. Mum ended up sitting with the girl, talking to her, while they waited for the ambulance.'

'And was she okay?'

'No, that was the thing. She died before it arrived. She died in my mother's arms, there on the roadside.'

'Oh, God. That must have been terrible.'

'I can't imagine it, but to watch a young girl dying like that by the roadside when she had five children of her own . . . It really affected her.'

'In what way?' Clearly this was leading somewhere.

'At first she was just shocked and upset. She wanted to go to the funeral but the girl's parents wanted to keep it small. There was a lot in the local papers at the time.'

'Did she meet them?'

'No. She asked the police if she could but they didn't want to talk to her. Maybe it was too hard for them, knowing someone else was with their daughter when she died. I can kind of understand them not wanting to meet Mum.'

'But it might have helped her.'

'We'll never know. Afterwards, Mum couldn't get it out of her mind. She had nightmares and she stopped driving so she had to give up her job. She ended up staying at home and becoming very withdrawn.'

'That must have been difficult.'

'It was. I was the only one living at home at the time. Jackie and Alan had left and Kirsty'd just started nursing. Tessa still came back in the holidays – she'd just started her teacher training – but really it was just Mum and Dad and me, and Mum appeared to opt out.'

That sounded familiar. 'Did she see anyone?'

'Just the doctor, who suggested counselling, and I think she went once or twice but it didn't seem to make a difference, and then . . .' He paused. 'This is the weird bit.'

'She found God?'

'Yes. She'd gone to church before, not all the time but at Christmas, Easter, maybe some Sundays, but then she started going more and she seemed happier. It clearly helped until . . .'

'What?'

'She decided to go and live at this convent.'

'She became a nun?' I was more shocked by that idea than by Abe's description of the accident.

'She couldn't because she was married. At first she just went to stay on some kind of retreat, but she was happy there. She wanted to stay. She works in the office now and helps with the running of the place.'

'So she's there for ever?'

'Kind of indefinitely.'

'And do you see her?'

'She's allowed visitors on Sundays. I see her when I can and Dad goes once a month, but the rest of the time, no. It's a closed order and, although she's not a nun, she lives by the rules.'

'But she's your mother.'

'I did feel abandoned. Dad too. I guess at first we both thought she'd come home but she's been there nearly ten years. It doesn't seem very likely that she'll ever leave.'

'God, that must be really hard.' I thought about my own mother and how she'd changed. People said it was her condition, not her reaction to it, that made her depressed and unpredictable. And I thought about the risk factors that flew around in my head, which I ignored as best I could. I knew I should tell Abe: he deserved to know that things were not straightforward at home for me either. But he looked so drained, having just told me what he had. The time didn't seem right.

'I'm sorry,' he said. 'I still find it hard to talk about.'

'I'm glad you've told me now.'

'Can we go for a walk or something?' he asked.

We'd both finished our drinks.

'Yes.' I picked up my coat and put it on as we went to the pub's door.

Outside, Abe put his arm around me, and mine circled his waist, squeezing him to me as hard as I could. We wandered in no particular direction, ending up in Bloomsbury Square.

'Shall we sit for a bit?' Abe asked.

We sat side by side, our legs touching, no longer talking. It was a beautiful night and the stars were clearly visible.

'Look at the sky,' I said, breaking the silence. 'So many stars.'

'And we are all stardust.'

'Is that a song lyric?'

'No. It's science!'

'Are we?'

'Every atom of your body came from a star that exploded. We start out as particles floating around the universe and we end up back out there.'

'That's a lovely sentiment. It's a more positive way of thinking about death.' I wanted to tell him about Mum. I had to explain soon. But I couldn't quite bring myself to start, not just then.

Later, when we were back at his house and had made love, I wasn't sure if he thought I'd fallen asleep and wouldn't hear him when he said quietly, 'I love you, Ivy.'

It was my idea to go to Hampstead Heath. I wanted to have good memories of the day, in case, when I told Abe, things started to unravel.

I'd only recently discovered the swimming ponds and,

since the weather promised to be warm, I'd suggested we take a picnic.

'You really love swimming don't you?' he'd said.

'Well, yes. '

I tried to swim once or twice a week and sometimes I'd met Abe afterwards or left him early in the morning to swim before work.

'You always seem to be happiest when you're heading towards a swim,' he said. 'Even when it's in a duck pond in the middle of a city.'

'We don't have to go if you don't want to.'

'I'd like to. It's a lovely idea. I'm not much of a swimmer but I'll try not to show you up.'

'I'm not planning on doing laps around the ducks or anything! I just wanted to have a day out with you. We could go somewhere else if you prefer?'

'Nope. I want to do laps around the duck pond!'

I'd bought a proper picnic: taramasalata, olives, cold chicken and ham. I'd packed beers too. The weather obliged. The pond was surprisingly empty for a sunny London day and Abe was less appalled at the prospect of swimming in a duck pond than I feared.

'It actually looks quite tempting.'

'Just imagine you're in the middle of the Swiss mountains.'

He screwed up his eyes. 'Not quite getting it. Maybe the Sussex countryside. Can we go for that?'

'If it helps you enjoy yourself.'

'I am,' he said. 'I almost can't wait to dive in.'

We lay on the bank for a bit, warming ourselves before we took to the water. It wasn't cold and the ducks kept their distance and we messed about with other bathers, jumping from the jetty, seeing how far we could make it out into the water. I felt like a kid. I felt happy, sun-kissed and energized.

After we'd had lunch, sated by food and a bit light-headed from the beers, I stretched out on my towel, next to Abe, who turned on to his side and looked at me. 'Are you happy?'

'Yes. I feel like I'm swimming in warm water.'

'As good as it gets.' He laughed and I tried to hold on to the moment a while longer.

It felt like having to tell someone you'd done something terrible, something you didn't want to tell them in case they despised you and could never forgive you, in case being honest with them, knowing that if you weren't you might lose them, might be the very thing that caused you to lose them.

'So good that I don't want to spoil it,' I said.

'Why do you say that?' He eyed me quizzically.

'The other day, when you told me about your mum, there was something I needed to tell you too, about myself . . . about my mother.'

'I thought so. Whatever it is, tell me. You can tell me anything.'

'I'm scared it will change things.'

'It won't.'

'It might,' I said. 'That's why I've been trying to find the right moment.'

'Go on.' He was stroking the side of my stomach as we lay on the grass facing each other.

'My mum's not well.' I took a deep breath. 'She's got Huntington's disease.'

Would he know anything about it or would I have to say more?

'Is that serious?'

'Yes. Very.' I paused. 'I only found out myself a few years ago what it was that had been making her ill. It started about ten years ago but it wasn't that noticeable at first. It's a neurological condition. It affects muscle control and mental ability. At first Mum just seemed a bit moody and forgetful and clumsy. But it's much worse now. She needs a lot of help.'

'I'm sorry,' Abe said, but I had to carry on.

'There's no cure and most people don't live more than twenty years after their initial diagnosis.' I swallowed. I still found it hard to acknowledge my mother was probably only a few years away from dying.

'Ivy, I'm so sorry,' Abe said. 'I should have been more sensitive. I should never have gone on the way I did the other day. I only did it because I wanted you to know everything.'

'It's okay,' I said. 'You've got nothing to be sorry about. I should have told you before but it's hard, and when you told me about your family, it just didn't seem right to blurt it all out.'

'Still. You were so understanding and you've got all that going on. But you're still wonderful and warm and loving and unafraid.'

He gazed at me intently, as if he really did love me, as if he really did mean everything he said.

'But I'm afraid,' I said quietly.

'Of course you are. I didn't mean . . . I just meant . . . I'm not expressing myself very well, am I?'

'No.' I smiled. 'But it's not just Mum. It's me too. Her condition, Huntington's, is hereditary. It's genetic. The chances of my having it too are fifty–fifty. I won't know until I start to show the signs but it might be the same for me. I could get it tomorrow and be dead in fifteen years. I don't know.'

'Jesus.' He sat up and looked at the pond for a while. Eventually he asked, 'Is there a way of finding out?'

'There's no test. I didn't know when I was younger that Mum's dad had died of it. Mum never talked about him much or told us how he'd died.'

'Did you know him?'

'He died before I was born. Apparently I get my red hair from him. So I definitely have some of his genes.'

'And is it related? To having red hair?'

'No. That was a red herring.' I caught myself. 'Sorry. That was an unintentional pun.'

'And no one ever told you he'd died of this disease?'

I shook my head. 'It was only when Mum was diagnosed that all the details began to come out. He died when she was in her twenties. The awful thing was, apparently he drank a bit. Not so much that things were really difficult but he'd go to the pub every evening after work and come home a bit pissed.'

'Did that make it worse?'

'I don't think anything can make it much worse than it is. It's a horrible condition. But when he first began to show the signs of Huntington's everyone just thought it was the drinking – that it had got worse, that it was causing all the muscle spasms and the raving. It causes a kind of madness, too. In the past, people got locked up in asylums.'

'So they didn't know what was actually wrong with your grandfather?'

'I don't think so at first. It's all a bit unclear. Gran never talked about him. Mum didn't either.'

'But they knew when he died?'

'Gran did. She didn't tell Mum until she decided to get married. She hadn't known when she married Granddad that the condition ran in his family. She thought Mum needed to discuss it with Dad before they went ahead with their wedding.'

'And your dad was okay with it?'

'Yes, but . . .' I paused. I was assuming things that I didn't really know to be true. 'I think, because he'd never known Grandad, because he'd never seen anyone with the condition and because he knew there was a chance she might not have it . . .'

'Go on.'

'I don't think he realized how bad it would be. But if he did, he took the risk anyway. I don't know what he'd have done if he'd known for sure, back when he asked her to marry him.'

Abe was silent.

We both knew what I was saying.

'Some of the symptoms are just things that are normal anyway,' I told him. 'I didn't know until Mum had deteriorated what it was. Initially she would stumble for no reason and she was a bit forgetful and moody. I thought it might be the menopause. I'd never heard of Huntington's.'

'And you never thought it might be more serious?'

'I suppose I had a sort of subconscious inkling but nothing more. Sometimes, especially at the start, she'd get upset about something that didn't really seem to matter. If she dropped something, she'd get tearful and Dad would ask her if she was okay. In hindsight, he was more than usually concerned. But I was a teenager at the time. I didn't think anything of it. I was concerned with other things.'

Abe began plucking handfuls of grass from the bank and throwing them a little distance away. He plucked so much that a bare patch of earth appeared. I had to put out my hand to stop him and that disconcerting sense of *déjà vu* came over me.

'Say something,' I said.

'It doesn't make a difference,' he said. 'I still love you.'

But it did make a difference. How could it not?

'You need time to take it in,' I said, as gently as I could, trying not to let dread filter into my voice. 'It took me a while to get used to knowing.'

He remained quiet. Eventually he said, 'I love you, Ivy, nothing else matters.'

But it did matter, not at first, not when the two of us were together, but when he met my parents. Even though he behaved impeccably, I could tell he was shocked. He was taken aback by the way Mum's body jerked so uncontrollably, by her slurred speech and the way she dribbled and slopped her food when she ate.

He didn't know how to react when he tried to talk to her but she didn't appear to notice, or what to do when she suddenly shouted at my father, a really angry vitriolic rant that came from nowhere and left her exhausted and almost choking.

It's not a pretty condition. It must be easier having a mum who was a virtual nun.

When I was a child I used to romanticize the Victorian illnesses I'd read about. I liked the idea of having consumption, like Helen Burns in *Jane Eyre*, or scarlet fever, like Beth in *Little Women*. I imagined looking pale, and people coming to sit on the edge of my bed to read to me while I slipped away. I knew now that those diseases were more painful and frightening than literature made them out to be. I also knew that the genes that accounted for my hair and eye colour also had a fifty–fifty chance of being marked with a disease that was cruel, especially to those who had to watch a loved one disintegrate over a prolonged period, knowing that there could be only one conclusion.

If I asked Abe to carry on loving me, that was what I might be asking of him. And if it went further, I'd be asking more of him too.

'Do you think you want to have children, Ivy?' Abe had asked, when we drove home after I'd taken him to meet Mum and Dad.

'Yes. I do.'

'Even if . . .' He didn't finish the sentence.

'Yes, I think so,' I said.

'But if you knew now?'

'But I don't. And I won't.' I wanted him to see it from my point of view, although I could also see it from his. 'There's only a fifty–fifty chance I might be carrying the faulty gene. It's the same for all of us, Jon, Cathy and me. Maybe we all do. Maybe one of us is lucky. Maybe one of us will and the others won't. Maybe we're all free. When you see Mum like that, it looks like a higher risk, but it's only a fifty–fifty chance. I could be fine. I have to live my life as if I am.'

'You're such a glass-half-full person,' Abe said, looking at the road, but I could tell he wasn't concentrating on it.

'I have to be. I don't want to spend my life worrying about what might be. There are so many what-ifs. You can't worry about them all or you'd never get out of bed in the morning.'

'I know but some things are –'

'I could be run over by a bus. We could all be wiped out by a nuclear war. This is my life, whatever happens. I want to dive in.'

'You're only ever one remove from a swimming metaphor.' He glanced across at me and smiled ruefully.

'But I mean it.' I said. 'I have to live my life. It's the only way I can cope.'

'You're right,' he said, and gripped the steering wheel so tightly that his knuckles turned white.

Abe's father, Greg, seemed genuinely delighted when we told him, getting up, hugging Abe and kissing me, slightly awkwardly, the way men of that generation do. They're not really comfortable with showing physical affection.

'I'm so pleased,' he said. 'Really happy for the two of you. Have you told your mother, Abe?'

'Not yet,' Abe said. 'We wanted to tell you first, Dad, and I didn't really want to tell Mum over the phone. I guess we'll have to go down one Sunday.'

'She should be here now,' Greg said, as if he needed her, more than ever, to tell him what he should do next.

'I feel bad that we didn't find a way of getting them together,' I said to Abe later.

We were making the sofa-bed in Greg's study for us to sleep on. They'd recently sold the family home near Oxford, given a lump sum to each of the children, and with his half of the remainder Greg had bought a small flat in Hampstead. He'd also left his university job and was working for the Foreign Office.

What he did was a source of mystery to me. He'd been to Washington twice, where he'd met President Reagan, and Margaret Thatcher had briefed him before he'd left.

'It was time for a change,' was all he would say about the job, and 'I was rattling around in it all by myself,' about the house. 'It made sense to move to London with Kirsty, Alan and Abe all here.' He never said he'd given up hoping that Pam would come home. But it was implicit in the changes he'd made to his own life.

'She could still go and live with him in London if she decides to leave that place,' Abe said.

He always called it 'that place' or 'the place': it was his way of showing that he was angry with his mother.

'It must be difficult for him, living here without your mother.' I took the cushions off the sofa and piled them near the bookcase.

'It's difficult for all of us. He's happy for you and me, though,' Abe said, as if I needed reassuring.

Greg had sent Abe out with some money and told him to buy champagne. 'I'm driving, Dad.'

'Why don't you both stay? You're here for dinner anyway. You can leave first thing in the morning if you need to get back. I've got the sofa-bed. Someone's got to use it sometime.'

'Ivy?'

'I'd love to.' I suspected our news had made Greg feel lonely.

'It's wonderful news,' he said again, to me, as I stood at the sink washing potatoes while he prepared fish.

Greg's a good cook. I suppose necessity had made him one, just as it had my dad. He was removing bones from a lemon sole, concentrating on the fish while talking to me.

'I'm glad you think so.' I was scraping mud off lumpy Jersey royals.

'It doesn't feel right, Pam not being here,' he continued. 'But I'm really happy. It's the best news, Ivy. It's what I'd been hoping for but when you told me . . .'

'I know.' It wasn't necessary for him to finish his sentence. 'We'll go and see Pam and tell her too. And you'll both be at the wedding?'

'Of course we will. Of course. She wouldn't miss Abe's wedding. I just wish . . .' A pause. 'I wish she knew you better. She'd love you if she did.'

'There's plenty of time for that,' I said, as Greg took a jar of capers and began sprinkling them liberally over the fish.

'I hope so. It hasn't been easy for any of the children, Pam being . . . well, especially for Abe. And I know you've got your mother's illness to deal with and everything that goes with it. I'm just happy you and he have got each other. Life's easier if you have someone to go through it with.'

I wondered how hard it had been for Greg to say that. I felt I owed him something in return. 'I know there's always going to be the uncertainty,' I began.

'Oh, Lord, Ivy, I don't want you to think . . . I wasn't for a moment suggesting . . .'

'I didn't think you were. But I don't exactly come with "happy ever after" stamped all over me . . .'

'It's an uncertain world, Ivy,' he said. 'If I was young now, I'd want to just get on with my life, the way you two are. There are bigger what-ifs out there.'

'I know.'

'I'm sorry, Ivy.' He cleared his throat. 'I didn't mean to diminish what you have to live with. What I'm trying to say is you're a wonderful young woman and I'm so pleased that you're going to be a part of the family.' He cleared his throat again.

'Thank you.'

I hadn't thought of it like that before. When Abe asked if I'd marry him, three days earlier, after he heard he'd got the job he wanted, I was only thinking about the two of us, that I would get to spend the rest of my life with the man I'd wanted from the moment I'd met him. It hadn't occurred to me until Greg voiced it that I would become part of his family and he mine. I'd only really thought about the possibility of us having our own family and I still worried Abe hadn't fully grasped the implications of that. We'd discussed it, of course, but children were still only a vague possibility. I worried that, when the time came, he might not want to have them.

So, I felt flattered by Greg's words and a certain weight of responsibility. I wanted to make Abe happy and to have a family, but was I being naive in thinking I could when there was a sword dangling over my own?

We'd been to visit my parents a couple of days earlier. I'd phoned Dad and said there was something we wanted to tell them, adding, 'Nothing bad,' as we all did, if there was ever news of any kind.

'Mum's not great today,' he said, opening the door to us and nodding towards the living room where I could see her, sitting at a peculiar angle in her wheelchair.

'Mum,' I said, going to her. She barely reacted.

'She doesn't always recognize people any more,' Dad said, as I waited for her to try to speak.

'Mum,' I said again.

It was increasingly hard for her to speak but when she tried I could usually understand what she was saying. She dropped her head to one side, letting it rest against the handle of the wheelchair and stared blankly at me.

'I'm sorry, love,' Dad said. 'Let's get you both something to drink. What would you like?'

Dad didn't drink much, these days, and the alcohol on offer was usually the dregs of whatever was in the drinks cabinet.

'There's Dubonnet,' he said, opening its doors. 'Not sure how long that's been there. And there's some beer in the fridge, Abe.'

He fetched Abe a beer and one for himself. I made myself a coffee and we sat in the living room: Abe and I on the sofa, Dad in an armchair and Mum completing the circle in her wheelchair.

'We've got some good news,' I said, hesitating, thinking it needed more of a preamble but unable to think of one. 'Abe's asked me to marry him.' I put out my hand to show them the ring, searching my mother for some sort of reaction but there was none.

Dad tried to make up for it. 'Oh, that's superb news, love,' he said, getting up to hug me and then Abe. He was more physically affectionate now than he'd ever been when we were young, as if he needed to make up for the things he no longer got from Mum.

'I'm so pleased for you both,' he said to Abe, adding a quiet, almost inaudible, 'Thank you.'

I wondered what he'd meant. Was it a thank you for the moment, which seemed to have made him happy, or was he thanking Abe for taking me on?

'Did you hear that?' Dad said to Mum. 'Ivy's to get married.'

'I'm sorry,' he said, to both of us this time. 'She doesn't seem to know what's going on a lot of the time now. But don't let it spoil your wonderful news.'

We hadn't known what to expect and, naturally, I was disappointed. There was nothing celebratory about our visit to my parents, so I was grateful to Greg for sending Abe out to buy champagne, while I helped him prepare dinner.

'Everything okay?' Abe suddenly appeared in the room, removing tissue paper from a bottle of Moët et Chandon. We hadn't heard him come into the house.

'Couldn't be better.' Greg put his hand on the bottle. 'Ah, good, it's already chilled. I'll get some glasses.' He opened a cupboard and began taking out tumblers so he could reach the champagne flutes at the back.

'Are you okay?' Abe lowered his voice.

'Of course.'

He asked me again later, as we dragged spare bedding from the cupboard where Greg kept it and made up our bed. 'You're happy, aren't you?'

'Of course. You know I am. I couldn't be happier.' I expected him to say something but he was too busy putting pillow cases on to pillows. 'Abe?'

'I still find it weird, coming here to see Dad. It never feels right.'

'Maybe the wedding will . . .'

'What?' He looked at me.

'Well, maybe your mother will want to be more involved.'

'You'd have thought she might want to be involved in the sale of the family home but she wasn't.' There was bitterness in his voice.

Abe piled the pillows on to the bed and shook a duvet over it. 'Right, that's ready. I'm just going to the bathroom to take my contact lenses out or do you want to go first?'

'No, you go,' I said, suddenly anxious.

We were with the travel agent, looking into our honeymoon, when I knew for certain what I'd already begun to suspect.

My parents were doing the wedding. They'd insisted – well, Dad had, and he was hoping we'd get married in the village. I was the youngest but I was the first child in our family to get married. And despite Mum's condition, he kept saying, 'It will make your mother happy, especially if it's at the church,' as if repeating it would make it true.

It was important for Abe's mum too. She'd leave the convent for the whole weekend. She said she'd stay at the flat the night before and go with Greg. It was the first time for years that they would be together for more than an hour or two. There was so much more than just a wedding going on. I felt the pressure of that. I knew Abe did too.

'The vicar is really nice,' I'd told Abe, worried that he wouldn't want a church wedding. Maybe he'd think it hypocritical since neither of us ever went to church, and, anyway, he harboured an understandable antipathy towards it. But I was only considering it to please my parents and his.

'Actually,' Abe had responded, 'I'd be much happier getting married in a church than a register office.'

'Really?' I was surprised.

'Yes,' he said. 'If I'm going to get married, I don't want it to be in some seventies concrete council building. I want it to be a building with a flint stone wall and a Norman tower!'

I should have guessed aesthetics were guiding his reasoning. And I didn't care where the ceremony took place, as long as I was marrying him.

Dad had stopped working altogether now so that he could look after Mum, but although it was time-consuming and exhausting, he seemed to need another project to distract him, to keep him going. The wedding seemed to fulfil that need and, where once my mother would have been trying to sort out flowers, I now took regular phone calls from him asking if I wanted them on every table.

'That sounds lovely, Dad. But if the cost's going up, it's not important.'

'I want it to be a good day for you, love.'

While Dad was throwing himself into the preparations, Greg had offered to pay for our honeymoon. I was hesitant, at first, about accepting the money because he'd already given us some from the sale of the family home to use as a deposit for the flat. 'It's not a fortune,' he'd said at the time. 'Pam won't take anything but there's still money there for her if . . .' He didn't finish the sentence.

Abe's eldest brother, Jackie, was an academic and lived in Sheffield. He reckoned he could buy a whole house with the money but Alan, who was renting a bedsit in Hackney and performing comedy, had plans to take himself to the Edinburgh Festival.

'The girls are still not ready to settle,' Greg had said, when he told us his plans. 'I don't think Kirsty wants to stay in London for ever and she could nurse anywhere. And Tessa seems to be planning on living at Greenham Common for the foreseeable future. They don't want to do anything with it yet. But you two could use it as a deposit on a place.'

He'd also asked if we might have Fred, the tortoise, to live with us. 'If you can find somewhere with a garden, it will be better for him in the summer,' Greg had said. 'I don't like him being cooped up in the flat.'

So I worried that if he paid for the honeymoon, too, he might be leaving himself short.

'Maybe his London flat is paid for by MI6,' Dad said. He was convinced that Greg was a spy. His decision to leave his job as professor of history and join the Foreign Office was, to him, otherwise 'inexplicable'.

'Who exactly do you think he's spying on?'

'The Russians, I suppose. Or maybe the Arabs.'

However Greg supported himself, the money he'd given us put us in a good position. We had enough for a deposit, we both had jobs, and the building society was happy to lend us more money than we needed, which seemed to make it harder rather than easier for us to buy a place.

'We could buy a house, rather than a flat, with that sort of money,' I'd said, after our first meeting at the building society.

'We don't really need a house, though, do we?' Abe seemed uncomfortable with the adult nature of it all.

'Not yet.'

'What do you mean by "not yet"?'

'Nothing.' I felt defensive. 'Just that maybe one day we will want a house. People do.'

'But I thought we both liked living in central London?'

By this time we were spending most of our time at his house in Bloomsbury and had talked about trying to buy a flat somewhere not too far out.

'We do. All I said was that, with the amount of money they're prepared to lend us, we could buy a house somewhere. But if you want to look for a flat not too far from where we are now then that's what we'll do.'

'Fine.' He was clearly not.

'What is it?' I asked him, taking his hand, as we walked home.

'Sorry. It's just . . . I feel a bit overwhelmed, to be honest.'

'By the thought of buying somewhere to live?'

'Kind of.' He refused to look at me.

'You're going to have to explain.' I stopped.

'It's not buying somewhere *per se*,' he said. 'It's just . . . it's a lot all at once. I'm still finding my feet with the new job and there's the wedding to think about. Trying to buy somewhere to live at the same time just feels like too much.'

'Is that all?'

'Yes.' He appeared to relax a little.

'I agree, really. We've got enough on our plates without spending every weekend looking for somewhere to buy. Let's wait until after the wedding.'

'Thanks, Ivy,' he said, and then he kissed me in a way that unnerved me. It almost felt as if he was taking his leave. I think I knew then, deep down, but I didn't want to admit it.

It was only in the travel agent's that I knew I was going to have to confront him.

'So where were you thinking you'd like to go?' the travel agent asked.

'Italy,' I told him.

Abe said nothing.

'We wanted to have a few days in a city, maybe Rome or Florence – neither of us have ever been – and then a week somewhere in the country.'

Alex, my boss, had said we could go cost-price trekking in Nepal.

'It's a honeymoon, Alex!'

'You'll love it.'

'It's very kind of you but we want to do something more . . . relaxed.'

'Well, the offer's there. I'd suggest something more relaxed if we had anything but you know the score.'

I did. It was adventure travel. If we wanted to go white-water rafting or mountain climbing I knew exactly where to go, but we wanted something different.

'Abe?' I tried to get him to say something now.

'Yes, that's what we thought,' he said.

'Abe works for a firm of architects.' I felt anxious, and when I'm anxious, I babble. 'So we'd like to spend a few days seeing some of the buildings first before going somewhere to relax.'

'In that case perhaps Florence,' Harry Tebbit said. 'Then you could take a train to Pisa for the day if you wanted.'

'That sounds interesting. Can we fly direct to Florence?' I looked at Abe, waiting for him to say something.

Harry Tebbit was pulling heavy books out of drawers, checking flight routes and tour operators. 'Or perhaps Greece?' he suggested, while he rummaged. 'You could fly to Athens, then visit one of the islands. Have you been?'

'I have.'

Abe was still saying nothing.

'It would be nice to go somewhere we can swim too.'

Still nothing.

Harry Tebbit turned and reached for a brochure from the shelf behind him. 'There is this lovely *pensione*, about half an hour outside Florence where you could go for the rest of your stay. I can highly recommend it.' He opened the brochure and showed us a large house surrounded by hills, with a pool and rooms that looked as if they were still inhabited by Renaissance princes.

'It looks beautiful.' I wanted to go.

'Yup, great.' Abe gave it no more than a cursory glance.

On it went. Harry Tebbit did his best. He came up with

suggestions; he checked out flights and accommodation; he showed us pictures and tried to enthuse us. He showed us Rome and Pisa, Berlin and Salzburg, Athens and Nafplio, hotels on cliff-sides, country retreats and beachside villas. He seemed aware that Abe was lukewarm. 'So,' he said eventually. 'Perhaps you'd like to go away and think a little about it all, then let me know if you want me to book the flights and accommodation.'

'That's a good idea. Shall we go and have a coffee somewhere, Abe?'

'Sure,' he said, getting up too quickly.

'Here's my card.' Harry handed it to us. 'These flights are unlikely to be fully booked at the time of year you wish to travel. You don't have to let me know immediately. Give me a call when you've had a think.'

'Thank you.'

'What was all that about?' I demanded angrily, once we were outside.

'Not here, Ivy,' was all the reassurance Abe could offer.

'What do you mean?'

'Let's go somewhere.'

'Where?'

'Let's go for a walk.'

He started walking fast towards Primrose Hill, forcing me to break into a run to catch up with him. 'Shall we go to the top?' he asked, at the entrance. 'We could sit on the bench up there.'

'No. It's too much of a landmark.'

'What?'

'That bench is too iconic. I don't want to be reminded of whatever it is you're going to tell me every time I see it on a postcard or in some film. '

'Okay,' Abe said quietly, walking towards one at the foot of the hill, far enough away from the perimeter fence and the children's playground to afford us some privacy.

'Just tell me,' I said, as we sat down. 'Whatever it is. Just say it.'

'I'm sorry, Ivy. I'm so sorry. I don't want to do this to you because I really love you but I can't go through with it. I just can't take it all on. It's too much.'

There was more, of course: Abe's attempts to explain, my incomprehension – although I did understand, sort of, just not why he'd let us get to this point. There were tears, recriminations, and declarations of love that were pointless if this was the beginning of the end. They might have been genuine but they were still pointless.

If you call off a wedding, if you can't go through with it, if you're scared of loving someone, it damages the relationship too much to carry on with it. We both knew that, however much neither of us wanted it to be that way.

One of the few things that August didn't know about
her was that sometimes when she looked at her
collection of pictures she tried to imagine and place
herself in that other, shadow life . . . She tried to
imagine this life playing out somewhere at the
present moment. Some parallel Kirsten in an
air-conditioned room, waking from an unsettling
dream of walking through an empty landscape.

Emily St John Mandel, *Station Eleven*

Tel Aviv, September 1974

It was my decision to go, to leave him, even though I knew
I'd hurt him, and I'd have done anything to avoid that –
anything except stay.

I didn't know what I wanted to do after school. Abe knew
exactly. He had it all planned out: art foundation, then architecture at university. I wasn't sure. University didn't appeal,
although I wanted to get away from home and the atmosphere
that didn't get better, which I didn't understand.

Ironically, it was Abe's neighbour, Barbara Van der Zee,
who told me about a family in Paris who were looking for an
au pair. It came up in a casual conversation when we'd been
round to use her pool. She'd asked me what I wanted to do
after A levels and I'd said I wanted to travel.

She'd put me in touch with them. They were keen. I was
keen. It was not for long. It was all so easy. Or it would have

been, if it weren't for Abe. Telling him was worse than I'd anticipated. More final than I'd expected.

'But we could have gone somewhere together.'

'But we hadn't planned anything. And you've got a job lined up.'

He had work with a local firm of architects over the summer.

'I could have had a holiday first, after or even during. We could have gone to Greece or somewhere.'

'But I want to do something more. I want to travel. I want to see the world. I need to get away. I'm not like you. I don't have my life planned out but I want to do something with it. I can't just sit here. It's too good an opportunity to turn down.'

'I know. I just wish you were staying.'

'It's only for three months. I'll be back after that.' I'd thought so at the time.

'But things will be different.'

'They'd have been different anyway. We've finished school now. I'll have to find something to do.'

'You just found something a bit sooner than I expected.'

'But it's not for very long. Do you want me not to go?'

'No, of course not. It's just . . . It all feels so . . .'

'What?'

'Final.'

'It's not the end of us, Abe,' I said.

But it was the beginning of the end.

In Paris I worked for the Cahns, a husband-and-wife team who ran a fashion-importing business in the Marais. I took their children to school and to the park afterwards. I had French lessons in between. It was an experience but a little lonely. I didn't meet many people my own age.

It was Isaac Cahn's idea that I should go Israel. 'If you

want to experience a really different way of life, then you should apply to work on a kibbutz.'

He helped me apply from Paris for the visa and permit so that I was able to travel straight there.

I wrote to Abe. I said it wasn't fair to ask him to wait. In my mind, it was a break not a split. But we were both young, too young to be tied to each other. I missed him, maybe less than I would have done if I'd been the one stuck at home while he went off travelling. But I did miss him.

I'd push him to the back of my mind, especially when I was with Nathan in Israel, but he was always there.

I could tell that Nathan wished he'd said goodbye at the entrance. Now that we were in the check-in queue, and looked likely to be in it for some time, he was twitchy. The time between being about to say goodbye and saying it was stretching out. Making him irritable.

'Jeez, are they going to take everything out of every single bag?'

'I don't care if they do. I'd rather stand in line for a little longer than be . . .'

A week previously a TWA Boeing 707 had crashed into the sea en route from Tel Aviv to New York. It was flying via Athens and Rome and went down in the Ionian Sea half an hour after leaving the Greek capital. Everyone on board was killed. News reports said a young Palestinian boy had brought the bomb onto the aircraft: the first time an Arab would board a plane in an apparent suicide mission.

I scanned the passengers around me. People looked nervous.

'They're not going to pull the same stunt twice in a fortnight,' Nathan muttered.

'Well, it's still reassuring that they're making checks. For everyone.'

'Sorry. Sorry, Ivy. I hate goodbyes and all this.' He nodded to the Israeli gun-toting soldiers patrolling the airport.

'Look, I'm fine. You can go now, if you like.'

'No. No. Sorry. I didn't want it to be like this.'

The news was a week old but it had made us jumpy with each other ever since. A vague plan we'd had to fly to Athens and visit the Greek islands before I went home added a what-if to the various things the bomb had triggered for Nathan. What if we had decided to go to Greece? What if the bomb had gone off before the plane landed at Athens? What if we'd been on that flight?

There'd been a sense of shock among everyone at the kibbutz, a prevailing notion that the attack was somehow personal. It was a notion that I couldn't quite accept. Yes, it was a targeted act of violence but the target was impersonal and random. There's a huge gulf between 'almost' and 'actually', between the possibility of something happening to you and it happening.

I didn't understand why Nathan needed to feel he could have been caught up in it any more than he understood my detachment.

Perhaps it was my naivety about the political situation in the Middle East that had begun to get to him. The way he started talking about Fatah and the proximity of the kibbutz to the border with Lebanon showed up my ignorance. He was irritated if I asked questions to which he felt I should know the answers. And, out of the blue, the fact that I was not Jewish seemed to matter too.

'You've no idea what it's like to be hated,' Nathan said, as if he resented me for not feeling whatever it was that he felt so keenly.

I didn't understand him any more than I understood the mechanics by which bananas and avocados, like the ones I'd spent so much time picking, would in the future be manipulated. 'It will make them bigger and better and more resistant to disease.' Nathan tried to explain the process and its potential application. 'Genetic modification will help eradicate famine and hunger. It could even be used to prevent disease in humans.'

He was going to study biochemistry at Harvard. He wanted to be at the forefront of gene technology. My inability to grasp the subject had frustrated him as much as my ignorance about Middle Eastern history appeared to now. The tension between us, which had been brewing, made our parting something to be got out of the way, not quite the sweet, sorrowful closing that the romantic in me might have imagined.

I'd had a wonderful year and Nathan had been part of it. He was everything that had been exotic and exciting in male form, but I was ready to go home now, to the people I was missing and the familiar comfort.

'Smoking or non-smoking?' the girl at the checkout desk asked, as her colleague opened my rucksack and began pulling out its filthy contents.

'Non-smoking, please.'

'Window or aisle?'

'Aisle.'

She handed me a boarding card and I walked in silence past the security officers.

'So, this is it,' Nathan said, and kissed me, a kiss laden with various emotions none of which I could accurately describe.

'Bye, Nathan,' I said, heading towards the departure lounge.

When I turned around, he was walking away. He never looked back.

I watched him, wondering what I was feeling. Loss, yes. But for the place where we'd been and the time we'd spent together more than the man. As I watched his departing back, it was Abe I really missed.

'Every time you fall in love it will be because something in the man reminds you of him.' I'd read that somewhere and I wondered if it was true. Would I spend the rest of my life looking for someone who reminded me of someone I'd loved only fleetingly but first?

'Was he Jewish?' Nathan was quizzing me about Abe.

What seemed to define my relationship with Abe was that someone was always asking me questions about it: Lisa, my parents and now Nathan.

'No.'

'Abraham's a very Jewish name.'

'His dad's a professor of American history. He named him after Lincoln.'

'So how did you two meet?'

'At school. We were in the same maths class.'

We were on the beach at Rosh HaNikra, at the foot of the white cliffs that reminded me of England, and Nathan was taking me back to a time and a place that sometimes seemed much further away than just last year and the far end of the Mediterranean.

I was a different person here. I hardly thought about home. The days were too preoccupying, the people too new and too different. Nathan was unlike anyone I had met before and exciting to be with. Our relationship was new enough for him to be jealous of my ex – for him to need to know about him. 'So he hadn't been at the same school as you before, then?'

'No. He went to another school in a different town.'

I'd had this conversation with Abe too. 'How come you went there?' I'd asked him. He lived in the country, midway between two villages, stuck between two schools.

'I don't know. My parents decided.'

It was just one of those things, but it seemed important for us to wonder at it.

'Imagine if they'd decided otherwise. We'd have met when we were kids.'

When we reached the sixth form we thought we were adult.

'And maybe had nothing to do with each other. I was very shy when I was little.'

'I'm sure I'd have liked you.' I was. But then you are, aren't you?

When you first meet someone, you imagine you'd have liked them whenever you met, and that you'll always find them as compelling as you do at the start. You think it will go on for ever. Even though you know it never quite works out that way.

'What if we'd met on our first day at primary school?' I said to him. 'Do you think we would have been friends?'

Abe had this look. He'd say something and look momentarily sad, then catch himself and smile, a big, wide, inviting smile. The look and the smile always made me want to kiss him. This time I just arched my eyebrows.

'What?'

'That what-if thing.'

I suspected I knew what he was thinking. That if they'd all gone to a different school, then maybe Tessa would not have been walking there at that particular time on that particular day. And then she'd be okay.

'Sorry.'

We'd talk about something else, or occasionally we'd talk about the way things were. Maybe that was what drew us to each other – the fact that our home lives were a little odd. We weren't typical teenagers. We didn't have responsibilities, but our worlds were slightly out of kilter.

*

'When did he ask you out?'

That was Lisa, miffed that I hadn't filled her in on every twist and turn.

'He didn't exactly.' We were lounging on the floor of her living room, which was so much better for lounging on than ours. They had floor cushions from Habitat, four times the size of normal ones. They were covered with a kind of thick brown corduroy.

'Corde-du-roi,' Lisa's dad said. 'The cloth of kings.'

'*Nouveau*.' My dad threw another French word into the mix when I repeated the phrase.

I didn't know what he meant, any more than I understood why he thought having a colour TV was 'vulgar'.

'So how did you get together?' Lisa turned down *Ziggy Stardust*.

'It just sort of happened.'

'Where? What? When?'

'Oh, you know.'

'No. So tell me.'

I didn't really want to. 'Going out' was something private, between two people, and the world should not be privy to every detail.

Abe often got the same train to school and sometimes we'd walk halfway home together, occasionally taking the path through the woods. 'Stop a minute,' he'd said one day, pausing by a log that rested alongside a stream.

We sat and he told me about his sister, about what had happened and how that made life difficult for his mother.

And I told him about my mother, as much as I under-stood, and how her condition made me feel.

It was an exchange. We'd revealed a little of ourselves to each other. It was enough to make kissing inevitable, as we sat on the log, and again, when we stood up to go.

'We walked home through the woods and he kissed me.'

'Is that all?'

'Yes.'

'Girls!' Lisa's mum called from the kitchen.

'Spaghetti bolognese is on the table.'

'What did he look like?' Nathan asked me now.

'Tall, dark and incredibly good-looking! Like a film star. Like Sean Connery.'

'Seriously?'

'No, Nathan. I'm teasing you. He was nice looking. Ordinary. Unruly hair, thick glasses, badly dressed.'

'No, but seriously.'

'I'm being serious. That's what he looked like. Ordinary.' Should we be having this conversation? It didn't feel right.

'So what was it about him?'

'He was nice.'

'Nice?'

'Yes, nice! Jesus, Nathan, what do you want me to say?'

'That he was a bastard and you hated him!'

'He was a bastard and I hated him.'

'Is that true?'

'No.' He was a lovely bloke and I loved him.

'You went out with him for over two years. It's a long time, Ivy, when you're sixteen.'

I ran my hands through the sand, pushing it into a little hillock at my side, ignoring Nathan's question.

'I'm interested.' His tone was less challenging. 'I want to know all about you.'

'He was funny. He made me laugh. And he was kind and interesting, and interested in the world and people around him. A bit like you.' Deflection by flattery.

'Really?'

'Yes, really.'

'Sorry, Ivy.' He put his arm around my shoulders, which were warm from the evening sun, and kissed me. 'You're so . . .'

'What?'

'Lovely, sweet, funny, intoxicating. I'm a little bit jealous of Abraham Lincoln.'

We lay back in the sand and did things that should have pushed Abe from my mind. They did for a bit, until Nathan patted the top pocket of his shirt. He had a johnny there. 'Ben and Josh are going to the cinema tonight,' he said.

Nathan had an understanding with his dorm mates and there was a lock on the door. It was always a rush to get dressed and vacate the room before anyone came back. It made the lovemaking lack intimacy, somehow. It made me feel strangely detached from Nathan. Maybe I was. Maybe I was chasing a closeness I'd experienced before that wasn't going to happen – not here, not now, not with Nathan.

Abe and I had always found it easy to talk about things. He had told me, not long after I'd first encountered him, a little about his family as we walked between classes: two older brothers – one just finished university, the other in his final year. His older sister, Kirsty, was training to be a nurse in London. And then there was Tessa, who'd been about to go and work abroad in America when the accident happened.

If it hadn't I might never have met him. His father had just been offered a professorship at Oxford. During the summer they were going to move and Abe would have gone to school there.

But Tessa had been walking home from a friend's house one evening when a lorry travelling down the lane began to shed its load: hay bales piled in a tower that was as precarious as it looked. The driver of the car behind swerved instinctively, to avoid the bales, and veered up onto the verge, hitting Tessa.

A moment later.

A moment earlier.

Had Tessa been walking on the other side of the road, had she stayed five minutes more at the house of the friend she'd just been to see, things would have been different. But she was where she was and the car hit her. Her back was broken in several places.

She was lucky to be alive but she couldn't move, not yet. She'd lie immobilized in the hospital for nearly six months before she was allowed home with her back in a brace. She would learn slowly to walk again, with some difficulty and considerable pain, which doctors told her might remain for the rest of her life.

But she was lucky to be alive.

Abe's father took the job anyway. He was too far down the line not to. He stayed in Oxford four nights a week, returning at weekends and during the holidays. Mrs McFadden and Abe stayed where they were. Abe gave up his place at an Oxford school and applied to the one I went to. Mrs McFadden visited Tessa daily, with Abe when he had time.

I'd been to meet her too. I liked her. How could anyone not when she was so full of smiles and laughter, despite the pain and the traction?

'She always seems to be happy,' I'd said to Mum accusingly.

Mum had shaken her head and said nothing.

'Abe really likes you,' Tessa said to me once, in hospital, when he went to get drinks.

I didn't know what to say.

'You make him happy.' She took my hand and held it.

I guessed she was lonely lying there, out of touch, lacking

273

much human contact, but there was something about what she'd said and the gesture. It made me feel included, part of the family, not just Abe's girlfriend, a little more.

His mother made me feel the same way. I liked her easy company and her calmness. I liked standing next to her at the sink, doing the dishes in companionable silence, not feeling on edge as I did with Mum, wondering if she was going to get angry or tearful, or have one of the peculiar spasms that made her drop things. Mrs McFadden didn't seem to feel a need to talk to me, even though I was a guest, which I liked too.

And I liked it when, on Tessa's birthday, Mrs McFadden asked if I'd come to the hospital with her, Abe, Mr McFadden, who was home, and Kirsty, who was down from London. I felt included as we sat round Tessa's bed, chatting as she opened presents and talked excitedly about her plans for next year. Maybe I felt it more because my own family seemed bizarrely fractured by something I did not understand, and my mother was often angry and upset with me.

'Ivy, come downstairs now.'

'Why? What have I done?'

Mum was furious. Standing at the bottom of the stairs, holding on to the banisters to steady herself, as she often did these days, losing her balance and her temper at the same time.

'What?' I came out of my room.

'In the kitchen.' She jerked her head to the left, a deliberate gesture.

'I know it's not easy, Ivy,' Dad would say to me, 'but your mother's nerves are not quite right.'

What exactly did that mean?

'I know she seems unreasonable sometimes, but try to be

patient. Try not to react. It doesn't help.' Dad was affection-ate when we had these chats in a way he was not normally. He'd pat my arm, sometimes stroke my hair or tell me I was a good girl.

'Dad, is there something wrong with Mum? I mean seriously?'

He'd close off again. 'It's just her nerves. You're cooking tonight, aren't you?'

'Yes. I said so. Is it okay if Abe stays for dinner?'

'Yes. Of course.'

'Abi says her mum was really weird for about a year when she went through the change and then she was okay again.' Lisa had tried to make me feel better after one of Mum's irrational outbursts.

I hated confrontation so I tried not to get into arguments, to wait for whatever was making Mum tense to pass.

'What's up?' I said now, sitting opposite her at the kitchen table.

'This.' She slapped something on the table.

'Oh.'

'Is that all you've got to say?'

'It's not mine.'

'Then whose is it?'

'I found it.'

'You found it?'

'Yes. Really. Have you been going through my pockets?'

'I was going to wash your jacket, Ivy. Where did you find it?'

'On the train.'

Why had I picked it up? What had induced me to slip the waxed paper and cellophane package into my pocket? Curi-osity. I wanted to see what they looked like. I wanted to know what they felt like. I wanted to see how they worked.

'You found a contraceptive on the train?'

Mum didn't believe me.

'Yes, really. It was just there tucked down the side of the seat. I thought it was litter.' I'd known exactly what it was. 'I was just going to throw it away.'

'Ivy. I know you and Abe are close.'

'But we're not. Honestly, Mum we're not . . .' We weren't.

But Mum was never going to believe me.

Except she did. 'You're not?'

'No. I promise. I just picked it up on the train.'

'You haven't?'

'No.' I don't think either of us wanted to be having that conversation.

'Okay.' She appeared to relax. 'It's just . . . you need to be careful, if you're going to. You don't want to get pregnant.'

'I'm not going to.'

'If you are, I can make you a doctor's appointment.'

That wasn't what I expected. 'I'm not, Mum.'

'It's important that you don't get pregnant. Not yet. Not now.'

'I know that. I'm not going to.' That was the last thing I wanted.

'Ivy. It's not just . . .' She was becoming tearful.

'Mum, I'm not going to get pregnant.' I couldn't stand it when she cried. It was awkward.

'Okay.'

And that was the last time she brought up anything like that.

There's an empty space between my seat beside the window and a young English man sitting on the aisle. I wonder if this is a random seat allocation or if the check-in girls deliberately match nationalities. Around us there are several men in skull caps with side curls. A young couple with a toddler and a baby are seated across the aisle. Everyone seems to be speaking Hebrew and smoking.

My seat is in the row just in front of the last row of smoking seats. The differentiation is pointless.

'Hi,' I say, as I force him to stand up while I get in. He's a redhead too, his skin pale and freckled. I wonder how he's managed in the heat. I find it hard, but at least my skin tans, eventually.

Sitting a foot away from him and heading home, I'm aware that I'm newly full of myself and bursting with it all: bursting to share my experiences and wear the stamps in my passport on my sleeve. In a way I'm already doing that. The leather sandals bought from the market in Tel Aviv, the loose tunic from a stall in Haifa, the Hand of Fatima – a present from Nathan – which I am wearing on a chain around my neck, and the suitcase Madame Cahn in Paris had given me.

I must surely look like someone who's seen something of the world. I want to latch on to someone, to engage them in conversation, to let them know I've seen things and been to places that have changed me. And I need to talk so that I don't think about the possibility that, amid the sea of Jewish faces, there are a couple of Arabs. I don't want to think what I'm sure a lot of the other passengers are thinking. I don't want to think the way Nathan had revealed he'd been thinking. I don't want to be suspicious of these men just because they're Arabs.

I put my copy of Hermann Hesse's *Siddhartha* in the pocket of the seat in front of me and stick the small canvas bag containing my passport and a few oranges under the seat in front. Rachel, who shared my dorm at Rosh HaNikra, gave the novel to me when I left.

'Have you been in Israel long?' I ask the English bloke

'A month or so.' A pause. 'I was working in Tel Aviv.'

'Oh.' That isn't what I expected. I expect everyone to have been working on a kibbutz as I have. 'Where?'

'At an architect's.'

He could be Abe a year down the line.

'Tel Aviv's an amazing city,' he continues. 'Did you get to see it?'

'A little.'

Nathan and I had taken the bus down the coast a couple of days earlier and checked into a cheap hotel. It was basic but all the better for saying goodbye in. Somehow its tatty décor and fraying edges had begun to rub off on us so that by the time we were at the airport saying goodbye wasn't as hard as I'd thought it might be.

'It's got the greatest concentration of Bauhaus buildings anywhere in the world,' the Englishman is saying now. 'But it's going to change. It'll get a lot bigger – probably end up looking more like New York than Jerusalem. They'll probably have towers as high as the World Trade Center in New York in a few years' time.'

I'm about to ask him if he'd seen the Frenchman who'd thrown a tightrope between the Twin Towers and danced his way from one to the other, but we're interrupted by the arrival of the occupant of the middle seat. A tall elderly man who says something in Hebrew as he sits down and nothing further for the rest of the flight.

I didn't see my parents at first, when I emerged through Customs and scanned the rows of faces waiting for loved ones to arrive. Then I saw Dad towards the back of the crowd. I'd been away for less than a year but he seemed older. Maybe I'd simply forgotten exactly what he looked like. Perhaps you never really take in the details of the people you see every day and only notice them properly after a prolonged absence.

I couldn't see Mum, but as I walked towards him, I spotted her, sitting on her own, a few feet away.

'Mum!'

She glanced around, eyes darting, until she eventually focused on me. 'Ivy.' She smiled but remained seated.

Then Dad was beside me, kissing me stiffly and saying, 'Go over to your mother.'

Mum was standing up now, with a stick for support. 'Ivy,' she said again, and tried to hug me, but it was awkward with the stick and she shuddered as she held me, almost pushing me away. I stood back. 'You look so different,' she said to me. 'Your hair's lighter. The red's nearly gone.'

'I've faded in the sun.'

It's a redhead trait to get lighter as you grow older, progressing from red, through strawberry and dishwater blonde until you eventually reach a silvery grey.

'But what about you? Have you had a fall?'

'I'm just a bit unsteady . . .' Mum stopped as another shudder convulsed her. 'I've lost my balance a bit.' She screwed up her eyes and shook her head.

'Let's get you home, Ivy,' Dad said. He gave his arm to Mum for support. 'You're probably tired, after travelling, and you must have lots to tell us.'

I walked beside them. We went slowly to the car and they kept asking me questions, the sort of questions I'd expected.

'What was the weather like?'

'Was it hot?'

'What were the other people like?'

'Were they all from Israel?'

'Was it hard work?'

'So you picked bananas as well as avocados?'

'There were reports on the news about Arabs crossing the border to attack the Jews. And we knew you were close to the border although, of course, you're not Jewish, but even so.'

I'm not sure my father had ever asked me so many questions or said so much in such a short space of time.

'We thought you were probably having a marvellous trip but, still, we worried.'

'I was fine. I always felt safe.' I felt bad now. 'I should have written more often.' I didn't tell them I'd barely thought about home: I'd been too caught up in what I was doing. But now that I was back, I was worried too – about them.

I suppose I'd known before I went away that there was more to whatever was going on with Mum than 'the change'. I noticed now that the moments of clumsiness, the mood swings and memory lapses had multiplied and magnified. Where previously she'd sometimes lose her balance or drop something, her body often took her by surprise, jerking in a way she couldn't disguise. She was forgetful and angry most of the time.

Had she got so much worse while I'd been away? Or had I just been blind to the symptoms that had crept up on her so gradually that she seemed normal?

It was normal not to talk about illness, to behave as if all the signs and symptoms and outward bodily changes were unremarkable.

'Why is Mrs Brown in a wheelchair?' I remember asking Mum, of a woman who went to the same church as we did and had been healthy and able-bodied.

'She had an operation,' Mum had replied, as if that was explanation enough.

I'd presumed the operation had left her weak and that the

wheelchair was temporary. Only when she died did Mum tell me she'd had cancer. Only when she died did her own children discover that was the cause of her weight loss and diminishing ability to breathe. I knew now, looking at my mother, that there must be more wrong with her than her nerves.

Dad made the dinner that evening. I hadn't seen him cook before. He might have made the occasional boiled egg or beans on toast but not a proper meal. Now he was brandishing saucepans and stretching for ingredients as if he was in some sort of elaborate choreographed routine.

'I've made a pie,' he announced. 'And I'll do some fried potatoes. I've even got an avocado to make you feel at home.'

'At home?' I felt as if I'd left home and come back to a strange discombobulating place. I thought I'd grown up, but here I was feeling like a child again, uncertain and a little scared.

'They're from Israel.' Dad brandished the avocado. 'Bought it in Marks & Spencer's. Perhaps you picked it.'

'Maybe.'

But what I really wanted was familiar food that made home feel more like home.

Before I left, avocado was a colour not a fruit – the colour of Lisa's bathroom suite. Nobody bought or ate them.

And a pie? And fried potatoes? It was unnerving enough that Dad was cooking but at least if he'd been cooking bangers and mash I'd have felt vaguely reassured.

'When did you start cooking?'

Dad looked at Mum, who was taking cutlery from the drawer and moving it carefully to the table. It was clearly an effort. 'I burned myself a few months ago, Ivy,' she said. 'I knocked a pan of boiling water off the hob. I get these spasms.'

'Are you going to tell me what's wrong?'

'Tell us about what you've been up to first, Ivy,' Dad said. 'There's so much.'

Dad poured me a glass of homemade wine, and Mum sat, awkwardly, twitching every now and then, her head jerking away from me as I talked.

I told them about Paris: about my attic room in the house on the rue de Lille, overlooking the Seine. I told them about the Cahns and their children, how Isaac Cahn had suggested I apply to work on a kibbutz and helped me. I told them that Israel had seemed like a different world, with a different landscape and climate, unfamiliar food and people speaking a strange ancient language I'd never heard before, alongside English.

I described my room at the kibbutz and my room mates: Rachel, from Düsseldorf, Emma, who was also British, and Maria, from Spain, who each morning at breakfast said, '*Viva el té de Tel Aviv*,' which meant 'Long live Tel Aviv tea.' She said it even though we were in Tel Aviv and the tea was always weak and lukewarm. She said it because it was a palindrome and it pleased her.

I described the games room and the bar and the social areas and told them that, as well as the Mediterranean Sea being nearby, there was a communal swimming pool that was several times the size of the Van der Zees'.

'I bumped into Peter Van der Zee in the village,' Dad said then. 'They said they'd like to see you.'

'And Paula Turner.' Mum mentioned a school friend. 'She's got a job in Sun Alliance. You might want to see if they're taking people on, when you've got used to being back.'

I wouldn't. I was back but not ready to slot into anything that vaguely resembled my life as a child or the life of my parents. I wanted to be off again. I thought I might learn to teach English as a foreign language and spend a few years in Europe. But I didn't tell them that, not yet.

Neither did I tell them about Nathan. I didn't tell them we'd worked the same shifts on the avocado plantation when I'd first arrived. I didn't tell them he played the guitar and I'd first noticed him when he was singing a song I recognized from somewhere, 'This Land Is Our Land'.

'It's a Woody Guthrie song,' Emma had told me. 'But he's changed the words. It's supposed to be "This Land Is Your Land".'

I didn't tell them he was a few years older than me or that other kibbutz members would agree to be absent from their rooms at certain times. I introduced him into the conversation in a roundabout way. I told Mum and Dad that some of the people on the kibbutz were Israelis but others came from all over the world. For example, there was an American boy called Nathan who was studying biochemistry at Harvard and had chosen that particular kibbutz because they were pioneering some sort of plant technology that I didn't really understand.

'They alter the genetic makeup of plants in a lab,' I tried to paraphrase what Nathan had told me, 'so that they'll be stronger and can withstand disease.'

'This is probably the point at which we should tell her, darling,' Dad said.

And I knew then that it was serious because Dad never used terms of endearment, and my mother only when she was cross. I used to think 'darling' was a swear word when I was younger because Mum would snap it at Dad when they were arguing.

'Tell me what?'

'Do you want some tea or coffee? We can leave the washing-up for a while.'

It must be serious, I thought. 'I'm being allowed off washing-up?' I tried to lighten the mood. 'Is that because I'm adopted?'

'This might be easier if you were,' Dad said.

After dinner Jon came round. He was a solicitor, the kind of job that made my parents happy and proud but that struck me as dull. He dealt with wills and probate for a local firm and still lived in the village. I'd never understood why he'd chosen not to leave, not to go somewhere more exciting, at least the next town, if not London or abroad.

Now it was beginning to dawn on me. Maybe he felt he should stick around.

'He's got a new girlfriend,' Dad had told me. 'A lovely girl. It's early days yet but . . .'

But what? I wanted to ask. Do you want them to get married? Are you hoping for grandchildren? Do you worry she might have ambitions to move elsewhere and he won't be on the doorstep to help you? Does she know too? Did she know before I knew? Does she know and might she still marry Jon? And have his children? Will anyone ever want to marry me?

But I couldn't say any of those things to my parents.

I think I said something like 'It's going to take a while for it all to sink in.'

When Jon arrived, Mum said she had to go to bed. Dad helped her because she couldn't manage to undress by herself, even though she was only in her forties.

Jon and I were left alone, facing each other across the kitchen table.

'I hadn't thought coming home would be like this,' I began.

'They didn't want to spoil your trip by telling you earlier.'

'It's so shit. I can't take it all in.'

Jon fumbled in his jacket pocket. 'Mars,' he said, producing a half-eaten bar. 'Want some?'

'Yes, please,' I said, and smiled because, for the first time since I'd come home, something felt normal and familiar.

Time forks perpetually towards innumerable futures.

Jorge Luis Borges, 'The Garden of Forking Paths'

Deauville, 1969

I spotted them when we arrived, swarming out of the bar, happy and noisy, a large family group. They were a blur of teenage boys and girls but one swam into focus as they passed through the hotel lobby, where we were handing over our passports and waiting to be allocated rooms.

He looked nice, the boy, about my age, and he appeared to pause as they made their way towards the staircase, as if I had come into focus for him too, rather than simply being part of another family group.

He smiled, then bounded up the stairs two at time, but he had made an impression because he was a boy and I was fourteen, and if a boy smiled at me, it made an impression.

'So, is this your first time in Deauville?' the hotel receptionist was asking Jon.

'It's our first time abroad,' Jon said.

It would turn out to be a week of firsts: the first time man landed on the moon, the first time Mum had one of her 'incidents' – or, at least, the first time I noticed. And the first time I saw something that had seemed almost as unbelievable as man landing on the moon. The sighting, and what followed, another first, lodged in my mind for longer than it might have otherwise.

*

'Looks like it could be any time soon.' Dad glanced up from yesterday's *Times*, which marked him out as British, and eyed a basket of croissants, as if he didn't quite trust them. 'They might actually land on the moon.'

'I feel like we've landed on the moon.' Mum waved her hand at the room and the windows that opened on to an enclosed garden with sculpted hedges. It wasn't that strange but it was definitely 'foreign'.

The weather was hot, the language alien, the food different. Even the bathroom in the hotel was weird. 'What's that for?' I'd pointed at the low-level sink. 'Is it for children?'

'It's for washing your feet after the beach,' Dad said.

'It's not,' Jon contradicted. 'It's for washing your –'

'Jonathan!' my mother warned him, as she took her flannel out of her washbag and hung it over the edge of the basin.

I wasn't sure why.

Later, when our parents were out of earshot, he told me. 'It's for washing after shagging.'

'How do you know?' I was shocked and intrigued.

'I just do. The French do it a lot.'

'Do they?'

'Yes. That's why the bed in Mum and Dad's room jiggles too.'

'They said it was to relax you.'

The bed in their room had a switch, which made it vibrate. It was bizarre, like so many things here.

Only the jams and spreads looked familiar, and the boy standing by the table they were arranged on, the one who'd smiled at me in the lobby the previous evening.

'There's the boy who was having drowning lessons.' Dad nodded to him.

Dad had been up at the crack of dawn, strolled along the seafront before breakfast and taken in the grounds of the hotel.

'What's the pool like?' I'd asked, as we were shown to the table where we would eat breakfast for the next seven days.

'It's not as big as the Van der Zees' but the water felt warmer and there was a boy having drowning lessons.'

'Before breakfast?'

'It was half past seven. I'll give you all a franc to spend if you swim before breakfast every day for the rest of the holidays.'

'How much is that?' Cathy asked.

'About a florin.'

'What do you mean "drowning lessons"?' I wanted to know more about the boy.

'Well, he obviously couldn't swim, and the instructor's method seemed to be to drag him out to the middle of the pool, with a metal pole, then take it away, so he had to swim back to the edge.'

'So, he could swim?'

'Only just.'

'I'm going to get some honey,' I said, but I hovered shyly as the boy arranged several individual servings of jam, spooned into miniature glass saucers, in the palm of one hand.

'Hi,' he said, without looking up.

'Hi.'

'You arrived yesterday?'

'Yes, with my family.'

'Me too.' He smiled.

I spooned some honey into one of the glass dishes and tried to think of something else to say.

'I'm Abe, by the way.'

'Oh, I'm Ivy.'

'Like the Mamas and Papas' song?' he asked, and I didn't know how to answer.

I was so used to people saying 'like the plant' that I'd been expecting that, and I'd never heard of the Mamas and Papas but didn't want to admit it. 'I suppose so,' I said.

'My brother listens to them all the time,' he said, as if to explain why he'd asked and to excuse me my ignorance.

A win on the football pools had brought us to France. Previous holidays had involved caravans, or the Hillman Imp with a tent in the West Country. 'I thought we'd go somewhere different this year,' Dad had announced one evening, just before we all got up from the kitchen table and began our allocated kitchen-tidying tasks.

'Where?' Jon asked.

'The Lake District?' Cathy suggested.

'Scotland?' I tried.

Abroad didn't enter anyone's mind.

Dad removed the checked napkin from his lap, folded it into a square, rolled it up, slowly and deliberately, and pushed it through the centre of one of the bone rings that had been a wedding present, along with a set of white napkins, which Mum kept for a 'best' that seemed never to materialize.

'France,' Dad said, setting the napkin down so that the ring knocked the table with a tiny triumphant thud.

'France?' Jon asked. 'How come?'

'Yes, France. Because I had a bit of luck with the pools.'

'When?' Jon helped him fill in the coupons.

'Last week.'

'When I went to stay with Simon?' He looked put out.

'Yes.' Dad sounded defensive.

'How much did you win?'

'Four hundred and fifty pounds!' He thumped the table with his hand, but Jon was not so easily put off.

'How did you select the teams?'

'I closed my eyes and brought the pen down.'

I could tell Jon was miffed, despite the win. They had a system, the two of them, and random selection was not part of it.

'I just wondered what difference it might make if I gave it no thought at all.'

'That's great,' Jon said, quietly, clearly miffed that Dad had done it without him.

'It's enough money for us to get a new battery for the car, buy a new washing-machine and all go to France for a week. We'll get the ferry from Dover to Calais and drive to Deauville from there.'

'Deauville?' Cathy asked, diverting the conversation from the means of the win to the result.

'It's on the coast, in Normandy,' Dad said.

And now we were there, and Dad was full of relentless bonhomie. It was as if he thought we'd all follow suit – or maybe it was just Mum he wanted to cheer up. She was strangely quiet and occasionally snappy.

She certainly wasn't herself in the bar that evening, when Dad insisted on us having 'an aperitif' before dinner with one of his oft-repeated 'When in Deauville!' exclamations.

The bar was empty, except for the barman, setting up a television in the corner.

'*Deux Dubonnet*,' Dad ordered for himself and Mum, '*et un Britvic*.' That was for me.

'Would you like a beer, Jon? Or a Dubonnet? You too, Cathy? When in Deauville . . .'

'I'll have a beer,' Jon said.

'Dubonnet.' Cathy caught my eye, smoothing the fabric of her new cheesecloth dress and watching as the TV was manoeuvred into place.

'*C'est pour la lune*. It is for the moon,' the barman translated. '*Demain*. Tomorrow.'

'*Ah, oui. Oui. Oui!*' Dad replied, animated. 'The moon mission.'

'We have to watch it,' Jon said, as we settled at a table by the window.

'I still don't believe they'll be able to actually land –' Dad began, but we were interrupted by the arrival of another British family in search of aperitifs.

Abe's.

'*Bonsoir.*' Dad half rose.

'*Bonsoir,*' Abe's dad said, awkwardly, then, 'Evening, everyone.'

'Hello,' we mumbled, all so obviously English.

I caught Abe's eye.

'I'm Richard.' Dad began a general round of introductions.

'This is Pam,' Abe's dad responded, 'I'm Greg, and these are Jackie, Kirsty, Tessa . . .' He paused. 'Our older boy's at university and didn't want to come. And you've met Abe.'

'I saw you swimming first thing this morning,' Dad said.

'Yes.'

'Where've you travelled from?' Dad asked his father.

'We live near Lanark, in Scotland,' he said. 'How about you?'

'Sussex. Small village you won't have heard of.'

'Try me.'

'Pulborough?'

'Know it!'

'Really?'

'Yes. We used to live in Sussex, not far from there. We moved before Abe started school.'

'Well, what a coincidence,' Dad said, as if it was. 'So why did you move? For work?'

'Initially,' Abe's father said.

'Greg got a job in Oxford and we were there for a while,'

his mother expanded. 'We moved to Scotland a couple of years ago.'

'Pam wanted to be near her family.' He put his arm round her. 'Five kids are a lot to cope with.'

'Quite a clan!' Dad smiled, and raised his glass as if toasting them. 'Is this your first time here?'

'Pam and I came to France years ago, before the children were born, but not this part. We tend to holiday at home. This year I was invited to speak at a conference in Paris . . .'

'Greg teaches at Glasgow University,' Abe's mother interjected. 'American history.'

'Very nice,' Dad said, looking at his watch. 'I'm sorry but we should be getting going. We're having dinner down by the harbour.'

I was old enough to have an inkling that Dad was put out by Abe's father being a university professor, by his having been to a conference en route, by their having been to France before. He did that thing he always did when he was bothered by something, humming under his breath. As we got up to go, he held his arm out so Mum could walk ahead. I could still hear him as I followed, then his sharp intake of breath as Mum tripped, losing her balance and clutching a table to steady herself.

'Steady on, Janet,' he said, cross, not concerned.

'Are you all right?' Cathy went to her.

'Yes.' She held on to the table, as if she still needed its support.

'Your mother's had a bit too much Dubonnet,' Dad said, his tone jovial but I could tell he was annoyed.

'I only had a glass. I just tripped,' Mum protested, but there was an edge to her voice I'd never heard before. She was angry and upset.

'Are you squiffy?' Dad asked. Then he looked at her more

closely and something registered. His whole demeanour changed. 'Are you all right, Janet?' Now he was concerned.

I felt uncomfortable.

'Yes,' Mum said, but even in that one syllable I heard her voice crack.

Over dinner, she talked a little but her mind seemed to be elsewhere.

'Are you going to try an oyster, Ivy?'

'Do I have to?'

'No, you don't.'

'But you won't get pudding unless you do.' Dad's pleasure-pain principle at work.

'What do you think?' Mum asked, as I washed the horrid slippery thing down with a glass of water.

'They're disgusting.'

'At least you tried one. When in Deauville!' Dad said again.

Mum ignored him. I couldn't interpret her look. 'I think they're disgusting too,' she said, smiling at me conspiratorially.

Later, Dad, Jon and Cathy stayed up to watch the moon landings, but Mum said she was tired and would go to bed. I went up with her. 'Are you all right, Mum?' I asked, as we walked up the stairs to our adjoining rooms.

'I'm fine, Ivy.' The annoyance was in her voice again.

'Are you enjoying the holiday?'

'Yes.'

'I really like it. I'd like to come back.' I was prattling.

'I'm sure you will.'

'I'd like to go to other places too. Other countries on the continent, maybe even to America one day.'

'You'll have to be an air hostess, then.'

'What do they do?'

'They're like hostesses on aeroplanes. They look after people on their flights. You'd get to travel a lot.'

'Maybe.' I thought there must be other jobs that involved travel. I wasn't sure I wanted to be stuck on a plane but I didn't say so. 'Night, Mum,' I said, when we reached the door of my room.

I waited for her to say something motherly, to ask if I'd be happy on my own in the room until Cathy got back, perhaps to come in, draw the curtains and turn back the covers on my bed. But she didn't.

'Goodnight, Ivy,' she said, in a tone that was unfamiliar.

When Cathy came in, much later, I woke as she closed the bedroom door. She climbed into bed beside me.

'Cath?'

'Sorry, did I wake you up?'

'Did they land?'

'Yes, they did.'

Silence. I tried to imagine it. I'd looked up at the sky hours earlier when I closed the curtains and had seen the moon suspended in the night. It seemed almost impossible that someone might be about to climb out of a rocket and walk on it. I wished now I'd stayed up and that Mum had too.

'Do you think Mum's all right?' I asked quietly.

'Why?' Cathy said, settling into the pillows.

'I don't know. She just seems a bit . . .'

'What?'

'I don't know.'

I expected Cathy to say something dismissive, like 'Why are you worrying, then?' but she didn't.

'Neither do I,' Cathy said. 'I'm sure she's fine, though. Are you?'

'Yes.' Why wouldn't I be?

'And you're having a good time?'

'Yes.'

'Your friend seems nice. They were just coming in as we went up.'

I knew whom she meant, but 'My friend?'

'The boy in the bar. The one who has swimming lessons.'

'I haven't really spoken to him.'

'Maybe you should.'

'Night, Cathy.'

'Night, baby.'

Sometimes she called me that. She was only two years older but it was a hangover from when I was born. She used it when she was feeling protective towards me.

'Night.'

The next time I saw Abe he was alone by the pool, lying on a towel, no sign of his family. The pool was quiet at that time in the afternoon and I planned to do lengths. I hadn't anticipated finding Abe there and I felt awkward.

'Hi.' He waved.

'Hello,' I said.

Abe stood up. 'Are you on your own?'

'Yes. The others are still in their rooms.'

'Are you going swimming?'

'Yes.' I didn't know whether to sit next to him or settle somewhere else. To join him seemed too forward, but to sit elsewhere unfriendly.

'Tessa and Kirsty are playing tennis. They said they'd come over when they're done. I'm not very good at it.'

'Neither am I,' I laughed.

I was bad at all forms of ball games. That was partly why I liked swimming.

Abe nodded towards the ground. 'Do you want to sit with me?'

I spread my towel next to his, a foot or two between them, and tried to think of something to say.

'Did you watch the moon landings?' It was what everybody was asking.

'Yes. We went to a barber's shop in town.'

'A barber's? Where you get your hair cut?'

'Dad saw a sign there earlier saying there was a television and it would be open half the night. He thought it would be fun to go there. And it was. Did you watch?'

'No.' I wished I had now. 'The others did but Mum and I went to bed.'

'It was weird seeing them there on the moon, the same moon we saw over the sea when we went out to dinner.'

Then he took off his T-shirt so that he was just wearing his trunks.

'Are you going swimming?' I asked.

'Not yet. I will in a bit.' He lay back on his towel.

'Right.'

Shyly, I removed my top to reveal the swimsuit I was wearing underneath.

'Are you going in now?'

'I might wait for a bit too,' I said, enjoying the warmth of the sun on my skin. 'Warm up a bit first.'

I glanced across at Abe, wanting to study him without him noticing. I breathed in, aware that my fledgling breasts rose as I did. Did Abe notice? He smiled at me, then closed his eyes.

'Ivy what?'

'What do you mean?'

'Have you got any other names?'

'Trent.'

'Middle name?'

'I haven't got one.'

'Why not?'

'They couldn't think of one for me.'

That was what my parents said when I asked the same question.

'I've got three.' Abe opened his eyes again.

'Three?'

'Abe Craig Joseph Aiken McFadden. Aiken was my mum's name but we've all got it as a middle name.'

'That's a lot of names,' I said, then worried that I might have sounded critical. 'But it must be good having so many.' Chatting wasn't coming easily to me. 'Abe's an unusual name.' I tried instead.

'It's short for Abraham.'

'I've never met an Abraham before.'

'I've never met an Ivy.'

'You don't have an old aunt called Ivy?'

'No.'

'Most people do.'

'It's an old-fashioned name . . .' he considered it '. . . but it suits you.'

'Thanks!' I felt the ice had broken.

'I didn't mean —'

'I think it might be time for your swim!'

'I think it is.' He grinned, and I wasn't sure if he winked at me as he stood up. Maybe he just squinted into the sun.

Dad must have exaggerated the drowning lessons. Abe wasn't a brilliant swimmer but he could stay afloat. I joined him. I swam a few lengths with my head under water before pausing and blinking the water from my eyes.

'You're a good swimmer, Ivy.'

'I swim at the local pool a lot. They have a club.'

'I'm going to get out now.'

I watched the dark hairs on the back of his legs glistening as he climbed the steps and ran his hand through his hair to get it out of his eyes.

Then I put my head under water again and began swimming, counting the lengths. I planned to do fifty. I tried to ignore the fact that Abe was probably watching me. But I was conscious of his presence, as I tried to concentrate on elongating my strokes, as the instructor at our local pool at home had shown me.

When I finally got out Abe's mother was there, sitting on the grass beside him, the other side of my towel. 'Hello, Ivy,' she said.

'Hello,' I said, bending to pull my towel off the grass and wrap it around me.

'You're a good swimmer.'

'Thank you.' I felt my earlier awkwardness begin to return but his mum was nice.

'Abe's been having lessons here.'

'Yes.'

'Maybe by the end of the week he'll be as good as you.'

'Mum,' Abe said, but he smiled at her as he said it.

'I came to give Abe some money to go to the shops. We're going on a picnic tomorrow. He needs to practise his French and I want him to buy some cheese.'

'I can't really speak French,' I said.

'Nor can I!'

'Well, I'm sure you'll find a way of buying cheese.' His mother laughed. 'Bring it up to our room when you get back. Bye, Ivy. Nice to meet you properly.'

'Bye,' I said, laying my towel down and sitting on it. 'So you have to go and buy cheese?' I asked Abe.

'Soon. Why don't you come with me?'

'Into town?'

'Why not?'

I didn't see him again for a few days. We went to Mont Saint-Michel on one of them and Dad had given us each another franc when we reached the monastery at the top of the rocky island promontory. 'For being good climbers,' he said.

Jon and Cathy had looked at each other and raised their eyebrows, as if there was another reason, and Dad had said, 'Okay, because I'm feeling generous, then.'

We'd all laughed, not because Dad wasn't generous but because it was unusual for him to hand out money that had not been earned by climbs or dawn swims here and at home by various chores.

'Are there any jobs need doing?' I'd asked before we left, keen to bring some money to spend on the holiday.

'You can iron Dad's handkerchiefs,' Mum had said, and handed me a pile, folded and creaseless. She'd already ironed them but money had to be earned. It was never just given away.

'He's certainly in holiday mood,' Jon had said, as we made our way down through the streets of the village that lay below the monastery. 'Shall we go into town tomorrow and look for souvenirs?'

Jon, Cathy and I wandered through Deauville, pausing to look at the arrays of beach shoes, shells and pottery.

'What about one of these?' Cathy suggested, as we stopped outside a shop with piles of bowls, each painted with an image of a French man or woman and a series of individual boys' and girls' names.

'They're nice,' I said, looking at one with 'Claudette' painted on the side. 'Do you think they have an Ivy?'

We found an Isabeau, Ignatia, Ila and Inès, but no Ivy.

'There's a Catherine,' I said.

'You know I hate that.' Cathy pulled a face.

'I might get one.' Jon picked up a bowl with a woman's name.

'Jean?' I said.

'It's Jean, stupid.' He pronounced the J like 'zh'. 'It's French for John.'

We'd laughed.

'Did you three have a good afternoon?' Mum asked that evening, as we gathered in the hotel bar before dinner.

'Yes.' It had been nice to spend time with Jon and Cathy. 'I didn't buy anything, though,' I said, scanning the bar.

'Looking for Abraham Lincoln?' Jon asked.

'No.'

'Where did you two slope off to the other day, anyway?'

'Nowhere. We just went to get some cheese.'

'Cheese?'

'Brie,' I said. 'And Camembert.' I said the names, hoping to impress him. Mum referred to all cheese that was not Cheddar as 'smelly cheese'.

'French cheese?' Jon said, and I tried to think of something to counter his insinuating tone but we were distracted by Mum.

She'd just picked up her drink and was about to carry it to a nearby table when she dropped it. The glass shattered as the wine cascaded over the floor. 'Oh, I'm sorry,' she said to the barman.

'What happened?' Dad asked.

'It just slipped from my hand,' Mum said. She looked confused.

'But how?'

'It was an accident.'

But there was something else.

Something about the way they looked at each other.

'But how did it happen? Did someone jog you?'

'No, Richard. It just happened.'

The barman began to wipe the floor as Dad ushered Mum to a table.

'I was just clumsy.'

'Are you sure that's all?'

An uneasy silence followed. None of us was sure what to say.

I was the first to break it. I was trying to help. 'Shall I ask the barman for another drink for you, Mum?'

'Ivy, keep out of it,' Dad snapped, and the awkward silence continued until Cathy announced that she wanted to buy a pair of espadrilles.

'What are they?'

'Rope-soled shoes.' Cathy hadn't mentioned them when we were shopping earlier.

'They sound weird. I bet they're not comfy.'

Uncomfortable shoes were more comfortable territory.

After that Dad's bonhomie seemed to disappear and Mum was strangely withdrawn. I was glad of the chance to get away when it came, surprised at my own lack of hesitation in taking it.

'Ivy.' I recognized Abe's voice as I went into the dining room later that week.

'Hi.' I tried to appear casual.

'I haven't seen you lately. What have you been up to?'

'We went to Mont Saint-Michel. Have you been?'

'We were going to go yesterday but Mum said it was too

hot so we ended up driving to a beach instead. It wasn't that nice, not as nice as the one we went to the day before.'

'How was your picnic?' I asked, remembering.

'Good. We might go to the same place again tomorrow.'

'Oh.' The chance of spending time with him seemed to be disappearing.

'Are you here today?' he asked, as if he was thinking the same thing. 'Will you be by the pool later?'

'Probably, after lunch. We might be going to a museum this morning.'

'Good,' he said. And then: 'We're going to the beach we went to on Wednesday again tomorrow. It's our last day. I wondered if you might like to come too. Jackie and Tessa don't want to go again so there'll be room in the car.'

The beach was about a half-hour drive. I sat in the back of the car with Kirsty and Abe. His dad wore a black fisherman's cap to drive. His mother sat next to him but turned round every now and then to say something to us.

'So this is your first trip abroad, Ivy?'

'Yes.'

'Are you doing your O levels next year?'

'Yes.'

'Abe does his O grades. We don't have O levels in Scotland.'

She faced forward again and spoke to Mr McFadden as a lorry carrying hay bales drew out of a side road ahead of us. 'Don't get too close, will you? They never look safe to me.'

Kirsty raised her eyebrows. 'Mum's always spotting potential accidents.'

'Better to be safe,' Mrs McFadden said.

'If it's going to happen it will,' Abe's dad said, glancing in the rear-view mirror. 'Murphy's Law.'

'I thought Murphy's Law meant that anything that can go wrong will,' Kirsty said.

'That's the pessimist's interpretation,' Mr McFadden replied. 'I think it just means that everything that is going to happen will happen. You can't do anything about it if it does. It doesn't necessarily mean it will happen to you. Your bread might not land butter side down but someone's will.'

'Look out for the field with the donkey. I think the turn-off for the beach was shortly after that,' Mrs McFadden said.

We left the main road and drove down a smaller lane, until a row of sand dunes topped by a strip of grey-blue sea hove into view.

'Have you ever been to Cornwall, Ivy?' Mr McFadden asked, as he parked.

'We've been to Devon a few times but never to Cornwall.'

'The beaches here are very similar.' He opened the car door. 'The two land masses were joined thousands of years ago and you get the impression that one beach starts where the other left off.'

'Shall we just go, Dad?' Kirsty asked.

'Sorry.'

Their mother got out, opened the boot and pulled out a striped canvas bag with two plastic handles, which she handed to Kirsty. To Abe she passed a large tartan rug. 'Greg, can you take this one? It's got the drink in it. And, Ivy, do you mind carrying the bread?'

I took the paper-wrapped French sticks she handed me. 'Can I carry anything else?'

'No, thanks.'

Mr McFadden was already striding with purpose, search-ing out a picnic spot. The rest of us followed.

'Shall we set up here?' Abe's mum asked, gesturing to a crescent of sand half enclosed by dunes.

'Let's have a photo of the two of you,' Mr McFadden said, as Abe and I laid out the rug and anchored it with pebbles. He kicked off his shoes and produced a camera, motioning me to stand next to Abe. 'Smile!'

I smiled shyly and was surprised when, moments later, he handed me the photo he'd taken. 'A souvenir,' he said.

'But how?' I'd never seen a Polaroid camera before. 'How come you didn't have to wait for it to be developed?'

'Modern technology.' He laughed. 'Are you going to have a swim before lunch?'

We did go into the sea before lunch. It wasn't really swimming.

'You won't go out too far, will you?' Mrs McFadden asked, as we set off.

'Mum! We'll be fine.' Kirsty grinned at her mother.

The sea was rough and we stopped when we were waist deep and jumped over the waves.

'Let's try surfing,' Kirsty said, and tried to explain to Abe and me at what point we should launch our prone bodies on to the waves. 'I did it with Aunt Katrina at Pease Bay . . . Try this one,' she urged us, as a wave rose a few feet from where we were standing. We threw ourselves into the water and tried to roll with it but our attempts were not exactly successful.

'Rubbish,' Kirsty said. 'Let's try a few more times then go for lunch.'

More of the same. More being dunked by the waves until eventually I hit one at just the right moment, stretched my arms in front of me, the way Kirsty had shown me, and the wave carried me to within a few feet of the shore. Fantastic.

'Well done!' Kirsty was shouting.

'That was brilliant,' I said, when I'd walked back out to the two of them.

After a few more attempts, Abe was complaining: 'Argh, I just keep going under.'

'One more wave and then we'll go in?' Kirsty suggested.

I rode the next wave too. It was exciting.

A few minutes later we were back with Abe's parents.

'Ivy's like a fish,' his mum said, handing me a piece of bread and gesturing at the picnic. 'Dig in.'

After lunch Abe and I walked along the ridge of sand dunes.

'Mum and I might have a wee nap,' Mr McFadden had said, as he wrapped leftover bits of cheese and ham and put them back in the basket. 'Why don't you three go and explore?'

'I'm going to read my book,' Kirsty excused herself.

'Shall we go up to those woods?' Abe pointed out a cluster of pine trees about a mile away.

'Okay.'

We threaded our way along the path that crossed the dunes towards the patch of green.

'It was nice of your parents to let me come,' I said, wondering if mine would have let someone encroach on their holiday so willingly, and feeling shy alone in his company.

'They like having people around. Shall we go up there?' Abe pointed to a path that seemed to wind around the edge of the dunes.

He took the lead. We chatted at first, about this and that: school, friends, family, pets (Abe had a tortoise called Fred), the music we liked, previous holidays, until we fell into a silence that surprised me by not feeling awkward. It was eventually broken by the sound of people. Not voices, not laughter. But people making sounds that were something between strange and familiar.

As the path dipped into a bowl created by the surrounding dunes we found the people and discovered what the noise was. They were surrounded by the remains of a picnic: a bottle of water, leftover bread and a couple of apples. Discarded shoes lay in the sand – rope-soled shoes, like Cathy wanted – a bikini hung to dry on a tuft of couch grass and a towel was spread on the ground. Next to it, too obvious when they should have been tucked neatly into a bag, was a pair of knickers and a crumpled shirt.

All the details seemed to jump out at me. These people had had a picnic and been for a swim. I took in all of that, as if it might make what was really happening go away. The boy, who looked a few years older than Abe and me, was wearing a pair of faded blue shorts. But they were down around his ankles, and his buttocks, which were white, contrasting with the tan of his back and the dark hairs of his legs, were moving with purpose on top of the girl beneath him. Her dress was ruched up around her waist and her legs were clasped around the boy.

It was only for a second or two that we stood there, rooted by the unexpectedness of what we were seeing, not sure whether to go on past, ignoring them, or turn round and find another route. But in those seconds I found myself strangely mesmerized by the movement of their bodies, the sounds they were making and their obliviousness to our presence.

Then the girl turned her head, saw us and raised her hand, flicking us away in annoyance rather than embarrassment. Her gesture distracted the boy, who turned his head and grinned.

The only embarrassment was between Abe and me, as we turned and beat a retreat. We were unsure what to say to each other and the silence between us was uneasy now.

Abe spoke first. 'Typical French.' He shook his head, as if he stumbled across French couples making love in the dunes all the time.

'Yes.' I tried to appear nonchalant.

The woods, once we reached them, were fenced off.

'We can't go in.' Abe looked at his watch. 'We should probably head back anyway.'

'Yes.'

'Shall we go along the shore?'

'Maybe we should.'

'I think I'll take my shoes off and carry them.' Abe sat down and began to unlace his plimsolls. I sat next to him and he shifted slightly, moving closer to me so that our arms were touching.

'Cathy wants to buy these shoes with soles made of rope,' I said, as I leaned forward to unlace my own shoes and kick them off.

'Espadrilles?' he said, as I sat up. 'Kirsty got a pair the other day. Blue ones.'

His chatter about shoes made the fact that he'd put his arm tentatively around my shoulders seem normal.

'She wasn't wearing them.'

'She thought they might get wet.'

'Oh.' The feel of his arm around me was delicious. I wanted to lean in, put my head on his shoulder, but I didn't.

'Okay?' Abe asked, and I nodded.

'It's such a beautiful place,' I said, wondering, What next?

'Ivy, can I ask you something?'

'Yes.' I looked at him expectantly, without being quite sure what I was expecting. He seemed a little scared. 'What is it?'

'Can I – can I kiss you?'

'Yes.' That was it.

Neither of us moved. Then Abe leaned towards me, put his arms around me and pulled me to him. His lips were on mine, tentative at first, but I found myself pushing my body closer to his so that I could feel my breasts against his chest and clasp my hands around his back.

It wasn't the first time I'd kissed a boy properly. There'd been awkward attempts at school and embarrassment after-wards. But with Abe, I liked it, I really did. I liked the way it felt as if he was tasting me, and I wanted it to go on and turn into something more – not what we'd seen on the beach but something else.

Abe's hand was moving down my side, almost touching my breast but not quite. I began to feel something new, something bold and slightly scary. I shifted slightly, and felt his hand brush my breast through the fabric of my shirt. I wasn't wearing a bra. I usually did, a flimsy teen bra that was more of an acknowledgement that I'd reached puberty than support, but it had been too complicated, changing on the beach after our swim, to put it on.

He kissed me again and his hand came down to rest firmly on my chest. 'Thank you,' he said, after a while, stopping and looking at me.

I reddened. 'We probably should go back.' I reached for my shoes and started to put them on, without looking at Abe.

Then we walked back along the beach, the same people who had left the family picnic less than an hour earlier but who had changed in themselves and in relation to each other.

Before Abe's family left, we exchanged addresses, but there was only ever one letter, which I kept for a while, wrapped around the Polaroid photograph of the two of us, in my secret box under my bed. It didn't really say anything, although I searched for something between the lines and tried to believe Abe was telling me more than that Fred, his tortoise, had been missing when they'd got home, but they'd eventually found him hiding in a flower bed.

I never wrote back. I wanted to. I started a letter a few times, but something always stopped me completing it.

Philosophically, the universe has really never
made things in ones. The Earth is special
and everything else is different? No,
we've got seven other planets. The sun?
No, the sun is one of those dots in the night sky.
The Milky Way? No, it's one of a hundred
billion galaxies. And the universe – maybe
it's countless other universes.

Neil deGrasse Tyson

Sussex, 1965

I was so pleased for him that I completely forgot my own
disappointment. 'You won? That's so clever!'

'Yes.' Abe seemed anxious rather than excited. 'You don't
mind?'

'Why should I? It's really good.' I wanted to hug him but
something about his demeanour stopped me. 'I can't believe
you won out of everyone!'

Cathy had pointed out the 'Design a Flower bed' competition in the local paper.

'But I don't know much about flowers and I'm not that
good at drawing,' I'd said to her.

I wasn't keen at first but the prize was a ten-shilling book
token and there was a book I wanted, more than anything: a
copy of *Gulliver's Travels*, with a red leather cover on which
the title was embossed in gold. The pages were thick and

creamy, tipped with red at the edges. It was the most beautiful book I had ever seen.

'I'm sure we've got a copy somewhere.' Mum hadn't understood that I wanted this particular book.

Abe and I had decided to enter the competition on a rainy day when we were stuck inside. We sat at his kitchen table, with the Cuban cigar box that contained coloured pencils between us, and sketched our flower beds. As soon as Abe began drawing, I knew I hadn't a chance of winning. My sketchily crayoned blocks of colour couldn't compare to his.

He'd used a book to look up actual flowers and created a cascade of blooms of different heights and colours. My neat rows of indeterminate pinks and reds were pretty, but Abe's flower bed came alive on the paper.

'You should have won,' I said to him. 'Yours was the best.'

I could barely contain myself. I was so happy for him. And the council would make the flower bed just by the traffic lights on the edge of town. Everyone who drove through would stop there and see it. And it would be Abe's.

'But it was your idea to go in for the competition and –'

I cut him off. 'It was Cathy's idea and it doesn't matter.' I'd never thought I'd win and it hadn't seemed possible that Abe would either. The competition was open to so many people. The whole of Sussex. How could two ten-year-olds compete with all the artists and gardeners in the county?

The book token was forgotten. I'd asked for the book for my birthday anyway.

'I'm so pleased,' I told him, and his face broke into a huge grin that went right up to his eyes.

I'd spotted him on my first day at school: he was standing alone on the other side of the playground, pressing himself against the wire fence that surrounded it, as if he thought he

311

might disappear if he pushed hard enough. He was wearing enormously thick glasses, ill-fitting clothes, and must have been a good two inches taller than any other four-year-old in the playground. He seemed ill at ease, and had the sort of awkwardness that made other children keep their distance. I wanted to talk to him.

I had a tangerine in my pocket. 'Be good.' Mum had pushed it into my hand like some sort of good-luck charm.

I concentrated on peeling it as I walked towards the boy, trying to keep the skin in one long snake. He looked up and half smiled, unsure. 'Do you want a pig?' I offered him a segment.

'A pig?' He looked confused.

'A piece of this.'

'Why do you call it a pig?'

'Everybody does.' The expression was a relic of my mother's Irish roots. Everyone but her called pieces of citrus fruit 'segments'.

'Thank you.'

'Do you want to jump off those?' I nodded to a part of the playground where a flower bed was bordered by an assortment of small rocks trailing on to the concrete and forming a line of stepping-stones across it.

'Why?' He'd moved forward, ready to follow me, still unsure.

'For fun.' I willed him to come and try it.

'Fun,' he repeated, but he followed me as I stepped on to the first rock then jumped off it onto the concrete. I looked back at him, smiling, encouraging him to follow.

We jumped for the next few minutes: from rock to rock, from rock to the ground, round and round, smiling without saying anything, until 'It is fun!' He laughed.

'I'm hot.' I took my coat off and hung it on the fence by the nametape sewn inside the collar.

On cue, he asked my name.

'Well . . .' I hesitated '. . . that says "TRENT".'

'Is that your surname?'

'Yes. The nametapes say "Jon Trent Catherine". Jon and Cathy are my brother and sister. My mum sews under whichever name isn't the right one. I just get Trent.'

'I have old clothes,' he said, shrugging off his coat and taking a step closer. 'What's your Christian name?'

'Ivy.' I hated my name. I'd been called after my maternal grandmother, one of the many relatives on my mother's side who had died before I was born. It was an old person's name or the name of a poisonous plant. It couldn't be shortened or trailed, the way the plant could, only commented on.

'That's a nice name.'

Relief and a surge of warmth. 'What's yours?'

'Abraham.' He shuffled awkwardly. 'But everyone calls me Abe.'

'Ivy and Abe.' I liked the way the two names sounded.

I'd got used to hearing our names, rolled into one 'Ivy'n'Abe' when it happened.

I knew because of the way Mum and Dad were talking to each other that something bad had taken place. They didn't talk to each other much. It wasn't a deliberate ignoring, rather that family life didn't leave much room for the two of them. It was unusual when one specifically solicited a word with the other.

They never did our bedtimes together either. It was Dad first, for a quick chat and a kiss, Mum after.

Dad was sitting on the edge of my bed, reeling off an account of his day, which, to me, sounded so exotic he might as well have been reading from *The Hobbit*.

'You'll never guess what Mr Piper did today?' He'd imbued his boss with the mystique of Gandalf.

'What?'

'He ate a yoghurt at his desk!'

'He ate a yoghurt at his desk?' I was delighted. It was the daftest, silliest thing anyone could do. A grown man, who worked in an office, eating yoghurt at his desk? Who even ate yoghurt? Nobody.

I could hear the phone ringing, unusual at this time of night, but Dad took no notice. 'He did! He keeps a spoon in his drawer, specifically for the purpose!'

Just wait till I told Abe. He'd laugh as much as I had.

Mum came in. 'Can I have a word?'

'But he's saying goodnight. And you haven't kissed me.'

Mum walked over to my bed and did so.

That was it. The nightly routine was all messed up. Mr Piper and his yoghurt were no longer funny. But I didn't know why.

I listened to their footsteps on the stairs, heard the doors, then murmuring directly below my bedroom but not what was said.

Maybe ten minutes later, maybe three-quarters of an hour, Mum came back up again. I pretended to be asleep as she bent down, smoothed my hair and kissed my cheek. Her face was wet.

'Mum?'

'I thought you were asleep.' Her voice was all wrong.

'What did you need to talk to Dad about?'

'Oh, Ivy . . .' she took a deep breath ' . . . I'll tell you in the morning. You get some sleep now.'

'But –'

'Go to sleep. There's nothing for you to worry about tonight. I'll see you in the morning, sweetheart.' The give-away endearment. Terms of affection were as rare as Mars bars and swear words. And when someone doesn't tell you what's wrong immediately, you imagine the worst.

*

Mum and Dad sent me to school the next day, with reassurances that everything was 'fine', but as soon as I got there I knew it wasn't.

Abe was not at school.

I needed his reassuring presence. I wanted to tell him about Mr Piper eating yoghurt at his desk. I wanted to make him laugh. I might even have told him that Mum and Dad were behaving oddly and perhaps he'd have told me that something was worrying his parents too.

But I understood, at school that day, that something was not right. Abe's desk was empty and our teacher was behaving strangely. She didn't read Abe's name when she took the register, as she usually did, even if she already knew that a particular child was absent.

'William?' she'd say. Then, 'Oh, no, William's not well today.'

When she reached the place in the register where Abe's name was, there was no 'Abe?' she just skipped his name and moved directly from Rachel to Stephen.

I put up my hand.

'Yes, Ivy.' She busied herself with something on her desk.

'You didn't call Abe's name. He's not here today.'

'I know, Ivy,' she said, in a voice I'd never heard before.

The teacher supervising playtime found me crying. 'Oh, Ivy. You poor little thing. '

'Why?'

'You're bound to be upset,' she said kindly, gesturing for me to sit beside her on the playground wall.

'Has something happened to Abe?'

'I thought you knew, dear. He's quite all right. He'll be back at school in a few days. You don't need to upset yourself. Perhaps we should ask your mother to collect you and take you home.'

'Ivy! Come and join in!' someone in a group of girls skipping called.

I ran to them.

'I've got doughnuts,' Mum said, when she picked me up. 'I stopped at the baker on the way here.'

'For tea?' We never had doughnuts for tea.

'Yes.'

She allowed her mouth to smile but the rest of her face was not involved. There was no light behind her eyes or crinkles spreading around them.

'What's happened?'

'At tea.'

We walked home in silence.

Abe was the youngest of five siblings. Alan was three years older than my brother Jon, Jackie in the year above him at school. Kirsty was in the year between Jackie and my sister Cathy, and Tessa in the year below. They lived in an old farmhouse in the country, equidistant to our school and another in a different village.

'If you'd gone to that school we'd never have met,' I used to say to him.

Sometimes Abe's mother picked her children up from school in the car. If the weather was good, they usually walked. Occasionally, if one of the older ones decided to cycle, Abe was allowed to ride his bike with them.

Sometimes in summer, if I went home with Abe after school to have tea and roam in their large garden, or play in the disused barns, his mum's car would get stuck behind a lorry piled high with hay bales. They moved slowly and Mrs McFadden would brake, maintaining her distance.

'Ivy, something bad has happened.' Mum sat next to

me at the kitchen table. 'You know how Mrs McFadden always likes to keep her distance from those lorries carrying the hay?'

I nodded.

'I used to think she was a bit too anxious,' Mum took a sip of her tea, 'but there was one on the road the day before yesterday, just after school, and the bales weren't secure. Not at all.' She paused. 'Kirsty was cycling home.' She took a deep breath. 'If she'd been just a second or two later it would have been all right. But she was cycling behind the lorry, and when the bales fell, one hit her and she came off her bike.'

'Is she hurt?'

'Ivy.' Mum put out her hand and took mine. 'They fell from such a height it must have been like being struck by a large rock. And then she hit the road.'

I said nothing.

'She fractured her skull, Ivy,' Mum said.

'But she'll get better?'

'No. I'm so sorry, love. The ambulance took her to hospital but they couldn't do anything.'

'You mean . . .' I couldn't say it.

'She died, Ivy, before they got her to hospital.'

I nodded and tried not to cry

'Shall we walk the dog, love?'

When Abe came back to school, after the weekend, I wanted to say something to him but I couldn't think what. It wasn't just me. There were fewer than a hundred pupils at our school. Everyone knew Abe and Tessa, and everyone knew Kirsty had died, but no one said anything to them.

'Abe, would you help me put the books away?' our teacher said, at the end of the morning's lessons on his first day back.

It was a solicitous gesture and I echoed it when I took out my tangerine to eat during break.

'Would you like a pig?' was probably the closest I came to offering condolences.

The McFaddens had never taken holidays, even before Kirsty died. Mr McFadden occasionally went away on work trips. He'd been to Berlin, and seen the Wall, and to Washington and New York, which he'd loved. He'd brought back gramophone records bearing names I'd never heard of: Little Richard, Ray Charles and Woody Guthrie, who looked out from beneath a hat, like the one Mr McFadden had, on the cover.

'I'd like to take the family to America one day,' he said. 'But it's expensive. We'll have to wait till I win the pools.'

'Which will be a long time coming, since you never actually do them,' Mrs McFadden rejoined.

She didn't seem to mind about holidays. Instead, they had a huge tent, which could take up to ten people. They put it up in the back garden for the whole summer. I'd camped in it. 'Can Ivy stay?' Abe would ask his mother.

'Of course,' Mrs McFadden replied, as she cut us both a slice of cake. 'How many minutes, Ivy?' She divided cakes and tarts into minutes rather than approximate sizes or fractions.

'Four, please! Is it really all right if I stay?'

'Of course. You don't need to ask – you're part of the family.'

I liked it when she said that and I liked the nights in the McFaddens' garden better than the holidays we'd spent in a caravan in Wales. There were always so many people.

'Abe, you and Ivy go and fetch wood.' We were happy to take orders from Jackie as he supervised the building of a campfire.

'Everyone keep quiet. It's Ivy's turn.' Tessa would force

everyone to listen to me, as we took it in turns to tell a story while we were sitting around it, line by line.

'Push the blade away from you, Ivy.' Alan taught me how to whittle a stick and use it to toast marshmallows.

They all made me feel part of the family and I loved being with them, but I looked forward to the point in the evening when everyone retired in groups of two or three to the separate sleeping compartments and I could snuggle down in my sleeping bag next to Abe.

In the mornings we were woken by Fred, Abe's tortoise, whose name I'd helped paint on his shell in large white letters in case he got lost. Abe left him in the outer area of the tent, free to roam and eat the grass, and when the sun rose, we'd hear him exploring the canvas of our sleeping compartment with his nose and feet, snuffling noisily, as if asking to come in.

But the summer after Kirsty died, the tent never went up.

Erecting it was a monumental team effort. There were so many poles needing to be pushed into the right bit of canvas at the right time. It took all of the McFaddens a good day to put up. It was like building a giant Meccano structure and covering it with complicated folds of canvas – one of the rituals of summer that Abe loved most. Seeing the steel structure of the tent take shape gave him as much pleasure as the buildings he screwed together in his bedroom.

But two weeks after Kirsty's funeral, when the summer holidays began, the tent stayed in its bag in the barn. I still went round to the McFaddens' house, played in the woods and the barn, but Abe was quieter – subdued. We didn't talk about Kirsty.

I wanted to ask him if he missed her but I never seemed to find the right moment or the right words.

'It's a shame you don't have the tent up this year.' We were sitting on a log by a stream, which ran through the woods at the bottom of the McFaddens' garden.

Abe was picking bits of bark and throwing them absent-mindedly towards the stream.

'Did your dad not want to put it up?'

'I don't know.'

'He probably didn't.'

'I don't think it's even occurred to him that he should.'

'No.' I nodded. 'It's a shame it's so big.'

'Why?'

'Well, it's too big to put up without your dad and everyone helping,' I said. 'Because I know they can't.'

'We've got another tent,' Abe said suddenly, looking at me.

'Have you?'

'Yes, a little one. Jackie took it to Scout Camp one year.'

'And it's yours?'

'Yes. I think it's in the garage.'

'The garage?'

'We could put it up easily.'

'Maybe we should ask your mum and dad if that would be all right?'

'They won't mind,' Abe said, jumping down off the log.

'I think we should. They might not want anyone camping.'

'Why not?'

'They just might not.'

'Well, we'll ask them,' Abe said. 'But I don't think they'll mind, not if we can put it up ourselves.'

He was right.

'Of course,' was all Mrs McFadden said when he asked.

She didn't seem interested, or when Abe asked, 'Can Ivy stay tonight, if we put it up? Will you ask her mum?'

'Whatever you like, Abe.'

'I don't want to be a nuisance,' I said. 'It was just an idea.'

She smiled a small sad smile. 'Oh, Ivy, you are sweet.' She got up from the kitchen table and stroked my head briefly, muttering something about 'Titian' as she walked towards the hall. 'I'll phone your mother now.'

When Mum appeared later with a sleeping bag and my overnight things, we were in the garden and the tent almost up. 'I'm just going to say hello to Mrs McFadden. I'll come and say goodbye before I go home.'

She hadn't come out by the time we'd finished, so we went in to find them in the kitchen. Abe stopped ahead of me. 'Let's go upstairs and get pillows.'

'But . . .' I saw what he'd already seen through the kitchen doorway: Mrs McFadden sitting at the table, her head in her arms, her body heaving. Mum was beside her, her arm round her shoulders, saying nothing.

She came out later, looking sad but being extra jolly. 'Bye, Ivy.' She poked her head through the tent flap. 'Gosh, it looks cosy in here. Don't be a nuisance, will you?'

'I won't.'

Mrs McFadden was fine again by suppertime. 'We're having ham and salad,' she said.

Everything seemed normal, which was what made it feel so odd.

We had supper. We helped to wash up and tidy the kitchen. We went out to play in the garden, then came in and got ready for bed. We said goodnight to Mr and Mrs McFadden, who were sitting in the living room with cups of coffee on the table between them.

It was all normal but not quite right.

Lying in the dark of our tent, I asked Abe, 'Is your mum all right?'

'I've put the torch in this pocket by the door,' he replied.

'Oh.' I changed tack. 'I like this tent. Funny that it's been in your garage all the time.'

'Why's that funny?'

'Just that I didn't know.'

'There's other things,' Abe said, 'that you don't know.'

I couldn't tell if he was cross.

'Mum's supposed to take these pills. But she doesn't always. Dad found the bottle in the bathroom cabinet this morning and there were too many left. So he knew.'

'Oh.' I felt embarrassed because I'd found pills in the bathroom once before. I'd been there after school and Abe had a headache. He'd left his glasses at school and Mrs McFadden thought that might be the cause. She had told me to look for aspirin in the bathroom cabinet. 'I can't find any.' I came back, holding the only packet of pills I'd spotted. 'Only these.' They were tiny tablets, smaller than aspirin, in a foil strip. Each one was marked with a day of the week. Half had gone.

'Give them to me!' She had snatched the packet and Jackie had laughed. 'Jackie, that's enough.'

'I'm sorry,' I said, unsure what I'd done wrong.

'I'll go and have a look.' She took the packet with her upstairs and Jackie smirked.

'What?'

'They're Mum's contraceptive pills, Ivy.' Jackie watched me as if expecting some sort of reaction but the only one he got was of slight confusion.

'Oh.'

'To stop her getting pregnant, silly.'

He grinned and I could feel myself blushing.

I knew what had to happen for a woman to get pregnant. I didn't know that people kept doing it, even after they'd already had five children. Was Jackie telling me his mum was going to have another baby? I didn't dare ask.

'Is it because of Kirsty?' I asked instead, in the darkness of the tent.

'Yes. Sort of. I'm going to sleep now.'

He turned away, pulling his sleeping bag up around his neck.

'Night, Abe.' I pretended to be asleep.

I don't know how long we lay there before Abe started to cry. 'Abe?' I whispered, because it was night and quiet. I'd never seen him crying. Not ever.

'Sorry.' The quiet sobs grew louder.

'What for?'

He didn't answer. I could see the contours of his back, heaving beneath the sleeping bag. I pushed my arm tentatively out of mine and rested it on his shoulder. 'What's the matter, Abe?'

He turned over and even in the darkness I could see his face was streaked with tears. 'Sometimes I just can't stand it.' He pushed his sleeping bag down and moved towards me, so that my arm was now right round him.

'It's all right,' I said, in the way my mother spoke to me, when I was really upset. I moved closer and stroked his hair, trying to soothe him. Eventually his breathing grew quieter, and when I thought he was asleep, I moved my arm ready to shift back to my side of the tent.

But he wasn't asleep. 'Stay,' he said. 'I don't want to be by myself.'

I pulled my pillow nearer to his, sat up slightly so I could nestle into the crook of his arm and we fell asleep. I was still there when Mrs McFadden unzipped the tent and peered in. 'Oh,' she said. That was all.

She left the flap and walked away.

Abe was still asleep as I eased myself out of the embrace we'd fallen into. I wasn't sure how much of the night before he remembered, but I felt odd when we went in for breakfast and his mother asked if we wanted toast as well as cereal.

'I've got to go into the village after breakfast, so I'll drop Ivy home,' she added.

I felt odd, sitting next to her in the car too. I didn't know what I'd done wrong, or if I'd done anything wrong at all.

Not long after that there was another phone call.

I answered it, in the early evening.

'Is that Ivy?' It was Abe's father.

'Yes.'

'May I speak to your mother, please?'

He never called. Just as my father never made phone calls at home, no social calls. He made business calls from the office, and Mr McFadden sometimes made work calls from home. But he'd never ring here. Mrs McFadden did, to chat to my mum or ask about some arrangement to do with me and Abe.

'I'll go and get her.'

I hovered, wanting to know what was being said, but Mum flapped her hand at me, shooing me out of the hallway.

'What did he want?' I asked, when she'd finished talking.

'Abe's staying with us tonight.' No further explanation. 'I'm going to pick him up.' She was looking for her car keys.

'Can I come?'

'No, Ivy. You stay here. I won't be long.'

She was half an hour.

Abe looked confused when he arrived without his overnight things. Mum was fussing over him. 'Do you want a drink? Anything to eat? I'll find some old pyjamas of Jon's for you. Would you like to watch television? Ivy will sit with you.'

'Has something happened?' I asked Abe, when we were alone.

'Mum's been taken to hospital,' he said, without looking at me.

'Oh. Is she ill?'

'Jackie had to ring for an ambulance. He found her in the car in the garage.'

'Oh,' I said, as if I understood but I did not.

A year later, things were almost normal in the McFadden household. The house had begun to fill again with family and friends. The big news was that the neighbouring farmhouse had been bought by Peter Van der Zee, who was practically famous. He ran a chain of men's clothing shops in Surrey, Sussex and Kent.

At the time there was a Van der Zee shop in nearly every market town. It was where anyone with an office job went to buy their suits, shirts and ties. I'd been to the nearest branch with my mother, to pick up suits Dad had bought for himself but left to be altered. On one occasion I'd been to take back a tie he had liked, until he discovered that Mr Piper had the same one.

'Dad bought a new tie from Van der Zee's last week,' I'd told Abe. 'It was blue with a kind of red swirly pattern, so from a distance it looked more red than blue.'

'Outlandish,' Abe replied, opening his eyes wide, as he said it.

I'd never heard the word before and had no idea what it meant. 'He had to take it back. You'll never guess why.'

'Why?'

'Mr Piper had the exact same tie!'

'Oh.' Abe started making swirls in the dirt with the tip of his toe and I wondered if my repeated tales of Mr Piper bored him or if he was just more interested in Mr Van der Zee buying the farmhouse next to his home.

When we'd talked about the imminent arrival of Peter Van der Zee, Abe and I had created a fantastical creature who bore very little resemblance to the man who came to live in the house. It was his ownership of the men's clothing shops that lent him, in our imaginations, a touch of exoticism – and his name. If you were from Zee, you might as well have been from Samarkand or outer space.

So by the time the furniture lorry arrived and, with it, the family's car, we were expecting some sort of velvet-suited, cigar-smoking, pointed-shoe-wearing 'outlandish' character.

Instead, a very ordinary middle-aged man, his nice-looking wife and two children emerged from the car. The children were the wrong age for any of us to have much to do with. One was already at Oxford, studying Mandarin – a subject that made him almost as exotic as our imaginary Mr Van der Zee had been. The daughter, who was younger, was doing A levels at a boarding school in Dorset. So Mr and Mrs Van der Zee were effectively childless and semi-retired too.

They threw their energies into their new home, stripping out kitchens and bathrooms, putting up conservatories and gazebos, but in between they were friendly. They took their dogs for walks and said, 'Hello,' a little louder than anyone else. They stopped their car and wound down windows to engage in conversation, and Mrs Van der Zee, whose name was Barbara, invited women round for coffee and couples for cocktails.

Pam McFadden was one of the first and, because they lived next door, one of the most frequent recipients of an invitation for 'a mug of instant'. So she broke the swimming-pool news. The Van der Zees were going to build one. A proper outdoor sunken pool, not one of the metal stand-up ones they advertised in Sunday supplements.

'The pool's almost finished.' Mrs Van der Zee stopped her car outside the McFaddens' house. 'Do you want to come and see?'

'Yes, please.'

It was a thing of wonder. A big hole in the ground lined with myriad blue tiles and a few workmen. 'They're just sealing it,' she explained. 'But it should be ready to use by next week. The water will be a bit cold but come round and help us christen it, won't you?'

'Really?'

'Of course! What's the point of it if there are no children here to enjoy it? Now then. While you're here, would you like something to eat or drink before you go home? There's Coca-Cola in the fridge.'

'Yes, please!'

'Yes, thank you.'

I'd never had Coca-Cola or swum in an outdoor pool.

It was early May when the pool was ready. The water was cold but that didn't bother a couple of ten-year-olds.

'You can change in the pool room, if you like,' Mrs Van der Zee offered, the first time we went.

I'd arrived with my costume already on under my clothes and fussed about under a towel. A changing room was not a necessity. Not until a few weeks later when the weather and the water had warmed up and a sudden storm broke.

Mrs McFadden and Mrs Van der Zee were sitting at a table near the pool, with cups of 'instant', chatting. They kept glancing at the sky, as Abe and I tried to do proper breaststroke.

'You have to put your head in and move your arms and legs at the same time, like a frog,' I said authoritatively. I had no idea really but I loved the feel of the water. I wanted Abe to love it too.

'It always gets up my nose,' he complained.

'You have to breathe out when your head is under water so you can breathe straight in when you take it out.' I took a deep breath and buried my face in the water to demonstrate. I felt a few drops on my back. 'Stop splashing me and try it,' I said, coming up for air.

'I wasn't splashing. It's raining.'

Abe was right. Big fat drops were pummelling the water. His mother and Mrs Van der Zee were gathering up their coffee cups and heading for the house.

'Can we stay in?' Abe asked. 'We're already wet.'

'I suppose so.' Mrs McFadden looked at Mrs Van der Zee.

'I'll put your clothes and towels in the pool room,' Mrs Van der Zee said, scooping up our things.

'Thanks,' we shouted, as she headed for the wooden shed where they kept all the cleaning stuff.

'It'll stop in a minute,' Abe said confidently.

It didn't. The rain fell harder and the surface of the pool was almost choppy.

'I think I might get out now.'

'Me too.' Abe followed me to the steps and we ran the short distance across the concrete flagstones to the pool room.

Abe picked up his towel and began rubbing himself dry but mine was missing from the pile of clothes Mrs Van der Zee had placed on the wooden bench that ran along one side of the room. 'My towel's not here.'

'Oh, no! Well, you can use mine in a sec.' Abe wrapped it round his waist and shuffled under it, pulling his trunks off

328

and putting his pants on. 'Here.' He handed it to me, and I did the towel dance, wriggling beneath it out of my wet costume and into my dry underwear.

'We'll get soaked if we go out again.' Abe looked out of the window. 'What shall we do?'

'Do you think Mrs Van der Zee will mind if we use the mats?'

There were two foam mattresses that the Van Der Zees laid by the pool. They were propped sideways against the wall.

'We'll put them back,' Abe said, dragging them out and laying them side by side but propped up against the bench – a kind of comfy sofa-bed.

'Ow.' I tugged at the elastic band that secured my hair in the pigtail Mum said I had to put it in for swimming. 'There's too much hair caught in it.'

'Turn round,' Abe said, and I put my back to him, allowing him to free the end of my hair from the band and loosen the three plaited strands so that it would dry.

'Your hair's so dark when it's wet,' he said. 'It's like . . .'

'Not so ginger?' I hated it when people at school said it was ginger but I didn't mind referring to it like that with Abe.

'It's not ginger,' he said. 'It's red.'

'I still don't like it,' I said, which was true, but not so much the hair as the comments it attracted.

'I do,' Abe said, unwinding the final section of my plait. 'It's got so many different colours in it. There!' He smoothed the loose strands with his hand and I turned around.

'Thanks.'

We sat with our heads resting against the ledge of the bench, our arms touching.

'Did I tell you Mum's sister might be coming to stay?' Abe asked.

'No. What sister? When?'

'Auntie Katrina. She lives in Scotland.'

'So you don't see her very often?'

'No. She's coming on the sleeper train.'

'I'd like to go on one of those. I'd love to just go to bed on a train and wake up somewhere else.'

'Do you think it'd be easy to sleep?'

'I don't know.'

And I don't know if it was the fug of the pool room, with the rain outside, or that I was tired from swimming or just the talk of sleep, but I must have dozed off, while we were chatting.

I awoke to the sound of a door opening and Abe's mother's voice. 'They're still in here,' she said.

I opened my eyes and felt my arm, which was numb from the way I'd been leaning against Abe.

'Oh, yes!' Mrs Van der Zee was behind her, her head silhouetted by the sun, which was out again.

'It's stopped raining now,' Mrs McFadden said. 'Time to go home.'

We got up, put the mats back where we'd found them and gathered our wet things while the grown-ups waited outside. I didn't hear what Barbara Van der Zee said to Abe's mother but I heard her reply: 'They've always been like that. They're like an old married couple.'

I wondered vaguely who she was talking about.

'That's one of the things I'm worried about.' She lowered her voice. 'He'll miss her.'

A few months later I would replay those overheard snippets of a conversation.

It was my mother who told me. It felt like a huge betrayal. She wasn't to blame for the news she had to impart, any more

330

than she was responsible for the sequence of events that led to it. Nevertheless my childish mind held her to account.

Dinner had been normal – pork chops, mash, cabbage and questions.

'What do you want to do for your birthday, Ivy?'

'I want to see the dolphins at the Aquarium.'

'They sing happy birthday to you if you go on your actual birthday!'

'Dolphins don't sing.' Dad, the killjoy.

'They can.' Cathy backed me up. 'I went with Jenny last year on someone's birthday. They really do sing.'

'How?'

'They grunt.' Cathy demonstrated with a tuneful throat clearing.

We all laughed, except Mum, who shook her head, the way she often did when she thought a conversation or event had happened before. '*Déjà vu*,' she said, half laughing – too late.

Nothing about the meal made me think anyone was about to deliver bad news. It was only when we'd finished that I realized something was up.

'Ivy, you don't have to help with the washing-up today.'

'Why not?' It wasn't my birthday. I hadn't done particularly well at school. I wasn't ill. I'd stopped asking if I could be exempt from the task because I was adopted because it worried me when my parents went along with the ruse. I clearly wasn't adopted. Apart from my red hair, I bore a resemblance to my parents and siblings that was too strong for me to be anything other than part of the family.

Adoption was just a game that I tried to use to my advantage. 'Do I have to do the washing-up? I'm adopted.'

Sometimes, when my parents were feeling indulgent, they did let me off, despite protests from Jon and Cathy.

'You're not adopted.'

'Then how come I've got red hair and you haven't?'

'Cos it's a recessive gene. Our granddad had red hair. It just didn't come out in us.' Jon knew all about Mendel and his sweet peas. 'You're just lazy. And the youngest, so you get spoiled.'

But I didn't want to be spoiled today. 'I don't mind. I'll dry.' I jumped up, eager to put off whatever the bad news was that exempted me from after-supper duties.

'No, Ivy, you sit down.' Mum was adamant. 'I'm afraid there's some sad news.'

I already knew that. Mum hadn't made her 'Blancmange is a dish best served cold' joke, the one she made every time we had blancmange for pudding, the one everyone laughed at as if it was the first time they'd heard it, the one I laughed at too, even though I didn't get it. The one Jon never shook his head at and said, '*Déjà vu*,' to, the way he did to Dad.

I said nothing.

'I know you'll be very sad. I'm sad too,' Mum began. 'But I saw Pam McFadden today. Don't look so worried, love.' The endearment. 'It's not the end of the world.'

I shuddered. The Jehovah's Witnesses had been round a few days earlier with a definite date for that. Dad had insisted on inviting them in for coffee. He'd said he felt sorry for the children. 'They get dragged around on Saturday mornings spreading doom and gloom while you go swimming.'

'And resurrection,' Jon quipped. 'If you didn't get that bit you just wasted the best part of an hour and a half and a packet of Bourbon biscuits.' He resented the liberal offering of his favourites, when we were limited to three at teatime, more than the threat of the world ending.

In fact, he rather liked the idea of Armageddon in one

form or another. Four years older than me, Jon remembered the Cuban Missile Crisis properly. He was ten at the time and desperately seeking what-ifs that might really change the world, not little ones that seemed to make no difference.

'If Hitler hadn't been born, someone else would have led the Nazi Party,' he'd say to me. 'But if a comet hit the earth, you'd have about two seconds before it all ended.'

But the world was not about to end, not the wider one, anyway. Just mine.

'The McFaddens have decided to move,' Mum said.

'House?'

'Yes, house. But also, well, country, I suppose.'

'Country? Where are they going to?'

'Scotland. Just outside Edinburgh. Mr McFadden's got a new job and Mrs McFadden wanted to be closer to her sister after . . .' She was still unable to talk about the event that had divided everything in the McFaddens' world into before and after. 'Well, she needs to be near her family.'

'But what about their friends?' If they moved to Scotland, I might never see Abe again.

'It's not the same,' Mum said gently. 'When something like that happens, you need your family around you. I'm sure things would have been different if it hadn't been for . . .' Again she avoided saying it. 'It's been really hard for Mrs McFadden.'

'When are they moving?' I tried not to sound upset but I could hear the resentment in my voice.

'At the beginning of the summer holidays. Maybe we could go and see them. Not this summer but another one. We could have a holiday.'

I didn't want a holiday. I wanted the McFaddens to stay in Sussex. I didn't want Abe to go. We'd be starting secondary school next year and there was the summer holidays before that. We had a plan to camp outside for the whole summer. I couldn't envisage the next few months without Abe, let alone a lifetime.

'I'm going to my room.' I didn't know what else to say.

'Love,' Mum said again, as I brushed past her and went upstairs.

Later Jon came up to me. I'd taken a pack of cards and was laying them on the carpet, ready to play solitaire. I tried not to think about what I'd been told, about the consequences. I wanted the feelings I'd begun to have to go away. If I didn't think about it, maybe they would.

'Here. Your share.' He walked in, holding a saucer with a fifth of a Mars bar placed in the centre.

This was a treat. 'A Mars a day helps you work, rest and play' but no one in our house had ever eaten a whole bar. Occasionally, Mum bought one and cut it equally into five pieces. Sometimes she would forgo the treat and divide it into four. (Presented on a saucer, it was *nouvelle cuisine* ahead of its time.)

'You know it's not named after the planet?' Dad said, every time.

We did, because he'd said it so often.

'Everyone thinks it's part of the space race chocolate collective. You know? Milk Way, Galaxy et cetera. But actually it bears the family name of the manufacturer, Forrest Mars.'

'Really?' We'd feign interest but were more interested in the morsel of chocolate on offer than the titbit of information.

'And Trebor, as in Trebor mints, is Robert spelled backwards.'

'Really?' We'd heard that too.

Sometimes Jon would mimic Mum.

'*Déjà vu*,' he'd say, shaking his head to get rid of it the way she did.

'It's bad luck,' Jon said now, sitting next to me and laying the sliver of confectionery between us.

'You sound like Mum.' Her at her most sympathetic.

Abe had remarked on this once, a few years before when he'd come to play after school and fallen roller-skating. He'd put out his hands to break the fall and bloodied them spectacularly.

'Abe's hurt his hands.' I'd found my mother at the sink peeling potatoes.

'Bad luck.' She'd turned briefly to look. 'Better go and wash them in the downstairs cloakroom.' My mother never said 'toilet'. She said it was common.

'Your mum's odd,' Abe said, as he filled the sink and began soaping the blood from his hands.

'I know.'

'If my mum had been here she'd have come running and said something like "Oh dear! Oh, darling!"' He raised his voice to sound more like a woman. 'But yours just says, "Bad luck!"'

'I know,' I said now, to my brother, and began moving cards around.

'It's because of what happened,' Jon said.

He was trying to be nice and trying to make me feel better but I wanted to be left alone.

'Mum says Mrs McFadden will never get over it,' he continued. 'She says you never get over something like that.'

I ignored him, turning cards over, moving them around, placing them on top of others, so the lines shortened in places and lengthened in others.

'You'll get over it,' he added.

'Bloody hell.' I raised my voice, angry, using the worst words I could think of.

People didn't swear. They 'cursed', usually quietly under their breath, 'Damnation' or 'Hell's bells'. Very occasionally one of my parents would lose their temper and say, 'Bloody hell.'

It was enough to shock Jon. 'Ivy!'

'Just leave me alone!' I shouted, sweeping my arm across the cards and destroying the game.

'I wanted to make sure you were all right.'

'Bloody hell,' I said to myself, as he got up and left the room.

I didn't feel all right.

This was what loss felt like. It was normal. Time was a healer. Abe would become a distant memory. A good but distant memory.

I lay on my bed and looked at the mirror on the opposite wall. There was a mirror tile on the inside of the cupboard door too. The door was open and the mirror was aligned with the one on the wall, creating a series of endless reflections of my desk, with the red leather-bound copy of *Gulliver's Travels*, which Abe had bought for me, in the centre, the chair, a jumble of clothes hanging over the back, and the doll's house I was too old for but didn't want to part with.

I liked that view. I often lay there, mesmerized by image after image going back beyond the actual mirror: endless copies of my bedroom, as far as the eye could see. I liked to imagine that those rooms were occupied by a slightly different version of me: an Ivy with different parents, other brothers and sisters, who went to other schools with different friends.

And now, as the tears I refused to shed in front of my mother started to flow, I tried to imagine that in one of those other reflected worlds, I'd meet Abe at another time and things would be different.

Let your soul stand cool and composed
before a million universes.

Walt Whitman, 'Song of Myself'

Epilogue: London 2032

I'm waiting for Lottie, Jon and Abe. I'm meeting them for lunch in Granary Square. It's crowded in the sunshine and I've bagged a table outside but they're late.

I've not been here for a while, and I'm amazed by how the trees along the approach to the square have grown. When they first developed the area, I remember that there were hoardings with trees painted on them lining what is now an avenue. I take great pleasure from the way the tiny saplings have grown into mature trees. From my table, I can see their tops swaying gently in the breeze, which occasionally blows droplets of water from the fountains in my direction, spritzing my face with a fine spray.

Lottie is late but I put this down to her having two small children. Jon is only three and Abe not yet one. I remember how hard it used to be to get out of the house when Max and she were tiny.

'You don't mind, do you?' Lottie had asked anxiously, when Jon was born. 'My naming him after Uncle Jon?'

'Why would I mind? It's a lovely thing to do.'

'I just thought it might upset you, having to use his name all the time. Are you sure it doesn't?'

'It makes me happy,' I told her. 'It's a continuation of the family. There's little bits of Jon in little Jon. '

'As long as you're sure?'

'Of course.'

I wondered, if the next baby had been a girl, whether she might have considered Janet and if I'd have found that strange. Perhaps the two names together again would have been too much. But Lottie's baby was another boy, a strawberry blond, traces of my hair colour on his tiny head but not a real redhead, like myself and Connor, Max's eldest son, my first grandchild.

'We're going to call him Abe,' Lottie said, when I visited her in hospital.

'Short for Abraham,' Tim said, proudly.

'That's nice. I've never come across anyone called Abe – or Abraham. Only in the Bible.'

'We wanted a name that was recognizable but not really popular,' Lottie said. 'I know it doesn't have any resonance but we like it.' She looked at me anxiously, as if it was important that I liked the name too.

'It's a lovely name. A lovely name for such a gorgeous baby.'

I imagine the gorgeous baby has held her up today, needing to be fed or changed or woken from a nap, when she was trying to get out of the house to meet me.

It's the anniversary of Richard's death and it was Lottie who suggested meeting for lunch and the location too. 'Jon likes playing in the fountains and there's plenty of space outside for the buggy,' she'd said to me on the phone. 'Let's go there. Lunch is on me.'

'There's no need,' I said.

There is none. Treating my children and grandchildren is one of my greatest pleasures in life but I'm beginning to wonder what's holding them up, as the waiter approaches me, for a second time, to ask if I'd like to order.

Once more, I tell him that I'm waiting for my daughter and her children to join me.

And then I see her, hurrying across the square, looking a little flustered. Jon is holding the handle of the buggy so that he is being half dragged along by the speed with which she's pushing it.

Abe is all wide eyes and smile, to everyone and everything – even more so when he sees me. He's one of the happiest children I think I've ever encountered.

'I'm so sorry I'm late,' Lottie says, slightly breathless. 'I seem to have dropped my phone. I had it when I got off the Tube but Jon wanted a picture of himself in front of the fountains, and when I looked for it, it had gone.'

'Do you want to go back and see if you can find it? I'll look after the boys.'

'I've already been,' she says. 'That's why I'm late. I was already a little bit late anyway but I retraced my steps when I realized and couldn't see it. It's so annoying.'

'Sit down, now that you're here,' I say. 'Jon, do you want me to ask if they've got a high chair for you or are you going to sit on a big chair?'

'I'm going to play in the fountain,' he says.

'Sit down for a bit, love,' Lottie says. 'We want to say hello to Granny and order some lunch. You can go and splash about in a bit.'

He climbs up on to the chair next to mine, kneeling so he's better able to reach the table as Lottie unstraps Abe from the buggy. 'Oh, Lord,' she says. 'He's soaking. Sorry, Mum. I know I'm late and you've been waiting but I'll just take him inside to change him.'

'Don't worry,' I say. 'I'll be happy here with Jon.'

'There was a dead bird in the kitchen this morning,' Jon tells me, his eyes shining with the importance of it all.

'Oh dear. Did the cat bring it in?'

'No. It flew in the window and –' Jon stops when he hears my phone ringing inside my bag. His ears are sharper than mine. 'Granny, is that your phone?'

'Oh, yes, but I don't suppose it's important.' I take it out nevertheless, and look at the caller display. It's Lottie's number but obviously not Lottie calling.

'Hello, Ivy speaking,' I say.

'Oh, hello, Ivy,' a man says. His voice sounds remarkably familiar.

'Who is it?'

'I'm sorry, you don't know me, but I've found a phone just outside the station. It wasn't locked so I dialled "Mum". I presume it must belong to one of your children.'

'Yes. It's my daughter's. She thought she'd dropped it and went back to look but couldn't find it. She'll be relieved. Where are you now?'

'I'm at the entrance to the Underground.'

'My daughter's just gone somewhere with her baby,' I say, 'but she won't be long. Can I ask her to come and meet you when she gets back? I'm with my other grandson so that's probably the quickest way, if you don't mind waiting. Or you could hand it in at the station?'

'Where are you?' he asks.

'We're in Granary Square.'

'I'll pop it up,' he says.

'I don't want to put you to any trouble.'

'Really, it's no trouble. There's something I'd like to take a look at there anyway,' he says. 'I'll call you again when I get there so that I can find you.'

'That's very kind.'

'A nice man has found Mummy's phone,' I say to Jon.

'Good I want to take a picture.' He holds out his hand and takes an imaginary selfie as Lottie returns with a smiling, dry Abe.

'Good news,' I tell her. 'Someone's found your phone.'

'Oh, great. Should I call them?'

'He said he'd bring it up here,' I say, and in my peripheral vision I catch sight of an elderly but sprightly man with a thick head of not entirely grey hair walking towards us.

'Ivy?' he asks.

'Yes?' I'm slightly confused.

'I thought so,' he says. 'You said you had two grand-children with you.'

'Oh, I see,' I said. 'But how did you know my name?'

'You said it when you answered the phone.' He smiles and holds it out to us.

'Of course,' I say, as Lottie takes the phone from him.

'Thank you so much,' she says. 'I think I must have dropped it when I was carrying the buggy up the stairs.'

'Well, I'm glad you've got it back now.' He nods, as if to conclude the exchange.

I don't know what it is but something about him makes me want to detain him a little longer. 'Thank you,' I say. 'It was really very kind of you to bring it up here as well. What is it you're going to see? You said there was something you wanted to see in the square.'

'It was only the fountain.' He gestures towards the jets, which are sparkling in the sun.

'I love the fountain,' Jon announces.

'Do you, young man?' He raises his eyebrows, smiling. 'I'm very glad.'

Then he moves a little closer and bends down so he's at Jon's level and points to the Granary building. 'Do you know,

341

the four blocks of jets are positioned so that it looks as if the four big windows of that building are being reflected down on to the ground?'

Jon looks a little baffled, and the phone finder shrugs, then turns to me. 'I used to be a fountain designer,' he says.

'Really? How interesting.' I look at the fountain, then at the man, who seems to know so much about it. 'I've never met a fountain designer before.'

'There aren't that many of us.' He gestures to the plumes of water. 'Historically, fountains are an expression of life.'

'Really?'

'Sorry,' he says. 'I could go on for hours but I'll leave you to your lunch.' Then to Lottie, he says, 'I'm glad I was able to return your phone to you.'

'Why don't you join us for lunch?' Lottie says. 'As a thank you.'

'I don't want to intrude.'

'You wouldn't be. We'd like it, wouldn't we, Mum?'

'Yes,' I say. 'I'd like it very much if he joined us.

'If you're sure?' he says.

'I insist.' I pull out a chair for him to sit down. 'I'm Ivy, as you know, and this is Lottie, my daughter, and Jon and Abe.'

'Abe? That's an unusual name.' He looks at Abe. 'Hello, little fellow.'

Abe grins at the stranger.

'It's short for Abraham,' Lottie says.

'I know,' he says. 'I've just never met another Abe before.'

Lottie and I look at each other, not quite understanding.

'I'm sorry. There I go again. I haven't even introduced myself,' he says. 'I'm Abe too. Abe McFadden.'